EMERALD
TARGET

BOOK I
STARLING

EMERALD TARGET

BOOK I
STARLING

D.D.O'Lander

Blade Publishing House
Highlands Ranch, Colorado

EMERALD TARGET
BOOK I—STARLING
Copyright © 2015
Denise D. Ohlander writing as D.D.O'Lander

Cover Design: NZgraphics
Interior Layout: Denise Ohlander
Consultant: PBComposition
Editor: Word Shop Ink
Proof Team: Keith O. and Mary Ann L.
Tech Supervisor: Scott Ohlander

Blade Publishing House, LLC
Highlands Ranch, Colorado 80129

Emerald Target: Book I—Starling is a work of fiction. Names, characters, places and incidents are products of the author's imagination or are used fictitiously. Any resemblance to actual events or locales or persons, living or dead, is coincidental; while situations involving historical individuals are created for this narrative.

EMERALD TARGET
BOOK I—STARLING
D.D.O'LANDER
ISBN-13: 978-1492320012
ISBN-10: 1492320013

Fiction/ World War II/ U.S. Coast Guard/ U-boats/ Nazis/ Espionage/ Greenland/ Battle of the Atlantic

*To my thoroughly loved & greatly missed
Dad and Mom,
Paul and Lee Reddy.*

*Thanks for adopting me and
supporting me through
all my endeavors.*

ACKNOWLEDGEMENT

There are *many* people—family, friends, co-workers and contacts, near and far—who helped me get to this point in my life and with my writing. Some have played a more active role in this book, while others were always there to encourage me and keep me sane (though crazy is normal for my Scotch-Irish self). Please don't feel offended that I've not listed you individually. I truly do thank everyone. And I pray you know who you are and how special you are to me. Love D

NOTE TO READERS

Because of the original length of *EMERALD TARGET*, I needed to divide the book into three smaller novels: *STARLING*, *IRISH* and *PAWN*. Otherwise it might have ended up a very handy doorstop nobody would have wanted to lug around, much less read. Since it didn't seem feasible to give eReaders an unfair leg-up on the story, my son Scott thought it best to also divide the eBook, which came out first.

Hopefully, the dividing points will not seem too awkward, though everything gets pulled together by the end of the series.

On the other hand, every situation is not resolved.

For that to transpire, my next series, *INDIGO DEPTHS*, will need to be read. For now, please experience and enjoy *STARLING*.

A Few Terms In Emerald Target

bearcat	an attractive, hot-blooded or fiery girl.
bitter end	free end of last part of a rope or cable.
blottos	drunks.
Buck and a Quarter	Prohibition era Coast Guard cutter of one-hundred-twenty-five feet in length.
bunker tank	storage for bunker fuel oil or bunker crude aboard a vessel; the fuel tank of a *Buck and a Quarter* held 6,650 gallons and spanned the cutter's width amidships.
Cape Islander	lobster boats first built in Clark's Harbour, Nova Scotia, about 1905.
CO	commanding officer; captain of a cutter or ship; any rank.
davit	a small crane that projects over the side of a ship to hoist or lower a boat.
dero	Australian slang for tramp or hobo, probably from derelict.
flivver	usually an old, beat-up car.

das Hakenkreuz	hooked cross or swastika: either static—standing flat or mobile—standing on one point to show advancement.
Hooligan Navy	regular Navy term for the Coast Guard.
hoosegow	jail.
Joe Brooks	anyone who dresses to perfection; used by college students from the 1920s.
kedge; kedging	a light anchor; process of moving a small boat, particularly one that has run aground, by setting a kedge (anchor) further out and hauling the boat toward deeper water to free it.
Lebensborn	Nazi German program where young women were encouraged to become pregnant for the Reich; children were then raised by the State, the mother having no further contact.
OOD/Officer Of the Deck	officer on watch in charge of the ship when underway; when anchored or moored, Officer Of the Day is used.
painter	bow line for a small boat.

Palooka	a boxer.
Piker	a cheapskate; one who is overly cautious with his money; also a coward; used throughout the period.
piteraq	Inuit for "that which attacks you" referring to very strong winds (110-180 mph) which roar off the icecap and down the East Greenland Coast.
Puzzle Palace	slang term for Coast Guard HQ or administration.
Reuben (or Rube)	a hick; unsophisticated or naive person from the country; used during both Wars and in between.
der Ritterkreuz	Knight's Cross (of the Iron Cross).
root(ed)	Aussie slang synonymous with fuck(ed) in nearly all its senses.
Sam Browne belt	belt worn over a police or military uniform with a shoulder strap running across the chest (from late 1800s).
Schlicktown	meaning sludge town; the nickname of Wilhelmshaven, Germany's only deep-water port and largest naval base.

Schnellzug	an express train in Germany.
Sehr saftig!	German for "Very juicy!"
shite (like white)	another way of saying shit.
SS or Sig-Runes	"lightning bolt" insignia of the *SS* for *Schutzstaffel;* Nazi typewriters had a special key added for this symbol.
stem	upright post or bar at forward point of the bow of a cutter, ship or boat; cast, forged, welded or made of wood.
stern	after part of a ship.
Treasury Class	high-endurance cutters named after Secretaries of the Treasury, also known as 327s; called a maritime workhorse: dependable, versatile and long-lived.
Tschüss!	informal German for "Bye!"
Very pistol	a stubby gun, specialized to fire colored signal flares.

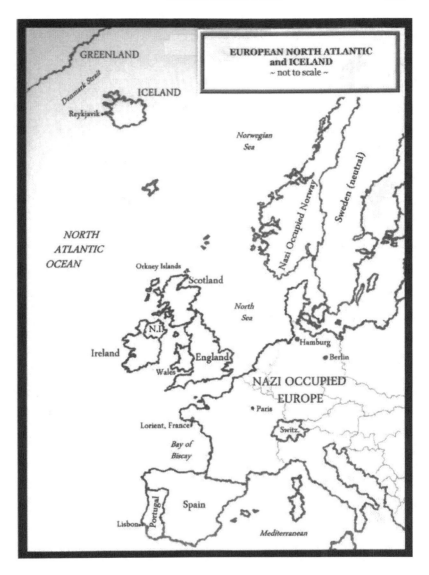

These maps were drawn by Karney Rork over a period of several days, while flying with the crew of Ice Sheila on their patrols between Christmas '41 and when Wendy flew him to Greenland in mid-January '42. Karney used a world atlas the Aussies kept aboard but left out their notations of where to find the best taverns, pubs, bars and brothels.

PROLOGUE
NAZI GERMANY

"*Liebling*, you forgot Hildie," the genteel *SS* officer called after his five-year-old daughter. After he'd given her the key to their flat, Anna quit listening to eagerly race into the apartment complex. He knew she would soon want the much-loved rag doll her mother had made her, but after the turbulent flight from Lisbon, Portugal, Anna was just glad to be home.

With an amused smile, Captain Brandt Gündestein tucked the doll under his arm and pulled the bags from their Volkswagen. Strolling inside, his thoughts drifted to this past week spent with his daughter and her mother Elise.

On leave from his Signals Battalion while Hitler's Norwegian campaign drew to a close, Brandt had turned his wife's mission for German Military Intelligence into a nice holiday. They had flown to Lisbon—a key location for *Abwehr* agents, like Elise, to funnel into England or reenter Germany. For her role as a double agent working for the British, Lisbon felt like a revolving door. In the dangerous game of espionage, she carried information out of Nazi Germany and returned with choice misinformation from Britain's MI-6. So far, no one suspected Elise's dual role, but Brandt still worried.

The trip to Portugal was to be a break from the war. Brandt's brooding almost spoiled it, but Elise and Anna banished his frets with giggles and sunshine. They made him realize how precious their time together was and that he shouldn't waste it on uncertainties beyond his control.

And much was beyond anyone's control these days.

Though not pleased that Elise hadn't returned to Germany with them, Brandt knew she had to go to England. Hesitation over any of the Reich's demands might garner unwanted attention. Any member of Hitler's spider-webbed police agencies—*Gestapo, SS* or *SD*—would be delighted to interrogate a prize agent like Elise Greer Gündestein. With the knowledge Elise possessed, the identities she knew, the secrets she kept, the Nazis would do anything to break her. If that happened, many would be compromised, including Brandt, his father Wolf and the cells of their German Resistance network.

Yet the *Abwehr* unwittingly gave Elise a way to warn British Military Intelligence of Hitler's pending plans. Within days Hitler intended to overrun Holland, Belgium and Luxembourg, rolling through the Low Countries to bypass the Maginot Line and invade France. Since the *Abwehr* covered Elise's expenses, the twist also appealed to his wife's Scottish frugality. What didn't appeal to either Brandt or Elise was the ill timing.

Elise would not be back in time to care for Anna when his unit, as part of the vanguard into Belgium, returned to the fighting. He'd have to leave Anna with *Opa* Wolf. His father loved Anna to pieces, spoiling her shamelessly. But Brandt hated for their daughter to be separated from both parents while Hitler's hostilities expanded.

Brandt had said *auf Wiedersehen* to Elise barely two days ago, but it felt more like weeks. However, Elise's path was set: Dublin by plane, Hollyhead by ferry, then Euston Station in London by train late tonight. It was a long, potentially dangerous haul.

Inhaling the cool evening air, the coppery clouds left by a dazzling sunset served to remind Brandt of Elise's tawny curls. *I'll be amazed if Elise can make it home in three weeks, much less six days,* he thought. *Dear Lord, please let her trip be swift and safe.*

Brandt and Elise loathed this double life but had vowed, on their secret wedding night in 1933, to fight the evil propagated by Adolf Hitler. They bound themselves to this course with daring and refused to look back. It was a risky life. Each faced different but equally hazardous levels of duplicity. Thus far, acute vigilance had kept them safe.

Once inside the building's foyer Brandt stopped.

A Wagnerian opera blared from the upper floor. *Mein Gott,* he thought, racing up the stairs, *Anna knows she's not to turn up our radio that loud. Frau Brügen will kick us out on the street. Or worse, she'll call the bloody SS!*

When Brandt reached their floor and saw light spilling from the open door of their modest flat, he sensed something was wrong.

Setting the suitcases down, with Hildie on top, Brandt unsnapped his holster. He withdrew his 9mm Parabellum Luger and edged toward the open door. His boots made the old floor creak, but the thundering aria masked the noise.

Double checking the hallway behind him, he peered between the door jamb and the open door of their flat. Brandt's heart froze.

Anna struggled in the arms of his sergeant. The bastard's bear-like paw clamped firmly over her mouth, his other arm wrapped tightly around her body. Anna's eyes were huge with fear and desperation. A sneer curled the big brute's lip.

In a flash reaction, Brandt knew a headshot was

feasible. As he brought his luger up, the muzzle of a weapon pressed into his neck with equally cold words of warning.

"Do not try it, *Hauptsturmführer*," hissed a voice from behind him. "You may be a remarkable shot, but in that same moment, Kühnstahl will snap Anna's delicate little neck like a dry twig. *Bitte*, hand me your weapon."

Unaware from where the gunman materialized, nor if he was alone, Brandt did as ordered. Any brash action he took could result in Anna's death. That must not happen.

The gunman stepped back, sliding Brandt's Luger under his belt. Recognition made Brandt's skin crawl: Lieutenant Colonel Joachim von Zeitz was a schizophrenic deviate who excelled at vicious Nazi tactics and relished brutality. Brandt had seen firsthand the delight von Zeitz took in abusing others. And Kühnstahl, supposedly Brandt's sergeant, would do exactly what the *SD* officer ordered.

Cut from coarser cloth, Kühnstahl was a bloodthirsty maniac apparently held in check only by his master's leash. In Poland and Norway, Brandt had been forced to keep the beast on a taut leash. Clearly, Brandt never truly controlled Kühnstahl. *How long has he been obeying von Zeitz and spying on me?*

"Slowly pick up the suitcases and carry them into the flat, *Hauptsturmführer*," von Zeitz ordered, taking a step back.

Brandt did as ordered and moved inside, while Kühnstahl retreated further back.

Brandt asked in a tone of guarded offense, "Whatever can you possibly want with us, *Obersturmbannführer* von Zeitz?"

"It should not be difficult to figure out," he sneered, "or did your frivolous holiday in Portugal leave your mind in blissful ignorance?" Lowering his pistol, von Zeitz said, "You, my dear boy, are under arrest for subversive acts against the Reich."

"Subversive acts? I am no traitor—"

The colonel's gun butt cracked into Brandt's skull. Falling over a suitcase, he crashed to the floor. The rag doll landed at von Zeitz's feet. Brandt fought to remain conscious. Over the thud of his heartbeat within his skull, Brandt tried to focus on Anna, her raggedy doll, the warm blood oozing behind his ear, his distorted image on von Zeitz's polished black boots.

"You are a traitor," von Zeitz seethed. "The most abhorrent kind." Picking up the doll, he ripped it apart, probing the rag-stuffed head with his fingers. He threw it aside.

Brandt's vision sloshed in a woozy muck. Fear for his young daughter kept his hate in check. Anna struggled to reach out to him. With a tender gaze, he tried to reassure her, but knew he had to wait for the right moment to act.

"Kühnstahl, take her away," von Zeitz ordered.

Battling to his feet, Brandt cried, "You cannot take—"

With spiteful amusement, von Zeitz shoved Brandt back onto the coffee table, shattering the glass. Brandt faintly registered a gasp from Anna, heard her muffled sobs. Glass shards viciously sliced his hands. Any thought of pulling his *SS* dagger ended when von Zeitz aimed his pistol squarely between Brandt's eyes.

"I take what I wish," the *SD* colonel snarled. "Though I dearly wish to splatter your putrid brains across this room, how can I question a corpse? However," he said, shifting his Walther P38 to Anna's delicate profile, "your daughter is expendable."

Despite knowing he might be killed as well if von Zeitz shot Anna, the sergeant grinned moronically.

Seeing Brandt back down, von Zeitz picked up the shredded ragdoll and threw it to Kühnstahl. "Give the brat this pitiful doll to stop her crying. Take her to the matron waiting outside."

As the oaf thudded down the stairs carrying his daughter like a sack of potatoes, Brandt yelled, "Anna, I

love you. Don't forget our gift, no matter what happens."
The colonel's boot smashed into Brandt's face. "The
Reich will provide all the gifts your daughter needs."
With those scoffed words, blackness devoured Brandt.

⊕

When Brandt came to, the apartment had been
ransacked, suitcase contents and papers strewn everywhere. Despite a whirl of chaos in his head, Brandt
managed to ask, "*Wo ist* Anna?"
Scowling down, von Zeitz threw aside a ripped pillow.
"Anna needn't concern you. She will be raised in
Himmler's Lebensborn Program and become a proper
Nazi. When she is old enough, I will impregnate your
daughter as service to the Reich. Just as I did your
beautiful sister, Brianna, before she so selfishly deprived
our *Führer* of another child by killing herself. To be
precise, Anna will cherish *der Führer* for the Supreme
Being he is . . . unlike her seditious *Vati* and traitorous
Scottish *Mutti*."
The mention of Brie's death confirmed Brandt's early
suspicions that his younger sister's death had not been an
accident. But the thought of this bastard raping his baby
daughter, even touching her, horrified Brandt. Yet he was
angst-ridden about what this brute knew of Elise. Boldly,
Brandt defended, "You are sadly mistaken, *Oberst*. Elise
works for the *Abwehr*. She's—"
"Shut-up, *du Scheißhund*. I know her exact role in all
of this. I trained her for MI-6. Elise knows me as an
upstanding British officer. Do you realize how difficult it
has been to avoid her, even in a city the size of Berlin? Not
that I wish to shrink from her presence, quite the
contrary." Unexpectedly, von Zeitz spoke in very precise
King's English, "I have always had a hard spot for dear
Elise . . . If you get my meaning?"
The man's chuckle scraped like broken branches

screeching against glass on a bitterly cold winter's night.

"You know, in God-awful Scotland, at Achnacarry, some other fellows and I dubbed our willowy STARLING, 'Lithe Ellie.' Always so nimble on those bloody obstacle courses. To be precise, she was better than most of the men."

Brandt felt sick. *Christ, this Schwanz knows everything.*

Again speaking German, the Nazi prattled on, "Also, to be precise, my dear Elise won't share your fate. Not yet anyway. She's much too . . ." he waved his hand as he thought of the right word, "luscious for such a routine death. No, I have my own designs on that svelte beauty with her tantalizing emerald eyes and such a provocative way of moving . . ."

Seeing von Zeitz distracted, Brandt carefully drew his knife from his boot and lunged. His movement was too sluggish. Blood, slick on the wood floor, made him slip. Easily sidestepping Brandt's attack, von Zeitz knocked the blade from his hand with a blow to his elbow. Brandt heard a muffled crack, like stepping on rotten boards, and knew his elbow was broken before pain registered in his mind. Brandt fell to his knees, Shoving him over with his boot, von Zeitz kicked Brandt solidly in the groin. Brandt crumpled in an agonizing heap.

Despite excruciating pain, Brandt struggled to rise. Though aware of Kühnstahl's return, the words of his former sergeant were little more than an annoying whir.

"The girl is gone. I found nothing in the *Volkswagen, Obersturmbannführer*, but I drove it several blocks away. What are we going to do with him?"

Emphasizing his frustration at not learning what he needed, von Zeitz cocked his leg back and kicked Brandt again. The sickening thud signified cracked ribs. Pain would soon follow. Brandt slumped back onto the floor. He lay in his own blood, motionless, struggling to breathe, knowing things would only get worse from here on out.

"Throw this pathetic wretch in the trunk of the *Horsch*. I don't want the bastard getting my upholstery all bloody." Grinning at the crumpled heap of Elise's soon-to-be-dead husband, von Zeitz contemplated his strategy. "Once we get him to *Gestapo* HQ, we can devote our full, undivided attention to this scum with a leisurely interrogation."

Feral eyes glowing like a rabid wolf, Kühnstahl grinned in vile anticipation. This was what he enjoyed about assisting von Zeitz.

PRINZ ALBRECHTSTRASSE 8
WED: 29 MAY 40

The leisurely interrogation dragged into days. Stripped naked, fed barely enough to keep a sewer rat alive, denied sleep, Brandt lost track of time. He endured the agony, every conscious moment stalked by fear. Not fear for himself. Brandt was reconciled to his fate. But fear he'd talk. To say anything would imperil his father's resistance network, which in turn, would put Elise and Anna in more danger.

Brandt knew he didn't have long to live. Though the guards revived him daily with icy buckets of water, he knew either von Zeitz would kill him outright or Kühnstahl would more than happily beat him to death.

Before I die, I must warn MI-6 of this Judas who can enter the governmental buildings of Whitehall or visit Buckingham Palace as boldly as he strides the inner sanctum of Adolf Hitler's Chancellery or Himmler's Wewelsburg Castle.

Just as crucial, Elise must get Anna out of this Nazi hell. But Brandt's hope began to fade . . .

⊕

Days, maybe weeks, passed. Bruised and bleeding,

bones broken, blind in one eye with a constant ringing in his ears, Brandt wanted to stay curled in a fetal position. He couldn't help but desire death. In the dark, permeating chill of this dungeon cell, he fervidly prayed Elise and Anna be spared the horror of von Zeitz's wrath. He also prayed that he'd neither betray his father nor die a coward. So far Brandt's refusal to talk never wavered. He also begged God for an end to his torment.

The brawny *SS* guards dragged Brandt, still groggy from a pain-racked, nebulous sleep, back to the same interrogation room. Harshly bound to a bolted-down chair, he knew his suffering would begin anew. One guard left, presumably to inform von Zeitz that Brandt was ready. The other guard, a newer man, whispered, "Wolf knows your fate." The man stepped out of the room.

Those four simple words were enough to put Brandt's mind at ease. *I'm already a dead man, but my father's aware of the truth and will take care of Elise and Anna. Dear God, thank you.*

When von Zeitz and Kühnstahl entered, both wore similar black leather gloves, reinforced to inflict maximum damage. Questioning resumed, the pummeling continued. Brandt's blood spattered the floor and walls. But within Brandt was a peace they could not break. After more senseless torture, the colonel began to realize this as well.

Despite a constant murmur in his blood-clogged ears, Brandt heard von Zeitz softly order, "Leave us, Kühnstahl."

The door grated open, then clanged shut. Through an orange haze, Brandt saw von Zeitz step closer. Grabbing a fistful of blood-matted hair, von Zeitz jerked Brandt's head back. Feeling the demon's hot breath on his face, Brandt saw pure malevolence in von Zeitz's eyes, sensed the rasp of conquest stroke his soul.

"I tire of your obstinacy, Gündestein. Tell me what I need to know, and I will let you die."

From between his broken teeth and swollen lips, Brandt spat blood and hatred at von Zeitz. "*Fick dich!*"

Fingers clamped onto Brandt's windpipe. With the back of his other hand, von Zeitz wiped the pink-frothed spittle off his face. The thin scar near his eye stood stark against a hate-reddened face as his grip tightened. "I cannot fuck myself, you *Schwanz*, but to be precise, your wife can and will fuck me."

Before Brandt passed out, von Zeitz released his throat.

"No . . ." Sliding a stiletto from his sleeve, von Zeitz thoughtfully said, "Choking you is too much trouble . . ."

The colonel strolled behind Brandt. Already coughing up blood, Brandt fully expected his throat to be slit. He'd die all right: slowly, in agony, blood pumping from slashed arteries and veins, lungs gasping but receiving no air, all the while knowing he had mere seconds to live.

"It is odd, Gündestein," the psychopath said, reappearing in front of Brandt, "I've no desire to prolong your inquisition." Rhetorically, he asked, "I wonder why? It's not like me to show pity to an enemy." Resting the stiletto just below Brandt's good eye, von Zeitz again demanded, "Where's the package you received from the Jew in Portugal?"

The same damned question. With no fight remaining— nor any answer—Brandt glared into the greedy eyes of his executioner.

"To be precise," von Zeitz's voice sliced through Brandt's hate-infused mind, "you lasted longer than I thought for such a weak excuse of an officer. However," he said as he pressed the knife until the tip punctured Brandt's cheek. Blood bubbled out. ." . . . rest assured, you pitiful cur, Elise shall be my own personal whore and she will play whatever games I desire. But in the end . . . she too must die. Just like you."

Without care, von Zeitz thrust the stiletto up through Brandt's blue eye, forcing the blade into his brain. Death came almost instantly.

As von Zeitz recalled Elise Gündestein's lush body, he

felt himself harden even more. Withdrawing the knife, he smiled with pleasure.

"Perhaps," von Zeitz wondered aloud, methodically tugging off his bloody gloves one finger at a time, "I should keep my green-eyed quiff on the edge of fear by stalking her?" His smile broadened. "To be precise, the mundane intrigue I've witnessed at MI-6 will be enlivened a great deal. Though I'm sure I'll be the only one to believe our poor delusional Elise . . ."

Chuckling softly at his private joke, von Zeitz withdrew a silk *SS* monogrammed handkerchief from his pocket and wiped the blade clean. He dropped the soiled fabric on the battered, broken and naked body of Brandt Gündestein.

Aware Kühnstahl watched through the spy-hole, he motioned for the perverted sergeant to enter. After Kühnstahl closed the door, von Zeitz ordered, "Dump his body in one of the Jew mass graves. He deserves no better. Then, make the usual arrangements for a flight to Lisbon for me. Lay out my civvies. I will change into my British uniform after I reach Godforsaken Dublin."

When von Zeitz contemplated his ultimate plunder, an icy grin tilted his rapier-thin mustache. With a flourish of his hand, he declared, "Not wanting to disappoint *Mein Führer*, this mighty warrior must travel afar on a quest for a most delectable woman, ripe with feminine charms and spicy delights: my most beautiful Elise Gündestein."

"To the greatest warrior belongs the most beautiful woman."

Adolf Hitler

SECTION ONE
GLASGOW BONNIE

CHAPTER ONE

Eleanor McCallister Greer braced her legs shoulder-width against the rolling swells and stared across the turbulent sea. This day, like this dead-in-the-water freighter, had vacillated like a bobbing cork. She'd been heartened when the Australian's big flying boat came back to report contact with a U.S. Coast Guard cutter to their north. But, just as quickly, her hopes had been dashed when the Aussies added that they'd also spotted a German U-boat. True to their word, however, the Aussie Sunderland had flown cover over *Glasgow Bonnie* for as long as possible.

Eventually their petrol had run low, forcing them to leave. Knowledge the Yanks were near didn't counteract the hush after the flying boat withdrew. The drone of the huge plane's engines had been like a mother's lullaby.

Now the melody was painfully absent.

Ellie, as her Uncle Bert and the crew knew her, felt

night creep over *Glasgow Bonnie*. She considered her own impasse. By boarding her uncle's old freighter, she'd escaped a two-legged lion stalking her in London only to take refuge in a wolf's den.

Like an inescapable shadow, trouble continued to follow her. Icy fingers of fate clawed at her heart. With a U-boat lurking near, Ellie feared *Bonnie*'s crew, including herself, might not live to see dawn. If they even made it that long.

Briefly closing her eyes, she bowed her head in prayer and resignation, hoping her instincts were wrong. As always, God alone knew, though over the years she'd learned to trust herself.

Entering the crew's mess, she took the food slopped on her metal plate and sat by herself. The scarred table tilted as *Glasgow Bonnie* rolled. Sipping tasteless, lukewarm tea, she surveyed her fellow crewmen over the top of her chipped mug. They glared back, if they looked her way at all. Fear, hatred, perhaps even a little lust, leered at her from their red-rimmed, exhausted eyes.

Ellie was the outcast; a woman; this freighter's designated Jonah; *Bonnie*'s bad luck on an already ill-fated voyage.

As one of *Bonnie*'s three radio operators, Ellie talked and acted like any other crewman: uncouth and gruff. Her appearance matched as well: flannel shirt, heavy wool sweater, corduroy pants, sea boots.

Underneath the garb, the crew knew she was a woman. She didn't belong with them.

This mangy lot was all a dilapidated freighter of *Bonnie*'s ilk could draw: salt-tarnished mariners with no other life but lingering loyalty to her uncle; second-rate salts not qualified for newer ships; British brig conscripts due to a shortage of any other able-bodied seamen.

To Ellie, the crew's character didn't matter. Reaching her cousin in Nova Scotia did. Fellow crewmen, even her uncle, had no idea what drove her to this end. They

STARLING — *GLASGOW BONNIE*   15

wouldn't care if they did. Unsure and uncaring about where any of their shaky futures might lead, Ellie continued to guard her own shadowed past.

Attacking the block of anemic meatloaf, colored only by a dousing of Tabasco sauce—its sole flavor—her fork screeched on the metal plate. Her thoughts of eating ended. Seasickness had never bothered her before, but with today's events, supper did nothing to help her queasy stomach. She pushed the plate away and withdrew a dog-eared Agatha Christie novel from her pocket. The cover had fallen off long before the mystery was solved for the umpteenth reading, but it was an escape.

"'Ey, li'l Sheba," a gruff voice dragged her back to the present.

Oh, God, nae Bilks. The brashest of the black gang stokers sashayed his bulk over to her table like a corpulent Casanova. Ellie braced for a clash. Bilks had badgered her since they cleared Liverpool. Until now, evening meals were the only time she avoided him.

The man's scraggly whiskers and soot-grimed face reminded her of a huge wels catfish. A stench of sweat, cigars and dried urine preceded him like putrefaction. His breath alone could shrivel an onion. Ellie's stomach rolled.

Parking his butt on the table edge, Bilks flashed a yellow grin. "Sweets, why ye keep tryin' to hide them loverly bubs o' yers under those frumpy men's clothes? I know they're jus' beggin' to be squeezed. How bout we go to me cabin and ye can suck on me li'l nipper an' gives us some hot cuzzy? I tell ye, sweets, me nipper's all loaded an' ready to fire. Whad ye say, Sheba?"

She met his gaze. At thirty-seven with all she'd endured—the past two years in particular—Ellie gave no hint of the real emotions she felt. Though she certainly didn't feel like it, she burst out laughing. Every man in the mess, if not facing them already, turned to see what was so funny.

"Kiss yer bloody pecker, Bilks?" Ellie asked in a coarse

Highland brogue, the only vernacular anyone ever heard from her. With a snort, she arched an eyebrow. "I'd sooner be blowin' a bloomin' shark than kiss the likes of ye. How do ye even find that wee blighter under all yer stinkin' blubber anyway?"

Black eyes narrowed. His beefy jowls reddened in rage, blooming into humiliation when men sniggered behind him. Bilks swung his mass around. The chuckling ceased. Then he turned on Ellie.

"You li'l strumpet." His meaty hand knotted a fistful of sweater, dragging her close. "I've half a bloody mind ta—"

Seizing his sausage-like thumb, Ellie cranked it back with an ease taught by the best hand-to-hand combat instructors in Great Britain. Bilks yowled as his own bulk tipped him off balance.

She twisted him onto the deck, bending his arm up into his back. Though Bilks squirmed like a harpooned whale, her grip held like the curved hook of a barb.

"God's sakes, Bilks, ye better nae be givin' me half yer mind or ye'll be comin' up bloody well empty," she snarled through clenched teeth. "Wha' might be on yer puny brain, anyway?" When he failed to answer, Ellie rammed his hand further up between his shoulder blades. He wailed in agony.

"Nothin' . . . nothin'," Bilks gasped out. "Don' be breakin' me poor arm. I didn't mean nothin', jus' don' break me bloody arm."

"Forget yer manners, Bilks? 'Don't break me arm' wha?" she demanded. With his hesitation, she applied more pressure.

Crying out in pain, Bilks pawed the deck with his free hand and sputtered, "Please . . . don' break me arm . . ."

With his dignity impaled, Ellie leaned close to his ear and, in a menacing whisper, said, "I'll only be tellin' ye this once, Bilks, so listen up good. Talk to me like that agin, I'll whack off yer wee pecker, cram it down yer fuckin' throat, then toss yer fat, bloated carcass in the drink for the bloody

sharks to feast on. Do I be makin' meself perfectly clear?"
Bilks nodded, too weak or too unsettled to speak.

Pushing herself up, Ellie dug her knee into his back. Laboring to straighten his arm, Bilks whimpered. Crewmen gawked till they saw the defiance in Ellie's emerald green eyes. Their gazes quickly averted; conversations slowly resumed.

The solitary sound of clapping arose behind Ellie with a loud, "Bravo, milady! Bravo! Encore!"

She placed the voice of her lone admirer as George Mathers, senior radioman. Besides Uncle Bert, George was the only other man aboard *Glasgow Bonnie* with whom Ellie ever willingly spoke. Though George was lazy and not very reliable, she liked the unassuming, out-of-work actor.

George sat and said, "Catch your breath, love," patting the butt-worn wooden bench beside him. "I must say, my honey-tressed beauty, you've some phenomenal moves. Ever consider fight-scene choreography for theater? Could pay well."

"Nae, George," Ellie sighed as an ebbing adrenalin-surge pounded in her ears. "Fights're nae what I be wantin'."

Even if I explained the truth, she thought, *he'd never understand.* Nine years of duplicity, fear and death in Nazi Germany left a gloom Ellie longed to lighten with love, honesty and life.

"Pity," George said. "Such potential." Falling silent as he spied her plate, his lip curled derisively. "Tonight's supper looks more hideous than usual. Are ya able to chew the damn biscuits? I'd hate to break a tooth. Hard to be a gap-grinned leading man." He flashed his bright white teeth as testimony. "Spot more limp tea, love?"

Ellie closed her eyes at the thought. "Nae, but thanks." As she hunted her place in the novel, George made his way into the galley.

Tea and a biscuit smeared with oleo in hand, he came back shortly. Rapping the powdery puck on the table, he said, "Bloody things give the term 'hardtack' an entirely new meaning."

Dunking the biscuit in his tea, George took a grimaced bite. Trying not to taste his food, he mumbled, "Ever decipher the mystery message I showed you earlier?"

"Nae," Ellie said, another lie easier than truth. Within moments after receiving the note, she had decoded it. The flimsy's words burned in her mind with the steadfastness with which George told her it had been sent: every forty-five minutes, thirteen times. A warning, she understood, in itself.

At MI-6, a former colleague's morose poem had summed up the meaning behind any such timed code:

> *If you hear the thirteenth chime,*
> *know the Nazis found your crime.*
> *Plan to spend a cold, dark night,*
> *running from their dogs in fright.*
> *You're in some Nazi sniper's scope*
> *or you'll swing from a bloody rope.*
> *Either way you'll be good and dead,*
> *should've stayed home in your bed.*

Since no response had been given, Ellie suspected the process would start to repeat thirteen hours later—another reference to the thirteenth chime. That would make the time 2250 or 10:50 tonight. It would definitely fall during her radio watch.

Jolting Ellie from her morbid musing, seven bells chimed half-past-seven, 1930 hours, reminding her of the seven words of the dark message. Ignoring her pessimism, she unlimbered her long legs from the stationary bench. "I best be headin' for the radio room, George. Enjoy yer feast."

George waved, gulping his tea to avoid choking on another bite of biscuit before calling to her, "Watch your back, love."

"Always do," she said, wondering: *Will I be spendin' me whole bloody life lookin' over me shoulder? 'Tis either damned Nazis after me, drunk sailors or lecherous leeches like that obnoxious prick Bilks. It'd be nice to have someone next to me to watch me back for a change.*

USCGC *ZEALOUS*
NORTH ATLANTIC
MONDAY

Lieutenant Karney Liam Rork lowered his binoculars. In the lime-green radiance of the Aurora Borealis there wasn't much to see except dark rolling swells and churned water from their depth-charge attack on a lone U-boat.

After starting the attack on a German submarine on a typically short December day, *Zealous* disengaged after a British Coastal Command Sunderland contacted them. Flying patrol over the convoy routes, the flying boat signaled the American cutter that a freighter named *Glasgow Bonnie* was disabled and left behind by their convoy. The Aussies would soon run out of petrol and daylight, so gave "*Lady Z*" the freighter's coordinates and informed them they'd fly cover as long as their fuel held out. *Zealous* shifted to a southerly course, though they continued hunting the U-boat.

"Whacha think, Tap?" His question hung in ghostly blurs of frozen condensation. Though Master Chief Petty Officer Miguel Tapia was subordinate to Karney, the Irish-born Yank respected the opinion of the stout Chicano. He also valued their friendship and the honesty they nurtured in this partnership.

Raising his binoculars, Tap said, "*Compadre*, I think we're wasting our time." As always, Tap's voice was soft with barely a hint of his Mexican heritage. His Mom had made sure all her kids spoke proper English.

After a muted grumble of agreement, Karney called below through the voice tube, "Conn, Rork. We picking anything up?" He knew sonar or hydrophones might be the only chance of locating that sub.

Petty Officer Mark Allison replied, "Negative, Skipper. Sternbach or Craig, neither one can find 'em, sir, ya know? Sorry."

Bracing his forearm on the flying-bridge's icy rail, Karney rubbed his forehead with a gloved hand, trying to keep his unraveling patience from fraying further.

Again calling below, his tone was resigned, "Bridge, finish out this grid so we can eliminate the quadrant."

In the shifting Northern Lights, Tap observed Karney's brawny shoulders slump beneath his salt-crusted underway coat. The long hours of chasing a German ghost were etched beneath the shadow of his helmet. Blue-gray eyes, mirroring the moods of the sea, would remain iced-steel as they had been since the hunt began.

Command of their little Buck and a Quarter had come to Karney unexpectedly, but he accepted the responsibility in stride. Karney remained calm even after Japan had attacked Pearl Harbor Naval Base in the Hawaiian Islands eight days ago. As declarations of war had flown fast and furious between the Allied and Axis Powers, Karney Rork had galvanized his emotions and steeled the crew behind him.

Admitting this U-boat had escaped was counter-productive to Karney's mindset.

Time dragged as lookouts continued to scan the last portion of this quadrant.

The voice tube whistled. "Rork here," Karney said, listened briefly, then replied, "Thanks, Allison. Stand down from general quarters; go to battle readiness. Come about on course two-one-zero. Speed six knots. Let's find our wallowing *Bonnie*."

Disappointment traced Allison's voice as he answered from below, "Aye, aye, sir, two-one-zero, six knots. Headin' for *Glasgow Bonnie*."

Karney added, "And, Allison, thank Jeff and Del. Tell

'em we'll have another crack at this Kraut before long." He recapped the tube.

Miguel Tapia grinned in the darkness. "Is your prophetic Irish sixth-sense talking to ya again, *compadre?*"

Scratching his stubbled jaw, Karney groaned, "Geez, I wish it were that simple. I'd just connect the Irish-soothsayer part of me to the helm and we'd sink us a U-boat in no time." He softly chuckled. "Sounds wilder than a Captain Nemo scenario."

In the nasally timbre of a self-opinionated radio spieler, Karney aped, "Folks, this just reported from the icy reaches of the North Atlantic: a U-S of A Coast Guard Cutter sinks a Nat-see U-boat. We can't let slip crucial details, but we do know an ultra-secret weapon was used during this battle. Fantastic as it may sound, and you heard it here first, folks, the key to this new weapon has to do with what the skipper ate today. Yessiree."

With a hearty laugh, Tap shook his head. Karney's sense of humor seldom, if ever, wavered. His optimism, as gentle as Irish mist, allowed him to tackle adversity head-on and still crack jokes.

Though dog-tired, hearing Tap's laughter lightened Karney's mood. It served as the lubricant to a strong friendship, carrying them through disappointments, danger and the loss of loved ones. After six years of serving together, the two men were closer than many brothers. Partly why Karney was godfather to Tap's youngest son.

Since they first met, Miguel Tapia's looks had hardly changed. With thick, black hair and a longer-than-regulation mustachio, Tap held a Pancho Villa zest of jalapeños caliente despite icy winds from Greenland and the frigid Atlantic around them. The only things missing were a flashy black stallion, bandoleers and a *sombrero* rather than a helmet.

The two men—non-commissioned enlisted and an officer—kept duty professional and friendship personal. But on a small cutter like *Zealous*, boundaries blurred.

Physically, the two were Laurel-and-Hardy opposites. However, they did share kindred spirits and interests.

Stretching his stiff muscles, Karney asked, "You eat, *amigo?*"

"Not yet, but neither've you, Irish," Tap said, referring to his friend by his more common nickname.

"Had a Hershey bar a bit ago. If I eat another one, you suppose my gut'll tell us where our Wagnerian pig-boat might pop up?"

"Doubtful." More grimly, Tap said, "I just wish we could've nailed those Krauts. At least kept them deaf and blind till we rescued that freighter's crew."

With a sigh, Karney spoke in Gaelic, "*I ríocht na ndall is rí fear aonroisc,*" then translated, "In the land of the blind, the one-eyed man is king." He shrugged. "Since we can't see or hear Jerry, he's already got a step up on the throne. Go eat, *amigo.*"

Tap headed down the ladder.

A bit later, Karney heard a hesitant voice. "Skipper?" It was Clark Hackerman. "Can you come down to conn? Kelley needs to show you something."

"Sure, Hack, I'll be right down." To the senior rating on watch, he called, "Barb, I'm heading below. Show's yours. Rotate watch in another few minutes or so. We don't wanna hafta fight any Krauts with a buncha frostbitten bananas."

Seaman Jim Barberio grinned. "Aye, aye, Skipper." With frozen chocolate-covered bananas on his mind, the young Italian raised his glasses to scan another section of cold North Atlantic.

Swinging down the ladder, Karney jumped to the bridge-wing with a thud that rang the steel and both his feet. He entered the wheelhouse lit by red, night-running lights. The warmth of *Lady Z*'s nerve-center seemed stifling after the icy air up top.

He greeted Mark Allison at the wheel. Tugging salt-crusted gloves from his numb hands, Karney surveyed this space crammed with crucial equipment. From here, *Lady Z*'s course was charted and steered; transmissions coded and decoded; shipboard matters logged; watches set; commands came in from GreenPat to be passed along to the crew. Experimental sonar—which initially stood for SOund NAvigation Ranging—had been recently packed into the space as well. When operating, its p-pinging served as a constant reminder of *Lady Z*'s harsh duty off the convoluted East Greenland Coast. They patrolled for marauding German U-boats and searched for their hapless victims—if any managed to survive.

Karney again wondered: *Is our little Lady even up to this task?*

Designated a sub-chaser prior to the war, *Lady Z* had a maximum "drawing-board" speed of 13 knots. That fell far short of a U-boat's top surface speed. *How can our little gal destroy an enemy she can't even catch? A U-boat might not wanna waste a torpedo on us, but their deck-gun'd sure mess up our camouflage war paint. God forbid our fuel bunker ever got . . .*

Karney deep sixed the image as he stepped past the barber-style captain's chair to duck into the "back office," as the crew dubbed it. Here sat their radio to keep *Zealous* linked to the world beyond the horizon. Charts were stashed in a half dozen drawers beneath the chart table.

Noticing Petty Officer Clark Hackerman hunched over the table, Karney wondered what he furiously scribbled on his yellow notepad. He seemed oblivious to all else. Petty Officer Roger Kelley shuffled through a sheaf of radio messages where he sat at the steel radio desk. With his headphones on, he too seemed preoccupied.

To get his attention, Karney flipped his helmet off and set it like some capsized turtle beside the radio chassis. "So whacha got, Kelley?"

"I can't put my finger on it, Skipper," he said, sliding the headphones off one of his ears, "but somethin's not right with some of these transmissions."

Karney unwound his scarf and tossed it into his helmet with his gloves. Like some age-old ritual, he removed his Red Sox ball cap, ruffled his mussed coffee-brown hair, resettled the cap and began thumbing through the flimsies—thin paper torn from a larger pad used by radio-telegraphers to decode messages.

"The long messages are hit and miss, but they're sharp and clear, sir," Kelley said. "They seem close. Maybe our elusive U-boat?"

His something-not-right hunch crept up Karney's spine like icy fingers, as he considered: *A convoy course radioed to Wilhelmshaven? Messages between U-boats forming a wolf-pack? A Nazi surface raider out here?*

Watching his skipper, Kelley noted his eyes shift to stormy gray.

Karney sorted the flimsies. Eight of the messages, each with seven words, were definitely different from the longer missives. Glancing at his radioman, he asked, "Is there a sequence to the short ones?"

"Yes, sir. That's the pisser. They're at forty-five-minute intervals. Kinda weird. Ya think it might be a U-boat stalkin' a convoy?"

Slowly shaking his head, Karney leafed through them, noting each time. "Doubt it. They don't match any I recall at ASW," he said, referring to his crash course at the Anti-Submarine Warfare School.

Cocking his head in thought, Karney said, "The longer ones could be coded convoy course coordinates." Despite the seriousness, a grin crept over his face as he clicked his tongue. "Man, don't try saying that after a few too many beers."

Solemn once again, Karney said, "No numbers. And even on a vicious zigzag pattern a convoy couldn't change course that—"

As if on cue, staccato tapping—the dots and dashes of Morse code—came over the radiotelegraph. Kelley jotted down letters forming the words of an unknown code;

probably indecipherable without the German ENIGMA machine. Glancing up, he said, "Short one again, Skipper." Karney's gaze shot to the clock: ten minutes till eleven. To no one in particular, he muttered an Irish phrase, "*Ní scéal rúin é ó tá a fhios ag triúr é.*" His absent-minded use of Gaelic was one of the reasons he was known as "Irish" to half the fleet.

Curious, Kelley asked, "What's that mean, Skipper?"

"'Tis not a secret if three know it." Pursing his lips, he shrugged. "Unfortunately, we're not one of the three in . . ."

"Kelley," came Hackerman's excited voice, "I think I got it. I . . ." Swinging around on the stool, his eyes flew open upon seeing Karney. "Oh, sorry, sir, didn't know you were here."

"That's okay, Hack. What kick-started your engine?"

"I think I know what the short ones say. Well, I mean, I don't really know what it says, but I mighta filled in the seven words." Handing over his tablet, Hack suddenly sounded timid, "Well, that's if I figured the code right, sir."

Scratched-out letters and words were like crazed doodlings of an insane writer till Karney noticed a pattern. Reading the final line, the tablet seemed to waver in his hand. He briefly closed his eyes. An image crashed into his mind of a blond man's naked and battered bloody corpse being thrown into a mass grave. Visions this clear did not happen to him often, but his Grandmother Reddy had warned him he'd probably inherited the Irish gift of "seeing" from his mother.

Karney found the incongruity of this image, at this moment, wholly unexpected and more than a little disturbing. Suddenly hit by a feeling of wooziness, he grabbed the edge of the desk. "What the hell . . ."

"You okay, sir?" Kelley asked, steadying his skipper.

Shaking off the grisly chimera, Karney said, "Geez, that was weird. Tap's right, maybe I do need to eat something." Trying to dispel the bizarre image, he smoothed out the page and read aloud: "Starling nest discovered, Wolf on scent, Tusk." Karney glanced at the junior radioman.

Barely eighteen and usually seasick, Hack defended, "I don't know what it means, sir. It's a buncha gibberish to me, but—"

Holding up his hand, Karney said, "Hack, I didn't figure you would know what it means." He pondered the scribbles, quietly observing, "But I'll betcha even-odds, your so-called bunch of gibberish means something to somebody somewhere out here."

GLASGOW BONNIE
MONDAY

Before heading to the radio room, Ellie MacCalister Greer paused to gaze at the intense greenish hues of the shimmering Aurora Borealis. Her gaze drifted down to its broken reflection on the water. *I hope the Americans are close.* An unexpected reply came in a single, muffled explosion. Ellie held still. Two more blasts, probably depth charges, followed in short order, but they were all a long way off. *I hope the Yank plaster the bloody hell outta Jerry.* Like counting the seconds from a lightening flash to a clap of thunder, she wished she could see the explosions to figure out how faraway the Yanks were. But depth charges, if that was in fact what she heard, only rumpled the water.

Stepping inside the superstructure of the freighter, Ellie mumbled to herself to break the oppressive silence, "Maybe me worryin's for naugh' anyway."

After taking over from *Bonnie*'s on-duty radioman, she settled in for a long night. *The Yank cutter may be busy for hours. They'll have a long night, too.*

Guardedly, she unfolded the flimsy with its cryptic words and read the decoded message one more time:
STARLING NEST DISCOVERED / WOLF ON SCENT / TUSK

The meaning coiled about her like icy tendrils of fog.

TUSK was her former controller at MI-6: Major James Fenton Strafford III. She'd known the major long before Hitler's *Blitzkrieg* tore Europe apart and the deaths of her husband and precious little girl had torn Ellie's heart out. James Strafford had guided her as the double-agent Elise Gündestein in Berlin for more than nine years. Ellie reflected: *James is an ideal spy—slick, wily, ice for blood along with martinis pumpin' through his veins. But even though he's handsome, he's far too aloof with an ego that voids any good he ever does. Heavens, according to James, we'll lose the bloody war if we dinna have his expertise and devotion to MI-6 to direct us.*

Then Ellie reminded herself of another reality and sighed. *If nae for James, I most likely would've died in Berlin.*

Thinking of his shameless side, Ellie scoffed. *But he's still a cad. He uses his charisma and sweet talk for more than just the spy game. With false promises and lies, he lures gullible "skirts" into his bed.*

Right. Gullible skirts like me. Nae, it was more than gullibility lurin' me to his lair of lust. Though fear drove me there, trickery proved me undoing. Thank the Lord I wasna mired any deeper in James Strafford's honey-sweet babble and sticky lies.

Ellie closed her eyes and shook her head in remorse.

The warning James sent from England, like his empty promises, only depressed her. *What good does it do me in the midst of the North Atlantic? I've certainly nowhere to run or hide, especially nae from any damned torpedo.*

And torpedoes were the fangs of the WOLF—German U-boats. Alone or in wolf packs, U-boats prowled North Atlantic convoy routes, staining the seas crimson with the lifeblood of England and Russia.

The only other Wolf I know is me father-in-law and, surely, Opa Wolf would nae have any reason to wish me harm. He assured me he loved me like his own daughter— even before I married Brandt.

NEST was *Glasgow Bonnie*, Uncle Bert's wallowing, rusty tub.

However, the most poignant of the seven words was STARLING. It too was a code name—a very personal one.

I am STARLING and Nazis still hunt me.

Ellie set a match to the flimsy and dropped it in a nearby ashtray. Adjusting her headphones, an electronic symphony of colliding air filled her ears. She spun the dial, hearing nothing to encourage her.

Anxious minutes passed into agonizing hours. Glancing at the clock, she noticed it was almost eleven, almost thirteen hours since the last warning. She wondered: *Where'd the Yanks go? Why have they nae sent any messages? Or any—*

Startled from her listening, Uncle Bert popped in. "Ah good, Lass. Better I've you here than that actor rake singin' a bloomin' tune to the purr Yanks like 'twas some bawdy Broadway audition."

She giggled, knowing Uncle Bert's droll opinion of George.

"See if ye kin raise the bloody Yanks, Lass. They're bein' a wee bit shy aboot wooin' our lady. Let the first mate know if ye git 'em. I'll be down in engineerin'." With that, Uncle Bert left.

Before she keyed the mike, the radio burst to life.

"*Glasgow Bonnie*, this is *United States Coast Guard Cutter Zealous. Bonnie*, this is *USCGC Zealous*. Do you read me? Over."

The deep voice sounded calm and professional, perhaps even stiff. Though jumpy at the message's timing, Ellie serenely keyed the mike and answered, "*Zealous*, this be *Glasgow Bonnie*. Hear you strength four. Over."

A long pause hung in the air before a reply came back. Ellie figured the fellow probably wondered what a woman was doing on board.

"*Glasgow Bonnie*, this is Lieutenant Rork aboard *Zealous*. To whom might I be speaking? Over."

"Leftenant Rork, ye be talkin' to Ellie McCallister Greer. Delighted to be hearin' from ye. Over."

"*Bonnie*, what's your present status? Over."

Well, nae socializin' here. "*Zealous*, we're in a jar of jam but we be needin' to know, did ya sink the U-boat? Over."

There was another hesitation between the time she heard him key the mike and when he spoke. An omen of his answer.

"Negative, *Bonnie*. Assuming you are armed, please ask your gunners not to shoot a hole in our scones. We'll get your crew aboard for a midnight snack. Over."

Ellie grinned. *They're near and that stiff leftenant does seem to have a sense of humor.* However, his next comment ended her musing.

"Have your crew ready the lifeboats. We don't want any delays, since we don't know where Jerry went. Over."

It suddenly occurred to her: *If the Yanks're close enough to have us ready the boats, the U-boat they didna sink might be even closer. Oh, Lord, this is nae good.*

Calming her worrisome mind, she answered, "*Zealous*, I'll notify the captain of yer request and—"

The reverberation of an explosion roiled through *Bonnie*: a torpedo. In a delayed reaction, the old freighter lurched violently. Ellie was thrown to the deck. Pain shot across her abdomen when manuals and a tool box flew off the shelf above the radio chassis. Fighting a sickening, slow-motion whirlpool, her vision swirled in a maelstrom of gaudy hues. She registered only one thing: *The bloody U-boat got to us before the Yanks.* The overhead bulb flashed out like the closing act of a tragic play.

Ellie felt as though she was trapped in tar pitch. Her stomach began to churn in sluggish heaves. Fighting down the putrid bile rising in her throat, she scrunched her eyes shut. Gradually letting them relax, she again opened them. The eddies calmed to uniform blackness. She still struggled against a sharp pain, however.

Grabbing the table edge, Ellie started to pull herself back up. Chaotic spinning overwhelmed every ounce of cognizance she possessed. Ellie's world washed black.

CHAPTER TWO

Before Karney Rork could wonder why the woman's words cut off, an orange fireball lit the night sky. "Son of a bitch," he swore, tossing his headphones to Kelley. "SOUND GENERAL QUARTERS."

A split-second later, the repercussion from *Bonnie* struck his ears. The blaring Klaxon sparked *Lady Z* to action: men raced to their stations, boots thudding, orders came sharp and loud.

"Harley," Karney called to his exec coming onto the bridge, "maintain present heading; flank speed. Kelley, try to raise *Bonnie*."

Darting up the ladder, Karney tried not to worry about the lady with the Highland lilt to her voice. Yet he couldn't help but wonder if Ellie McCallister Greer was awfully brave or terribly stupid for being out here. Nor could he deny the possibility that many of *Bonnie*'s crew might already be dead. But it was a damned sure bet, if *Lady Z* didn't survive this, those aboard *Bonnie* probably wouldn't make it either.

⊕

GLASGOW BONNIE
MONDAY

Ellie Greer opened her eyes. Garish swirls of color continued in a stomach-churning kaleidoscope. Repeating the motions from her first try at getting up, she moved more cautiously. She touched the table leg, but stayed down on the deck. A faraway voice drifted in . . . and out of her hearing. In and out. It persisted like a stuck phonograph record.

Between the babble and acrid pall of smoke reality crashed back upon her.

She felt for the torch that normally dangled from a short rope. Reaching further, violent pain again shot across her stomach. Gritting her teeth, Ellie grabbed the light. She sat still for a long moment, feeling the surge of swells rolling beneath *Bonnie*'s keel.

Turning on the torch, she oriented herself. The deck tilted toward the stern with a list to starboard. *But the old gal's still afloat.* Ellie needed to assess her damage. Gingerly, she tugged up her sweater and shirt, pushing her pants down just enough to see an ugly, red welt running from her hipbone to bellybutton. Seeing her injury, the pain seemed to increase. Dread rose like bile. Despair engulfed her senses. Her normally intense focus spiraled into chaos.

Ellie saw the heavy regulations manual she'd pushed off herself nearby. The culprit for her injury. *How mockin',* she thought, *that which is meant to help, ended up harmin' me.* She closed her eyes again. Finding it difficult to think, she opened them.

Swaying with the ship's roll, the headphones dangled before her. She caught the word *Zealous* and halted their swing.

The radioman's persistent, "*Bonnie*, this is *Zealous*, come in please," became a litany driving her to respond.

Awkwardly, she drew herself up, head throbbing

viciously. When she adjusted the headset, her fingers grew sticky with blood. She ignored it. Retrieving the mike ripped her last strength away. The kaleidoscope exploded anew. Crushed under another onslaught of pain, Ellie crashed backwards into a whirlpool of expanding blackness.

USCGC ZEALOUS
MONDAY

"Skipper," came Brad Shelton's voice, "I gotta bogey, about two points forward of the starboard beam. About two thousand yards out."

Despite crewmen dubbing the shy, baby-faced seventeen-year-old, "Shell-man," he had the best eyes on board. Karney trusted him. Gazing across the water, nothing was evident. Blood-colored waves broke upon themselves, their troughs impenetrable shadows of darkness.

Lady Z rose on a crest. A vague silhouette caught Karney's sight, then he lost it. His peripheral vision caught sight of it again. "Yeah, bogey's right. It's a U-boat." With his glasses trained on the enemy, Karney could not mistake the conning tower backlit by *Bonnie*'s fires.

"Ironic," he said in a whisper, "the hunter's marked by the wounds of its victim."

"Yessiree," Mark Allison's voice drifted over, "it sure is a U-boat, Skipper. And she's aimin' for the Scottish lass."

"Probably admiring their handiwork," Karney said, uncapping the voice tube. "Bridge, Rork. Right full rudder, course two-seven-zero. Both ahead two-thirds."

"Bridge, aye . . ."

To his surprise it wasn't Dave Harlan who answered. It was Miguel Tapia. *I left Harley at the helm. Where the hell'd he go?*

"Course two-seven-zero. Both ahead two-thirds, aye."

The diesels rose in pitch. *Zealous* swung west. A swell

hit her beam on, sloshing the foredeck, seawater almost instantly turning to ice. The cutter lurched to port.

Karney grabbed the rail. "We're gonna pay hell trying to hit that pigboat in this sea." A three-inch pop-gun was the biggest punch *Lady Z* could muster if the Germans remained surfaced. Neither *Lady Z*'s two 20mm anti-aircraft guns nor their antiquated Lewis machine-gun packed much wallop. If the U-boat submerged, depth-charges might be able to finish them off.

Yelling down to his gunnery chief, Karney asked, "Gallagher, you got that U-boat sighted-in yet?"

"No, sir," came his cry. "Can't get a range."

Another explosion split the night. Karney's gaze snapped up to *Bonnie*. Munitions near her stern blew-up in a violent display. The enemy was now vividly marked by the freighter's death pyre. Karney once more yelled to the gunner, "Gallagher, you need a damn invitation to shoot him?"

"No, sir, I got 'em. Got 'em like a sittin' duck."

"Then Goddammit: FIRE!"

The three-incher's *kawhoom* seemed deafening, its muzzle flash blinding on the cutter's darkened deck. Karney raised his binoculars.

Lieutenant Dave Harlan appeared at that same instant, demanding, "What the hell are you doing taking on another U-boat, Rork?"

Temper barely in check, Karney watched as the shot fell short. He lowered his glasses to glare at Harlan as if he'd jinxed their aim. With a second shot fired, Karney raised his binoculars and said, "It's our job, Mr. Harlan. We're in a fuckin' war. And it's not another one. It's the same U-boat." He then hollered, "Gallagher, adjust fire two points to starboard."

The gun crew rammed home another round. Gallagher adjusted the elevation, double checked his aim and fired. Like an ogling little kid, Dave Harlan moved to get a better look.

Karney's temper flared. "Mr. Harlan, what the hell're you doing up here anyway?"

"Skipper," Brad Shelton called, "they're turnin' toward us."

Harlan accused, "To see what the hell you're getting us—"

A sharp whoosh split the night air. The German shell erupted to port. It showered the deck, leaving an icy sheen on the deck. "Jerry's got our range," Karney muttered. After *Lady Z* fired again, he ordered, "Helm, commence zigzag."

"Aye, sir," Tap curtly answered. "Commence zigzag."

The Germans fired again. No one saw where Gallagher's shot landed. Both shells hit simultaneously. The noise intense. Instinctively, men ducked as frigid water drenched them. *Zealous* rocked as if launched sideways from a shipbuilder's ways.

"Son of a bitch," Karney swore, straightening his helmet as icy seawater trickled down his back. He glanced around to see if his men were okay. Flames aboard *Bonnie* glowed dimly in Harlan's eyes, wide with distress. It was evident the thirty-year-old college brain wasn't prepared for a fire-fight with any Germans tonight.

Irish temper afire, Karney hollered over the turmoil, "Mr. Harlan, abandoning your battle station is tantamount to desertion." He forced himself to calm. "Return to your post immediately or confine yourself to quarters. Then figure out what the hell a court-martial will do to your aspirations of command."

Defying Karney, Harlan stood firm. Before he could say anything else an incoming shell screeched overhead. After ducking beneath the inadequate protection of rails and roped-on canvas, he stood up and glared at Karney. Reluctantly, Harlan headed toward the ladder and the bridge below.

Focusing on the battle, Karney put Harlan out of his mind.

Gallagher fired again. It landed starboard amidships. The U-boat's cannon crew vanished in a miasma of fire, water and smoke. Their efforts were not impeded for long.

Lady Z's deck crew winced with another piercing whine. It hit just aft of the gun platform, behind the fuel bunker. Engulfing the starboard side, the blast blew the motor launch off a davit. Fire and shrapnel rained down, ripping holes in the steel deck, fortunately not any men.

Knocked off his feet and momentarily blinded, the concussion rang in Karney's ears. He dragged himself up. When he saw the damage, he grumbled, "More forward and we'll sink in twain." His words were lost beneath the ringing from a church's belfry on Sunday morning. Karney pressed his ears, working his jaw to try and stop the incessant dinging. Bells were replaced by another din.

A tremendous clanking wheeze came from starboard. Further smudging the night, smoke roiled out of *Lady Z*'s exhaust. Diesel fumes mixed with the reek of cordite. Another belch of murky smoke changed the cacophonous noise to a grinding complaint of mechanical pain.

Flames on deck were quickly extinguished by a damage control party under the direction of Ensign Jonathan Grange.

"Grange," Karney hollered through his cupped hands to the inexperienced younger officer, "check engineering and make sure the galley's clear."

The tow-headed Oklahoman yelled back, "Gotcha, Skipper."

Karney focused his binoculars on *Bonnie*. Lifeboats were being lowered, crewmen on the deck were backlit by fire. No details stood out. *What shape are they in? Is that woman with them?*

A *kaboom* from their own gun brought Karney's concern back to *Lady Z*. For now, *Bonnie* would have to fend for herself.

In a blossom of fire and shrapnel, *Lady Z*'s round engulfed the conning tower of the U-boat. The German's cannon did not respond, her crew taken out of action. Other *Kriegsmariners* speedily replaced them, again ready to shoot as the vessels closed.

Kicking scorched debris from the gun platform, Dwayne Russell manned the starboard 20mm anti-aircraft gun while Clair "Foghorn" Flores readied the port gun. Their intense staccatos joined the chaos. Next to Karney, Brad Shelton opened up with the steadfast Lewis machine-gun; not always as effective but reliable.

Fiery tracers arced through the night.

Gallagher's last shot hit near the U-boat stern. The sub was under the elevation of their deck cannon. *Lady Z's* cannon could aim no lower.

Though the U-boat seemed impervious, damage had been done. Verifying what he saw with Mark Allison, Karney asked, "Mark, is that pig-boat listing to starboard?"

Staring through his binoculars, Allison agreed, "Yessiree, it does look that away. Down by the bow, too. Our first shot musta messed with her divin' planes, ya know?"

Karney ventured, "Yeah, maybe, but that doesn't explain why she hasn't fired a fish at us yet."

"Maybe we busted her torpedo doors," Allison said. "But they sure's hell want a piece o' our ass, Skipper. They're aimed straight at us."

"Yeah, they sure—" His words choked off. *Lady Z's* course was arrow straight as well. "Bridge, where the hell's our zigzag?"

Submissively, Harlan answered, "Rudder wire's damaged. We can't turn. Grossage says, and I quote, 'It'll be fixed in a jiff'."

"'Fraid a jiff ain't gonna cut it," Karney grumbled. On their present course, the Germans would ram *Zealous* amidships. The bow, her strongest point, had recently been reinforced against ice. But *Zealous* had never rammed another vessel—accidentally or on purpose—and Karney wasn't keen on proving its worth. He saw little choice since

Zealous couldn't outrun the U-boat's path. With a silent prayer and no time to explain, he ordered, "Harley, starboard engine ahead full, drop port to one-third. Sound collision alarm."

"Rork," came his inevitable protest, "you can't—"

"*Harlan, execute my orders!*" he hollered over the clatter of machine-guns. "*Starboard ahead full—now! Port ahead one-third.*" He never received a reply but *Lady Z* surged in a slightly new direction. The collision alarm sounded.

Zealous cut through the swells, trying to turn within the U-boat's course. *Does our ladyship realize she might be ripped open like a sardine can if this fails?*

The gap closed rapidly. With the U-boat mere yards from their bow, Karney gave a critical order, "*Port engine, ahead full; starboard, back emergency full. Now!*"

Lady Z slowly swung to starboard. Her momentum tried to drag the little cutter in the opposite direction, but she slowly turned toward the sub. The U-boat was now square to *Lady Z*'s hull. The conning tower loomed large and the faces of alarmed Germans grew distinct.

Gnashing steel rent the night. *Zealous* rose up on the sub's foredeck, crumpling their cannon as if cast of tin. *Lady Z*'s stern slewed cockeyed to the U-boat. Her bow smashed the conning tower. Cries from men still on the U-boat's deck were lost under a shriek of steel rending steel. *Zealous* reared like a wild bronco.

Flung off his feet by the impact, Karney hit the Lewis machine-gun mount. His helmet clattered across the deck. "Son of a bitch," he again swore, clambering to his feet. Seeing they were still snagged on the sub, he yelled below, "*Harlan, both engines back emergency full.*" Then, quietly and quickly, he pleaded, "*Go bhfóire Dia orainn.* Get us off that pig-boat before they drag us under."

He heard searing protests from the diesels and saw an upheaval of black smoke. *Lady Z*'s deck tilted so steeply, almost no one could stand. The U-boat continued to plunge to depths forbidden to *Lady Z*. Then, imperceptibly, the groaning grew into a piercing wail. Lurching to port, *Zealous* rolled clear, nearly capsizing she was flung so far. The unearthly screech faded. The U-boat vanished beneath cloistering waves.

Rising stiffly to his feet, Karney stared into the sinister abyss. Cries of lost souls from more than twenty years ago came unbidden to his mind. Shaking those forgotten ghosts away, he called below, "Harley, all engines stop."

An eerie hush settled over them. The night seemed blacker.

He gave Allison a hand up, then realized Brad Shelton clung desperately to the Lewis machine-gun. "You okay, son?"

The seaman recruit slowly nodded. "I think so, sir."

"If anybody gives you that Shell man crap again, kid, I'll more than gladly set 'em straight. You can stay shy, just take care of your eyesight."

"Thanks, Skipper," came his faint voice from the dimness.

Still at the 20mm, Foghorn called in his languid Texas drawl, "Skipper, there's some Heinees down in the drink. They's either too shook to holler fer help or dead."

Karney removed a glove, wiped blood from a gash along his eyebrow, then gazed at the water as he heard a faint cry in German. Pulling his glove back on, he grabbed his helmet. "Hertzel, Russ, Foghorn, arm yourselves, take the port launch. Pick up those Krauts, maybe they can fill in some blanks for us. Brad, crank up the searchlight. If Jerry had friends, I wouldn't be giving any orders."

Receiving the necessary, "Aye, ayes," Karney turned toward *Bonnie*, miraculously still afloat. "Bridge, Rork, is the rudder wire repaired yet?"

"Skipper, it's repaired but port reduction gears seized up. Only starboard diesel is operational."

"Understood. Once the launch is away, close on *Glasgow Bonnie*."

"Bridge, aye. And, Mr. Rork, engineering reports only minor injuries, sir."

"Thanks, Mr. Harlan." He cocked his head. *His attitude seems to've changed. Wonder how long this new condition'll last?*

A disembodied voice hollered to Karney, "Starboard davit's repaired, sir."

"Thanks, Foghorn," he replied, recognizing the drawl.

Raising his binoculars to *Bonnie*, Karney took a deep breath. Chill air helped clear his head but could not remove the bitter taste in his mouth. In the span of a few minutes, *Zealous* had engaged their enemy; and, except for some of her deck crew, he felt the U-boat had escaped. Aware of the *Kriegsmarine*'s methodical training, Karney was not convinced his little cutter managed to sink them. And with virtually no maneuverability, *Zealous* wasn't about to try and hunt them down.

Karney headed forward to check their bow. Though proud of his crew, he felt more relief than elation after the clash with the Germans. "Maybe I'll feel a sense of achievement once we rescue *Bonnie*'s crew and that crazy Scotswoman's on board her."

GLASGOW BONNIE
MONDAY

Regaining consciousness, Ellie Greer concentrated on simply breathing: *in and out—slow and deep—in and out—force the pain from me system. Slow and deep—in and out—slow and deep.*

Not remembering what she had been doing, she set easy tasks for herself. "In and out—get on me knees—slow and deep—get to me feet—in and—" Another spasm shot through her abdomen like an electric jolt. Ellie doubled over. Swallowing the urge to throw up, she focused harder. "Just take it slow."

When *Glasgow Bonnie* gave a terrifying lurch, panic

threatened to bully Ellie into submission before she started. "Ye can do this, love, I know ye can," she said to herself, reciting words she'd heard from the finest instructor at Achnacarry when training was at its worst. When she thought she'd never make it, Sandy's words helped her get through.

Ellie stood up. Reaching for the cabinet over the radio, she was hit by another cramp that doubled her over. *Breathe slow and deep—in and out.* Opening the cabinet door, she took out the rum flask George stashed there.

Taking a long pull of the cheap liquor, Ellie felt its warmth flood into her. *God, please let it numb some of me pain.* Once she recapped the flask, she slipped it into the pocket of her mackinaw coat, which she never removed when on duty.

An eerie silence engulfed her. "How long was I out? Am I the only one on board? Is anyone else left? Where's George? What of Uncle Bert? Surely they didna leave me. If Bilks knows me plight, he'd deem it just rewards to leave me, the bloated wels."

She hunted around for her life-jacket. Holding onto the table, she felt along the walls and door, then shuffled her foot on the deck. "Nae one bloody vest. Am I alone?"

Fear of another kind gripped her. "Where's the Yank cutter?"

Ellie staggered out of the radio room. As she feared, no one was on the bridge. Blood spatters covered the deck and charts on the table. Blown-out glass crackled under foot. The foul-weather view-glass had shattered. An acrid stench from burned wires and electric cables stung her nostrils. This view, however, allowed Ellie to survey *Glasgow Bonnie*'s situation.

Though the decks slanted precariously, *Bonnie* was far from gone. Substantial bulkheads kept water from the huge forward holds. "Uncle Bert knew it'd take a lot to sink you, old girl. Still," she prayed, "Lord, please let *Bonnie* take longer to sink than for me to be gettin' off her."

Counting the number of lifeboats, Ellie's dilemma grew. Of the four lifeboats that should've been there, both starboard boats were gone, the davit lines dangling. A port-side boat still hung inboard, untenable due to *Bonnie's* list, which probably began soon after the torpedo hit. "How could one boat be lowered on that side at all?"

A flash to starboard caught her attention. Ellie stared, transfixed. Explosions marked an exchange of cannon fire; tracers arced between the two vessels. Neither was distinguishable at this distance.

As quickly as it began, the gunfire ceased. Then an unearthly screeching, like a banshee's ferocious wail, tore through the night. "What's happened? Who won?" Head pounding violently, her stomach knotted in fear. Cruelly, her pain intensified with the tension. "Dear God, is *Bonnie* to become me funeral pyre?"

Despite sharp pangs in her gut, Ellie suddenly recalled the radio and wondered how she could've forgotten it. Praying the Yank cutter was still afloat, she hobbled to the radio room. Dragging on the headphones, she keyed the mike with a shaky hand.

Ellie battled a string of what-if anxieties. "*Zealous*, this is *Bonnie*." Her voice was too soft and quivered. More determined, she repeated, "*Zealous*, this is *Bonnie*, come in." *Lord, please be there.* "*Zealous*, this is *Bonnie*, come in. Over."

A man's voice sharply came back, "*Bonnie*, this is *Zealous*. I read you five-by-five. Please wait one. I say again: WAIT ONE."

Hoping he summoned his skipper, she curbed her fear. Though she had survived worse than this, her frayed emotions desired to hear Lieutenant Karney Rork's resonant voice. She didn't know him from Adam but craved the confidence, constraint and courage she'd heard in his voice when they spoke. He was a man who took charge.

⊕

USCGC ZEALOUS
MONDAY

Karney slid the rails the second Dave Harlan told him Kelley had *Bonnie* on the radio. Assuming he spoke with Ellie, Karney yanked open the bridge door, muttering to himself, "What the hell's she still doing on that damned freighter?"

Pushing one side of the headphones under his helmet, Karney grabbed the mike. "*Bonnie*, this is Lieutenant Rork, why haven't you abandoned ship? Over."

"Leftenant Rork . . . it seems . . ."

Though her voice sounded reasonably calm, he perceived a tremor. Hesitation spelled trouble. He forced himself to wait for her next words.

"I was unconscious when the others abandoned ship. I guess nae one checked for me. The lifeboats are either inaccessible or have already gone . . . I wondered if—"

With a sharp intake of breath, her pain became audible.

"*Bonnie*, you still there?" Karney asked, fearful he'd receive no response. A long moment passed. "*Bonnie*, please respond."

Faintly, her voice came through, "Leftenant, could *Zealous* please assist me? Over."

"We're headed your way now. Can you reach main deck? Over."

"I'm nae too steady, but I'll try. Over."

"Are you seriously injured? Over."

"Na too seriously. But, Leftenant Rork . . ."

The pause lengthened. Karney wondered if she'd passed out or the transmission broke. Then she spoke.

"Leftenant Rork," the woman said, suddenly sounding frightened and frail, "I'm pregnant . . . about five months along. Over."

Fathoming her distress, he closed his eyes, heaving a sigh of, "Sweet Mother of God." Karney keyed the mike.

Knowing her dilemma made it much more personal. "Mrs. Greer, if you can, try to make your way to the main deck, then forward to the bow. I'll see you off *Bonnie* myself, but please, don't give up on me before I can reach you. Over."

"Aye, Leftenant . . . main deck and forward. Out."

Handing the radio gear to Kelley, Karney noted a drop in engine noise. *Zealous* rolled awkwardly with the swells. "Mr. Harlan, why are we slowing?"

"A lifeboat from the freighter's coming alongside."

Karney stepped outside. In the glare of their searchlight, he saw not one, but two lifeboats close amidships. Starkly lit faces of the men huddled together on the thwarts were grim. Many looked scared, some were in shock, burned, a few unconscious.

Jonathan Grange, Tap and Jess Taylor, *Lady Z's* corpsman, started the transfer. With a twang of Southern comfort, Grange kept *Bonnie's* survivors headed below decks to JJ's hot food and warmth. Tap and Jess triaged the wounded.

Calculating the time to clear the lifeboats and now knowing what he did about Mrs. Greer, Karney's distress grew. *Glasgow Bonnie* couldn't stay afloat forever. The freighter already sat low in the water, her stern nearly submerged. And even if the lady weren't pulled down with the ship, she's not last long in the frigid water.

He made a decision. Concern for its outcome, if he failed, slunk away from his determination without argument.

"Pebley," Karney called the coxsun's mate, "lower the starboard launch. Barb, Newly, strip outta your heavy coats. Keep your vests on. You two are coming with me over to *Bonnie*."

Hearing, "Aye, ayes," and seeing the required action, Karney stepped into the wheelhouse and shrugged out of his heavy underway coat. "Mr. Harlan, you've got command till I return."

"What the hell are you doing, Rork?"

With glib defiance, he answered, "Probably something stupid that'll hang me square from Captain Bryannt's yardarm."

"You're nuts, Rork!" Harlan declared. "You're going after her, aren't you? You're the captain, Rork. You're not supposed to do stupid things."

Karney ignored his objection. "Harley," he said, removing his helmet as well, "there's a reason they call me 'Krazy Rork, the Wild Irishman'." Snugging his life vest tighter, he said with a shrug, "If I don't come back, hey, *Lady Z's* your command."

Jamming his Red Sox ball cap securely on, he looked Dave Harlan in the eye. "Write the report any way you want, Harley. I won't be around to dispute it."

Before Harlan could say more, Karney was out the door.

"Shit, Rork," he muttered, "I don't want command over your dead body." Seeing Kelley staring at him, Dave snapped, "Don't you have a radio message to send, Petty Officer Kelley?"

Unflustered by the XO's sharp tone, Roger Kelley quietly asked, "You really want me to call GreenPat now, sir?" As he reckoned, Lieutenant Harlan ignored him and went back to his fuming.

CHAPTER THREE

Every time *Glasgow Bonnie* lurched or a metallic wail rose in protest of her untimely death, Ellie seemed to share the old girl's pain. Ellie moved slowly through slanted passages and down crooked companionways. The absence of other crewmen and the vacant decks was haunting.

Buckled doors and stifling heat, forced Ellie to detour and backtrack more than once. Afraid she would be trapped and suffocate, or worse, be cremated alive, she tried to move as quickly as possible.

Ellie took another swallow of rum, the only thing retarding her premature labor pains and felt despair creep over her like the steadily rising water on *Bonnie*'s decks. "Do I drink the rum to brace me failin' courage or slow me contractions? By the time I reach that Yank, I'll be thoroughly sloshed." She capped the flask.

"Ach, who gives a bloody damn?"

A flooded companionway forced her in a new direction. Ellie stumbled into an unfamiliar passageway. Suddenly disoriented, she stopped to take stalk.

Mumbling to herself, she tried to bolster her spirits, "For God's sake, where's me other self? The self-assured *femme fatale* gatherin' intelligence from beguiled Nazi officers? Am I nae the tough wee fighter who got resistance cells in Denmark up and runnin'? Where'd me tough self go? The self who survived bein' captured by those nasty turncoat Danes and interrogated by the bloody *Gestapo*?"

Dodging flaming debris crashing from the overhead, she hit the deck hard. She took a long pull of rum and drained the flask.

Ellie realized her other self shrank beneath the pain of her injuries and fear of losing her baby, a child she wanted desperately, even if she never wanted to see the child's father again.

Rork will nae abandon me. I've nae met him in person, but I know he'll come. His words were sincere. I canna give up.

Standing unsteadily, Ellie sought a new route. As she left the fires behind, she used her torch sparingly. Midway down a darkened ladder well, her foot slipped on a broken rung. In a futile attempt to catch herself and not lose the torch, she impacted the deck and a discarded fire-hose reel. It cracked into her already injured side. Despite the rum's numbing affect, acute pain seared like a branding iron.

Dazed, Ellie watched the arc of her torch's light roll lazily from side to side. With her head reeling, her vision seemed to double. Inhaled smoke ignited a fiery spasm of coughing. The deck plates felt hot beneath her palms. As fires crept closer, Ellie's hope began to crumble like ash.

⊕

Karney watched flames aboard *Glasgow Bonnie* burn like an ancient Druid funeral pyre. The freighter's rusted sides shone blood-red in the oil fires on the water. They lent a macabre air to the death of the aged behemoth. *Bonnie* was already well down by her stern. Karney prayed the old vessel wouldn't give up the ghost till he had Mrs. Greer safely in hand.

But he saw no sign of the pregnant Scotswoman. Was

she lying unconscious in a passageway somewhere? Had her access to the main deck been blocked?

He checked with Barberio and Newland, "You guys see her?"

Almost in unison they answered, "No, Skipper."

Pointing aft, Karney told the young seaman, "Make for that accommodation ladder, Newly. Might as well put it to use."

The launch puttered around patches of burning oil. They tried not to breath it in, but a bitter stench from the black smoke crept into their nostrils and throats. They heard only the motor's monotonous chug, the rush of wind-fanned flames and creaking steel plates stressed almost to fatigue.

"Newly, once we're off, wait outside the oil slick. Watch for my signal. Be ready to move in quickly. Understood?"

Nodding so vigorously his helmet bobbled with the gesture, he answered, "Aye, aye, Skipper." Newly threaded the launch away from the scattered flames near *Bonnie*, and drew closer to the ladder.

"Barb, I'll check the superstructure. You go around the exterior. The lady should be up top, but double check the holds if you can. And just so you know, the lady's name is Ellie Greer, and she's about five months pregnant. You ready?"

Thinking of his own young wife, desperate for a baby, Jim Barberio looked a bit startled, then swiftly answered, "Aye, sir."

The launch nudged the stair. Its lower rungs were slick with ice where the sea had sloshed over them. Only the uppermost steps were above water. Karney leaped across. Barberio followed. The aft deck was totally immersed; the foredeck coated by a sheen of ice. In a few places, internal fires thawed the deck ice, but the slant made footing precarious everywhere.

Cautiously, the two men split up and began to search.

The launch's mechanical growl faded. Heightening their isolation, an eerie wail rose from within the freighter.

Karney worked forward, along the superstructure, trying the doors as he went. Most had been buckled with the torpedo strike. Still seeing no sign of the woman, he crossed to port.

Heading aft, Karney slipped on the glazed deck, barely catching a stanchion to avoid sliding into the frigid sea. Further aft, the ice had melted. Here, fire and rising levels of seawater posed a greater threat.

Are all the port-side doors buckled, too? One left.

Flames continued to consume the upper structure. It seemed strange. Karney wondered: *How'd fires get so high in the superstructure when the torpedo strike was below the waterline?* Before he could give the mystery more thought, hot wind stirred up by the fire shifted and enveloped him in bitter smoke. Coughing convulsively, he reached blindly for the last door.

Methodically, he forced open the dogs—latches that maintained each door's watertight seal. Heat scorched his gloves. Standing clear, Karney jerked on the door. Nothing. With his options running out, he tried again. After several more attempts, the door gave. Smoke and flame abruptly belched out like fire from a dragon's belly.

Ducking under a thick, suffocating cloud, Karney scrambled inside. A ghostly, undulating glow lit his way. Negotiating a companionway to the next level, he checked each passage. Beneath a mangled ladder, he found the Scotswoman in a heap. Beyond her reach, on the deck, her flashlight rolled aimlessly.

Not hearing Karney's call as he worked around the ladder, Ellie reached up to grasp the rail. Reflexively, she yanked her hand from the hot steel, lost her balance and again fell. Karney caught her just before she crashed back to the deck. Over the roar of flames, he called, "Mrs. Greer, I'm Lieutenant Karney Rork."

She looked up, startled by his appearance. With her

face revealed, Karney was just as startled by the delicate beauty he beheld. Ellie McCallister Greer was nothing like what he had expected of a woman working a tramp freighter.

Stray curls, highlighted red by the flames, clung damply to her pale skin. Her eyes, stark in the firelight as she gazed up at him, were mesmerizing. Although her eyes might be captivating, they were glazed with shock.

Gathering his wits, he asked, "Can you walk?" A blank stare indicated she was too dazed to understand. "Never mind," he said. "It'll be better if I carry you."

Because of her pregnancy, rather than sling her over his shoulder in a fireman carry, Karney lifted her in his arms. He was surprised at how light she felt. Ellie Greer was a willowy gal beneath the bulk of her male garb. The smell of liquor on her breath, however, confused him. *Did I need to add drunken sailor to incredibly brave or terribly stupid?*

"Ma'am, are you sauced?"

"Aye, Leftenan', probably," she said, before a bout of coughing hit.

"Turn your face into my chest," he suggested. "It might keep you from inhaling more smoke."

Why the hell is she drunk? From the way she sounded on the radio, I figured she'd keep a level head no matter what. Not get plastered. I wonder what else is wrong?

Pressing his back to the partitions, Karney worked his way toward the door. His eyes watered uncontrollably from the blinding smoke, caustic with burning electrical circuitry. Desperately, he held his breath. Once outside, he set her down while he gulped in cold drafts of air between searing bouts of coughing. As Karney's hacking subsided, he again picked her up, noticing she no longer looked so dazed. "Did you get soused thinking I wasn't coming for you, Mrs. Greer?"

"Nae, Leftenan'. I star'ed havin' contractions an' did nae wan' me wee babe born here an' 'specially nae now."

The gravity of her response shook him. "You're going into labor? I thought you were only about five months?"

Karney could barely hear her evasive answer.

"Me side was injured, but the rum's helped a wee bit. Tha's why I be drunk, Leftenan'. Do nae worry, I'll be fine."

"Not worry?" he asked rhetorically, forcing himself to keep moving. *Pregnant, going into labor, injured and drunk. Sure, no worry.* His Irish soothsayer chimed in with the dull admonition: *Getting her off this hulk's only the start of trouble.* Karney struggled to keep his footing along the tilting deck.

Eyes tearing from the smoke, Ellie saw the gleam of fire on the lieutenant's worried face. A pounding tempo raged in her rum-sloshed head. Her side throbbed wickedly in time.

His courage braced her ebbing fortitude. His look of determination reassured her. Though his voice was hoarse, it offered comfort, even if his questions did not.

"Was your husband aboard *Bonnie*?"

In a voice as raspy as his, Ellie stated, "Nae, he's dead."

Though true, Ellie did not wish to reveal Brandt had died in 1940, along with their only daughter. This baby was illegitimate.

"How'd you end up on *Bonnie*?"

"I needed pazzage to Canuckada, and me Uncle Bertie needed a radioman, so I signed on. Very thrifty of me, doon ye think?"

Karney rolled his eyes, then glared down at her. Ellie suspected he didn't care for her being pregnant and aboard this freighter. More than likely because he didn't like risking his life to save her.

"Where's your uncle?"

"He wazz in the engineerin' room when the torpedo hit." Thinking of her sweet uncle, her heart sank. "Heez probally dead."

"*Lady Z* picked up two lifeboats, maybe your uncle's on one of 'em."

Feeling this unknown officer's optimism pervade her misery, Ellie's spirits revived somewhat. She whispered, "Maybe . . ."

At the accommodation ladder, Karney gently placed Ellie on her feet, but kept an arm around her so she wouldn't slip on the icy deck. "Barberio," he hollered.

Ellie saw a husky Italian-looking kid emerge from the smoke. As Barberio made his way aft, Karney signaled across the water with his flashlight. A small boat soon puttered toward *Bonnie* from beyond the flames, another young Coastguardsman at the tiller.

"Skipper, I can't see shit in—" Upon seeing the woman, Jim Barberio fell silent in embarrassment. Still coughing from inhaling smoke, he grinned sheepishly. "Glad the Skipper found you, ma'am." Softly, to Karney, he said, "Skipper, fire's spreadin' toward a coal bin that hasn't flooded. If the dust in there goes . . ." He left the prospect hanging like a pall of smoke.

"Pray it doesn't, Barb," Karney said. "Pray real hard."

Glancing at the lady, Barberio quietly said, "Already ahead of you, Skipper." The devout Roman-Catholic Coastie quickly crossed himself.

They need not have whispered. Ellie was well aware that the volatile joining of coal dust and flame would make the torpedo explosion seem like a firecracker pop.

A gust of oily smoke and rising heat prompted Karney to press her face in toward his chest. Ellie once more felt herself drawing on this stranger's strength.

When the launch reached them, the access ladder had all but vanished beneath the water. The seaman at the tiller tossed a bowline across. Barberio caught it and drew the launch closer. Karney helped Ellie onto the rocking boat.

Sagging onto the thwart, Ellie felt weak and grateful to the Yank lieutenant for keeping her steady. The spinning in her head had eased a bit, but her side still burned with raw pain. It was all she could do to keep from doubling over in agony.

After Barberio jumped into the launch, Karney ordered, "Newly, get us outta this hell." With a nod, the young man steered toward safety.

Barely clear of the oil-slick, a rumble rose from *Bonnie*'s heart.

"Sweet Jesus, Mary and Joseph," Karney exclaimed. He shielded Ellie with his body, pressing her further down into the launch. A massive blast erupted from deep within the freighter, the power of its surge made worse by the depth to which *Bonnie* had settled.

Before Ellie could anticipate the shock wave, the launch flipped like a child's balsawood toy. Cold water engulfed her. Numbing fingers dragged her into the abyss, clawing at the tiny precious life within her womb. Ellie gasped for air. All she swallowed was saltwater.

In the frantic seconds when the launch capsized, Karney lost his grip on Ellie. His lifejacket bobbed him back up to the tumultuous surface. Barberio popped up about the same time and swam toward Newland, apparently unconscious.

Karney couldn't find her and cursed himself for not giving her his life vest. Too much worked against the woman. Ellie might be too weak to swim. Shaking his head like a wet dog, Karney spat seawater from his mouth. "Barb, you see the lady?"

His arm holding Newland, Jim Barberio gripped the overturned launch and yelled, "No, sir, she's still under."

Though only a few seconds had passed, a growling diesel marked the approach of *Lady Z*. Her other launch moved toward them as well. Karney struggled out of his vest. "Barb, get Newly to the launch, I'll find Mrs. Greer."

Gulping a lung-full of air, Karney dove deeper into the cold. Beneath the rough surface, water pressure crushed *Glasgow Bonnie* even more. It echoed with deafening clarity on his eardrums. Scattered patches of oil still burned on the surface, mutating everything he perceived into a watery rendering of Dante's inferno.

By the fire's demonic glow, Karney caught a glimpse of Ellie several feet away. Though a strong swimmer, his muscles grew stiff in the frigid water. Drawing closer, he lunged for her coat. It came away in his hand. Letting it go, it floated upward.

Ellie continued to sink. Lungs aching, heart pounding, Karney swam deeper to come up under her. Lit by surface fires, her hair spread like fiery, gossamer tendrils of a mystical sea nymph. To his oxygen-deprived brain, the scene was surreal.

Finally reaching over her shoulder and under her other arm, he gave a powerful kick and fought his way to the surface. The combined weight of sodden clothes threatened to drag them further down. *Dear God,* Karney silently pleaded, *please help me outta this one . . .*

As had happened during previous emergencies, a surge of energy miraculously rippled through his fatigued muscles. Karney focused on the glare from *Lady Z*'s searchlight. Though his muscles wanted to cramp, he held tight and swam toward *Lady Z*'s light and the haven the cutter offered.

Karney broke the surface, gasped for air and forced his spent limbs to tread water. Half-frozen and disoriented, he closed his eyes, concentrating on just staying afloat. Ellie, however, was slipping from his grip. He clung to her all the harder.

"Let go of her, Skipper," came Tap's voice from above and behind. "*Compadre*, I got her . . . Irish, let her go."

Painfully un-crimping his stiff fingers, Karney released Ellie and reached for the gun'ale. He found Jim Barberio's out-stretched hand, while Ron Eidlemann's strong grip closed on his other arm.

"We got ya, Skipper," Eidlemann reassured Karney. "Just hang on till Tap gets the lady settled in."

With his strength sapped by cold and his struggle to reach Ellie, Karney realized "hang on" was all he could do. Grabbing Karney's gun belt Barberio dragged him bodily on board. Setting Karney down beside where the woman lay, Eidlemann draped him with wool blankets.

Through chattering teeth, Karney asked, "Is Newly okay?"

To his surprise, Newland respond in a quivering voice, "I gotta a helluva headache, Skipper, but I'll live."

Lethargically nodding, Karney fought to clear his refrigerated thoughts. Finally, he muttered, "Tap, Mrs. Greer's—"

"Barb told me, Skipper. We'll take care of her."

"How many—" He gasped in a shivering breath, then gave it another try, "How many others were picked up?"

"Twenty-one from *Bonnie*, three Krauts, one badly wounded."

"Where'd—" Karney's words suddenly froze up as shivers hit him full force. He eventually managed to eke out, "Where'd you put . . . put the prisoners?"

"The wounded kid's in a bunk. The other two are shackled to the table in the wardroom. Allison's guarding them. They're too shook to offer any trouble for now."

"Was the . . . was the captain of *Bonnie* . . . picked up?"

"No, sir. Someone said he'd been below decks and that most of the black gang were killed right off the bat."

"What shape are . . . are the rest of 'em in?"

"Two severe burn cases. Mostly minor injuries, burns and shock. Between Grange's southern hospitality and JJ's scrumptious chow, they're snug as bugs in a rug, Skipper."

Karney nodded. "Can we re— . . . recover the other launch?"

"*Mi Dios*," Miguel Tapia sighed. "The man escapes death by the grace of God and his Guardian Angel Sister and still worries about everything and everybody but his own frozen self. Irish, don't fret," Tap begged. "Just don't turn into *un estatuas de helios* either."

His movements stiff, Karney protested, "Too late, *amigo*. I . . . I'm already . . . an ice statue. At least . . . I feel like one."

"Yeah, but this time we can thaw you out. Once we get aboard *Lady Z*, take a hot shower, then we'll get some of JJ's hot grub and a mug of joe in you. You'll be warmer than a Santa Ana wind in September. As for the rest, I've got the bases covered, *Compadre*."

Karney heard that "trust me" sound in Tap's voice. It was a reassurance he knew well and trusted. Closing his eyes, he prayed: *Heavenly Father, thank you for bailing me out . . . again . . . and for Kelli keeping an eye on us and for my guys being here when I needed 'em most.* Gently resting his hand on Ellie's inert form, he added: *And please, dear God, watch over this woman and her unborn child.*

SECTION TWO
ZEALOUS

CHAPTER FOUR

In a shabby building on the edge of St. John's, Captain Rob Roy "Mac" MacCalister, Royal Canadian Navy, paced the length of his draughty office. "A bloody igloo'd be warmer than this place, eh?" Mac grumbled, rubbing his hands together. "Ah, but I shan't complain. I'll be home soon enough though." At the garrison in Nova Scotia, he'd only have his father's frosty temperament to weather.

In his office, numerous charts, maps and aerial reconnaissance photos of U-boats marked with grease-pencil dates and times served as his wallpaper. A virtual mound of photos cascaded over the stout table around which Mac strode. Chelsea, his Border Collie mix, her tan brows furrowed, watched her master. Widely, she lay under the table, well clear of the path of Mac's large, spit-polished boots.

Mac shuffled the photos to find the one eroding his

focus. Twisting the end of his handlebar mustache, he again gazed at its haunting image. Too little of the U-boat was exposed, however. Not enough information known by a longshot.

While rubbing his weary eyes, his stomach growled. Chelsea raised her head and whined softly. "Don't fret, girl, I won't let you starve. Just a bit more sorting, eh, then we'll go eat at the Crow's Nest." The tolerant dog's tail swished in understanding.

The telephone jangled in the outer office. His girl Friday bubbled with giggles. Marciá Gertrude Therkilsen was a striking blend of Danish and French with a dash of Polish for grounding. Born in Alberta, Canada, the buxom blonde with doe-like hazel eyes, had worked for Mac a year. After all this time, he still wasn't sure where her priorities lay: ruby-lacquered fingernails or finding a date for her nights off or was it winning the war?

But Marciá typed a mile a minute and followed Mac's often disjointed dictation flawlessly. The fact she spoke Danish was a windfall when handling members of the Royal Danish Minister for Foreign Affairs. Meetings were strained at best, yet Marciá's feminine wiles always warmed the icy negotiations concerning Nazi Germany's threat to Greenland's autonomy.

A moment later Marciá strolled into the room. "Cap'n Mac?"

She paused, waiting for him to look up. Despite the long day behind them, she smiled brightly. "Wendy's on the tellie, sir."

"And you want tonight off, eh?"

Feigning embarrassment, she said, "Thanks, that'd be swell, sir, but Wendy still needs to talk to you. Says it's important."

Mac came around the table, Chelsea at his heel. "Lord," Mac mumbled, stepping into the outer office, "the only thing important to Wendy is sex and payday."

Sliding onto her chair, Marciá crossed her legs and

adjusted her skirt to expose plenty of shapely leg and filed her nail. Perched on her desk corner, Mac ignored the view and only listened to Flying Officer Wendell Collins, his recon pilot and Marciá's on-again-mostly-off-again boyfriend. Mac seemed oblivious to Marciá's abiding infatuation. Sitting back to admire Mac, Marciá took in his broad shoulders and tight tush, letting her eyes rove down his long legs, hidden by crisply pressed uniform trousers. But in his dress uniform, a tartan kilt of his Naval Company— *Oooh, what a knock-out!*

Though he was old enough to be her father, he was a swoony—handsome, gem-green eyes, very tall with the rugged build of a lumberjack. And although Marciá had heard supplying lumber to Donald McKay for his clipper ships in the 1800s was how Clan MacCalister reputedly compiled their fortune, Mac hadn't been a lumberjack. He was strictly a military man.

From Mac's casual demeanor, most people never suspected he came from such a well-heeled family. Though never ostentatious, Mac freely bought rounds at the tavern and helped anyone needing an advance on their pay, most often Wendy. Down-to-earth and refined, Mac's sole fault seemed his drive for perfection. But it never stopped Marciá's daydreams. Like now.

She wished Mac's hair were longer. He kept a military-bristle buzz cut. Though deep tawny red with a few gray hairs of maturity, it was so short, she'd nary a lock to twirl her imagination around. His one extravagance was a luxuriant handlebar mustache, a lighter copper shade, with neatly waxed tips which Mac twisted avidly when worried.

There was a polished air about Mac which Marciá found romantic. But romance with Rob Roy MacCalister remained pure fantasy. The best looking guy in this miserable town that dangled on the far eastern tip of North America was a doting husband with six kids. The most Marciá would ever get was a birthday rose.

Oh well, she sighed checking her nails. *Mac's a fair and honest man. He gives me time off to see my Aussie flyboy. Though Wend's definitely no Mac MacCalister, at least Wendy appreciates me for more than my bloody typing skills and proficiency in Danish. And Wendy's no figment of my imagination when we—*

Mac thrust the phone at her, canceling her musings.

"Collins would like a word with you, dearie."

Returning to his office, Mac glanced at the skewed clock. He fixed it and realized he'd been sorting photos for hours. "Collins, you'd best not be too late, we're already hungry, eh?" Chelsea whined in agreement. Mac sat down, pulling a stack of photos in front of him and contemplated the mixed talents of Flying Officer Wendell Collins.

Despite a nose for trouble, the Aussie pilot had an uncanny knack for ferreting out U-boats in his Spitfire, aptly named *Snapper.* With a specially adapted radar in the Spitfire, his gift for catching the Germans on the surface was legendary. His aerial photographs betrayed much Jerry did not wish revealed. Some shots had been taken in the fjords of East Greenland or Denmark Strait between Greenland and Iceland, others in choppy North Atlantic swells.

Most photos showed U-boats in emergency dives with their bow down, conning tower sloshed in seawater, bridge equipment visible. A choice few caught Jerry with his pants down—the boat's insignia on the conning tower in sharp focus, their guns hastily manned or crews scrambling to reach hatches. Some snapshots, like this last batch, actually caught tracers from anti-aircraft guns arcing straight for Collins' plane.

Leaning back, Mac smiled at the irony. "If the Huns only knew these photos were taken by German Leica cameras from a British-engineered Spitfire, sporting nose art created by a Yank gal of Mexican ancestry and all flown by a misfit, far-from-home, irascible Australian pilot only comfortable in the air.

"No wonder they call it a world war," Mac sighed. "This one's definitely getting more insane than the last."

To keep this war's madness from making him crazy, he always took time to get to know the men he commanded beyond their official records. He also became familiar with the equipment they used.

Several months ago, Mac met Wendy, who at that time flew strictly for Great Britain's Coastal Command in a Mark II Sunderland flying boat named *Ice Sheila*. Flight Lieutenant Collins had been up for a promotion to squadron leader. But on a drunken dare, Wendy took *Ice Sheila* up late at night to prove he could set down in a blacked-out harbor with no landing lights. By Monday, though *Ice Sheila* was in pristine shape, Wendy's wings were stripped and he had been demoted two grades to pilot officer.

Because Mac had finagled Wendy's wings back from an uncompromising disciplinary board and kept him flying, Wendy willingly granted Mac's every whim and order—no matter how bizarre. What really mattered to Wendy was keeping his ass in the air.

At least the planes Wendy flew were more reliable than the pilot's behavior. The planes flew to destroy Germans, not their own reputation. Other than his well-executed drunken landing, Wendy's flight record was flawless. It was his conduct once on land that was flawed. For years before the war, Wendy had successfully flown expeditions in and out of Antarctica and into the outback.

Despite awareness of Wendy's discipline problems, Mac knew the Aussie was the pilot for OPERATION ICE PACT.

Pulling in favors, as well as leaning on his father's rank of admiral, Mac asked for and received special permission to run operations for both the Sunderland and Wendy's Spitfire. Utilizing the planes' capabilities with supervision of each mission flown, Mac gained a modicum of control over Wendy.

To date, the alliance had worked well.

When the bullets accompanying the tracers in these pictures, ventilated poor *Snapper* a few days ago, the Spitfire'd been grounded. Wendy was lucky to be alive, though the calamity had been pathetically exaggerated for Marciá. But to Mac's observations, Marciá tended to hang on Wendy's every word, regardless of whatever stupid things the Aussie spewed out. "The girl knows how to tease and appease."

Mac shook his head. "Ah, such are the wiles of lust."

Marciá tapped on the open door, interrupting his mumblings.

"Cap'n Mac," she implored with a subtle whine, "may I go? Wend's takin' me out hoofin' later, and I need to ritz up a bit."

Feigning shock, Mac teased, "Why improve upon yourself to dance with Collins, Marciá? You always look the absolute cat's meow."

"Oh, Cap'n Mac," she blushed, "I've got carbon black from head to toe after typing all those boring observation reports in triplicate and quadruplicate and—"

"Marciá," Mac raised his hands, "I get the picture. Just be sure you're in bright and early tomorrow."

"Of course I'll be, Cap'n Mac. I'm always on time."

"Yes, I'll grant you that. You've never been late. Yet."

Smiling provocatively, Marciá lightly spun on her toes. With a toss of her blonde tresses, she glanced back at him.

"By the way, Cap'n Mac, your clock's crooked again."

Mac groaned as Marciá sashayed out the door with a prominent swing step. "It's a wonder she doesn't throw her back out, eh?" Mac rose, again straightening the clock and considered how her hour-glass figure could wind-up any guy's heart-clock for a long time. "Why we fight to protect Canada from Nazi goose-steppers, eh?"

Cocking his head, Mac said, "I wonder, if Marciá knows she's the model for the nose art on *Ice Sheila* and *Snapper*?" Mac shook his head and answered his own question, "Doubt it. Wendy's still alive."

Mac sat back down. Chelsea emitted a bored sigh, lolling over on her side to go back to her doggie dreams.

Methodically, Mac began to sort the rest of the pictures. Most he filed. Others he tacked to walls with a fusion of pieced-together maps and charts. On the left wall, maps of Newfoundland and Baffin Island, along with sea charts of the Labrador Sea and Baffin Strait running north to Ellesmere Island were carefully arranged. Centered to the left of the door and unruly clock was a West Greenland Coast map, which included the new U.S. bases, known as the Bluies. Tucked near Narsarssuaq was Bluie West One at the southwestern tip of Greenland. Much further north at Kangerdiuqssuaq, was Bluie West Five near Gothavn on South Disko Island. Between them were several other Bluies, not necessarily built yet and not numerical.

Though Greenland's immense ice-cap was central on this wall, little, except lofty mountain ranges, were marked on its virtually unexplored interior. Largely inhospitable, even to the Inuits, it wasn't suitable for bases.

The rugged East Greenland Coast representing a convolution of deep fjords and numerous islands was Mac's main focus. Depths had been recorded from soundings taken by the U.S. Coast Guard. Miles and kilometers between inhabited settlements were marked for reference, while strings tied to pins led to concise notes regarding local population, if any remained, and terrain features.

On the adjacent wall to Mac's right, other sea charts took in the North Atlantic. For bearings, a sliver of the East Greenland Coast nestled at the corner of the room. From there a composite of maps and charts expanded across the walls to show the icy Arctic: Denmark Strait, Iceland and north to Spitzbergen Island. Spitzbergen, under Nazi control since Norway's surrender, was used as another reference point for Mac in the vast Arctic Ocean. Curving onto the ceiling, over the turn-of-the-century cornice, were more sea charts showing the polar ice cap and land masses

as far east and north as Norway and the year-round
Russian ports of Murmansk and Archangel.

Every chart was pinned with U-boat contacts: blue
stood for sightings; black pins indicated a U-boat sunk—
few existed; red designated lost Allied ships—these nearly
exhausted Mac's supply of red pins. Notes connected by
thread to each pin were dated and marked with the U-
boat's symbol and captain's name, if Naval Intelligence had
them. The polar-bear's share of sightings was in the vast
North Atlantic. Several key blue pins—the most intriguing
for Mac—were in Denmark Strait near East Greenland.

Eleven months ago, in late January 1941, Mac had
participated in a conference urging the United States to
take a more active role in Greenland's defense. Reaching
an agreement with Denmark, America received permission
to build and run bases in Greenland. Since then, events
avalanched: construction began; the Coast Guard formed
the Greenland Patrol to protect the waterways and created
the Sledge Patrol for land. Both groups had the nearly-
impossible task of locating remote German meteorological
bases to prevent the Nazis from transmitting weather
reports out of Greenland—considered the weather kitchen
of Europe—back to Germany.

Though the Yanks, for the most part, dismissed
rumors of U-boat bases anywhere on the East Greenland
Coast, evidence did exist. Fostering a professional and
personal rapport with Admiral Russell Waesche,
Commandant of the Coast Guard, Mac had also gained the
support of American resources for OPERATION ICE PACT.

Smaller American cutters, 125-foot "Buck and a
Quarters," already patrolled the waters near Greenland and
transmitted weather reports used by convoy planners. The
Coast Guard preformed other services for Greenland's
population: emergency services, medical care, delivery of
supplies and mail. A month ago, Admiral Waesche had
given Mac a list of several skippers commanding these
small vessels. Though most of the men were relatively

young, each was a seasoned ice pilot, familiar with the seas in this hard-to-patrol region. Mac had narrowed his choices down to three skippers he felt he'd be able to work closely with and could trust during ICE PACT.

Stabbing a red pin into Denmark Strait, Mac knew that decision would wait for another time.

He sat down, propped up his feet and contemplated the potential impact of a U-boat base in Greenland. After jotting a note on one of Marciá's pale-green steno pads, he knew more speculation could also wait. Following Chelsea's example, Mac closed his eyes.

With no idea how late Collins would be, Mac dozed off.

USCGC ZEALOUS
NORTH ATLANTIC
TUES: 16 DEC 41

The sullen prisoners stared back at Lieutenant Karney Rork and Chief Petty Officer Mark Allison with brazen hostility. Their earlier dazed and frozen condition had melted into pure hatred.

Though he knew German, Karney listened as each question was translated, for at least the third time. Allison's eyes met his gaze. The petty officer shook his head.

"Ain't too chatty tonight, Skipper. Gettin' him to fess up that U820 was the frickin' boat number may be all we get, ya know?"

Karney knew. His anger rose to match the Germans' unveiled hatred. His patience wore thin. Numb from his own dunking, Karney needed to assess the wounded and check on Mrs. Greer. The last thing he wanted, or needed, tonight was trying to get answers out of two defiant Krauts.

The kid, downy chin-fuzz his most discernible push toward manhood, looked more scared than mean. The lanky, older fellow, gaunt with a handsome face, gazed from Karney to Allison, not lingering on either one for very long. For all his bluster, Karney sensed he was as frightened as the boy.

"Ya know, Skipper," Allison whispered, "I think the older Kraut knows English."

Karney kept an eye on the Germans. "Why do you say that?"

"He takes too much interest whenever anyone's come down here to talk to me. But there's somethin' more . . ."

Though Allison was overdoing his sleuth speculation, Karney knew it wasn't everyday a Coast Guard cutter took U-boat prisoners.

"What more?" Karney asked.

Leaning close, Allison lowered his voice further, "One of the Limey's we rescued thought the guy looked like *Glasgow Bonnie*'s radioman, who happens to be missing as well, ya know? Coincidence? Maybe. But . . ."

Karney contemplated the possibility. "Maybe. Or maybe it explains those radio signals we picked up over the last few days." He watched the Germans for a moment, then said more loudly, "Just keep a close eye on 'em. If they gotta piss or take a crap, give 'em a bucket. I don't want 'em unshackled for any reason. And I sure's hell don't want 'em outta this wardroom."

"Gotcha, Skipper. They ain't goin' nowhere." Glancing at Karney, he asked, "Who'd you want to relieve me, sir?"

Thinking a moment, Karney said, "Dwyer, then Eidlemann and Morrison. If that's a problem, Mr. Harlan can fix it. Understood?"

"Aye, aye, Skipper."

"If these guys become orators," he added, "I'll be in my cabin."

"Okeydokey, Skipper." Before Karney started up the ladder, he asked, "Sir, is it true the lady you rescued's pregnant?"

Noting the older German's eyes register a transitory twitch of surprise, Karney guardedly answered, "Yeah, she is. Why?"

"Just hard to figure why she's out here, sir, ya know?"

After a moment, Karney said, "Guess she has her reasons."

The father of his own brood, Allison nodded and thoughtfully added, "I just hope she's okay, sir, ya know, her and the baby both."

Karney glared at each of the Germans in turn. "So do I, Mark. God knows I do."

ST. JOHN'S, NEWFOUNDLAND,
COMMISSION GOVERNMENT
OF GREAT BRITAIN
TUESDAY

Captain Mac MacCalister nearly fell off his chair when Wendy Collins' typical but uncouth greeting boomed in the silent room, "G'day, mate, how's it goin'?"

Dropping his boots to the floor, Mac noted the time on his once-again cockeyed clock and realized Monday had rolled into Tuesday. "You're late, I'm hungry and what's so damned important you couldn't tell me over the phone?"

Preceded by the scent of cheap cologne, Wendy sauntered into the room. "Hey, Cap'n Mac, it's nice to see you, too!" When Wendy heard a resounding thump-thump, he glanced under the table and kneeled down. "And a fine g'day to you, Chelsea dear," he said. "You're lookin' loverly as always." Wallops of her tail increased with receipt of a morsel of doughnut. A faint white trail of powdered-sugar was evident on Wendy's dark uniform.

Wendy flopped onto the cracked leather chair beside the table like an indolent king on his thrown. "How's the family, mate?"

"Collins, cut the crap, eh?"

"My goodness, we are testy t'night, ain't we?" Wendy rummaged through several pockets, extracting a crumpled pack of American Chesterfields and a lighter. "Wanna smoke, mate?"

Glaring at the average-height, average-built, anything-but-average pilot, Mac shook his head. He had no choice but to wait on Wendy's deranged sense of priorities—possibly a tad worse than Marciá. Even Wendy's lack of urgency meshed with her get-it-done-eventually demeanor. *Maybe they're too much alike,* Mac thought.

Though Wendy had changed from his flying leathers to a clean uniform, it looked like he'd slept in it for a week. Worry lines etched his face and shadows ringed his sky-blue eyes that, despite their usual bland expression, never missed a thing.

"So," Mac asked, "what do you have to tell me, Collins?"

"Nothin' really, I suppose. Just figured I'd report to you in person for a change. Shoot the shit with ya an'—"

Mac's leer ceased Wendy's words. "How much is your 'nothing-really-I-suppose' information going to cost me this time?"

"Well, if ya could spot me a tenner till payday—"

"Like the tenner I spotted you last payday, eh?"

"Aye, somethin' like that, mate." Wendy grinned stupidly.

Mac stood and dug into his pocket, pulling out his wallet. Sure he'd never see it again, he tossed a wad to Wendy. "Just remember our deal, eh, Collins?"

Stuffing the money, uncounted into a pocket, he said, "I haven't forgot, guv. Quote: Get busted for fightin' again an' ya won't be able to fly a bloody milk crate off a bleedin' outhouse roof from here to Singapore. Unquote. Or somethin' more or less to that effect."

"Close enough." Mac leaned back against the table, his legs casually crossed, arms folded. "Now, what's to report?"

Taking a drag on his cigarette, Wendy blew a smoke ring toward the ceiling and leaned forward, resting his elbows on his knees. "'Member that freighter you asked me to look out for?"

"*Glasgow Bonnie?*"

"Aye, that's the one. We come on her today. Give or take, about seven hundred miles out. Dead in the water."

Mac straightened up. "Torpedoed?"

"Not this run. Damage from shoddy repairs and a run of really bad North Atlantic storms is what done her in. Leastwise, that's how Davey read their signalman. Convoy left her behind last night."

"*Bonnie*'s alone?"

Glancing at his watch, Wendy shook his head. "By now a Yank cutter should be with her. A little one . . . one of those hundred an' twenty-five footers. Her name was somethin' like *Zealot* or *Zealous*."

"*Zealous*," Mac repeated the name, looking puzzled.

"Aye, that was it. Know her?"

Pondering Wendy's bombshell, his thoughts faraway, Mac said slowly, "Yes . . . I have a file on her acting captain . . . Leftenant Rork. He's under consideration for ICE PACT. *Zealous* and her crew as well. Like you and your men."

Wendy blew another smoke ring. "*Bonnie*'ll have no worries with the Yanks there, mate." Relaxing back in the chair, he added, "Less o' course Fritzy pops up again."

"Again? A U-boat?"

"Aye, we sent one under early this mornin', well, actually yesterday mornin'. She musta come up later 'cause the Yanks'd tangled with 'em by the time we'd flown over. Don't think Fritzy knew about *Bonnie* though."

Agitated by this second revelation, Mac began twisting the tip of his mustache. He paced the length of the table, started a return trip, then paused, looking at the chart of the North Atlantic.

Though Wendy continued smoking his Chesterfield, his gaze never left Mac. When the captain didn't move, Wendy asked, "What's so bloomin' important about that rusty old bucket anyway, mate?"

After a moment, Mac's eyes focused on the Australian. "My cousin's on the *Bonnie*." Turning, he paced away.

Wendy waved his cigarette like a semaphore flag. "Ah,

quit worryin', mate, you'll give yourself ulcers. The Yank Coastie can pick 'im up if anythin' happens. He'll be fine."

"That's not the worry, Collins."

His face drawn, green eyes jaded, Mac sat back down. "My cousin's name is Ellie. Being on that crippled tub with some damned U-boat lurking nearby is the least of her troubles."

Wendy stared at Mac, cigarette dangling. "Jesus H. Christ, Mac, what the bloody hell's a Sheila doin' out there?"

Mac stood up again, pacing around the table. "She shouldn't be there, but she is. I tried to talk her out of it, but—"

The phone jangled. A call at this hour was not typical. With no Marciá to answer the only phone line was just plain inconvenient. Mac hastened out of the room, grabbing the receiver by the third ring.

Following at a leisurely pace, Wendy heard none of the one-sided conversation, but knew the call wasn't good. Mac hung up with deliberation, his grip white-knuckle tight. Quietly, Wendy asked, "What's wrong, mate?"

Mac glanced up as if just remembering his presence.

"That was Torbay. *Zealous* radioed Coast Guard headquarters a bit ago that *Glasgow Bonnie* sank after she was torpedoed by your evasive U-boat. *Zealous* engaged them but didn't claim a kill."

Wendy waited, not sure if he should ask, but Mac seemed to need something else to focus on. "What about your cousin, mate?"

"Two Huns and thirty Brits were rescued. Ellie, thank God, was among them, but there's no word on her condition."

"She's safe, Mac, why worry till ya know more?"

Returning to his office, Mac said, "I worry 'cause Ell's out there. And *Zealous* sustained damage. She's apparently making slow headway. You'll fly out tomorrow, pick up my cousin and as many survivors as *Ice Sheila* can carry."

"Ya mean, after we fly you down to Sheet Harbour?"

"Don't worry about me, I'll get there somehow. It's Ellie I want looked after, eh? Then return her to Halifax—"

"But Mac—"

"Don't give me any crap, Collins, just—"

"I ain't givin' ya any shite, mate, but what happens if the sea's still runnin' high. We can't put *Ice Sheila* down under any ol' sorta conditions, ya know. 'Sides another blow's movin' in."

"Then fly out before dawn and beat the damned storm, eh? If you don't take more risks than normal, you should have an extremely wide margin of operation."

Wendy gave the Canadian a practiced look of skepticism.

Mac placed his large hand on Wendy's shoulder in camaraderie. "For a pilot of your skill, going out to pick up survivors from a Buck and a Quarter should be a scrumptious piece of cake. It's your call once there, but I'd be shocked if you can't pull this off, eh?"

"Just a bloody piece of cake, the big man says. You're one bloomin' crazy Scot. I'd be safer flyin' a bloomin' milk crate off a ruddy shitehouse in bloody Tokyo, Nips an' all."

Mac slapped him on the back. "It'll be your patriotic duty, Collins," then added more softly, "and a personal favor to me."

Wendy cocked his head. "Well now, a favor's different. Just don't feed me any o' that bloody patriotic shite. That's what'll get me killed." He checked his watch. "I better get over to Marciá's or she will kill me, especially since we can't go dancin' with our night shortened."

USCGC ZEALOUS
NORTH ATLANTIC
TUESDAY

It was well after midnight by the time Karney completed his tasks: radioed an update to GreenPat, the

Coast Guard headquarters in Newfoundland; spoke with Chief Grossage about the mangled port engine; checked repairs to their damaged bow, the starboard gun platform, the deck and wardroom; then made rounds of the wounded.

Lady Z had now settled back to her usual routine. Her crewmen assured their skipper that all was under control.

By one o'clock, Karney left Ensign Grange at conn and quietly entered his cabin. As he came in, Miguel Tapia, who had been keeping vigil on Mrs. Greer, crossed himself as he ended a prayer. Karney knew from Tap's expression, the mere thought of this lady losing this baby dredged up memories of the baby Tap and Lacy lost several years ago. That tragedy was the first of several shared misfortunes to tighten the bond between the two men.

After graduating from the Coast Guard Academy, Karney had been assigned to *USCGC Crawford* out of San Juan, Puerto Rico. He and Tap served together barely a year when trouble developed in Lacy's third pregnancy. Differences between the two men did not matter. Tap's family needed help; Karney was there for them. Just as Tap would be there for Karney later. Now they shared another concern.

Nudging his chin toward the broad bunk where the Scotswoman lay, Karney asked in a whisper, "Mrs. Greer any better?"

Tap shook his head. "If anything, she's worse. She's still bleeding and in a lot of pain." Grief filled Tap's eyes. "She's going to lose her baby. Rum or morphine aren't going to help her if she starts into labor again. It never helped Lacy."

Hunting hope, Karney asked, "Is she resting okay, though?"

"Yeah . . . for now." Tap sighed. "But I have a bad feeling about this, *compadre*. Getting bashed like she did, then nearly drowning in such frigid water . . . mi Dios, this lady's been through hell."

"Remember when that woman in Aguadilla went into premature labor after that hurricane?"

"Irish," Tap sighed heavily again, "that lady was only four weeks early, not four months. Besides, we had that doctor in Mayaguez on the radio to talk us through her delivery and any complications."

Karney heard the discouragement in Tap's voice and had no conciliation to offer. A similar feeling had haunted Karney ever since he laid his hand on Mrs. Greer's shoulder in the launch after they'd been pulled from the icy water.

Squeezing Tap's shoulder, Karney said, "*Amigo*, get some sleep. I'll stay with her till Barberio relieves me. Thank God we have some married guys in this mostly baby-faced crew. Which reminds me, could you check on Jess Taylor before turning in? He seemed a bit overwhelmed by the influx of wounded."

Tap nodded. "I'll say one thing for Jess, he held up like a pro, considering the severity of those burn cases."

"He's a good man. And here I am helping him get a transfer. I must be nuts."

Standing up, Tap's hefty shoulders sagged. "It's for a good cause, Irish." Tap's indigo-blue eyes met Karney's, sizing him up. "You sure you're okay? You still look blue around the gills."

"Yeah, I'm fine." Grinning crookedly, he tried to sound lighthearted, "You know, Maurie says blue's my best color."

Tap turned before reaching the door. "*Compadre*, I don't think your sister meant your skin color."

"I dunno, with Maurie's sense of humor, it's hard to tell."

Tap chuckled weakly. "I'll check on Taylor. Night, Karn."

Sinking onto the vacated chair, Karney opened his Thermos of sugar-laden, black coffee and filled his mug. Rather than sip it, he merely wrapped his cold hands around the hot mug.

Time dragged by slowly, somberly. Though he tried to relax, concern for this pregnant lady kept his nerves on edge.

To do something besides stew over her, he withdrew his Navy Colt .45, dropped the clip, cleared the chamber, set it on the desk, then unbuckled his webbed holster. Like everything else, it was drenched from the launch capsizing. After Karney stripped, cleaned and very thoroughly oiled his sidearm, he found only his hands had been busy. The process was so automatic, his thoughts never left the injured lady.

Ramming home the ammo-clip, he holstered his weapon and cleared off his desk. The sweet scent of gun oil lingered. Leaving only the desk lamp on, he saw that Mrs. Greer lay in shadow. With a sigh, he knew music was the only remedy for his worries.

Battered travel guitar in hand, he tilted back his chair, propped his legs on the desk and tuned the strings. Quietly, Karney strummed tranquil sea chanteys, ballads, a few favorite hymns and practiced some Christmas carols trying to lift his spirits. *Lord*, he thought, *Christmas is only ten days away. Or is it nine now? Where the hell's peace and goodwill?* He shook his head. *It sure doesn't feel much like it's gonna be Christmas that soon.*

Pain continued to send spasms through Mrs. Greer's body, contorting her pale, fever-dampened features. Karney felt helpless with nothing to do except stay nearby.

After about an hour, Karney dozed off, still holding his guitar, still pondering this gorgeous and mysterious Scottish woman whose life had suddenly capsized his orderly existence aboard *Zealous*.

CHAPTER FIVE

Lieutenant Dave Harlan, two mugs of steaming coffee in hand, entered the small wardroom from the crew's mess. Taking stock of the German prisoners, he felt a blend of fear, curiosity and revulsion.

So these guys epitomize Hitler's master race, destined to remove Jews from the world. Jews—he used the term loosely, like calling all dogs mutts. Though Dave was a mutt himself, he sometimes wished he could forget his Jewish pedigree.

However, Jewish was a birthright that Baba, his Polish grandmother, never let him forget. She raised him after his parents' deaths—his father committed suicide after he lost all his finances in the stock market crash; his mother was committed to an insane asylum shortly thereafter. Taken in by his father's mother, Dave rebelled against Baba's strict rules and tried to deny his Jewish heritage.

In his fall semester at graduate school, Dave's plans were radically changed by two people: Baba's niece Miranda—and Adolf Hitler.

Miranda had escaped Warsaw mere days after Hitler's invasion of Poland, literally steps ahead of Nazi killing squads rounding up Jews and brutally executing men, women and children. Miranda witnessed her elderly parents' execution and watched them tumble into graves they had been forced to dig themselves. Terrified and alone, she fled south by a risky, twisted route through Nazi-held Czechoslovakia to Hungary, then down the Danube to the Black Sea. Eventually she was smuggled aboard a tramp freighter bound for the Americas. Though Miranda divulged her perilous escape to both Baba and Dave, the cruelty and terror she endured remained a secret revealed only to Dave after he found her sobbing uncontrollably in the middle of the night.

To Dave Harlan, Miranda's shocking account of Jewish massacres became more than hearsay and fabrications, easily dismissed. Dave saw through Miranda's eyes the calculated extermination of the Jewish people of Europe. Her account rang like a battle cry in his heart and mind. He lost all focus on his graduate studies.

After barely skimming through the spring semester of 1940, Dave applied to the Coast Guard officer-candidate school. Though a year older than normally accepted, his determination, a bachelor degree in marine biology and top physical shape from sculling helped him get into the 17-week program at the Academy. Officer's training, however, hadn't prepared Dave for meeting these Nazis face-to-face.

Now, here he stood and there they sat in the confines of the wardroom aboard *Zealous*. It was more personal than navigational skills and sea laws presaged.

Dave observed the prisoners up close. They looked like any rescued survivors: dejected, withdrawn, harmless. Yet their eyes held undeniable malice toward him. Real or imagined? Dave couldn't tell. *I don't look particularly Jewish—whatever the hell that's supposed to mean. But their stares make me uncomfortable.*

As if to deny their existence, he turned his back on them, handing a mug to Mark Allison. "Have they been any trouble?"

Allison leaned nervously to one side to keep an eye on his captives. Though they were shackled to a bolted-down table, Allison didn't trust them. "No, no trouble, sir." He set the hot mug beside him on his narrow, uncomfortable perch halfway up the ladder leading topside. "They been quiet. Worn out, ya know."

"Take your break while I'm here. I'll watch them."

Standing, Allison started up the ladder. "Yeah, lemme just take a leak an' I'll be right back, sir."

"Take your time, Allison. I'm not going—"

Dave sputtered as he was yanked toward the groping hands of the young German by his companion. Hot coffee sloshed from the mug, burning his hand. Fear gripped him as he felt his Navy Colt wrenched from its holster. The young German's arm encircled his throat.

Allison, almost through the door leading to the main deck, realized something was wrong below, but his reaction was slow, his position to help awkward.

Averse to altercations, Dave knew this was a fight to the death. *Mine, if I don't win.*

Out of the corner of his eye, he saw his pistol sweep up. He rammed his elbow into the German's gut. A loud whoof shot out. Grabbing his weapon, Dave clamped his hand firmly over the ejector slide. The struggle instantly became a wrestling match. Dave was on his own.

Half-falling, half-jumping on the older prisoner, Allison had his hands full. He grappled with the German to keep him from helping his accomplice and getting the .45 from Lieutenant Harlan's grip.

Dave recognized the younger man's inexperience. Forcing the German's hands backwards, Dave tried to manhandle him to the deck. The boy squirmed away but did not relinquish the weapon.

Catching the German's shackle with his foot, Dave jerked him off balance. He jammed his elbow into the boy's throat. Eyes bulging, the lad gasped and fell backwards. Dave crashed on top of him. In a loud expelled whoosh, the

German grazed the table. He rolled awkwardly to the deck, dragging Dave with him. The deafening repercussion of the Colt exploded in the cramped space of the wardroom.

⊕

Karney woke with a start. Straightening up, he first checked Mrs. Greer. She still slept, though fitfully. Something had jarred Karney from sleep, but he didn't know what.

Staring at the clock, his eyes slowly focused on the hands: 0255. It seemed like hours since he'd come in here. His thermos was empty; the last of his coffee cold. He swished the black liquid to stir the sugar, drank it down, then put his guitar away.

A moan from Mrs. Greer drew Karney's attention back to her.

She convulsed in pain. Feeling her cheek, Karney realized her fever worsened. He opened the voice tube just as she grabbed his arm. The fierceness of the grip left no doubt of her urgency.

Her eyes blazed with fear and panic as she pleaded, "Please, Leftenant, help me . . . me baby cannae come—"

A contraction seized her, violently doubling her up.

Karney rapidly broke open an ampoule of morphine. Drawing the amber liquid into a syringe, he injected the drug into her upper buttocks. Again starting to call the bridge, he realized someone summoned him. *I need help,* he grumpily thought. *Why the hell're they calling me?* "Rork here."

For the first time Karney recalled, Grange's voice was high-pitched with distress. Not pausing, the Oklahoman's torrent of the new crisis flooded into Karney's ears.

"Skipper, Mr. Harlan just shot one of the Krauts, the kid I think, he tried to get his gun from him an' it was all Mr. Harlan could do to wrestle him down so he didn't get shot an' his gun went off an—"

"GRANGE," Karney barked, ending the ensign's unremitting narration, "calm down. Is Dave wounded?"

"No, sir, but that little—"

"Grange, was the boy killed?"

"No, sir, but if'n it was up to me—"

"Who's with Harlan and the prisoners now?"

"Allison was already down there and Del Sternbach was about to relieve me when I got the call. Del headed down there an' had me call Taylor, but I got Chief Tapia, so—"

"Grange," Karney interrupted again when he felt *Lady Z* roll awkwardly with a swell, "mind your helm. You're falling off to port. Come right, back onto course one-niner-zero."

"Golly, Skipper, I don't know how the heck you do it, but you're right. Sorry, sir. Correcting to course one-niner-zero."

Zealous swung back on course, the swells no longer struck her abeam. "Grange, I can't leave Mrs. Greer. She's going into labor again. When the prisoner situation is under control, send Tap or Taylor down here. I need some help. And don't let our heading fall off one-nine-zero. Understood?"

"Aye, aye, Skipper. One-niner-zero."

Closing the voice-tube, Karney turned back to Mrs. Greer. The morphine should've begun to work through her system by now, but she still writhed in pain. As Tap warned, the opiate had no effect. The sheets became soaked with blood, diluted by her water breaking. She struggled less, but her battle was lost. He knew he was on his own.

Karney's heartbeat rushed into an agonizing death— the fetus aborted before he could think of what to do to save her baby—if indeed there was anything anyone could have done.

Staggered by this tragedy, he held the tiny body of a baby girl. His hands seemed huge in comparison to the incredibly formed child—nearly perfect in every way except the ability to survive. She weighed ounces that should have been pounds.

He'd dealt with various bloody wounds and death before, but never had he felt queasy. Breaking out in a cold sweat, Karney felt a panic he'd never experienced. His head swam as he fought the urge to throw up.

Hands trembling, he wrapped the little baby girl in a clean, white towel. Noting the time—0313—tears stung his eyes. Karney couldn't concentrate. His only thought was: *What a bizarre and heart-rending death to record in this cutter's logbook.*

"*Mi Dios . . .*"

Still dazed, Karney slowly looked up. Tap stood in the doorway.

Crossing himself, Tap's voice quivered when he spoke, "Irish, I got here as soon as Grange told me . . ."

In shock, Karney stared down at the wrapped body resting in his blood smeared hands. Looking back up, he noted Tap's pasty-gray face and knew his friend's pallor more than likely reflected his own.

Tap softly asked, "What do you need me to do, *compadre*?"

⊕

Hours later, Karney gingerly shifted his position. He sat with his feet propped up. As usual, his long legs proved impossible to accommodate in such tight quarters.

Subconsciously, Karney listened to Ellie Greer's breathing.

Initially spent after her near-drowning only hours ago, the ordeal she just went through was far worse. She slept and Karney hoped she would continue to sleep. In his mind, time wavered between minutes and years. Though morphine kept her sedated, it was only a matter of time before she woke up to face the bleak reality of her loss.

A new noise pricked his attention. Gingerly, Karney

dropped his chair back on all fours and stood. He heard a plane. The Sunderland?

Before he called the bridge, a soft rap sounded on the cabin door. He opened it to find Lieutenant Dave Harlan. "Rork, the Aussies are back. They signaled they're to pick up the woman and the others. They're on final approach. Do you want me to stay with Mrs. Greer, while you talk to them?"

Karney turned to look at her tranquil sleep. "Yeah, if you could," he said. "I'd rather she not be left alone."

Grabbing his winter gear, Karney left the cabin.

Up on deck, a glaring sun, frozen barely above the horizon, pained Karney's eyes as he dug out his service-issued Ray Bans. Knowing it was a little after 0830, Karney thought: *Christ, the Aussies must've taken off from Newfy in total darkness.*

He stood beside Tap, watching the flying-boat smack the choppy waves, bounce, then plop back down. The plane's great weight settled into the water. She wallowed like a winged-whale suspended in mid-breach—half in the water, half out.

Ice Sheila came to rest a hundred yards to starboard. Karney heard Tap groan. A closer view of the buxomy-bombshell nose art Karney noticed yesterday bore the unique style of Tap's wife, Lacy. Her delicate lace-like signature was also clearly evident. The model wore a military flight jacket, zipped at the bottom and barely covering her lush breasts. An Australian flag, rippling back upon itself, hardly concealed the rest of the blonde's nakedness. The lady appeared so lifelike, Karney almost felt he should return her salute.

Thumping his friend's back, Karney felt empathy for Tap who had to deal with his talented wife's wild side. It was a topic they'd discussed before. No words were needed to explain the back-slap.

Assisting *Bonnie*'s wounded into the launches, Karney noted the sailors' faces were a strange blend of eagerness and foreboding. The pitching gyrations of the flying boat lent a rather bleak welcome to these survivors.

Miguel Tapia asked, "You think Mrs. Greer is up to this, *compadre*?"

"No, she's not," Karney asserted, climbing into the first launch. "Just hope the Aussie's won't have to violate any orders, 'cause that lady ain't goin' nowhere."

As the launch approached *Ice Sheila*, a sandy-haired fellow wearing the pilot's cap and a Mae West life jacket appeared at the Sunderland's open door. He braced himself against the tumultuous rolls. Though his light-colored eyes seemed impassive, a friendly smile warmed his bland features.

"G'day, mates," he called as a line was tossed to one of the Aussie crewman and made fast. "Welcome to *Ice Sheila*, our little 'ome away from 'ome." The man stuck his hand out to assist the American officer aboard first.

Leaping across, Karney slid his Ray-Bans into his pocket to make eye contact. "Morning, I'm Lieutenant Karney Rork, Skipper of *Lady Z*, officially *USCGC Zealous*."

The man's brow creased as he leaned around Karney, peering into the launch. "Flying Officer Wendy Collins here, mate."

The Sunderland's crewmen began transferring the survivors into the cavernous interior of the flying boat. The Aussie pulled Karney further inside, out of the way.

Karney asked, "How many can you fly back?"

"We got room for all of 'em and then some, mate. Where's the Sheila? I guess she's comin' with the next batch, eh?"

"No, she's not," Karney sternly answered. "Mrs. Greer's in a lotta pain and in no condition to be moved. She and the prisoners stay aboard *Zealous* till we reach Newfoundland."

"Looky here, mate," Collins said, sounding edgy, "I got her cousin, a bloody Canuck cap'n, name of MacCalister, and a ruddy admiral, as in her uncle of the same clan, breathin' down me bloody neck, insistin' she come back with me."

Karney glanced around the plane. "Guess they bailed out on the flight out, chum. 'Sides, *Lady Z*'s American, not Canadian. What I say out here goes. The lady stays."

The gears ratcheting in Collins' head were almost audible. Even if the Australian produced written orders, Karney would not budge. Before Collins spoke, Karney gave an alternative view. "Look at it this way, she stays, I'm accountable. You fly her back and she gets worse, your ass'll be in a sling. This way, my butt's left hanging."

It took a scant second for Karney's logic to sink in. "Gotcha, mate. We'll get our *Sheila* loaded up and bugger on home 'fore that blow shuffles into town. Course, you do know there'll be a bloody blow waitin' in Hali' when I fly in without her."

"Collins, assure the Canuck brass that I'm taking excellent care of Mrs. Greer. I'll catch the flak on this one, not you."

"Hope you're right, mate. Last bloody thing I needs is Mac MacCalister gettin' all pissed at me and sendin' me to bloomin' Tokyo."

Raising an eyebrow, Karney wondered why he thought he'd be sent to Tokyo of all places. Karney figured: *Somewhere some squirrel's looking for the nut that escaped his stash.*

"Oh, 'nother thing, koala piss has it, right up till *Bonnie* got hit, there was a lotta fishy Morse-code chatter goin' on out here. A mate at Torbay figures it might've been the U-boat you tangled with and some rotten dingo dung aboard *Glasgow Bonnie*. Take it for what it's worth, mate, but one of your Fritzies might know somethin'."

Karney merely nodded. He'd already figured as much.

When the transfer was finished, they shook hands. Collins prepared for takeoff; Karney returned to *Lady Z*. Though not keen on crossing swords with either Admiral or

Captain MacCalister, Karney hoped Mrs. Greer's family understood why he had kept her on board: it was best for her. Karney just prayed he was right.

Watching the flying boat struggle into the air, Karney felt sure he had not heard the last of this. But Wendy's commanders were the least of his concerns on this wintry December morn. Karney had a baby to prepare for burial and a German to interrogate.

⊕

Karney cocked the hammer of his Colt .45 and jammed the muzzle under the chin of the sleeping prisoner. His eyes snapped open. Jerking upright, to see what rudely woke him, the German cracked his head against the back of the wooden bench seat.

The German prisoner's gaze focused on an icy pair of slate-blue eyes, then he glanced over at Allison. The Coastie stood placidly and quite indifferently nearby.

When the American officer spoke, his voice fairly seethed. "Listen close, Fritzy, or whatever the hell your name is. I've just sewn the body of a tiny, premature baby girl into her burial shroud, and I'm not in a real forgiving mood right now. Were you *Glasgow Bonnie*'s radio operator?"

Waiting for his words to sink in, Karney watched the man's dark eyes. There was no doubt he understood what Karney said in English. The German's gaze darted between his captors. Sweat glistened through the stubble on his upper lip. But the fear in his eyes gave way to something Karney could only describe as arrogant Nazi gall; like the hatred he'd seen in Hitler's eyes in newsreels.

As if denying his knowledge of English, the man answered in German. "You cannot threaten me, *Leutnant*. I have rights under the Geneva Convention. I am not required to answer your questions."

Karney had never willingly taken a human life—

especially not in cold blood. But at this moment, he was closer to pulling the trigger than he ever thought possible. It apparently shone in his eyes as he again rammed his .45 harder into the German's throat. Fear registered anew.

This time, Karney spoke in German. "Rights? Like *Bonnie*'s crew had? You gave up those rights when you betrayed them. Right now, the only damned thing between you and a bullet through your fuckin' brain is my finger on this trigger."

Blinking nervously, the German reconsidered his situation. He glanced at Allison and knew no help would come from that quarter. Karney's voice drew his gaze back.

"I'll ask one more time: Were you *Bonnie*'s radio operator?"

The Kraut's voice sounded strong, but quivered conspicuously as he replied in English, "Yes . . . yes, I was."

"How'd you signal U820?" Karney asked in English.

"At specified times, I would key the mike and tap out our position and any known course changes."

"That's how they knew where and when to pick you up before they torpedoed the freighter?"

"Yes."

"What if they didn't get your signal?"

"If they didn't . . ." His tone changed. "I don't know. I was just following orders."

Though Karney knew the man lied, he eased off on the pressure. He figured the Kraut's fear of lying to a Yank— and being shot—was more favorable than what might befall him if his Nazi taskmasters learned he talked. Karney still pushed for answers.

"How many are radioing convoy headings to U-boats?"

The haughty air rose again. "Dozens, perhaps more than a hundred."

Viciously, Karney jammed the enmity .45 under his chin again. The Kraut's head thudded loudly against the wood. "How many?"

"I don't know, I swear, I don't know. I've heard of only

a few others. We pick up our assignments in Halifax, Montreal or Liverpool."

"From whom?" Karney asked, keeping the pressure on his pistol.

"It's a blind drop," the German hurriedly answered. "A code on a postcard tells us what to do and when. It varies. That is all I know, I swear, that's all."

Releasing the hammer, Karney leaned back. "I need to bury a baby. While I'm up top, you give Petty Officer Allison your name and answer all of his questions. If you don't cooperate, I'll sink you tonight with the garbage. Dead or alive, I don't give a damn."

Karney stood, holstered his Colt and turned to Allison, "If he tries anything . . ." He glanced over his shoulder. "Anything. Shoot him."

With a lopsided grin, Allison answered, "It'd be my pleasure, sir."

As Karney started up the ladder, the Nazi radioman called to him, "*Leutnant?*"

Turning back, Karney glared at his captive.

"My real name is Georg Aldistreich, and I am truly sorry about Ellie's baby. I did not realize she was pregnant."

Staring at the German, Karney's mind locked on the lifeless body of a baby girl. When he finally spoke, his voice was as chill as the ocean sloshing past *Lady Z*. "You're way past the point where your regrets matter to anyone, you sorry son of a bitch."

⊕

The sea appeared like glistening golden scales of some mythical mermaid in an ancient mariner's tale. Wind-torn mares' tails fanned high above *Zealous*. Clouds near the horizon split the sun's rays into saffron ribbons, causing Karney Rork to wonder: *Did heaven's radiance break the gloom to bless this service?*

Still shaky and in pain, Ellie was bundled in a chair

next to the rail on the main deck. She felt Karney lean closer.

He whispered in her ear, "This gentle sea and that absolutely gorgeous sunset . . . are gifts straight from God to your Nikki."

Looking to the west, Ellie beheld the young officer's meaning. Though cold, this afternoon was blessedly calm—the first she could remember since leaving England.

Crewmen not on duty stood at parade rest on deck. Ellie held Karney's strong hand desperately, grateful for his presence. As Karney began the funeral service, Ellie felt his tenderness sustain her, both emotionally and physically.

As Karney Rork's words carried across the ocean, Ellie's thoughts gently drifted with them. She wanted to sail away on them, far from her despair and sorrow. Her world was collapsing again, just as it had when Brandt and Anna died.

Fearful of losing all control, Ellie steeled herself by focusing on the Coast Guard ensign as it rippled from the mast at half-staff. Alternating red and white vertical stripes formed the background, except in the upper left corner where a white field held the dark blue symbol of the United States of America. On the second red stripe from the outer edge, she could make out the crossed-anchor symbol of the Coast Guard. It was a proud and defiant insignia to which she could link her heart.

A gust of wind whipped the flag, almost like a reprimand, to draw her attention back to the lieutenant's resonant voice and her baby's service.

". . . a life, never born into this world, yet a victim of its cruelty nonetheless. Unto Almighty God, we commend the tiny body of Nicole Elaine Greer to the deep, in the sure and certain faith of the resurrection unto eternal life, when the sea shall give up her dead, in the life of the world to come." After a moment, Karney softly ordered his men: "Proceed . . ."

Crewmen snapped to attention. The plank was tipped

toward the sea. From under a Canadian flag—a crewman's gift—a small canvas bundle with her baby's body, slid into the water. A three gun salute cracked the stillness. It echoed hollowly across the icy sea, heightening her sense of desolation. Glancing up, she realized Karney's gaze stared straight forward, his jaw tight. A tear ran down his cheek.

With his next order, the Coast Guard ensign again snapped boldly as it was hoisted to the top of the mast. It settled calmly as if nary any gust had blown.

In a rich, deep baritone, Karney began to sing *Amazing Grace*. Every note came from the depth of his soul, each word from the bottom of his heart. All was hushed.

Hearing this traditional Scottish hymn—so loved and familiar—Ellie felt goose-bumps prickle her flesh. In solemn dignity, Karney sang the third verse again:

> *Through many dangers, toils and snares,*
> *We have already come;*
> *Tis grace . . .*
> *that brought us safe thus far . . .*
> *And grace . . . shall lead us home . . .*

Karney's last note lingered, like the twilight call of a lone bugler's taps. No one moved. The wind stirred, though barely a sigh, to ruffle the flag, then stilled once more.

Eyes moist, Miguel Tapia bent his knee without touching the deck and held out the folded Canadian flag. "Mrs. Greer, from the officers and crew of *Lady Z*, I present you with the flag of your native country. *Via con Dios* . . . God be with you."

Not trusting herself to speak, Ellie nodded her thanks and gratefully accepted the flag. Scanning the downcast eyes of these stalwart men, she lost her battle. Tears ran down her cheeks, and her gaze drifted back to the gilded sea.

Karney gave the order to dismiss the men, then

squatted down beside her. "Mrs. Greer, do you wish to go below?"

"Would you be mindin', Leftenant," she hesitantly asked, "if we stayed till the sun sets?" Gazing into his serene eyes, Ellie saw the depth of his sorrow and compassion. In their color she beheld the billowing, blue-gray clouds of a summer rainstorm.

"No, I don't mind. I'll stay right here till you're ready."

He stood, still holding her hand. It made her wonder: *Is the leftenant reluctant to go below as well? Does he see twilight's enchantment?* Recalling his earlier comment, she knew he did. *Today is a gift from God to me baby daughter—God's leadin' Nikki home on golden rays of sunshine.*

Though comforted, Ellie felt lost. Nikki, like Brandt and Anna, was gone; Ellie's future again blown off course, her compass broken. After losing her immediate family, the exacting work at MI-6 had rushed into the breached hold of her life. Now, Nikki's death felt as though icy water flowed into the unfathomable abyss of her heart. And this time no demanding duty filled her time or abated her pain.

The key was to seek a posting in Nova Scotia. Though Ellie swore upon boarding *Glasgow Bonnie*, she had left the spy-game for good, Nikki's death changed the rules. Ellie wanted—no needed to be—back in the game. *The Nazis will pay.*

Ellie began to understand her father's obsession with destroying Nazi Germany. His vindictiveness over crippling wounds received in the Great War were justified. It was readily apparent that Hitler and his Reich were extensions of that first war. *They must be stopped. Lord, please, let me nae insubstantial skills be used against those—*

Karney gently squeezed her hand as he hunkered down beside her. When he spoke, his tone was softened by Gaelic, *"Dá fhad lá, tagann oíche."* He translated just as softly, "Even the longest day has its end."

Ellie realized the clouds were stained deep red, the crimson of spilt blood, the color of vengeance.

"I better get you below. If you catch pneumonia out here, your Uncle-Admiral will definitely hang me from a yardarm."

With a sigh, Ellie said, "Aye, Leftenant. I would nae want him to be mad at you. Besides, I am startin' to get a wee bit chilly."

Aware that Ellie was still weak from her ordeal, Karney carried her below to his cabin. He sat her on the bunk and helped her remove his much-too-large winter gear before gently laying her down. He then covered her up.

Weary from the long day, Ellie closed her eyes. Sensing the rhythm of the small cutter on the swells was calming. Though she must have dozed off, when Ellie opened her eyes, the handsome officer sat on the side of the bunk, his foot propped up on an open drawer below. Karney's head was bowed, his eyes closed. Crossing himself, he opened his eyes to gaze at her. A sad smile failed to touch his serious eyes.

Avoiding her own misery, she asked, "You be Catholic?"

He looked baffled, then, with a soft chuckle of embarrassment and a crooked grin, said, "I crossed myself, didn't I?"

Smiling faintly, she nodded.

Shrugging, he said, "Da started us out Catholic but Ma was Protestant—that age old Celtic clash between the Green and the Orange." He glanced down at his hands. "Truth is, I'm more spiritual than religious. I tend to settle for middle of the flag: the peace of white. In Boston, I usually attend Gunnar's Episcopal Church, Catholic when in Ireland or visiting my sister in Quincy and—," He smiled softly. "I really don't care where I go if they preach Christ. But the only time I cross myself is when I feel lost, so I must be more worried about you than I realized."

Karney hopped down, his hand on the bunk edge and

closed the drawer with his foot. Ellie touched his hand. "Leftenant, the service you performed for me wee babe was beautiful. It meant a great deal to me, and I thank you for yer carin'."

With a reserved smile, he said, "You're quite welcome, Mrs. Greer. I'm just sorry we—," The voice tube shrilled. "Excuse me, please." Flipping open the cap, he snapped, "Rork here."

The words were garbled to her, but he clearly understood them.

"Okay, Tap, I'll be up shortly." Closing the tube, Karney gazed down at Ellie, his expression somber. "I'm sorry, but I—"

She lay her bandaged hand on his. "You've nae any need to explain, Leftenant. The sea has been in me clan for centuries. I know the demands. But can you do me a wee favor?"

"Anything," he tenderly said.

"Please, call me Ellie. Mrs. Greer seems a wee formal for all I've put you through." Though she hadn't told him Greer was her maiden name, it still seemed too starched for the circumstances.

This time his smile touched his eyes. "Then Ellie it'll be, if you call me Karney, or Irish. Every time you say 'Leftenant Rork', I feel I should jump to attention, snap a bloody salute and break into a chorus of God Save The King."

Ellie giggled despite her misery. "Please, do nae salute me, Karney." Pausing, she repeated, "Karney . . . 'tis a grand Irish name. I rather like the way it feels rollin' off me tongue."

His eyes took on a dreamy quality. "Yeah, I rather like the way it sounds rolling off your tongue."

Eyes enlarging, he was evidently startled by the impropriety of what he'd said. It seemed all the more endearing to Ellie.

"I better get topside," Karney stated, grabbing his

helmet and other gear. With a smile, he said, "If you wanna read, there's C.S. Forester's Hornblower books, Mary Shelley's *Frankenstein* or H.G. Wells and some Edgar Rice Burroughs. Several westerns by Max Brand and Zane Grey. But if mysteries are more your cup of tea, there's Arthur Conan Doyle and a few Agatha Christie's. A couple of history books, sailing manuals and even some Shakespeare, I think. Basically, it's sort of a shotgun approach to our library." He pointed behind her. "Most of 'em are in those racks Gunnar installed on each side of the porthole. More are in the wardroom. Sorry it doesn't follows Dewey's system. Heck, I don't even think it comes close to being alphabetical."

Ellie glanced at the long row of books. There was plenty to read. "I think I can find some something, if I feel like it. Thank you," she said.

A touch of mischief brightened his sad eyes. Karney bowed like a knight of old and flourished an imaginary cape.

"Milady, duty calls." Pausing, he added, "Books may relax you, but sleep's probably more important for you right now." With a quick wink, Karney was out the door, boots thudding up the stairs.

Entering the wheelhouse, Karney was completely back to cutter business. "Why's GreenPat wanna talk to me direct, Hack?"

"It's not HQ, Skipper. It's some Admiral MacCalister, Royal Canadian Navy. And, sir, the transmission's in the open."

Plunking his helmet upside-down beside the radio, he tugged off his gloves, one finger at a time and set them in his helmet. Each motion was slow and deliberate as he contemplated what was coming.

"Sir," Hackerman hesitated, "he sounds a little miffed."

Forewarned, Karney put on the headphones, then keyed the mike. "Admiral, this is Lieutenant Rork, U.S.

Coast Guard. How may I be of assistance, sir? Over."

"Leftenant, why is my niece still on your bloody little vessel? She was supposed to be in Halifax late this afternoon with those blasted Aussies. Over."

Hack's "a little miffed" was a mild understatement. Clearing his throat, Karney replied, "Admiral, I determined that her condition was too unstable for transfer. Over."

"And just who the bloody hell do you think you are, Leftenant, to have taken it upon yourself to disregard my orders to Flying Officer Collins and refuse to release my niece into his care? Over."

Jaw muscles flexing, he checked his temper before daring to speak. "Admiral, I'm a qualified medical officer, besides being skipper of *Zealous*. I understand your concern, sir, but making a demanding trip like that would cause her needless strain. She is resting quite peacefully now, sir. Thank you. Over."

"She should be resting quite peacefully in a hospital in Halifax, young man, not in the middle of the North Atlantic on some God forsaken boat for chasing rum runners."

A pause and a heavy sigh traveled the miles to Karney's ears. Teeth clamping like a vise, his thoughts exploded. *Who the hell does this guy think he is? Lady Z's not chasing any damn rum runners anymore. And we're not going to Halifax. Hell, we barely have fuel to make Newfy, much less Nova Scotia.*

Finally the admiral demanded, "When do you intend to dock in Halifax? Over."

Again keying the mike, Karney said, "Sir, GreenPat has our ETA and destination, and I'm not at liberty to, nor will I, divulge such information on an open transmission. Over."

"Leftenant Rork, perhaps you misunderstood me . . ."

Contempt burned through the headphones like hot tar.

"I am Rear Admiral Richard Gregor MacCalister, Royal Canadian Navy. I asked you a direct question, young

man. And I demand a straight and proper answer and I
DEMAND IT NOW. Over."

Staring up at the overhead, Karney took a deep breath
before keying the mike. "Sir, it wouldn't matter if you were
Winston Churchill himself, though any Kraut listening out
there knows who you really are and to whom you're
talking. I will not transmit any more information in the
open than has already been divulged. Over."

A lengthy pause followed. Karney had no trouble
imagining the admiral's teeth gnashing and fists clenching.
Braced for the next verbal barrage, he was surprised when
another, much more staid but similar sounding, voice
greeted his ears.

"Leftenant Rork, this is Captain MacCalister, RCN."

Ah, Karney thought, *this must be Cousin Mac.*

"Captain Wharton apprised me of your difficult
situation. I apologize for any complications, however. Your
excellent care of my cousin has been duly noted and much
appreciated. Can you let me know her present *condition,*
please? Over."

His sensitive tone rated the captain far above the
haughty uncle-admiral, who was presumably his father.
Mac MacCalister seemed to be a decent guy, genuinely
concerned for Ellie. Gently, Karney answered, "Captain
MacCalister, your cousin is all right, but, I'm sorry to say,
she lost her baby. Funeral services were held at sundown.
Part of why she stayed with us. Over."

When Mac MacCalister spoke again, the sadness in his
voice was undeniable. "Your message is understood,
Leftenant. I look forward to meeting you when you reach
port, eh? Thank you, Leftenant. Out."

Evidently, Captain Wharton, the Naval officer *Zealous*
had been reporting to since November, had informed
Captain MacCalister of *Lady Z'*s anchorage and estimated
time of arrival.

Karney handed the headphones back to Hackerman,
relieved that Mac MacCalister had umpired the call with

his dad. But Karney couldn't help but think: *I sure's hell hope I've not made a new enemy. The admiral may be Canadian, but he can make waves that'll make a tidal wave look like ripples on Frog Pond.* "Go bhfóire Dia orainn," he said in dismay, then translated, "God help us."

RCN Training Garrison
Sheet Harbour, Nova Scotia
Tuesday

The moment Mac MacCalister took off the headphones, his father, already glaring at him, demanded, "So, what did that smart-alec, self-important Yank have to say for his bloody self? And why the devil were you so conciliatory?"

Still sitting on the table edge, Mac handed the headset back to Chief Clevell. Mac stood and looked down at his father. "Admiral, we need to talk in private." With that, he walked out, leaving his father in stony, bewildered silence.

Mac negotiated the memorable halls of his family's manor on the southwest edge of Sheet Harbour, Nova Scotia. Turned into a training base to teach Canadian seamen everything from codes to meteorology, the estate now resembled a military garrison of most any nation at war. Its clandestine role—Mac's real purpose in being here—was not so well known.

In the mid-1800s the architect had designed the manor to portray the Holy Trinity when seen in plan-view. Over the years, the advent of steam-powered vessels and Clan MacCalister's strong bond with seafaring, turned the significance of the design from religious to nautical, representing a three-bladed propeller.

The once grand and cordial home, built on high ground above the harbor's western shore, was now a methodical hodgepodge of living quarters, offices, training and support facilities. Sentries—not butlers in livery—were stationed at every entrance. Machine-guns, mounted behind sandbags at strategic points and on the rooftops, were manned day and night. Checkpoints guarded the entry road and a contingent of sentries patrolled the perimeter.

The north-wing upstairs was considered officers' country. The first level housed RCN administrative officers. The lower, or garden level, had been transformed into RCN training offices and classrooms, complete with an updated gymnasium and sauna.

Non-commissioned officers were billeted in the west-wing, upper level. On the main level an enormous mess hall and kitchen served the numerous trainees expected to filter through the facility as well as officers and enlisted men, Mac's boys and all support personnel. A portion of the garden level, reinforced as a bomb-shelter, held the crucial Communications Center: the RCN's ears on North Atlantic radiotelegraph transmissions. Two radio towers perched on hills south of the manor with a third closer to the sea.

The South-wing held suites for Admiral MacCalister, Mac and private quarters for visiting officers. The study became the admiral's office, while the grand dining room now served as a map-operations center—the room where Mac's array of charts and pins would soon reside. The garden level became headquarters for Mac and his men.

One unaltered domain was the manor's library. Open to all personnel day and night, Admiral MacCalister worked a deal for an exchange of materials with Sheet Harbour's small library, which also accessed the Halifax Public Library. Since martial law created a guarantor at the manor, there was never a problem with late books.

Enlisted men had constructed their own barracks west of the manor beyond the gardens and a stand of red spruce. To the southwest stood the Infirmary, backed against the stable's paddock. This offered a tranquil scene for recovering patients since horses usually grazed here. This part of the grounds would still have appealed to Mac's

Mom. It definitely recalled a more peaceful time far from the war—even if the firing range was just over the hill.

For the most part, Mac was relieved his mother never beheld what a madhouse her beautiful home had become. The laughter and playful squeals of kids was one thing. The brusque orders of exasperated officers and harsh swearing of a slew of roughhewn chiefs and petty officers, quite another. *At least Mom's noble horses get exercised by the guys who'd rather ride off their stress than drink it down at the Tartan Banks.* Mac smiled thinking of the horses, despite the pending confrontation with his father.

Entering Admiral MacCalister's office, Mac sagged down onto the green brocaded, wingback chair near the crackling fireplace. He turned his thoughts from the garrison to Ellie. His father knew Ellie was returning to her native Nova Scotia; not that her journey began because she was pregnant.

Added to the cauldron was Karney Rork, Mac's key choice for ICE PACT. Sizing him up during their radio chat, Mac liked the Yank. He wouldn't buckle under if grilled by a brass-ass—like his father.

As if on cue, Admiral Richard MacCalister stormed in through the double doors, slamming the heavy oak behind him. "So, why the bloody hell did the Yank refuse to put Eleanor on that damned plane?"

Mac sounded blasé. "You know she hates to fly—"

"That's no bloody excuse," he snapped, glaring at his son. "Why the devil didn't the Aussie pick her up, eh?"

"It wasn't up to Collins. Leftenant Rork made a judgment call because he's dealing with a predicament of which you're not aware, eh? His actions were wholly justified in my book."

"Explain this predicament, Captain," he ordered.

Sighing, Mac met his father's pale-green eyes. "When *Glasgow Bonnie* sailed from England, Ellie was five months pregnant. She lost her baby after *Bonnie* was torpedoed. That's why Leftenant Rork didn't want her leaving *Zealous*. Ellie was in no condition to travel nor, might I add, did she wish to leave."

Admiral MacCalister stared at Mac for several long seconds before sinking into the matching wingback chair opposite him.

"Eleanor returned to have some misbegotten child?" His face red, he jumped up and began pacing. "That's preposterous. What sort of conduct is that for a lady of Clan MacCalister? You'd think she was a naive farm girl on her first trip to the city, not a mature, well-educated woman of thirty-seven. Unwed and pregnant. It's a bloody disgrace. Not to mention wholly unacceptable." The admiral wheeled on his son.

Sensing their age-old feud about to boil over, Mac felt his defense mechanisms coil for a strike.

Stabbing at his son with a gnarled finger, Admiral MacCalister alternately accused and demanded. "And you knew all the while? Why wasn't I told? Did Angus know of her condition? With five brothers, why the devil does Eleanor always turn to you whenever she finds herself in trouble? Blast that girl anyway! And why do you always help her without giving any thought to the consequences?"

Standing, Mac glared at his father, several inches shorter. "Uncle Gus insisted Ellie have an abortion to protect the Greer family name. Her truculent father is the reason Ellie was on her way here. As for Ellie's five brothers, only Robert was in any position to help and he, just as callously, stayed on the holier-than-thou side of stone throwing. The same as you are doing now, Father."

Head pounding, Mac rubbed his brow. "Everyone's so damned worried about our family honor, they don't see the hell that Ellie's been through. Rather ironic, don't you think, that an American Coast Guard officer cares more about your niece than her own bloody family!"

"So, you took it upon yourself to support Eleanor in this shameful debacle? How long have you known she was pregnant?"

His dad had not heard a word. "Since she lost her baby, this argument is pointless. At least, Leftenant Rork saved Ellie's life." Mac's rage boiled over. "Goddammit, Father, you should just be thankful Ellie's still alive."

"Don't you swear at me, Captain MacCalister."

"Don't pull rank on me when we bicker family matters." As his father stiffened with shock, Mac took a quick breath, then slowly let it out in a sigh. "From what Ellie told me in her correspondence, this baby— misbegotten or not—meant a great deal to her. And, by God, I'll not allow her to be further chastised or alienated from our clan. Uncle Gus and Robert have been callous enough for three lifetimes."

The admiral's eyes smoldered, but he said nothing.

"Father, you're blind to all but your own self-centered and stringent ideals, you always have been. And right now, Ellie doesn't need them crammed down her throat. One mistake doesn't erase her good nor all she's accomplished. And as Aunt Elaine's only daughter and the only female left in this clan, you should love Ellie no matter what the hell has happened. Don't forget she is your only niece."

With the mention of his younger sister's name, the fire in the older man's eyes was quenched. The admiral stared at the floor, clearly still feeling guilt for not being able to prevent his sister Elaine's suicide.

Though Mac didn't want to hurt his father, it was Ellie who needed protection, not the Old Man's walrus hide.

Sagging back onto his chair, Mac offered, "I suppose the best way to look at it, Father, is if Grandpa Kaid had maintained such chaste standards, Clan MacCalister would've died on a hurricane swept North Carolina beach during America's Civil War."

The admiral looked up at Mac. Though a thin smile tugged at the corner of the old man's wrinkled mouth, he said nothing and merely glanced away.

"If I'm going to see Liz and my kids before I return to St. John's, I'd better leave soon." When his dad didn't respond, Mac asked, "Want to join us for supper, Father? Get your mind off work and see your grandkids before they forget what you look like."

Eyes brightening, the admiral looked back up. "That's a grand idea. Sergeant Folks can drive us, so we can discuss your Leftenant Rork. And a leftenant he will stay, if I've any say in it. He's one of your candidates for ICE PACT, is he not?"

Guardedly, Mac nodded.

"Then we have much to discuss. Rork sounds like some typical cocksure Yank, absolutely full of himself, disrespectful with no . . ."

As his father's harangue rose, Mac's spirits drooped. *The Old Man never changes.* Though Ellie was out of the line of fire, Karney Rork was centered in his cross-hairs. And Mac knew he'd soon be, too. Karney Rork's promotion to lieutenant commander along with the formal transfer of *Zealous* to OPERATION ICE PACT was already in the works.

CHAPTER SIX

Recalling the feathery clouds at Nikki's funeral service and the opulent burgundy sky at sunset, Karney had groaned this morning when greeted by a similar wine-red sky. His aching shoulder corroborated the old nautical proverb as well: *Red sky in the morning, sailor take warning; Red sky at night, sailor's delight.*

Throughout the morning, though the temperature was mild for this latitude, the barometer fell. By noon they ran straight into the front. The barometer plummet as a low pressure area sucked the storm down on top of *Lady Z.*

As weather rapidly deteriorated, Karney took the dog watches, 1600 to 2000 . By the end of his shift, he knew midwatch would last even longer. In darkness, *Lady Z* struggled in near-gale conditions with wind velocities registering as Force 7 on the Beaufort scale. Winds blew between 28 to 33 knots as waves thrust upward to almost fifteen feet. Growing swells broke in upon themselves as foam blew off the tops in streaks.

Karney's aching shoulder remained a harbinger of worse weather to come; just how worse it didn't predict.

$\oplus$

USCGC Zealous battling the North Atlantic's winter fury.
At only 125' in length, Buck and a Quarters faced a daunting challenge
in such violent storms. Only two ever lost their fight to a hurricane off
Cape Hatteras: USCGC Bedloe and USCGC Jackson on 14 Sep 1944
Original pencil and watercolor drawing by D.D.O'Lander.

FRI: 19 DEC 41

By midnight, Mother Nature upped the ante with winds more than 50 knots and waves higher than the bridge. Snow shrieked around *Lady Z*, glowing with ghostly incandescence. Foam streaked off towering waves as if wraiths fleeing the graves. Every wave tried to turn *Zealous* on her beam end, creating a gut-wrenching scuffle to right herself.

Crewmen fought to keep ice and snow accumulation off the decks. It was an exhaustive chore. But they had to win this fight or *Lady Z* risked becoming a statistic: LOST AT SEA—NO TRACE FOUND.

Swinging his sledgehammer into a glacial mass near the fantail, Karney morosely wondered: *Should I have forced Ellie to leave with Ice Sheila? God, I hope she sleeps through this.*

Tethered by safety lines, a mere thread of protection, men wrestled to keep their balance on lurching, glass-slick decks as they chipped and hacked ice off the deck. To be washed overboard meant a battering against the hull, burial under huge waves and disorientation. In pain, possibly shock, prayers were their only certainty.

No one eagerly sought ice detail. Yet each knew they had to tackle this hazardous duty. It kept *Lady Z*'s medical corpsman quite busy.

Karney labored beside his men, catnapping when no emergency demanded his attention. Though he had faith in the men, Gunnar's absence was felt as keenly as the bitter cold. Concern grew with escalating winds. Danger stalked in the wake of their lone engine. Patience drained like seawater skimming through the scuppers.

Sensing a cold hint of dawn lighting the raging sea, Karney tried to steady his binoculars and focus past sheets of near horizontal snow. Mountainous waves and the overhanging crests filled his vision. Strips of foamed water shred like fabric torn by some vengeful Gorgon. It reminded him of Medusa's hair, but rather than serpents, this hair writhed with rimed strands of seawater.

Zealous now battled a Violent Storm, Force 11. Their little cutter, struggling for all her worth, seemed an absurdly puny, fragile speck amidst the fierce upheavals of the ocean.

The day dragged on. Nothing changed. An unseen sunset turned ominous clouds from slate-gray to soot-black. Karney was numb to all but his cutter, her men and the sea's vicious, pitiless mood.

Zealous continued to plunge into deep troughs. Water crashed over her bow. She struggled up the steep slope of one wave only to be hurled headlong down the opposite side. Water poured over her gun'ales. Lurching and straining through each drenching, *Lady Z* somehow managed to stay upright and afloat.

Taut nerves frayed to breaking. Hot meals were impossible. Any sleep for those off watch was a dream; warm dry clothes, a distant memory; relief from toil was a hope drowned in the sea's onslaught. Sheer stubbornness was the only barrier against death.

SAT: 20 DEC 41

The storm abated noticeably after another midnight had passed, though waves continued to surge over *Lady Z*. Inspections were made, injuries and damage assessed, repair duties assigned. Returning to the bridge, Karney found an equally exhausted Dave Harlan at conn.

Dave scrutinized Karney. When he spoke his voice was hoarse and incongruously sympathetic. "You look like something the cat dragged in, Rork. You need some sleep. I have the conn."

Shivering in sodden clothes, bruised and battered after his own harsh sentinels, Karney eyed Dave suspiciously. Never before had he volunteered to assist in anything.

Aware of Karney's skepticism, Dave said, "I had sort of

a hot shower, ate some sort of hot grub and sort of slept a little. If you don't do the same, you'll drop in your tracks. I can take midwatch. We can argue about morning watch later."

Karney pondered his offer: a hot shower, possibly dry clothes, sleep. It sounded heavenly, though it made him wonder about his exec's fresh outlook. "This change of heart have anything to do with your run-in with that Kraut kid the other night?"

"I wouldn't go so far as to say 'change of heart', Rork," he growled. "I just realize there are bigger fish to fry out here than arguing about who runs our sardine can."

"Yeah," he agreed, trying to get the blood flowing in his numb fingers. "*Lady Z*'s pretty much a sardine compared to a Kraut shark. Not to mention this God-awful storm." Karney tugged his gloves back on. "As for morning watch, wake me by 0400, okay?"

Nodding thoughtfully, Dave said, "Can do, Skipper."

On the bridge wing, Karney repeated, "Skipper?" *Dave never calls me skipper.* He headed down the ladder, reasoning, "Maybe that scuffle rattled a few obdurate planks of pride loose. Guess having a crazy Nazi waving my own gun in my face'd broaden my horizons a bit, too."

A few steps from the foot of the ladder, Karney tugged open the door to enter the deckhouse. Grateful to be out of the wind, he dogged the watertight door behind him.

Transverse to the cutter's centerline was a passageway about midway within the cutter and atop *Lady Z*'s fuel-oil bunker, her most vulnerable spot. From where Karney stood, the grinding of the engine was painfully audible beyond the slim door, leading aft to the catwalk over the engine room. Forward and below lay the sleeping quarters: officers to starboard, enlisted men to port with separate stairs but a door to pass between spaces at the bottom.

Lost in concerns for *Zealous* and Ellie Greer, Karney took a step down the steep stairs to his quarters. He should've paid more attention to where he was. A fierce wave slammed into *Lady Z.*

One second the top stair was underfoot, the next instant Karney found himself at the bottom of the ladder, flung against the bulkhead. It wasn't an uncommon occurrence in violent storms to be tossed about, but it was usually better to have the lurches take you up rather than down the companionway.

A mutter of obscenities rolled off his tongue, starting in English, then Gaelic, Portuguese, Chinese, German and some words he had learned so long ago he didn't know what they meant anymore. His litany did nothing for the pain wracking his shoulder.

⊕

Ellie Greer was awakened from an anything-but-peaceful sleep by a garbled string of swearwords. Though not too loud, she knew the voice. A few seconds later, Karney entered the cabin. She closed her eyes, pretending to be asleep.

At the desk, she heard the lamp click on, smelled wet canvas, damp wool and leather. Ellie sneaked a peek. Karney looked awful. Even if she felt sociable, with his demeanor, silence seemed a prudent choice. She watched him from the shadows.

Like coal smudges, exhaustion ringed his deep-set eyes. His cheeks, above scruffy whiskers, looked raw. Holding his shoulder, Karney slowly rotated his arm, unintentionally groaning. He removed his life vest and hung it on the door, then took off his underway coat, dumping it on the deck. Everything he wore looked soaked.

No wonder he strung his swearwords together. Curious now, Ellie scrutinized him when she realized Karney hadn't noticed her.

He tipped his helmet into his hand and set it upside down like a turtle-shell. His soggy gloves and wool scarf were spread on the shelf above the desk. In the helmet went his Red Sox ball cap, wristwatch and the double-silver bars of his rank. Unfastening his holster, he wrapped it around his .45 and set them directly on the desk.

Propping each respective foot on the chair seat, he bent to the task of unlacing his boots. He worked them loose, kicking them off to land with a mushy thud. Karney tugged off several pairs of socks and flung them on top of his soggy boots.

Stretching from side to side, he worked kinks out of his back as he pulled off the suspenders of his rubberized bib overalls and peeled them off. Tugging a sodden sweater over his head, he unbuttoned his flannel shirt with obviously stiff fingers, dragging it from his broad shoulders. He then wrestled his turtle-neck and a t-shirt off, followed by his corduroy pants. The small heap of wet garments had grown into a mountain beyond hope of drying.

Stripped to only his wet drawers, Karney turned the chair around and sagged onto it with a heavy sigh.

Never having seen Karney with his shirt off, much less most everything else, Ellie took in his solid build. His sturdy shoulder muscles merged with his arms like thick ropes aboard a sailing ship, spliced and braided for strength. A broad back narrowed to a slender waist, hips, a tight tush and his obviously muscular legs, beneath mostly sodden, baggy long-john bottoms.

An angry scar slashed down his back. It reminded her of her brother Andrew's burns after his Spitfire crashed. But Karney's wound was far older. *A childhood injury?* Though curious, Ellie realized it did not detract from his physique in the least.

Leaning back, Karney sat still for a long while. A very long while.

Softly, Ellie said, "Irish?"

Sounding half-asleep, he gave a drowsy, "Umm?"

Her antisocial mood evaporated to sympathy. Despite her own pain, Ellie scooted back, patting the bunk. Loud enough to rouse him, she said, "Sit up here. Maybe I can rub some of the kinks out."

Ponderously heeding her suggestion, he stepped on the chair to sit on the elevated bunk. Despite the wrappings on her burned palms, Ellie used her finger tips to gently massage Karney's tense, knotted muscles, starting with his right shoulder.

He groggily whispered, "Ohhh . . . yeah . . . right there."

Kneading his back was a peculiar break from her grief over Nikki. Her memories slid back to times she had rubbed Brandt's back. This intimacy with Karney made her feel awkward, yet it also made her appreciate being more than a barnacle hitching a ride to Nova Scotia aboard *Zealous*.

Softly, she inquired, "The storm 'tis a bad one, nae?"

Clearing his throat, Karney croaked out, "Yeah, but we're through the worst of it."

Leaning around his shoulder, Ellie scrutinized Karney's exhausted face. "And where, pray tell, did your poor, wee voice go?"

Karney chuckled hoarsely. "My dear Scarlet," he said in a credible imitation of Clark Gable's Rhett Butler as he swept his arm out. With a groan, he quickly lowered it, finishing in a more subdued tone, "it has inextricably gone with the wind."

Recalling the matinee of "Gone With The Wind" she'd seen at the Ritz Cinema in Leicester Square in London's West End, Ellie shyly impersonated Scarlet to say, "Why, Rhett darlin', I do declare, you've wrenched your poor li'l ol' shoulder somethin' fierce." Gently massaging the strained muscles and, in her own voice, Ellie quietly asked, "How long has it been botherin' you?"

"Forever," Karney moaned. "Since I hurt it about tennnn minutes ago." Turning his head, he winked. "First time was actually about ten years ago. 'Nother nasty storm, completely different ship. And a lot bigger than *Lady Z*."

Curiosity aroused, Ellie asked, "What happened?"

Karney was quiet so long, she wasn't sure he'd answer. Finally, he shrugged. "I was on a Portuguese freighter, the *Danica*, during the summer of 1930. A hurricane smashed into us off Cape Hatteras. She broke up, and I pulled a buddy to safety against an outgoing wave, which was pretty stupid." Karney paused. "Not 'cause I helped Jamie; just stupid timing on my part. Seriously popped my shoulder out, tore up the ligaments, ruined my summer and doused a great pipe dream."

"What was your dream?"

"I fancied myself a major league pitcher before the *Danica* sank. No such luck after my shoulder was injured."

"Could you nae play baseball anymore?"

"Oh, I could play, just not pitch with any accuracy for the next few years. Not only that, but it totally nixed my nickname."

Kneading his muscles, Ellie asked, "And that was?"

"Strike Zone," he said, with a definite trace of pride. He shook his head. "Good thing I already had an in with the Coast Guard. Seemed the big league scouts were only hunting pitchers that season." With another shrug, he said, "So, here I am."

Karney fell silent. She'd already sensed he was a private man and wondered if this glimpse of his life was all she'd get. Though not difficult to talk to, he made it hard to get to know him. Really know him. In a more hushed tone, she repeated, "Strike Zone, huh?" and received a minimal nod.

"Now people just call me Irish." After a moment, he offered, "You really don't have to keep doing this . . ."

"If it does nae feel good, I'll stop."

"No . . . no," he groggily said. "That's not what I mean. I feel like I've died, gone to heaven and been assigned the chief masseuse for all the angels. If I got treatment like this after every gale we bucked, I'd die an absolutely happy man."

Karney's cavalier talk of death bothered Ellie. Brandt had been much the same. And he was dead. She said nothing to Karney, though the thought hovered like a wicked apparition. She continued rubbing his shoulders and neck.

He tilted his head back, probably as much from weariness as to let stiff muscles relax. Without thinking, Ellie ran her fingers through his damp hair, reveling in its thick texture, stroking his scalp. A soft, almost sensual moan rose from Karney's throat.

Trying to distract her mind from their intimacy, she asked, "How'd you ever get so bloody wet anyway?"

Karney sighed, slowly answering, "Wrong place, wrong time. Or, if you were that breaking wave, maybe right place, right time."

Her hands stopped. "You were almost washed overboard?"

"Came closer than I like, but I snagged the rail. 'Sides, I was hooked to a safety-line. So long as it holds, I'd only be bashed about till someone reeled me in like the catch of the day. Hopefully."

"What if the line did nae hold?"

Karney again glanced over his shoulder. "We wouldn't be having this conversation." Sensing her alarm, he turned partway around. "Ellie, don't go borrowing trouble. I got drenched, not drowned."

His lack of concern fueled the same annoyance that mothered her brothers and male cousins for so many years. "Aye, drenched you bloody well be. 'Twas nae very smart stayin' wet so long."

"The bridge was warm and I—"

"That's nae the point. You'll be catchin' pneumonia waitin' to change like you did. 'Twas foolish, Irish."

Turning further around, a hard edge braced his words. "I don't exactly have the luxury of taking a hot shower every time my feet get a little damp."

"A little damp?" she scoffed. "Karney Rork, you be

bloody well soaked to your drawers. You should've been down here changin' first chance you had. Nae putterin' round the ship."

"I wasn't puttering." He hopped down and faced her, a storm cloud rising in his eyes. "And who the hell designated you my mother?"

His question stung and angered her at once. Sagging against the bulkhead, Ellie glared back at him. "'Tis apparent somebody bloody well should. You do nae take very good care of yourself. You've nae slept for days, you've barely touched your food when you've eaten with me and your skin feels like a bloomin' iceberg. If you did nae want to change here, then you should've gone elsewhere."

"Look, lady," his voice rose heatedly, "*Lady Z* ain't exactly the *Queen Mary* for accommodations. Even if I could've left my post, which I couldn't, there wasn't exactly any 'elsewhere' for me to go. You're in my cabin and so're all my clothes."

Karney stood, bowing in feigned apology. "Forgive my disturbin' your beauty rest, milady," he said, mocking a pompous Brit. "In the future, I'll have the steward herald my arrival," his accent died as he finished, "before entering my own damned quarters."

In an adverse way, he reminded her of James Strafford, her former controller, whom Karney didn't even know. Ellie snapped back, "You do nae have to be so bloody sarcastic." Taking a deep breath, she tried to soften her brogue, which seemed to serve as a barometer for her temper. The change was negligible. "I didna mean to sound like your mum; 'tis you just seem to be in need of a keeper. I'm sorry."

Standing quietly, Karney lowered his head and closed his eyes. When he opened them, their hue had softened. "I'm sorry, too." A half-hearted grin teased his chapped lips. "I better not bark at you or my next back rub'll be from a hungry shark after you deep-six me."

"Dinna be startin' that again."

He pulled his kit bag from the wooden locker in the corner. "Start what?"

"Talkin' about dyin' and sharks and gettin' thrown overboard. You treat death with such wretched nonchalance."

"Nonchalance?" His voice rose again. "Death keeps pretty close tabs on us out here, lady, and as the Irish say," his brogue grew conspicuous, "May I ne'er take life too seriously or I'll not get out of it alive." A subtle Boston Yankee finished. "I'm sorry if my boorish humor offends you, but I wasn't the one who planned your wee voyage." Karney's motion emphasized his frustration as he added, "Or should this be considered a venture?" He loudly snapped his fingers. "Better yet: a misadventure."

Ellie's spine stiffened. "A venture? You be thinkin' that's what this is to me? Some kind of venture? Or misadventure or whatever?"

Stuffing clean briefs in his kit bag, he stared over at her, his eyes a turbulent sea with annoyance floating barely beneath the surface. "I'm out here 'cause it's my duty. You're here 'cause you made a damn foolish decision—"

"Foolish?" Her cheeks flushed hotly. "'Twas nae foolish at the time I made it." In a heartbeat, memories flashed in her mind of nights spent in fear of a psychotic creep, who stalked her for weeks, then would abruptly disappear. With constant emergencies arising from German bombing raids, the police offered no help. Her father doubted her story. Finally, she'd turned to James Strafford, the only one who wasn't judgmental and believed she wasn't losing her mind.

Rage at her helplessness, then and now, erupted at Karney. "Just who the bloody hell're you to be judgin' my decisions anyway?"

"Lady, I ain't judging anything," he said, his voice steely. "Cause-and-effect speaks for its own damn self on this one," he said, snatching another pair of boots from his foot locker.

Inanely, she asked, "And what're you meanin' by that?"

"For God's sake, Ellie, are you nuts? You're sitting on a U.S. Coast Guard cutter, seriously injured, with your baby girl buried at sea not more 'an four days ago."

Tears stung her eyes. She hastily wiped them away, knowing this was exactly where his words had been headed. "You do nae have to be so blunt in remindin' me my wee babe is gone."

"Well, someone sure's hell better remind you of something or you're gonna go off half-cocked on another stupid scheme. Only next time you need to be pulled outta harm's way—"

Stopping, his eyes suddenly softened with a baffled, almost timid expression. His anger sank into a sea of compassion.

"Next time . . . I might not be there to rescue you."

Ignoring his sincerity, her Scottish stubbornness rose up like her Gregor ancestors at Glenfruin near Loch Lomond. "Ye'll nae be responsible for me e'er again, Leftenant Rork. I'd rather die than be holdin' you to any such worrisome obligation."

"Swell!" Karney grabbed his robe. "Forget it! Let some other poor schmuck risk his life to save yours. Then he can worry about you!" He stormed out.

Frustrated by Karney's swift retreat, Ellie bitterly swore at the closed door. "You holier-than-thou salt. Why'd you rescue me anyway? You should've let me drown . . ." Her voice trailed off. "I should be dead with me loved ones. Why'd you have to be me bloody knight in shinin' armor anyway?" She started to sob. "Why . . .?"

Waves of remorse crashed over the bow of her crippled soul. She foundered in a sea of grief and self-pity, wishing Karney would come back, so she could pour out her sorrows, perhaps find some solace in his tender embrace, a gentle—

"No, I can't do this." She rolled away from the door

and tugged the covers up trying to ignore her emotions. *I've been here before. All me fears and grief only brought me pain and misery. I need to bury my feelings, give me heart to no one, then no one can hurt me.* Sniffling, she found the kerchief Karney had left for her earlier. "But if I believe this, why canna I stop these tears from flowin'?"

⊕

Though Karney's brief shower barely warmed his chilled body, it quite sufficiently cooled his temper. The tiff with Ellie had been fueled by a dozen problems plaguing *Lady Z. And I damn well knew it. Unfortunately, Ellie became the match to ignite my powder keg. I shouldn't've blown up at her. Ellie needs empathy—not wrath.*

Entering his cabin, Karney softly called her name, but received no response. He assumed she slept. *For the best. She needs rest more than my apologies, sincere though they are.*

Karney finished dressing, hung up his wet clothes and started to climb onto the narrow upper bunk. Hearing a stifled sob, he stepped back down. "Ellie? You okay?"

Though she didn't answer, he saw her body quiver from repressed sobs. He sat on the bunk, touching her shoulder. She shrank away. His hand hovered indecisively.

Though Ellie felt Karney's weight sag the mattress, the touch of his hand still startled her. Unintentionally, she jerked away.

"Look, Ellie . . ." he gently said, "I truly am sorry."

Hearing the tenderness in his voice, stirred something very unexpected in her. His presence began to lift her sorrow.

Karney continued, "I shouldn't be mad at you 'cause you wanna be my keeper. Lord knows I need one. And I really shouldn't've said what I did. Please forgive me?"

Flustered because Karney caught her crying and too afraid to admit how scared she felt, Ellie tersely answered,

"'Twas you who said it first, Irish . . . so, forget it."

His weight shifted, but he did not leave. The tangy scent of Old Spice enveloped her as she felt him lean closer and draw the hair back from her face, caressing her tear-damp cheek.

"It doesn't seem you've forgotten it."

Ellie gently brushed his fingers away. Unconvincingly, she said, "Please, leave me be." Part of her still wished Karney had let her drown. Another part desired his comfort, desired it desperately.

"Ellie, look at me . . . please."

Though not sure why, yielding to him scared her. During her time aboard *Lady Z*, when Karney was near, even working at his desk, his presence calmed her. He helped her rise above the storm and glimpse a ray of sun-filled hope. Listening with her heart, she heard the soulful plea of his hoarse whisper.

Pushing away her fear, she gingerly rolled over. Her heart felt as bruised as her side. Karney's eyes were the same soft gray she recalled shortly after Nikki's service. She saw he'd showered and shaved. His hair, combed and damp, looked black. Dressed in clean, dry clothes, he no longer looked so miserable.

Softly, shyly, he confessed, "Till I said what I did about your decision, I'd not seen how deeply Nikki's death upset me."

Shaking his head, his shoulders sagged. "In the past, I've saved people who later died, but never anyone like Nikki . . . so tiny in my hands . . ." He stared at his calloused palms still seeing Ellie's baby. A tear crept down his chapped cheek, his big shoulders rounded even more. "I'm sorry I blamed my failure on you."

Karney's words caught her by surprise. Having never realized the true depth of his empathy, until now, she sat up.

Placing her hand in his, she said, "Karney, Nikki's death was nae your fault. Her wee life . . . and her death . . .

were my responsibility alone." Wiping her tears away, she found it hard to talk. Taking a ragged breath, she added, "Mine, from the moment I decided to return to Canada in the midst of this bloody war. And, with all things considered, 'twas a foolish decision."

Her tears began anew. She could not stop them.

Against a warning bell, as loud as any Klaxon, going off in his head, Karney pulled her into his arms. Her trembling body felt fragile within his embrace. "Shhh," he cooed, "it'll be all right. God's watching over you, but His healing takes time."

Karney dug out another clean, dry handkerchief from his back pocket. "Everything is happening too quickly for your emotions to catch up. Heaven sakes, Ellie, you just lost Nikki. And the lingering effects of morphine aren't helping any either. Time is what you need to regain your strength and get your life back on course."

"But, Irish . . . I've always been so . . . so strong and now . . ." Her voice trailed away as her thoughts stumbled into the same quagmire of pain into which she'd fallen after her father had told her Brandt and Anna were dead.

"Ellie, you've been through hell these last few days."

The warmth of his voice brought Ellie back to the here and now, the strength of his arms helped sustain her.

"For now," he urged, "let me be strong for you. Okay?"

He received his answer when she wrapped her arms around his waist, her head nodding silent consent. Closing his eyes, Karney rested his cheek on her amber curls. Holding her like this felt completely natural. Gradually, Ellie's tears subsided.

Stroking her hair, Karney soothingly said, "Gram Reddy used to tell me tears were heart-rain washing away your sorrow. When you cry, tears cleanse your soul and refresh your spirit."

Trying to lighten their mood a little, he added, "'Less of course you're up at the North Pole, then tears just kinda freeze on your face."

Ellie glanced up at him, her emerald eyes holding a hint of sparkle. A smile teased her lips. It was a hopeful sign. Yet her gaze remained pensive as she pulled back slightly.

"Have you really been there or are you teasin'?"

"Some of both. We were close, but we didn't quite make the actual North Pole. A severe blizzard turned us back. But I spent my eighteenth birthday north of Ellesmere Island. Started late my first year at the Coast Guard Academy but, believe me, it was worth all the razzing and work they dumped on me."

"You've led an adventuresome life for one so young. Nae enough time to be a lad. What else brought you to here and now?"

Not feeling young in the least, an edge honed his words, "I was born in Ireland, twenty-seven odd years ago. Lost my folks and older brother in a shipwreck when I was seven. Spent most of every summer in Ireland with family till I turned fifteen. Then, with a lie and my guardian's sanction, I joined the Merchant Marine. I was a fairly normal kid in high school, except for going to sea each summer. Originally, like I said earlier, being a Coast Guard officer wasn't my first ambition. But it's my life and I don't regret any of it," he finished with a definite note of defiance.

Sitting back, her eyes searched his face. "I did nae mean to suggest anythin' about your youth, Irish. 'Tis you remind me of Mac. When his older brother was killed in the Great War, Mac enlisted at fourteen, intent on revenge. Me Uncle Richard was furious. Even Mac gettin' decorated and receivin' a commission did nae ease the friction between 'em. Mac 'twas nae a lad for long either."

Before she looked down, Karney caught the sadness creeping back in to her expression again.

She said, "None of us are strangers to death, are we?"

Their conversation had again turned. *Lord sakes,* Karney thought, *talking to this lady is like anticipating the*

*waves when trying to land a dinghy. If you don't act quick
enough, you can flip.*

"No, we're not," he said sadly, thinking of his loved
ones who'd died: *Ma, Da, Jeremy, Julianna, Jen-Mai.* Not
wanting to reveal his own sorrow, he briskly said, "There
was something else Gram Reddy said." His brogue again
lilted: "Whenever sorrow starts ta get ye down, ye only
need but wait three days."

"What difference can three days be makin'?"

"Three days represents the time between when Jesus
of Nazareth was crucified and Christ arose from the tomb.
In three days the world went from being pretty bleak to one
filled with a hope never known before." After a moment,
Karney timidly added, "The hope of Christ is why I know
Nikki's with God right now, and I'm sure she doesn't want
her mum staying sad."

The emerald of Ellie's eyes became translucent
wellsprings of tears. Her bottom lip quivered. Karney again
wrapped his arms around her, whispering, "It's all right,
Ellie, just let your heart-rain wash away the sorrow."

Though Karney's hug was very reassuring, Ellie barely
knew the man. *How can the closeness of a virtual stranger
be so comforting?* More tears escaped.

Ellie felt Karney's sea-roughened hand touch her
cheek, catching a tear before it fell. Sliding his finger under
her chin, he raised her head, compelling her to look into
his eyes. In the span of a heartbeat, she thought he might
kiss her.

Abruptly, fearing their intimacy, Karney let his hand
drop away. He glanced at the clock. "We'd better . . . ah, get
to sleep. Are you all right?"

Nodding meekly, Ellie considered his almost-kiss and
how he now seemed so unsure. *Does Karney regret nae
kissin' me? Or fear the consequences if he had?*

His hug barely tightened, then he held the covers up,
allowing her to slide beneath them more easily. Tucking
her in, Karney gazed down. "Night, Ellie, sleep tight."

Baffled by her raw emotions, she whispered, "And to you, Irish."

Karney turned off the lamp and vaulted into the upper bunk with practiced ease. Laying still, no tossing or turning, not even snoring, Karney seemed to fall into a deep sleep in mere seconds. On the contrary, Ellie could not still her mind.

Unable to get settled, she rehashed past relationships, wonderful or disastrous, in an effort to find which way to go, one thing scared her: *For no longer than I've known Irish, he has hold of me heart. His compassion has already bridged painful rifts in me life.*

But a dark awareness coalesced her random fears: *Ever since me Mum's suicide, I seem to be the common denominator in deaths of people I loved, no matter how they died. Did I bring them to that end? What if I get involved with Irish and he dies? Will he be another link in this chain of guilt I drag through life?*

Oh, Lord, 'tis probably foolish, but I can nae be responsible for anyone else dyin' 'cause I care for them.

Hearing Karney's deep, peaceful breathing, she again found solace in his nearness. Shadowy fears released their grip. With a prayer for guidance, Ellie drifted off to sleep.

CHAPTER SEVEN

Karney heard Ellie's painful whimper. Turning on his reading lamp, he slid to the floor. Touching her cheek, he felt warmth, but she didn't feel feverish.

Ellie grasped his hand, softly asking, "Brandt, *wo ist* Anna?"

His mind translated from the German: Brandt, where is Anna? Confused to hear her speak the enemy's language, Karney was not sure if he should wake her. The voice tube whistled negating a decision. He checked the time—0347. "Rork, here."

Dave Harlan's voice traveled wearily down the tube, "Rork, it's your morning wake-up call. All's quiet up here."

Distracted by Ellie's renewed murmurs, Karney said, "I need to speak with Mrs. Greer. Be there by four."

Turning back to Ellie, Karney stroked her face as she struggled through her nightmare. As he had before, he gently lifted her into his arms. Speaking in the soothing tongue of his native Gaelic, he felt tension ease from her body. He held her long after she had moved out of the dream. Though Ellie rested calmly again, his thoughts were in a turmoil. *Her husband must've been Brandt, but is Anna another daughter she lost? Why did she speak in*

German? Am I dealing with another Nazi spy? No, Georg gave no indication Ellie was a spy. But then, why would he? Are they both Nazis, working separately with no knowledge of the other? Dear Lord, I hope not.

The mystique of Ellie MacCalister Greer deepened. With reluctance, Karney laid her back down, snugging the blankets around her. He stood, watching her. It was hard to leave, even pale and bruised, she enchanted him.

Sensing more to this woman than mere beauty, Karney prayed Ellie wasn't a Nazi. *Mother of Christ, please not that. I like her too much.*

When they'd talked, Karney glimpsed her quick wit and a nimble sense of humor. *And, by God, this woman has backbone.* Yet he could also see her lighthearted side was repressed by mourning and physical pain. Though little had been said about *Bonnie*'s torpedoing, when the subject of Nazism came up, her eyes became like the cold jade of a sharply cut Himalayan stone. Loathing for Hitler was all Karney perceived.

Either Ellie's a superb German spy or she's not one. My vote's for not. I think her hatred of Nazis is no different than my hate of the Japs for what they did to Jen-Mai.

He mentally weighted his thoughts and impressions with a chain and let them sink into his subconscious. They were marked so he could dive for them later if need be.

Ellie's depth, however, was an uncharted sea he ardently hoped to explore. Not sure what drew him to her, Karney just knew he wanted to know Ellie MacCalister Greer on a much more personal level. *Is this my prophetic Irish soul speaking? Or my sister-guardian angel giving me a shove?* Karney again sighed. Duty had to come first.

⊕

Ellie woke up, sensing Karney at his desk. Peering over the bunk edge, she saw he wrote in a journal. With his lips pursed to whistle, only silent puffs came out. Whenever he paused in thought, so too, did the soundless whistling. He would rub his jaw, furrow his brow, then resume writing along with the muted whistling.

Is he always so deliberate? No, just passionate about his work, like Mac. And, remembering how Mac disliked interruptions, she said nothing. Yet she wanted to talk to someone and Karney was here.

Rising up on her elbow, she softly said, "Irish?"

"Yeah," he replied, glancing at her, "Whacha need, angel?"

She felt suddenly shy, wondering what possessed him to call her angel. It was a sweet endearment and crumbled her loneliness like a wave washing footprints off a beach. She'd never thought of herself as much of an angel. Noncommittally, she asked, "What are you whistlin'."

His face went blank. "The tune you mean? Ah, oh, *"Moonlight Serenade."* Couldn't remember I do it so habitually."

"Glenn Miller's songs're bonnie. Do you like his band?"

"Yeah, he has a great sound. Caught his band live a couple times in Boston. You like him, too?"

"Aye, but 'twas nae always easy to hear him in England. His records were hard to obtain, so we danced to copy-cat bands."

His face lit up. "You like to dance?"

"Love to, though I do nae feel much like it now."

His grin broadened. "Think maybe you'd feel like kickin' up your heels for some dancing by New Year's eve?"

Karney looked chagrinned with the leap of his presumption. Not retracting the question, he simply amended it. "I mean, if you don't mind a date? I don't wanna rush you so soon after losing your husband and . . . with everything that's happened."

His clarification stymied Ellie until she recalled: *I never told Karney the truth.*

Looking at her with a sense of dread, he decided to give her a way out. Karney returned to his journal.

"D'you have much more to write?" she asked.

Rather than answer, he shook his head, wrote one more line, signed the page, then turned to face her, a crooked grin on his face. "Finished. Now what can I do for you, sweet lady?"

She watched his eyes. "I need . . . to make a confession."

Grinning self-consciously, he said, "Look, Ellie, I may've started out Irish-Catholic, but I'm definitely not a priest."

"'Tis easy to see that, Irish." A blush crept into her cheeks as she fussed with her covers. "I just want you to know somethin' . . . somethin' I did nae tell you . . . when you rescued me. Or since."

Leaning closer, elbows on his knees, he was tempted to make a wisecrack, but she looked so serious, he thought better of it. "So what could you possibly confess to a lowly Coastie?" Scared, he decided, fit her expression better.

As if afraid she'd lose her nerve, Ellie didn't meet his gaze as she said, "When I told you my husband died, I . . ." Having his full attention made her uneasy. She finally said, "I did nae tell you Brandt, my husband, was killed in May 1940." She fussed with the gauze on her hand. "You see, Nikki's father was a British officer. And even though I knew he was married, I sought his help and things . . ." Ellie hesitated, not quite sure how things really had happened, so finally just declared, "Nikki was illegitimate."

Though neither sure what she expected of him nor why she had not mentioned Anna, presumably her daughter by Brandt, this glimpse of Ellie's past further melted Karney's heart. He asked, "And you figured since you were an unwed mother, I'd keel haul you or set you adrift or some equally nasty thing?"

Flustered, she said, "Nae, I'd just rather you nae be thinkin' ill of me or me Nikki. Regardless of all else, I loved her with me whole heart." Tears glistened. "She was still me wee babe."

Taking her hand, Karney said, "Ellie, God creates pint-sized miracles called kids, so we see love in a whole new light. I'm not gonna throw stones 'cause you got mixed up with some married guy and got pregnant. It happens. In war, doubly so. Truth is, I've an adorable seven-year-old niece 'cause my little sister got in a similar bind in high school. And Maurie didn't even have the war for an excuse."

A brief smile touched Karney's lips, then disappeared the moment a disconcerting thought entered his mind. Though he wavered, Karney felt compelled to ask, "You still love Nikki's father?"

The question clearly caught Ellie by surprise. Her gaze darted around the small cabin. Apparently unsure how to answer, she looked anywhere but at Karney.

Feeling bizarrely threatened by some guy from Ellie's past, Karney waited with impatience. *She might not've been a good judge of this guy's moral fiber, but she knew him well enough to get knocked up. She must still have feelings for him.* Her reluctance to answer proved unsettling. His spirits did a nose dive. *Irish, when're you gonna learn not to ask such damned fool questions?*

Veering from the confusion his query caused, Ellie countered, "Does my past shock you, Irish? Does keel haulin' me suddenly seem like just punishment?"

Dismayed, Karney said, "I wasn't thinking that at all."

"Why d'ya seem to be upset?" She flipped his question over. "What're you thinkin'?"

His mood went from defense to distress to resolve before he finally said, "Okay, I wondered how you could still love a guy after he two-timed his wife and apparently stole your self-respect?"

The table flipped. Her rage flared, but she forced herself to stay calm as her mind weighed: *Though I donna love James now, never really did, he did save me life. And*

I'm indebted 'cause he cared when everyone else thought I ran from ghosts and shadows.

Ellie steadied herself, knowing that wasn't what Karney wanted to hear and said, "I never said I loved him."

Karney pointed out, "Nor did you say you didn't love him." Not wanting to start a new argument, Karney stood, shoving his chair in. "I have afternoon watch. JJ, our cook, will bring you lunch. Try to get some rest." Turning, Karney left the cabin.

Ellie stared at the door. Though she never answered Karney directly, she didn't understand his bitterness. *Is he jealous? Beguiled? Did Irish fall under that spell Mac insists I cast on the opposite sex? I never plan it, it just happens.*

"Aye, it happens," she whispered to herself. "Like meetin' out here in the midst of the North Atlantic, in this bloody war without any bloody common sense to nae fall for each—" A soft knock sounded at the door. She cleared her throat. "Come in."

The door opened. A covered tray appeared first, then a man, black as licorice and just as slim, entered. "Miss Ellie, I'm JJ, *Lady Z's* cook. Skipper thought you'd be ready for lunch about now."

"JJ, please, come in. I guess I am a wee bit hungry."

"That's good," JJ said, setting the tray down. "With that gale we were buckin', it's been hard to fix anything hot for anybody. Things are starting to settle back to normal, though. Thank heavens."

JJ removed the tray cover. The hearty aroma of potato soup drew her senses to the tray, which also included Saltines, Jell-O and hot tea.

"These are a few goodies I've kept stashed for special occasions," JJ said with a warm smile, his white teeth stark against his skin. "Like having a lady on board."

Ellie grinned. "You must've read my mind, JJ. Your potato soup smells divine. Just what my stomach needs about now."

"Well, Miss Ellie, I know when I'm feeling punk, only thing perks me up is hot soup, Jell-O and tea. Now you take your time eating, ma'am, I'll pick this up later."

"Might you be able to stay a while, JJ?" she asked.

Pulling out the chair vacated by Karney, JJ again grinned. "Don't mind if I do. Vinny's got KP duty, so I'm off the hook, for now anyway."

While she nibbled crackers, sipped the delicious soup and tea, then slurped the cherry-flavored Jell-O, they chatted about many subjects. She found JJ widely read and a fascinating gentleman. More scholar than cook, he thought the world of Karney. And, like Miguel Tapia, JJ had transferred from Caribbean warmth to stormy North Atlantic seas and the Greenland Patrol when Irish was promoted to executive officer aboard *Zealous.*

"Why are you so devoted to Irish?" she asked.

Flashing a broad smile, sarsaparilla eyes danced and crow's feet crinkled when he answered, "Ma'am, that's easy. Irish never asks a man to do anything he hasn't done or wouldn't do himself. He's always been one squared away fella. He's honest, gentlemanly and absolutely colorblind."

She frowned. "What's his eyesight got to do with loyalty?"

"Not that kinda colorblind, ma'am. The kind that doesn't care if my skin's black or Chief Tap's half-Mex or Mr. Harlan's Jewish, though he seldom wants to claim it." Then JJ chuckled. "Skipper never even fusses if young Hack's seasick-green half the time."

JJ stood up. "I enjoyed our visit, ma'am, but I need to get some sleep, maybe dream up something better than peanut-butter-dumpling stew for supper." Taking her tray, he added, "I'll talk with you again when I can. Afternoon, ma'am."

Leaning back, Ellie glanced at the books on the makeshift bookrack, while she considered JJ's words. Her mind began to weave a tapestry of Karney's life. JJ added many colorful strands. Though not yet large, she saw its intricacies, rich texture and complex patterns quite clearly. Tugging C.S. Forester's book from the shelf, she tried to read.

Her mind wandered in weary frustration, so she closed her eyes.

A knock woke her from a nap to find Tap with her supper. After an exchange of pleasantries as she ate, Ellie said, "JJ told me you and Irish are good buddies. 'Tis that nae odd for a non-com and an officer? What brought you two together?"

Tap smiled. "Guitar music, baseball and kids for starters."

"Similar interests, aye, but what keeps you friends?"

"Adversity. We weathered some tough times together when we were stationed in Puerto Rico." Tap paused, then slowly went on, "We were there for each other when things in our lives went south."

Ellie had the impression Tap was leaving a lot out, but respecting their privacy, she didn't press the issue.

Tap went on thoughtfully, "Mutual respect binds us as well. Our age, size and rank don't match, but, in other ways, we mesh like cogs of a well-oiled machine. And these days, unfortunately, it happens to be a war machine."

Chuckling, he added, "When we sing at the orphanage, Sister Margarita introduces us as 'The Coast Guard's Mutt and Jeff.'"

Uncertainly, she asked, "*Mutt and Jeff?*"

"Comic strip characters. Mutt's a tall, chronic gambler, horse racing originally, then just get-rich-quick schemes. He's sort of a dimwit. Jeff's a shrimp-sized, lunatic with a bushy mustache and muttonchops. I'm not exactly a shrimp nor a nut-case and I lack the muttons but I do have a mustache. And although Irish plays a mean hand of poker and can pick a winner at the racetrack, he's not chronic about it and he certainly isn't a dimwit." Tap ginned. "We're just opposites and buddies."

Wait," Ellie said, her gaze faraway. "That was the

musical comedy on Broadway me Mum took me to when I was seven or eight. It was a grand trip and where me love of acting began. I remember some good songs came from the show. I just didn't realize it was a comic strip as well. I guess '*Mutt and Jeff*' was more an American thing."

"Yeah, probably is," he said. "Funny that I forgot about that. It was back before the last war. I think one of my favorite songs to come out of it was '*Let Me Call You Sweetheart*'." Tap smiled with a fond memory.

Still curious about their friendship and history, Ellie asked, "What orphanage?"

"Karney's been helping at St. Aidan's for ages. The orphanage was his home before Captain Bryannt became his guardian. Irish got me and Lacy involved, now about half of *Lady Z*'s crew help out in one way or another. All the kids need love, and Irish has plenty to give."

"So," Ellie casually asked, "Karney's nae married? I'd be thinkin' with his hunk-of-heartbreak good looks, he'd have a bevy of sweethearts pinin' after him in every port."

A look of uncertainty crossed Tap's face. "Oh, I imagine there's a bevy, but they only dream of being his girl." He shook his head. "Irish never gives his heart easily, but when he does fall in love again, only one woman will own it."

Ellie did not miss Tap's "again" and mused: *So, Irish has at least been in love at some point before. His devotion in romance seems much like Brandt's had been.*

"Karney's heart is something my Lacy will never fathom." Tap chuckled. "She only sees Irish as a handsome, chivalrous and extremely eligible gentleman. She forever plays match-maker. I tell her to let Irish handle his own affairs, to which Lacy inevitably replies," His voice rose higher with a decidedly Mexican lilt in imitation of his wife's words, "'Amor conseests of more dan a night on de town danzing wit chor leettle seester Rosa and her friends'."

Laughing with Tap, Ellie wondered: *Why's he confidin'*

so much about Irish to me. Might he be doin' a bit of his own match-makin'?

"I love Lacy to pieces," Tap declared, "but there are times I swear she'll drive me nuts and I will end up as nuts as Jeff." Tap glanced at the wall clock and stood. "Miss Ellie, I need to get topside."

"Thank you for spending time with me, Tap. 'Tis easy to see why Irish likes you. He's lucky to have you for a friend."

Rather embarrassed by her praise, Tap said, "No, ma'am, I'm the one blessed by Karn's friendship. Try to rest." With that, he left.

More interesting designs and pleasant hues were woven into Karney's tapestry. Even Jess Taylor, *Lady Z*'s corpsman, who came in to change her bandages, added a few colorful strands.

Jess explained, "Skipper sponsored me for enrollment at Boston University Medical School. Sad to say, war forced the Puzzle Palace, what we call Coast Guard HQ, to cancel time needed for the program, but," Jess grinned, "Skipper pushed through my transfer to the Naval Hospital which'll let me work with doctors and take some of the classes I need. He's a swell guy." Suddenly flustered, Jess tied off the bandage protecting her palm, then hastily packed his kit. "I hafta check on the other wounded, ma'am, but I'll be back tomorrow. Evenin', Mrs. Greer."

'Tis nae a wonder his men like and respect him so much. Can I do anythin' less?

She opened C.C Forester's *Beat to Quarters* but soon grew fidgety. It was late, but Ellie wanted to be up and about, not laying around like some pampered bonbon-stuffing prima donna. "Surely I've slept bloody long enough to shame even old Rip Van Winkle." Recalling Washington Irving's tale, she wistfully added, "Though it would be nice to sleep through this bloody war."

Scooting off the wood-trimmed bunk, she held onto the desk, gingerly lowered her feet to the deck and stood.

Her head didn't whirl in dizziness. Ellie took five short steps to the door and back. By lap seven, however, fatigue claimed her. She paused against the wooden locker.

Barging in the door, Karney nearly toppled her over. Angrily, he demanded as he caught her arm, "What're you doing?"

Grasping the locker with her free hand, Ellie glared at him. "I was tryin' to walk till you scared me half to death." Pulling away from him, Ellie tottered toward the bunk. Before she made it, her knees gave out. Karney caught her.

He lifted her on to the high bunk. Surprised, Ellie met his intense icy-blue glare as he barked, "Look, Miss Go-get-'em, just because you're wearing my gym stuff doesn't mean you need to run laps or do push-ups. You need rest."

"I was, but I got bored, so I walked back and forth a few times. 'Twas you, after all, who started this."

"Me? I never told you to get up, much less—"

"Nae, but you gave me Horatio Hornblower to read with all his constitutionals. I grew restless. You and Tap practically carry me up to the head. And that 'tis nae what I call walkin'."

Karney's glare settled to guarded understanding. "Please, don't push yourself till a real doc can check you over, Ellie." In a pirate's brogue, he said, "So me eager hearty, thar'll be no more sail riggin' nor deck swabbin' till land's ho."

Grinning, she gave a British sailor's knuckle salute. She realized, though, Karney was already lost to another concern, his eyes distant.

He tipped off his helmet, clanking it on the desktop, where it spun. Throwing his scarf and gloves in, he shrugged out of his underway coat, jamming it in the locker, then slammed the door on it. Briefly removing his ball cap, he ruffled his hair before settling it back on. Karney removed his gun belt and rolled it around his Colt and ammo pouch, setting them on the shelf above the desk. Every motion seemed abrupt, even angry.

She felt like the catalyst. "Are you mad at me, Irish?"

When his gaze shot to her, it was as if her voice startled him. "I'm sorry, what'd you say?"

"I asked if you're mad at me."

His eyes answered before a grin eased his tension. "I'm not mad, at least not at you. Exasperation's a better word. But then I figure with you it's a perpetual state," his grin broadened. "Sorta like a bee's constant buzz in a garden. Getting stung's a hazard you accept in order to enjoy the beauty of the rose."

The twinkle in his eyes was beguiling. Shyly, Ellie returned a smile. "Will you play your guitar for me?"

Pondering his options, he countered, "If I do will you believe I'm not mad?" His eyebrow raised. "Better yet, will it help you sleep?"

"Maybe," she teased "if you sing me sweet songs, maybe some Christmas carols, so me dreams will be sugary, instead of—" Ellie fell silent as a vague memory of Irish holding her in the throes of morphine-twilight nightmares entered her mind.

Perceiving her thoughts, Karney grinned and accused, "Geez lady, you drive a hard bargain." She smiled hesitantly. "Then again . . . I think music's what I may need as well." He retrieved his guitar.

Sitting, Karney pushed his ball cap back on his head and tilted his chair onto two legs. He propped his boots on the tiny desk, seemingly oblivious to *Lady Z*'s roll, and began to tune the strings of a well-used, though obviously loved guitar.

Soon, his graceful fingers danced across the frets as fluid notes poured forth. The melodies floated down as softly as snow falling on poinsettias. Watching his face, Ellie felt the serenity of each song. It was magical. Whatever doubts came in the cabin with him, soon drifted away on unseen musical notes. The only reality for Karney was his guitar and the music he created.

Drawn into another world by his velvet voice and the

guitar's rich tones, her eyes closed. Beloved Christmas carols filled her heart with peace. It was a gentle tranquility far removed from the demanding horrors of war.

As she relaxed, it only seemed natural when Karney sang *"Silent Night"* in German, it was, after all, written in Austria more than a hundred years earlier. Drifting toward sleep, Ellie could not help but think, *I shouldna enjoy this man's company so much nor the sound of his deep voice like I do. It creates a conflict. Or am I the cause of it?*

SUN: 21 DEC 41

By morning, Ellie felt rested and stronger. She was sitting on the edge of the bunk, feet dangling, when Karney entered.

Meeting her gaze, his eyes sparkled as he teased, "Ready for your mornin' constitutional with Cap'n Hornblower, matey?"

"Nae. The captain'll be walkin' alone. I want a bath, though Tap said you've only saltwater showers, so that'll hafta do."

Emphatically shaking his head, Karney said, "Un-uh, no, absolutely not in the cards. You're still weak and—"

"I feel much better. I want to bathe and wash my hair—"

"Ellie, I don't think—"

"Oh, Irish, for heaven's sake, do nae be so silly. 'Tis nae the ruddy English Channel I wish to be swimmin'."

Though Karney considered numerous arguments, he also knew she'd shoot them all down. "Okay, but you gotta keep it short?"

She raised her hand. "I swear, since hot-water's limited."

"I see Tap's informed you of our shortcomings."

"Aye, but *my* biggest shortcomin' is clean clothes."

He loaned her his robe—soft with patched elbows—a towel, saltwater soap and a brush. He started to open a drawer beneath the bunk, then snapped his fingers and turned to the locker. "These'll be better than a sweatshirt and pants."

Pulling a package from the shelf, he shook out a new pair of light-blue, flannel pajamas with dark-blue piping.

"What'll you be sleepin' in if I take these?"

He flashed a crooked grin. "I don't wear PJs."

"Then why do you buy them?"

"I don't. Maurie does." He glanced at the wall calendar of two scantily-clad female elves wrapping a big box with red-foil paper. "And since Christmas is Thursday I'm due for a new pair." Seeing Ellie's expression, he shrugged. "It's easier to accept my sister's gifts than argue. Inevitably," he gave the PJs to her, "someone needs 'em."

"Will your sister nae be offended?"

"Even if I told her, she'd still buy me more."

"Does she nae listen to you?"

With a mischievous glint, Karney said, "About as well as you do. Though she's hardheaded Irish, not Scottish."

Feigning anger, Ellie remarked, "'Tis more like decisive. And I daresay I think I like her already. If e'er we meet, perhaps we can compare notes. On you."

"Good Lord, that's scary," he groaned, opening the door.

Still within the wheelhouse, Karney escorted her up to the officer's head. Tiring before they got to the top stair, Ellie said nothing for fear Karney would nix the whole deal. And she wanted a shower.

"I'll be right out here if you run out of steam. And, sweet lady, I don't mean hot water."

From his expression, it was clear Karney had little faith in this undertaking. She refused to consider he might be right. Closing the door behind her, Ellie teased, "Look who's borrowin' trouble now."

Though she tried to hurry, her muscles slogged in molasses, which grew thicker with each passing minute. As Ellie rinsed her hair, her vision shrank, the cubicle walls wavered. Acute pains shot through her abdomen. Turning off the water, she battled severe wooziness. Afraid she might pass out, she sat on the cold floor. By the time her dizziness subsided, she was chilled. Standing up, blackness swept over her.

"Irish . . ."

Uncertain she spoke aloud, she soon felt Karney's arms lift her.

Wrapping his robe and the towel around her, he carried her down to his cabin. Angry for giving in to her request, he grumbled the whole way. "Why am I always such a pushover when it comes to beautiful dames? I knew I shouldn't've let you do this. I knew it would only lead to trouble."

Pulling up the covers, he tugged the wet robe and towel off her naked body in a vain attempt to be discreet and get her into the PJs. It wasn't easy. Toweling her hair till it was no longer sopping, Karney couldn't help but feel guilty. Anxious, he sat on the edge of the bunk.

When finally her eyes fluttered open, Ellie glanced away as if embarrassed. Not wanting to pass judgment, Karney was nonetheless worried. "You okay, angel?"

Guardedly, she looked at him and said, "I must've gotten a wee bit light-headed."

His eyes popped open in shock. "You call passing out light-headed?" He couldn't keep the cynicism from his voice. "I guess that must make pneumonia the sniffles." When he realized how harsh he sounded, he forced himself to calm down. "What's wrong?"

Sensing her aversion to answer him or meet his gaze, Karney persisted, "What else is wrong, Ellie?"

She barely eked out, "I've very bad cramps again."

Pushing back a strand of damp hair from her forehead, he saw the fear on her face. She rolled over and curled up into a ball. With her legs tightly drawn up, she reminded him of a frightened little girl.

"We're still quite a ways out from Newfoundland," he

spoke gently but added more firmly, "I don't want you even sitting up till we moor at Argentia." He broke a morphine ampoule, carefully drawing the dose into the hypodermic needle. "I'll start you back on morphine. I'd rather you sleep till I get you to the Naval hospital there and a real doctor can check you over."

Ellie frowned like a petulant child not wanting to take her medicine. "But, Irish—"

"No buts," Karney said with finality. "You're in pain and you need this. So tug your britches down and take your medicine, young lady. No pun intended."

Pushing her PJs down to expose her buttocks, she registered what he meant by 'no pun intended'. It almost made her smile.

When done, he gently pulled them back up and tucked her in.

As the dose of morphine took hold, Karney quietly said, "Ellie, I'm so sorry this has happened. I don't know what I did wrong, but I know they'll take good care of you at the hospital—"

"Irish, 'tis nae your—"

"Shhh," he whispered, tenderly pressing his fingers against her lips. "Close your eyes. Argue later." Tenderly, he stroked her cheek. "Sleep now, *meu anjo*."

Her eyes closed before he finished speaking. Caressing her cheek, her skin felt silken beneath his sea-roughened hands and much too warm with fever. Suddenly acknowledging the intimacy of his gesture, he jerked his hand away, bewildered by the power of his emotions.

He slumped in his chair, wondering, almost painfully: *When did concern for a survivor turn into love for this winsome lady? War's no time to be falling in love. Didn't the Nips already prove that to me when they killed Jen-Mai? Haven't I already experienced enough heartache to last the duration?*

"Aye," he agree with himself, leaning back to stare at the overhead, "but you know what they say, laddie?"

Karney answered in his beloved tongue, "*Giorraíonn beirt bóthar*—two shorten the road." His gaze focused on Ellie.

Sighing, Karney knew his fight had already been lost. "War or not, what does duty to God, country and the Coast Guard matter when Ellie MacCalister Greer has, without a doubt, stolen my lonely heart?"

CHAPTER EIGHT

U.S. NAVAL HOSPITAL
ARGENTIA, NEWFOUNDLAND
COMMISSION GOVERNMENT
OF GREAT BRITAIN
MON: 22 DEC 41

Karney jumped from the back of the ambulance as it came to a stop. Before he could help the driver lift Ellie's stretcher out, a pair of husky orderlies came up on either side of him.

"We'll get her, sir. You'll need to take the reports in."

Entering the recently completed hospital, he stepped to the side of the double-swinging doors as they carried Ellie into the facility. Trying to collect his wits, Karney muttered, "I damn well never shoulda let her take that shower. She was doing okay till then." He slowly shook his head.

Before *Lady Z* reached Argentia, his composure was shredded by guilt. His men had to field his line-drive temper. Tap pinch-hit to ease tension, but his reassurances fell on deaf ears. *Of course Tap can say she'll be fine, he isn't falling in love with her.* That notion again exploded in his mind. *I hardly know her. How can—*

"Irish," a voice intruded into his thoughts, "you okay?"

Turning, he found Lieutenant Mary Paulson, senior nurse and a good friend of Gunnar Bryannt, *Lady Z*'s skipper. Despite her petite size, she stared up at him with impatient obsidian eyes, waiting for an answer. Her eyes matched her stony approach to life.

"Are you admitting yourself?"

"No, ah . . ." Karney pointed down the empty passage, "I came in with . . ." He halted: fatigue and anxiety kept his mind from connecting with his tongue. "Dammit. Here." He shoved the medical clipboard, with Ellie's report on top, at Mary.

Taking it, she read the concise notes in his distinct penmanship. "No wonder you look shell-shocked." Her eyes narrowed reading a note on the chart. "Wait here."

Mary left him standing for several long minutes before hurriedly returning. "Irish, what's your blood type?"

Woodenly, he answered, "Oh-negative."

"You're a universal donor. C'mon." Dragging him down the hall, she said, "Get your gear off, Lieutenant. That gal needs blood. We're out of her type right now."

Dazed, Karney handed Mary his helmet and unbundled himself. He knew his blood was valuable, he could donate to any blood type, often had. But this was more personal. This time Ellie needed it, not an unknown somebody he had never met.

Mary opened a door. Stepping into an area screened off from a large room, Karney dumped his gear on a chair. Glancing up, he stopped cold. Ellie lay on a gurney, her arm immersed in a tub of presumably hot water—a trick used to distend the vein prior to a transfusion. But her skin was as blanched as the bedding beneath her. *Was she this pale aboard Zealous? Why didn't I notice? Do the overhead lights in here give her that deathly pallor?*

"Betti, this is Lieutenant Rork, our blessed oh-negative." Mary patted the empty gurney. "Lay down, Irish," Mary ordered.

Doing so, he rolled up his sleeve. "How bad is Ellie?"

"Bad enough," Mary confirmed, not looking at him. "Betti, he's all yours. Holler if you need me."

As the door shut behind her, the plump Navy nurse told Karney, "Lieutenant, just relax. I'll be ready in a sec."

Focused on Ellie, Karney paid no attention until Betti stuck a needle, attached to a small rubber hose, into his arm, then taped it down. His blood was slowly drawn into a glass flask that Karney estimated would hold about a liter of liquid.

"Gently pump your hand, like your heart beating." Karney did as told and noticed the blood flowed more steadily. "Good. That's doing the trick. We'll have enough for your lady friend pretty quick."

Betti regularly picked up the flask and swirled the contents around.

"What're you mixing it with?" he asked, observing the flask into which his dark lifeblood flowed.

"Sodium citrate. It's an anticoagulant. Your lady friend will get the blood fairly quickly, but it's a good precaution. It's rather an antiquated means of doing transfusions, but in a pinch, it's worked well since the First World War. I learned this in the Spanish Civil War in '36. What a mess that was," she said with a sigh and fell silent.

Karney said nothing more either.

After a short while, Betti clamped off the tube from Karney's arm and carefully set the flask aside. She returned to his arm, pulled out the needle, placed a gauze pad on it and instructed, "Keep pressure on that for the next few minutes."

Working quietly and efficiently, Betti reversed the process with the addition of a bulbous affair she'd attached to a side tube he'd not noticed before. He realized this filled the role of his pumping hand to get the blood from the flask into Ellie.

As the glass flask gradually emptied, Karney swore Ellie's color improved, though it was most likely his desire to help heal her.

Periodically, Betti clamped the line into the needle in Ellie's arm and checked her progress. Before he had a chance to ask her anything more, Mary showed up.

"Let's get your batteries recharged, Lieutenant," the older nurse curtly said, then started dragging him out the door.

"Whoa, I wanna stay with Ellie, make sure she's okay."

Mary's eyes glittered with finality. "You can't stay."

Far more understanding, Betti smiled at him. "Don't worry, Lieutenant, I'll take good care of her. It just takes longer putting it in than getting it out. She'll be fine, but you do need to go with Mary and get your batteries charged."

Feeling lost by this dismissal, Karney buttoned his sleeve and mumbled, "Thank you, Betti," as he grabbed his gear and rushed after Mary, already halfway down the hall.

Mary held open the door to the staff lounge, still to be finished, giving Karney no choice but to enter. A hot potbelly stove heated the room to the likely temperatures of the South Seas travel posters pinned to naked plywood. Two painted walls, in tropical colors as well, battled to cheer the raw décor. A threadbare sofa, three folding chairs and a card table, relocated from a previous home, were the sole occupants. Other signs of life did exist: a dented coffee urn, mugs on a rack, dirty dishes in the sink, a cracked mirror perched above lipstick tubes on a narrow shelf and a 24-hour clock over a bulletin board besieged by shift schedules, change requests and personal notices.

Without asking, Mary poured Karney a mug of coffee and set it beside a plate of donuts covered with foil. "Help yourself to all the sugar you want, Irish, but, if you like your java blonde and sweet, we don't have any milk, canned or otherwise."

Again removing his helmet, ball cap still in place, he dumped his gear and absently shook his head. "Sweet's fine, thanks." He sat.

"I need to see how Betti's doing. Make yourself at home, Irish."

Karney washed down three sinkers with the stout

coffee, got a second mug and stared at the clock. Straining to hear beyond the silence, he felt the lonely solitude of a morgue would seem more fitting in this Quonset than the welcome peace of healing.

Ice-laden winds careened outside. The clock continued to tick a somber litany. His sense of loss grew with each minute. Already tired and having just been vampirized, he realized not even strong coffee could keep his fatigue at bay. Fighting to stay awake, he stood and wandered into the empty hall.

His despair deepened. Back in the lounge, Karney slumped on the sofa, burying his face in his hands to pray. For the first time since his mother had died, more than twenty years ago, fear for another life clouded his ability to talk to God. After several tries at "Dear Heavenly Father," he leaned back and closed his eyes . . .

Karney jerked awake. Almost an hour had elapsed. Hearing a noise, he stood up as Mary entered. "How's Ellie?"

Mary again avoided his eyes. "What happened to Mrs. Greer is known as an incomplete abortion. The fetus expelled after her water broke, but not the entire placenta was removed. There wasn't anything you could've done, especially not aboard *Zealous*."

A diagnosis wasn't what Karney needed. Or wanted. Resolute, he again asked, "Mary, how is Ellie?"

The older woman remained quiet too long. Karney's dread rose in proportion to the nurse's delay. Finally, she stated, "She's in serious condition and is being transferred to a civilian hospital."

"Transferred?" Karney repeated. Then, sounding more hostile than the Arctic wind outside, he clarified, "As in already left?"

Mary looked uneasy. "Plans to move Mrs. Greer were underway even before *Zealous* moored. I wouldn't release her until she had your blood in her, though."

"Headed where? Halifax?"

"I'm not authorized to reveal that information."

His temper blew. "Why the hell didn't you tell me?"

"She was unconscious, Irish. Besides," irritation bled into Mary's tone, "you are not related to her."

"So imperious Uncle Richard said I wasn't to know where she was taken?" Karney snapped. "Or did you just take it upon yourself to park me outta the way down here?"

"Don't raise your voice, young man," Mary barked. "I'm sorry Mrs. Greer lost her baby and you had to care for her. But you are outta line, mister." Her eyes burned. "I have to follow orders just like you do. And this one came down from RCN Admiralty, kid-gloves all the way. Your duty in this lady's life is finished. Whatever happens from here on out isn't your damned business. You are not her husband!"

Her harsh words hit home. His rage sank into reality. *Mary's right. No matter how I feel, Ellie isn't my wife.* He sat back down. *The admiral does have the last word.*

"Forgive me," he softly said, "I shouldn't have blown up. I just meant—" Not sure what he meant, he sighed and closed his eyes. He'd not been so irrational since he received word of Jen-Mai's death.

Sitting down, Mary reached across and squeezed his arm. "Irish, I'm sorry I read you the riot act. I know you've been through hell."

Yanking off his ball cap, Karney angrily rubbed his head in frustration. Hopes of staying with Ellie longer washed away like the tide receding. With it, went part of him. Yet the tide always comes back in. Karney looked Mary in the eye. "Which hospital?"

"Irish," her tone stony, "I can't tell you that either."

Though moving Ellie was undoubtedly best for her, it certainly didn't help Karney any. He was surprised by the heaviness in his heart.

Quietly, Mary asked, "You've got it bad for this gal, don't you? You saved her life and gave her blood, Irish, but you'd better back off before you tangle with her jealous husband. And you know Gunnar would throw an absolute conniption fit if he learned you were getting involved with a married woman."

His temper ignited anew. "What I do with my life is none of Gunnar's business. Nor yours either. He was my guardian when I was a kid. He doesn't butt into my life these days, unless it directly interferes with my duty. And this doesn't."

Standing, Karney shoved the chair into the table. Though angry with the turn of events, he regarded Mary's weary face and found guilt softening his voice as he told her, "Ellie's husband died in 1940." He left the math up to Mary if she wanted to bother figuring it out.

RCN CATALINA
EN ROUTE TO HALIFAX, NOVA SCOTIA
MONDAY

Morphine caused Ellie's stomach to churn as if on a plane bucking headwinds. *Lady Z doesn't lurch like this.*

Opening her eyes, she saw her uncle's weathered face. *Am I dreaming?* Beyond him she saw tiers of white-sheeted bunks, the majority filled with patients. *'Tis a medical transport. I'm nae dreamin'. 'Tis a nightmare.*

She forced out, "Irish?"

Uncle Richard's bony hand tenderly clasped hers, fully waking her to this reality.

"Don't talk, Eleanor. We'll be in Halifax shortly."

"Halifax? I do nae want to go there. Where's Karney?"

Not answering, her uncle motioned for the orderly to come to them and adjust her IV. Fog once more engulfed her. She couldn't speak.

Ellie's thoughts echoed hollowly within her foggy brain: *Where's Karney? Why isn't he here with me? I want to be with Irish . . .*

⊕

U.S. Naval Hospital
Argentia, Newfoundland
Commission Government
Of Great Britain
Monday

Mary watched Karney put his ball cap and helmet back on, then shrug into his salt-stained underway coat. His face was drawn with fatigue, his eye color leaden with worry for this woman he'd rescued and for whom he obviously cared. Just before he reached the door of the staff lounge, Mary quietly called after him, "Irish?"

Karney stopped, then slowly turned to meet her gaze.

"Mrs. Greer will be admitted to Victoria General in Halifax. But, Mr. Rork," Mary cautioned, "you did not hear it from me."

Karney nodded, giving a brief salute of thanks and left.

Outside, he stared into the whirling snow: lost, angry and frightened for Ellie. He didn't know Ellie well. But Karney knew his own heart. Jen-Mai had been the only other woman to stir his emotion this deeply. *Japs took Jen. Did Nazis indirectly take Ellie from me before we even had a chance to know each other better?*

He sighed with a new thought: *If I told Ellie this very second I loved her, she'd think I was absolutely nuts.*

Scooping up snowball after snowball, he threw them with the powerful arm in demand at Coast Guard scratch ballgames, especially against Navy Seabees. He nailed the red cross of a parked ambulance dead center every time. Despite the pain tweaking his shoulder, it was more acceptable than the sorrow in his heart.

"What's wrong, *compadre*?" Miguel Tapia softly asked, coming up beside his commanding officer.

Startled, Karney glanced at Tap. "How long've you been here?"

"Since you more than likely struck out Babe Ruth, Ty Cobb and Lou Gehrig."

Karney thumped snow from his gloves. "They flew Ellie outta here. She mighta been halfway to Halifax before I even knew she was gone."

Sensing his distress, Tap said, "*Compadre*, I'm sure you'll see Ellie again. It'll work out. Just give it time."

Karney nodded but changed the subject as Tap knew he would.

"Were you looking for me?"

"Captain Wharton wants you in his office at 1300."

Karney checked his watch. "Crap, I'm almost late now."

Tap asked, "Anything you need me to take care of?"

After a moment, Karney said, "Yeah, have Harley set up leaves and preparations for the guys to catch transports home for Christmas, yourself included. Don't worry about me 'cause I won't see Beantown anytime soon anyway. The captain's probably gonna ream me a new asshole for the battering *Lady Z* took."

"I doubt it, *compadre*. We never fought a U-boat before."

With a half-hearted shrug, Karney trudged off and was soon lost to Tap's view by the ranks of forlorn Quonset huts.

"I do believe *mi amigo* is falling in love." Tap softly prayed in Spanish, "Dear Heavenly Father, please, for both their sakes, watch over Ellie on this journey, heal her body, mind and soul from her tragic loss and enfold both her and Karney within your loving grace."

GREENLAND PATROL HEADQUARTERS
ARGENTIA, NEWFOUNDLAND
MONDAY

Having had no time to shower or shave before his meeting with Naval Captain Wharton, Karney felt downright uncomfortable. The fact that *Lady Z* was in even worse condition compounded his unease. He could only hope Teddy Wharton would understand. As temporary commander of the Coast Guard's Greenland Patrol under the affable, but determined, command of Rear Admiral Arthur Bristol, Captain Wharton was a busy man with a myriad of shifting duties.

Upon entering the captain's office, however, Karney found his attention wasn't on Captain Wharton. It was his imposing visitor. A Royal Canadian Naval captain perched on the cracked leather sofa. The equally odd, but reassuring, presence of a Border Collie mix lay at the Canadian's large feet.

Teddy Wharton was his usual animated self. The Canadian seemed much more reserved, though not particularly aloof.

Karney jumped to a conclusion: I bet this is Cousin Mac. *Why's he here though? Surely, he knows Ellie's headed to Halifax.* His sixth-sense might be working overtime, but Karney felt sure this was not the usual debriefing after a patrol—their U-boat engagement aside.

Seeing Karney, Wharton unstuffed the eternal cigar from his mouth, greeting him with a raised arm. "Irish, there y'all're. Prompt as usual, sonny."

Karney had forgotten the strong twang of Teddy Wharton's Alabama drawl. In contrast, Jonathan Grange's dialect seemed docile. Snapping a crisp salute, Karney said, "Lieutenant Rork reporting as ordered, sir."

Wharton casually returned the salute, cigar smoke wreathing the gesture. "Y'all take it easy, sonny. Ain't no formality here."

Stripping out of his Arctic gear and ball cap, Karney nervously finger-combed his hair, thinking: *What the hell am I getting into?*

He didn't have long to wait for the mystery to untangle.

Indicating his guest, Captain Wharton said, "Irish, this here gentleman is Cap'n Rob Roy MacCalister, RCN, Special Forces. Mac, Lieutenant Karney Rork, U.S. Coast

Guard. W'all call him Irish roun'cheer, though. 'Cause he's always spoutin' them Gaelic proverbs and such."

Captain MacCalister rose to his feet like a life-size Paul Bunyan, reaching out to shake Karney's hand in a bear-paw grip. A good three inches taller than Karney, he had the honed look of a seasoned warrior, but the affable smile of a friend.

In the ballpark of forty, he was amazingly what Karney had envisaged. Except his eyes: lighter green than Ellie's with a more jaded edge. A buzz-cut contrasted his large handlebar mustache—neatly twirled and waxed—both a coppery color. Taking note of the rows of fruit salad—campaign ribbons—Karney was amazed the Canadian, even for his stature, didn't list to port.

"Call me, Mac," the big man grinned pleasantly. "Too damned many syllables in Captain MacCalister, eh?"

"Mac," Karney greeted, matching the firm hand shake and hearing the subtle, but distinct, speech pattern of a native Canadian.

Mac's dog, black with a white ruff, three white paws and tan eyebrows, sat up, paw out-stretched for Karney to shake. Squatting down, he asked, "And who's this lovely charmer?"

"My shadow, conscience and pal, next to my wife of course. I don't dare forget to add that. This sweet mongrel is Chelsea."

"Chelsea," Karney said, shaking her big paw. "My pleasure. Impeccable manners, my dear, especially compared to my mountain-sized mutt back home." Rising again, Karney addressed Mac, "And nice to finally meet you, sir."

Chomping his cigar, Wharton asked, "Y'all're acquainted?"

Surprised Wharton wasn't aware of the situation, Karney wondered if his arrival interrupted their meeting prematurely.

"A brief exchange by radio, Captain," Mac said with a

grin. "Leftenant Rork was there with *Zealous* to rescue my cousin off the *Glasgow Bonnie.*"

The sparse explanation seemed to satisfy Wharton. "All the more fittin' y'all're here then. I need ta turn this parlay into a double fandango, though, like runnin' two coons up one tree."

Rummaging in his desk drawer, Wharton pulled out a small box and tossed it to Karney. "Sorry it ain't nothin' too fancy, Irish, but y'all're promoted. Congratulations, Lieutenant Commander Rork."

Karney stared at the box, then slowly opened it. Finding a pair of sea-tarnished gold oak leaves pinned on the blue velvet inside, he glanced up at Wharton. "Captain Bryannt's oak leaves?"

"Yours now, Irish. Gunnar sent 'em up with his blessin's for a Merry Christmas and charged you with the lovin' care o' his precious li'l gal, *Lady Z.* She's your command now, son."

Dubious, Karney asked, "A promotion? But what about Captain Bryannt?"

Wharton wouldn't meet his eyes. "Guns had a little flare up after his surgery, but y'all don't need to worry 'bout that now."

Not only did Karney not buy Wharton's good-ol'-boy sorghum, he sensed something else wrong. He let it slide and shook Wharton's out-stretched hand. "I'll put 'em on when I get cleaned up, sir. Thank you."

Grasping Karney's hand, Mac shook it with a hearty thump on his back. A bottle of Jack Daniel's whiskey materialized on the desk and Wharton generously sloshed out equal portions into three tumblers.

Karney's weary mind couldn't take it all in. He hadn't expected his promotion for months. On the other hand, like most everyone else, he hadn't figured the Japs would attack Pearl Harbor Naval Base little more than two weeks ago either.

Mac proposed the first toast. "To Leftenant

Commander Rork, hero and friend of Clan MacCalister."

With Wharton's accord, the three men downed their drinks. The amber liquid burned its way down Karney's throat. A second round was poured, and Karney raised his tumbler first. "To Ellie, a woman with the fortitude to show us all how to win this damned war."

Mac raised his glass with a soft spoken, "Aye, to Ellie."

Wharton looked perplexed. "Who the begeezus is Ellie?"

Gulping his drink, Mac answered, "My cousin on the *Bonnie*."

"Your cousin?" Wharton blurted, his voice rising nearly an octave. "A woman was who Irish rescued . . ." Wharton sputtered. "Hell's bells, I won't even ask what the devil she was doin' on that old bucket, but Irish deserves another toast for savin' a scared damsel in distress," he said, eagerly refilling the glasses.

Ignoring the buzz in his head, Karney drank eagerly, hoping to dull the distress over Ellie's sudden departure. Trouble with that, it might take the whole bottle.

"Captain Wharton," Mac's voice grew suddenly somber, "may I talk privately with Commander Rork somewhere around here?"

Wharton glanced at his watch, asking, "This place do?"

Mac nodded. "It'll do fine, eh?"

Karney politely objected. "I'm glad we met, Mac, but I need to get back to *Lady Z*. We've a lot of repairs and—"

"Don't worry 'bout *Lady Z*, Irish," Wharton said. "From what I hear, it's gonna take more 'an spit and bailin' wire to get her shipshape again. I won't be comin' back t'night, anyway. Guh'night, gents."

With that, Captain Wharton bundled up and left.

Like a trapped wolf, Karney faced Mac and challenged, "This really doesn't have a damned thing to do with Ellie's rescue, does it?"

⊕

Bedford Basin (circa 1942)

BEDFORD BASIN HARBOUR MASTER'S OFFICE
HALIFAX, NOVA SCOTIA
MONDAY

Willy Christensen, a lanky blond lad, marched brashly into the harbor master's file-crammed office. The stout harbor master of Bedford Basin, Arthur Boggs, waved languidly at his young assistant.

Ignoring the gesture, Willy asked, "What's going on in the harbor?" He waited in classic impatience for his boss' sluggish response.

With a drilled period, Boggs finished his entry in the log book and set down his dull pencil. Lifting his considerable bulk from the chair, wheels and swivels squealing in relief, he ambled to the window overlooking the Basin.

Below him spread the world's second largest natural harbor. Dozens of ships were docked on the fringe or moored within its immense sanctuary. Each ship, returning from or heading to ports in Britain, frigid Russia or warmer climes in the Mediterranean, bore signs of fatigue, some braced by sheer temerity. Though no two ships looked alike, their objectives were similar.

Recognition flags from many countries fluttered in a stiff westerly breeze. Colorful pennants contrasted sharply with muted grays, blacks and rust-streaked hulls of vessels at anchor and the frigid blue-gray of the water. Willy's attention wasn't on any of the ships, however.

An RCN Catalina glided over the ruffled surface and settled gently onto the water. A sharp V cut in her wake. From a graceful bird of the air, the plane became an ungainly creature wallowing on the bay as she taxed to a dockside berth.

"That Cat?" Boggs shrugged, like a sloth humping his prodigious shoulders, giving an equally prodigious answer, "Some uppity admiral requested special permission to set down so he could bring his daughter or niece or some-such-type female directly to one of the hospitals in Halifax. The woman was returning to Canada when her ship was torpedoed. Rest of the convoy arrived earlier in the morning before you came in. Damn funny thing that."

Willy glared at his employer. With great deliberation, Boggs stuffed tobacco in the bowl of his meerschaum pipe. His rude habit of starting a sentence, then taking too long to finish it, whether for mystery or annoyance, infuriated Willy. Reminding himself poise was crucial to a good agent, he was forced to remain serene.

And Willy—born Willem Rask Krigeshaald in Odense, Denmark, twenty-three years ago—was a good agent. To his contacts in *das Dritte Reich* he was known as BLUE FOX. Working for Boggs was the perfect position for a spy, the intelligence that Willy gathered was of inestimable worth. Impatience could not spoil his cover.

His pipe sufficiently full, Boggs lit a match to it. After several puffs, he said, "Seems *Bonnie* was the only freighter hit out of fifty-odd ships." He relit his pipe, puffing to keep it going. "A west-bound convoy at that. As I recall, she was a rusty old hulk loaded with scrap-iron. Since Yanks are in the fight, I guess it serves as a warning the Huns are moving west, hunting any target, coming or going."

Turning away, Boggs sauntered back to his desk, stacked with schedules and reports, both old and new, as well as manifests and clutter—disorder Willy loathed.

Willy glanced below. Two men carried a stretcher to a waiting ambulance. Just as it drove off, Willy read: Victoria General Hospital.

His spirits lifted. A hot tomato in his Monday night class, Cynthia, worked at VG. Willy already knew she would do anything for some nookie. Especially something as easy as getting the name of a woman he suspected was the British agent STARLING. Willy's Nazi superior, JAEGER, had warned him she might arrive in Canada. Then his thoughts tumbled like crates from a broken cargo net.

What if JAEGER wants me to finish what the U-boat

could not? I'm not a killer. And I don't want to start now.
Someone else can murder the woman. After all, Willy
claimed to his conscience, *I gather seeds of intelligence;*
I'm not the bloody Grim Reaper. On the other hand, if I
kill STARLING, *might* JAEGER *reward my skill and—*

Boggs blew his titanic nose, a sound to rival the
Georges Island foghorn. Sitting back down at his desk,
Willy cautioned himself, *Routine in this office must come*
first. I'll worry about STARLING *later.*

GREENLAND PATROL HEADQUARTERS
ARGENTIA, NEWFOUNDLAND
COMMISSION GOVERNMENT
OF GREAT BRITAIN
MONDAY

"No, Commander Rork," Captain Mac MacCalister
answered, "it doesn't have a damn thing to do with Ellie's
rescue, at least not directly, eh? But it does have to do, in
an adverse way, with my father, Admiral MacCalister, and
what happens to you and *Zealous* from here forward, as
well as the prisoners she took. But we can cover that later."

Wholly focused on the word admiral, Karney heard
only the first part of Mac's comment. "Look, Captain, I
followed procedures on the radio—"

"I know, Irish, I know." Mac held up his hands to halt
his defense. "That's what tipped my decision. I don't want
or need an officer who'll knuckle under when some
crotchety old fart of an admiral barks at him. Even if the
admiral happens to be my father, eh?"

Ambling to Wharton's desk, Mac said, "Actually, I read
your service record long before you two tangled, both your
Merchant Marine and Coast Guard files. Honors for
rescues and awards for bravery, expert marksman,
aptitude for languages, including German, broad range of
experiences and a skilled nautical ice pilot to boot.
Impressive."

Karney eyed Mac suspiciously. He knew what was in his file and nothing said anything about German. In fact, the only people aware of that were Gunnar and their former houseguest, a German-Jew. Well, and Mark Allison aboard *Zealous*, too.

Wondering where this was going, he watched Mac pour another tumbler of Jack Daniel's. Mac offered him more; Karney declined. Sobriety seemed crucial. With Mac knowing so much about him, Karney felt like a harpoon was poised to strike. He had learned over the years: *Good seldom came of a higher ranking officer knowing more about you than you knew about him—Canadian or not.*

"I had the pleasure of speaking with Captain Bryannt when in Boston. Gunnar assured me of your competence, though not because he used to be your guardian. My father doesn't share my views. Admiral MacCalister believes you're too young, too inexperienced, too . . . how did he put it . . . cocky, I believe, eh?"

Mac waved his tumbler with an air of dismissal. "After more than twenty years as an officer in the RCN, the admiral doesn't see me as competent either. I think you can fill Captain Bryannt's shoes quiet capably. Of course, considering the first part of this mission, maybe I should say 'snowshoes'."

Cautiously, he asked, "Fill his snowshoes for what?"

Heading across the room, Mac motioned him to follow. On a huge oak table lay Wharton's equally large, unrolled map of Greenland, anchored at the corners by four heavy Navy-Reg manuals. Karney was very familiar with Greenland's features.

Mac ran his finger down the East Greenland Coast. "You know this coast." It was not a question. "Could the Germans establish a U-boat base anywhere along here?"

Karney's eyes narrowed as he frowned and scratched his beard-stubbled jaw. "It would be a good position from which to hit convoys but not very practical."

"Ice?" Though asked, it was more a statement.

"Yeah, ice is an issue, but why try. Bombers could probably knock it out before they'd even finish building it. The Nazis'd have to bring in generators for electricity, food, fuel, equipment." Karney smiled. "Greenland's East Coast ain't exactly a spur off the Atchison, Topeka and Santa Fe. And having an operational base up there would mean tons of supplies, a lot of men and torpedoes. It would need a helluva lot more than a corner market or the gas station down the road."

Leaning over the table, arms braced, Karney spoke as though viewing the island of Greenland itself. "But the key factor's weather. Summers are short, fjords can be icy the year round. And storms, even in July, are as unpredictable as frozen hell."

Mac twisted his mustache. "It's doubtful they could do it then."

Karney stared at the convoluted coastline. In his mind's eye, he pictured steep, jagged precipices rising from undefiled, deep, emerald fjords, often choked with ice, even in summer. He shook his head. "No one thought a U-boat could sneak into Scapa Flow, under the nose of the British Home Fleet, and sink *Royal Oak* either."

"So they might be able to man and supply a U-boat base up there?"

Looking Mac in the eye, Karney shrugged. "I doubt it, but I gotta nasty hunch you're gonna ask me to check it out."

A devilish grin crookedly tilted Mac's mustache. "You're bloody astute for a Yank who looks like he could use another drink."

Sensing the harpoon thrown, its barb not fatal, Karney strolled over to refill his tumbler. He definitely needed a drink now that he knew Mac's intent. Over his shoulder, Karney quizzed, "So what am I supposed to do? Knock on every hut and igloo up there and ask the Danes and Inuits if they've noticed any big blond Aryan types running around with swastikas and cigar-shaped boats?"

"Not quite. At this stage, you just need to contact one man: Dr. Bross Krigeshaald. I believe you've already met him?"

"Yeah, briefly, two summers ago on a mail run with *Lady Z*."

"Speak with Doc, since he knows the bloody Danes and Inuits. Perhaps do a bit of reconnaissance while you're at it."

Karney slowly shook his head and downed the contents of his tumbler. "I hate to remind you, Mac, but the pack ice is miles wide right now. *Zealous* has a reinforced bow, but she's no icebreaker. And I can't imagine a U-boat getting through either."

"True, but this is only the opening stages and you'll be going in alone. You'll be flown in. Plans will be made to meet Doc and have him give you a perspective on things, eh?"

"Swell, I get to do a pitiful imitation of Admiral Byrd. But I know this much, Mac, it's damned cold and damned unforgiving up there." Karney slumped on the sofa, absently rubbing Chelsea's head. She leaned against his leg, resting her head on his thigh. "Why'd you pick me if this is a Canadian operation?"

"It's not strictly Canadian. And why I picked you over several other qualified Coast Guard officers, is your time as Gunnar's XO and your Arctic junket with him. There's also the bond with *Lady Z*'s crew, which Gunnar insists you have, along with your judgment of their character and capabilities."

Mac sipped his whiskey. "That will all come into play at a later date. Right now, I need a Yank because of the relations your country has with Greenland. America has established a consulate at Godthab and your cutters have been running ice patrols since the Titanic sank. However, this is a joint Allied venture. Along with my Canadians and Americans, I have Brits, Aussies, Danes and some Frog-Canucks thrown in for good measure." He gave another lopsided grin. "I call it ICE PACT, eh?" Mac's grin faded. "It will be an aggressive mission to stop Nazi U-boats from slaughtering our men and convoys. We can't let them get any sort of bloody toehold up there." His voice rang with resolve.

Standing up, Karney refilled his tumbler, considering Mac's theory. "You gotta pretty wild imagination, you know that?"

"How so?" Mac asked, leaning back against the table, folding his arms over his chest and waiting for the explanation.

Karney moseyed back to the chart table. "Why do you think Jerry might plan to build a base in Greenland? Could this just be some Nazi *sub*terfuge to tie up our troops? Pun intended."

Mac raised an eyebrow as he lifted his battered briefcase that had definitely seen its best days a lifetime ago. Withdrawing a file, Mac spread several glossy photographs across the table. "These pictures. Note the dates, U-boat markings, their damage, locations." Again leaning back, he refolded his arms.

With a magnifying glass, Karney scrutinized each. Evidence for Mac's suspicions came into sharp focus.

The photos showed U-boats with damaged decks, conning towers and antennae. In later photos, they were repaired. Yet their locations and turn-around time were far too short for a refit in France or Norway; much less Germany. Karney again sorted through them. "Who took these? Houdini incarnate with a camera?"

Mac's laugh came easily. "Collins, the cantankerous Aussie you argued with over Ellie. He flies recon for me in a Spitfire. *Snapper* he calls her. At the moment she's air-conditioned from a number of Krupp munitions, souvenirs from even crankier camera-shy Germans. Besides uncanny luck and skill, Collins possesses enough piss and vinegar to fly any bloody plane he wants without benefit of petrol."

"Yeah, that I believe." The Aussie's attitude wasn't

easily forgotten. Karney nodded. "We didn't exactly see eye-to-eye at first."

"Collins doesn't see eye-to-eye with anyone. Definitely not with most officers. Unfortunately for his service record, he likes it that way. Wendy stays just within my bounds to keep his wings."

Mac glanced at his watch. "Speaking of.... How 'bout we swing by *Lady Z*, you get cleaned up, put your new oak leaves on and check your cutter, while I meet another officer down there. Then we can run over to Dunville for chow? Since Collins is back to flying *Ice Sheila* for a while, I'm sure he'll be eager to barter their flight report for victuals and their ration of grog."

Pulling his blood-red beret from his epaulet, Mac set it on his head at a jaunty angle. Chelsea sat up, wagging her tail. "I want you to meet the lads on a more even keel than the choppy North Atlantic. Especially since you'll be working with them, eh?"

Hands in his pockets, Karney stated, "I don't recall volunteering for this mission, sir. Why assume I'm going?"

"Come now, Irish. Deserved though it may be, who the bloody hell do you think helped push through your promotion?"

"I don't need to kiss anyone's ass to get my rank."

"Oh, for crying out loud, Rork. We're waging war, not some kiss-ass political campaign. I needed a leftenant commander for this operation. You had the quals, not the rank. I simply cut the bloody red tape. Much to the rancor of my Old Man when he finds out."

Pissed at being used, even if he benefited, Karney accused, "You used my promotion to snub your old man?"

"People aren't pawns to me." Mac's tone bore no rebuke, but his eyes jaded. "I chose you because you are a veteran who came highly recommended." His gaze bore into Karney. "Keeping my dad's petty indignation from interfering with my mission and your promotion was purely incidental."

Karney eyed the tall Canadian irritably. "Did your old man make sure Ellie flew outta here as soon as we reached Argentia?"

"He flew up here to get Ellie to Halifax, his timing also incidental." Mac raised an eyebrow. "You make it sound personal, Irish. Ellie stole your heart while you weren't looking, didn't she?"

Wary of possible ramifications to Mac's question, Karney wasn't willing to betray his emotions. "Even though you're Ellie's cousin and confidant, it's none of your damned business, Captain."

"Wasn't making it mine, Irish. I just know the effect Ellie has on men. She'd like to ignore it, but that's like Cinderella trying to ignore the fact she's running around with only one slipper."

Mac stuffed the photos into his briefcase. "I intend to recruit her as well. Ellie held the rank of leftenant in the WRENs till she resigned to come back to Nova Scotia. Before that, she spied for MI-6 in Germany for years. The impression of innocence my sweet cousin radiates is a far cry from the ordeals she survived. If you'd like, that lady can draw you a road map of Hitler's hell by heart."

Karney wasn't sure what to make of this new revelation. But Mac wasn't lying. *Christ Almighty, Ellie a spy? With the angelic qualities I bestowed on her, I'd've never suspected it. On the other hand, her seeming vulnerability mixed with a lethal dose of sexuality makes her an ideal spy. That gal holds more intrigue than I ever fathomed.*

Glancing at Mac, Karney said, "For a guy who supposedly doesn't use people as pawns, you play a damned wicked game of chess, Captain MacCalister."

"I don't use people, Irish, I just play their strengths. I also plan to win. So which is it? Serve your queen to snub the king? Or sacrifice a knight? Perhaps both?"

Still skeptical, he eyed Mac. "You buying supper?"

"And grog all around," Mac reminded amicably.

"Why do I feel like I'm trading my soul to Lucifer?"

Slapping Karney on the back, Mac said, "From what I hear, Irish, you've kissed the Blarney Stone with the best of 'em. This diplomatic junket will be a skate for you."

"Yeah, on very thin ice," he griped. "Ah, but don't forget, Mac: *'Bíonn grásta Dé idir an diallait agus an talamh'.*"

"Meaning?"

Skewing his grin and raising an eyebrow, Karney translated, "The grace of God is found 'tween the saddle and the ground. In this case, my butt and your ICE PACT." As he shrugged into his heavy coat, then settled his ball cap and helmet on his head, Karney headed for the door. "Let's go before you volunteer me to find the Holy Grail."

Mac chuckled. "Actually, I was thinking something more like finding the Arc of the Covenant. That would really brass Hitler and Himmler off if we found it first, wouldn't it, eh?"

CHAPTER NINE

VICTORIA GENERAL
HALIFAX, NOVA SCOTIA
MON: 22 DEC 41

Ellie couldn't remember where she was till her eyes managed to focus on the dripping IV above her, crisp hospital sheets beneath. She also noticed the absence of rolling waves. Images flickered through her mind like some out-of-order Kinetoscope. Her only bright, warm, agreeable memories were of Karney, Brandt and Anna. Other visions intruded as shadowy, distant and more devastating. Pleasant meditations refused to stay long.

A view of Irish grinning aboard *Lady Z* was exiled by a Danish trawler's chain locker, reeking of fish and fear, where she'd hidden from Nazis ordered to find and arrest her. The brave Danish fisherman, who tried to help her escape to neutral Sweden, shot pointblank as she was dragged up on deck. Sunlight sparkling on the waves as Brandt and Anna raced each other over warm sands on a Portuguese beach morphed into sadness as her father told her they had both died in a plane crash. Oil-fires dancing on the ocean when Irish rescued her from *Glasgow Bonnie* spread into Nikki's burial at sea. The striking radiance of the sunset blurred into the tears that Irish shed for her unborn baby on that solemn day. Though a sad image, it deeply touched Ellie's heart, bringing more tears.

The dank cell, where chilled, spent and naked, Ellie had been held captive in Copenhagen evolved into the antiseptic white of this hospital room where she felt welcome, comfortable and safe. James Strafford's licentious stare drifted into the sincere glow of Karney's compassion for her aboard *Lady Z.*

Reminiscing on Karney's deep, dulcet voice as he soothed her to sleep, Ellie slid beneath a numbing blanket of morphine. Here was a haven free of fear and danger, her past forgotten for the moment.

TUES: 23 DEC 41

Ellie's meager lunch set well, even tasted good, though she didn't finish it. She slept afterwards as if she'd feasted at a banquet. Her physical pain subsided, but her broken heart over Nikki would take far longer to mend.

Daydreaming about Irish, even just thinking of him, helped. *But is the design of Karney's Irish tapestry more fantasy than reality? How will I add more threads if I dinna see him again? Am I woven into the fabric of his life? Or is it all an illusion? And what of me fears about fallin' in love? Are those frayed edges I'll never complete?*

She considered Karney himself, knowing he held the answers to these questions: *Rather than riding a white steed, me Prince Charming pilots an Arctic-camouflaged cutter. But I so cherish his empathy and humor. Though he flashes an Irish temper, his apologies are endearin'. And his music, like an unbreakable thread, charmed me just like the tender strength of his embrace calmed me.* Ellie silently giggled with a memory: *I loved how he'd briskly rub his hands together, then transfer the heat to me bloody freezin' feet. What a delicious delight.*

Wrapping herself in memories, Karney's warmth became real. Thoughts of him shielded her from the embittered world beyond the hospital walls. A world she'd soon have to face.

Will Irish try to visit me?

Her thoughts were broken by a rap at the door, quickening her pulse. As the door creaked open, however, the weather-worn face of her uncle appeared.

"Eleanor?" he called in a strained voice, barely a whisper.

The look in his eyes revealed how out of place he felt. Her mother had told Ellie how ill-at-ease he felt around women and their maladies. *Good thing he had boys.*

Ellie tried to sound cheerful. "Come in, Uncle Richard."

Entering the room, he laid his coat on the chair and reluctantly stepped closer. His hands fidgeted in and out of his pockets like a puppeteers strings gone awry.

"Your color's much improved from yesterday, Eleanor dear," the stern admiral observed. "How are you feeling?"

"Actually," she lied, not wanting to worry him further, "I feel much better after me ordeal last night." His raised eyebrow made her realize he didn't need nor want to hear anything about any female procedures. "I'll be bonnie in nae time."

"Yes, well, mustn't rush things. Best if you're completely well before you get out on your own and such, eh? Elizabeth said you can stay with them after they've released you from hospital."

"For a wee while, but Mac's comin' back soon and I dinna wan' to be a bother to them. I intend to find work and get my own flat."

"Well, Rob Roy will not be returning until Christmas or later. And I daresay, Elizabeth and the children will delight in having you as their cherished guest. Having his dear, sweet cousin back on Canadian soil is a pleasure Rob Roy has looked forward to for weeks."

Uncle Richard had always used their Christian names sounding as stiff as a barrister in the House of Commons. Stifling a giggle, Ellie said, "I'll be delighted to see Mac too, Uncle Richard. But I need to find a job or I'll be livin' in the poorhouse, scrapin' porridge like Oliver Twist, mornin', noon and night."

"Ahem, well, yes . . . I suppose you would be in a bit of a wicket without any family. However, Rob Roy does have a job for you, Eleanor. If you wish to accept it, of course. He would've asked you himself, but foul weather further delayed him up in Newfoundland. He requested I speak with you when I called."

Curious, Ellie prompted, "Go on . . ."

"Well, nothing too fancy. We've not the assets of the home islands, eh? It shall be suitable: intel analysis, data comparisons, radiotelegraphy, some instructing."

Having not yet delineated her goals, Ellie knew this was what she sought: *A way to get back at the Nazis, gainful employment and get my life back together.* "When may I start?"

Caught off guard by her hasty acceptance, her uncle tripped over his tongue, "Ah, well, ahem . . . once you are up to snuff, ah, perhaps after the new year. We'll get the lighthouse keeper's cottage fixed up for you, painted, carpeted and such."

She was certain no one else at the garrison was handled in this manner. "Why such royal treatment, Uncle Richard?"

"Well, I daresay, Eleanor, you are my only niece and you'll need a place to live. Can't have you stay at the manor, it's been converted into bachelor's quarters, more or less. Besides . . ."

Ellie waited patiently, while he fidgeted some more.

"It will be nice to have you living nearby again."

Despite her uncle's abiding soft-spot for her, Ellie grew suspicious of his reason from his actions, not his words. Since arriving, he stood, sat, paced and incessantly wrung his gnarled hands. And it was more than being in a woman's hospital room.

But she dare not check the teeth of this gift horse.

Glancing at the unadorned wall calendar, Ellie asked,

"How 'bout the first Sunday after New Year's Day? 'Tis time enough?"

Uncle Richard's eyes brightened. "Yes, Eleanor, that would be grand. It shall also allow you time to lose that bloody Scottish brogue you reacquired. Besides, here you'll be quite safe . . . well taken care of, I mean, ahem, but there's no rush to your reporting for duty. I want you to start only when you feel up to it."

Though curious what he meant by safe, she didn't ask. "Uncle Richard, I feel much better just knowin' I have a job, a place to live and I willna be a burden on anyone."

"Eleanor," his smile carved a dram of warmth on his craggy face, "you've never been a burden. When you came back after your mother's death, you were sunshine to my dark and lonely days. After you left, the clouds rolled in again." Uncharacteristic for him, he took her hand in both of his and patted it gently. "I'm thrilled to have you back, my dear."

"Dinna be getting', oops, excuse me, don't get too sentimental, Uncle Richard, or the men at the garrison will know you play favorites."

"Eleanor, I never play favorites." A twinkle brightened his jade-green eyes. "Our relationship must remain professional. In fact, I insist you address me by rank unless in private." Giving her hand a final pat, he lay it on the bed and withdrew his hands.

"Ahem, which reminds me, we must work out a reason why a British WREN has been assigned to an RCN garrison." He gazed at the wall. "I will give it some thought. However, your cousin has been quite generous in doling out promotions, whether they're deserved or not, so consider yourself promoted to the rank of leftenant commander."

"A promotion?" She tilted her head and teased, "Oh, and you say you never play favorites, eh?"

"No, I do not," he insisted, stiffening slightly. "Rob Roy does. He wants rank for this mission to handle it properly. My signature may be required, at times, but Rob Roy runs the show. Whom he chooses is his affair. Even when I disagree."

Ellie again sensed there was more to his remarks than he revealed but she chose not to push.

Collecting his coat and gloves, he placed his hat on his silvered hair. "My dear, please get some rest. You still look a tad peaked, and I must get back to Sheet Harbour."

The admiral leaned over to kiss her forehead. "I meant what I said about having you back, Eleanor. I just wish it might have been under . . . better circumstances."

"So do I, Uncle Richard. At least it's behind me."

A shadow crept over his face. "Yes, ahem, well, take care of yourself. Though I shall visit when I can, there are several bloody conferences I must attend. It appears each and every brass hat in Canada needs to complete unfinished business they neglected to do in 1941. And the bloody war news certainly doesn't make the coming year look very promising. Bloody Huns."

With a wave, he closed the door. The haunting feeling that she had not been told everything lingered like a pall of smoke. *What is Uncle Richard hiding from me?*

Surprisingly weary from her uncle's visit, short though it was, she dozed off before she could explore any of those unsavory territories.

FRENCH ARMS TAVERN
DUNVILLE, NEWFOUNDLAND
COMMISSION GOVERNMENT
OF GREAT BRITAIN
TUESDAY

When Karney dined as Mac's guest last night, dark paneling, heavy timbers and warm firelight created a quaint mood in this nineteenth century tavern. However, in daylight the place wore its hundred-plus years far less gracefully. Even the Christmas tree looked rather gaunt now. But terrific food and wonderful ale made up for the old tavern's lack of daylight ambiance.

Having met Collins and his flight crew on cordial grounds, Karney realized their orneriness was simply part of the Australian's makeup. A savory meal, pints of ale and closely matched dart games thawed the Aussies' apathy at learning Karney would be the newest member assigned to the ICE PACT mission.

Since foul weather had kept *Ice Sheila* sea-bound today, Karney asked Collins to meet him here for supper. His impatience growing, Karney dipped his finger in his Molson and ran it around the rim of his glass mug to hear it sing—it didn't. The old grandfather clock ticked past five. Collins was late, and the waitress was driving Karney nuts.

In a sultry French accent, she kept asking if he needed anything. Karney kept saying, "No, thanks, I'm fine." She returned anyway, her carnal interest too thinly veiled not to miss. He figured her interest was to be expected with the war and the fact that this corner of Newfoundland wasn't exactly a teeming metropolis of males.

But Karney wanted nothing to do with this French tart and her blue eyes as prominent as her bosom, barely held in a colonial-period blouse and tightly cinched vest.

Finally, Collins, face ruddy from the cold, waltzed through the door. Keeping his hands in his pockets till he reached their table, he greeted, "Eh, good man, Irish, a table by the ruddy fire to keep me poor arse warm. A mate could freeze their ruddy jewels off out there it's so bloody cold." He sat and asked, "So what's on your mind, mate?"

Before Karney opened his mouth, Miss Tits showed up, eyes aglow at the sight of fresh meat. "May I get you somezing, *Monsieur* Fly Boy?"

Putting his arm around her narrow waist, Collins pulled her onto his lap. "Sure, sweets, ale and somethin' yummy for me tummy?"

Twittering in delight, her breasts jiggled like mounds of vanilla pudding. The Aussie's smile broadened. She was also pleased. Nibbling his ear, she said, "I'll bring your ale right back, Fly Boy."

"Buttercups, me name's Wendy. What's yours?" he asked, releasing her so she could stand back up.

With gauged grace, she bent over to set the menus on the table, her breasts mere inches from Collins ravenous eyes. "My name is Trudi, *mon chérie*."

Swishing her skirt, Trudi sashayed away, glancing back with a flirtatious wink. She blew Wendy a kiss before disappearing around the corner to the bar.

His voice laden with lust, Collins sighed. "Now that's one ripe tomato." His eyes still staring, he asked, "What were you sayin', Irish?"

Karney grimaced, trying to dismiss Collins' lude behavior. "You flying to Halifax in the next coupla days?"

"Hell, I dunno know, mate," he said, turning his attention back to the Irish-Yank. "Maybe tomorrow. Why?"

"If you do, can I hop a ride?"

"Why?" Collins persisted.

"I've some business I need to take care of down there."

"You Yanks got more bloody planes than our bloomin' air force. Can't one of your blokes give ya a buzz down?"

To this practiced troublemaker, Karney's silence rolled into designs of mischief. Wendy grinned, rewording the scenario, "Aw, I get it, you ain't got duty business, you got Sheila business, eh?"

"Something like that," Karney said noncommittally.

"Anyone I might know, mate, or you plan to introduce us when we get there?" the Aussie asked, the light in his eyes lecherous.

Guardedly, Karney answered, "Actually, she's the lady I wouldn't let you take off *Zealous*." He noted the light in Collins' eyes recede and his face visibly pale.

"You mean the admiral's niece? As in Mac's cousin? As in, do I look like a bloody bloomin' lunatic? You're outta your fuckin' head, mate. Ain't no way in bloody hell I'll fly you down there and land on the wrong side of that old codger, much less do somethin' to piss Mac off and have him retract me bloody wings again."

Just as Karney started to pose an argument, Trudi reappeared.

She bent over to set the ale down, making Karney wonder if she'd pop out of her blouse. Eyes bulging, Collins clearly hoped she would. When a group of Canadians came in the door, Trudi's services were drawn away from the drooling Aussie.

Karney resumed his appeal. "Collins, it's not like anyone's gotta know I go with you guys. I wanna get there, pick up some gifts, see Ellie and get back here by nightfall."

"Even if we go to Hali', which I ain't sayin' we are, we won't come back here. We're due back in Torbay Christmas mornin'."

"Even better. I gotta meet Mac in St. John's that same day. I can just hitch a ride with you to Hali', then—"

"Nothin' doin', mate. Trouble finds me without help. Mac'd figure it out and nail both our ruddy hides to his bloomin' map wall with all his bloody thumbtacks."

Karney's hopes washed out with the tide. Curbing further conversation, Miss Twin-endowments returned.

"Would *Monsieurs* care to order supper before we get busier?"

"Eh, darlin', how about you for supper?"

"No, *Monsieur*, you know I am no ze zupper. I am ze dezzert."

As Collins pulled her closer, Karney slapped his arm. "Just order off the damn menu, Collins. Play with your dessert later."

With more twittering, Trudi took their orders.

Their meal devoured and the dishes cleared, Karney still hadn't convinced Collins to play his chauffeur. Though their chatter ran from pole to pole—from Karney's Arctic excursions to Collins' work as an Antarctic pilot—the Aussie remained adamant. He still refused to chance crossing swords with Mac or Admiral MacCalister.

The other constant of the evening was Trudi, lingering with Collins' well-placed tips in her cleavage. He must've been paid and was looking for some payback.

Several times, tiring of Wendy's crass behavior, Karney visited other tables to speak with officers he knew. When a third waitress began her shift, Trudi's flirting grew even more aggressive.

By nine, snuggled on Wendy's lap, breasts pressed against his chest, Trudi was off work. Playing darts nearby, Karney was more aware of the clientele than the lustful birds. It was the reason he noticed some burly sailors enter the tavern.

Shoulder patches distinguished them as Free French. Rating insignias identified them as stokers—a black-gang— the men who kept fires fueled, boilers steaming. On any ship, the black-gang was formidable, not easily intimidated. Karney guessed not one of them weighed-in at less than two-hundred pounds, though their heights ranged between about five-nine to six-four, give or take.

Blinded by Trudi's headlights, Collins paid no heed. A huge bear of a Frenchman with sloped shoulders and a sneer beneath his thick black beard, called Trudi's name. She apparently didn't hear him. Like Goliath over David, the big stoker towered over the table where Wendy held court. With jealous spite filling his dark eyes, the Frenchman glowered down at Collins.

Collins' stupidity flowed more freely than ale from an open spigot. "Go 'way, mate, the Sheila's busy. If you want someone your own bloody size, a whale beached itself down the coast a ways," he heartily laughed at his drunken joke. "He's dead but his carc-ass might still be warm if ya hurry on down there."

Only Karney seemed to see Trudi's face blanch. Eyes filling with terror, she tried to squirm free of Collin's embrace. Finally wiggling loose, she faced the steaming Frenchman, rapid-firing excuses at him in French. Her arguments fell on deaf ears. The huge stoker gently picked her up and set her off to one side as if she were a mannequin being moved in a storefront display.

The challenge was met as Collins shoved his chair back, knocking it over. He tipsily stood, totally blind to the trouble he brewed.

Holding no hope of any Canadian patrons siding with this crazy, corked Aussie and one sincere, though slightly-sauced Yank, Karney knew he and Collins would have to face the ten big Frenchmen alone. The term "ally" only extended so far.

Trying to stop the fracas before it could erupt, Karney grabbed Collins' jacket and jerked him toward the door. It was already too late. Like a terrier straining against his leash to get at a much larger French bulldog, Collins slipped his grip.

Collins squared off against the stoker, spouting, "You bloody-bloated piss-swilling Frog, get outta my—"

A wicked right hook sailed at Collins' head. He ducked. It missed. Then Collins rammed his knee into the Frog's crotch, doubling him over. Before he could straighten back up, Collins followed with a stiff uppercut. At least the Aussie could fight.

Another Frog came to his friend's aid, yanking Karney back from his second try at hauling Collins to the door. Not waiting for his punch, Karney spun on him. A left hook deliberately sent the Frog sprawling into a table of Canadians.

Straightening his tie, Karney exclaimed, "Don't ever call the Canucks lazy, yellow-livered, Limey-kissers again!"

As one, the Canadians glared at the fellow on the floor.

Plainly not understanding English, the unsuspecting sucker struggled to his feet. A beefy fella helped him up only to send him sailing across the room with a mallet-sized right fist. Though the odds were still far from even, the donnybrook was definitely on. Allies included.

⊕

ST. JOHN'S, NEWFOUNDLAND
COMMISSION GOVERNMENT
OF GREAT BRITAIN
WED: 24 DEC 41

Taking one glance at the report Marciá had surreptitiously laid on the edge of the table, Mac barked, "MARCIÁ, HALT!"

She stopped in her tracks and slowly turned around, a vague sense of panic in her hazel eyes. "Yes, Cap'n Mac?"

With a growl she knew to respect, he instructed, "Telephone the hangar over at Torbay and get me your sweetheart Collins."

Shifting from one dainty foot to the other, Marciá timidly said, "I can't, sir."

"And why the hell not? Damned phones out again?"

"Well, I could phone Torbay, sir, but Wendy's not there."

Mac rose up. With an eyebrow arched with intimidation, he stalked around the table. "And just where the hell is he?"

"In Halifax, sir. Somethin' about picking up spare parts."

"Why didn't he clear it with me first?"

"Well, sir, you were at that meeting all mornin' . . ." She tried to stop wringing her hands. "And after that, well, I forgot, that's all."

Under Mac's scrutiny, Marciá visibly shrank.

"Marciá Gertrude Therkilsen," Mac addressed her like her father used to when she was in trouble, "you may've forgotten all the times Wendy's been out with other women, all the times he's stood you up and all the times he forgot to call, but you've never, ever forgotten to give me my messages. What the bloody hell's going on, and why'd you sit on this report from the French Arms Tavern?"

Fluttering her eyes, she began, "Well, Cap'n Mac . . ."

"Marciá!" His tone held warning enough.

"They did go for parts, the requisition's on my desk," she lamely pointed over her shoulder, then brushed back a blonde curl.

"The tardiness of the report?"

"Well, that nice Yank, the one you helped get promoted—"

"What's Rork got to do with any of this?"

"Well, he called from Halifax, sir, and well, you weren't here and Wendy was gone since they were together, so the damage was done." She winced at her choice of words.

"Did Rork want to speak with me?"

Marciá batted her hazel eyes again. "Well, no, not really, sir."

Sighing with displeasure, Mac sat on the edge of the table and folded his arms. "Marciá, let's try this once more. Why did Rork ask you to hold this report, and why did Collins fly down to Halifax? I want it all, from the beginning, eh?"

Though averse to tattling, Marciá was undeniably mad at Wendy because she knew the row started over some female. It wasn't the first time. Slowly, she unraveled the tale. "This morning, after I came in early to type all those long reports for you, Commander Rork phoned and asked if I could hold that particular report till this afternoon. Truth is, Cap'n Mac, you never had a chance to read it before now anyway."

He motioned with his hand. "Keep talking . . ."

"Well, Commander Rork told me damages at the tavern had been covered and, if you'd read the whole report, sir, you'd know no one was arrested and he said it really wasn't entirely Wendy's fault—"

"Nor was it NOT his fault," Mac interjected.

"Leftenant Commander Rork said some big French guys came in the tavern and, well, the waitress, who apparently belonged to one of 'em, happened to be sitting on Wendy's lap and the fracas began." She shrugged.

"Besides, what the Frogs did to Wendy won't be half as bad as what I intend to do to him. Sir."

Exasperated, Mac forcefully exhaled. "Okay, that explains the tavern. Why did *Ice Sheila* fly to Halifax?"

"Part business, picking up plane parts, partly so Commander Rork would be able to visit your cousin, Ellie, you know, sir . . ."

"Yes, I know she's my cousin. Is there another partly?"

"Ah . . . to meet a freighter just in from Australia—"

"To pick up a supply of Foster's Lager," Mac finished. "I should've known."

"Commander Rork said *Ice Sheila* will fly him back here, then Wendy and his crew will go to Torbay and be up and flyin' tomorrow mornin' bright-eyed and bushy-tailed."

"The only thing Wendy will ever be bright-eyed and bushy-tailed for is his own wake. Providing someone else buys the booze. You're sure Irish is with him?"

"Yes, sir, that's what he told me. Irish seems like a sweet fella, especially for stickin' by Wendy on this one."

"Marciá, don't you mean lying for Wendy?"

"I don't think he was lying, Cap'n Mac. But you know Wendy, sir, he tends to wear trouble like a campaign ribbon."

Mac shook his head. "You're too damned good for that man, Marciá. Too damned good."

The phone jangled. Marciá bolted out the door. Having Mac notice her when she was teasing him was one thing. Mac's interrogative glare was quite another. Marciá grabbed the receiver. Hearing a friendly voice, she sighed. *The Mounties to my rescue.* "Cap'n," she called, "it's long distance from Nova Scotia. Liz wants a word with you, sir."

⊕

VICTORIA GENERAL
HALIFAX, NOVA SCOTIA
WEDNESDAY

Willem Krigeshaald slowly pushed the metal cart with the wobbly wheel down the corridor as much to give him support as make him look as if he belonged in the white smock of an orderly. He kept repeating, "You can kill her. You can . . . you—No, I can't. I'll get myself killed. No, no," he argued with himself, "You can do this. You can and will. How hard can it possibly be anyway? Think of all the other difficult and nauseating things you've accomplished in the past."

His argument crumbled. His hands shook. He couldn't think. He halted at the room of the woman named Ellie Greer. JAEGER had always called her STARLING. And JAEGER wanted STARLING dead.

Willy hadn't wanted to know her name. It made this abhorrent business much too personal. But the only way to find her room was to know her name. Sweet talk in bed with Cyndi gave him the cake he needed. Hot cuzzy merely put icing on Cyndi's piece of it, not to mention release some of his pent up tension.

Wiping his sweaty palms on the smock, Willy listened at the door. Silence. *She must be alone. The willowy blonde's left.* As smoothly as his shaking hands allowed, he opened the door and peered in to the room. Ellie's back was to him. *What if she isn't asleep? What if she's merely gazing out the window? What if she's a light sleeper—*

She stirred. Hastily closing the door, Willy sagged against the wall. A bass drum thudded in his chest. Grabbing a pitcher, he tipped it up, gulping a mouthful. Icy water sloshed out the sides, running down his neck, soaking the smock.

The drink helped calm his mind, not his shakes. *I'll bring her the water. If she's awake, I'll chat while I fill her pitcher, then come back later. If she's sleeping . . .*

CHAPTER TEN

At the nurse's station, Karney set the wrapped package on the counter and waited for the plump brunette to look up. With her ivory blouse pulled rather taught across her generous bosom, he was reminded of a spinnaker sail straining against a stiff wind. Her name tag read Cyndi.

When she glanced up, Karney nodded. "Could you please give me the room number for Ellie Greer?"

With a flutter of dark eyelashes, the receptionist rose from her chair. "You'll need to sign the register, please." She turned it toward him. As he signed, she smugly asked, "American, aren't cha?"

Nodding, he turned the book back around.

Cyndi read his name and licked her lips. "Do you want me to escort you upstairs, Commander Rork? It's easy to get lost."

There was enough "come on" in her voice to make him realize her offer was a bit more than mere politeness. "No, thanks," Karney said, hoping his tone would suffice as a brush-off. "Just the number, please."

She sat to check the directory with her bosom pressed against her folded arm. The deep chasm of her cleavage was presented to his gaze; he didn't bother to look away.

Dreamily, Cyndi gazed up at him. "It says she's in room three-oh-four."

Before he could leave, she stood and grasped his sleeve and said, "If your lady friend's asleep, we could go to my flat for some moist cheesecake, eh? I'll be off duty in about ten minutes." She again licked her lips.

Though Karney refrained from rolling his eyes, he groaned inwardly. *Why's this gal coming onto me like this? Is the war atmosphere loosening women's morals a notch or two and unbuttoning their blouses a bit lower? It could get annoying.*

Leaning on the counter, Karney let his gaze wander back to the canyon between her breasts. "Tell you what, Cyndi . . ." Her eyes gleamed expectantly. "Before you go home, why don't you go dump a ward full of bedpans. Maybe that'll clarify my opinion of your offer. I came here for Ellie's sake. Not your lust."

Karney picked up Ellie's Christmas package. Taking the stairs two at a time, he wanted to put as much distance between himself and Cyndi as humanly possible.

HRADCANY CASTLE
PRAGUE, CZECHOSLOVAKIA
WEDNESDAY

"*Herr Obersturmbannführer* von Zeitz," articulated the aide-de-camp in a manner of pompous authority, "*Obergruppenführer* Heydrich will see you now, sir."

Lieutenant Colonel Joachim von Zeitz stood. Straightening his sharply creased black uniform, he ignored the aide and marched into Reinhard Heydrich's office. A violin concerto played softly on the radio. One meter in front of the general's highly polished desk, von Zeitz came to attention, clicked his heels and snapped a crisp Nazi salute.

"*Sieg Heil, Mein Obergruppenführer.*"

General Reinhard Tristan Eugen Heydrich stood and

returned the salute just as smartly. Stepping around his desk, Heydrich extended a slim, rather effeminate hand. "Glad you could stop by, Joachim. It has been a long while since we've chatted face to face."

Taking his hand, von Zeitz felt immense pleasure in the presence of such a great man. Heydrich represented many things von Zeitz wished to emulate. Utmost his level of power.

The phone jangled. "Excuse me, Joachim, I believe this is a call for which I have been waiting." Heydrich picked up the handset.

Joachim considered his superior. The graceful hand he had shaken could as easily play an impassioned violin serenata as fly a fighter or sign orders of execution for those posing a threat to the Reich—real or imagined: Jews, priests, clergy, primary-school teachers to college professors, journalists, communists, abortionists, Freemasons and political malcontents, aristocrats or homosexuals. Heydrich's logical and harsh tactics, combined with a wholly unsympathetic heart, earned him the name "Blond Beast" from his own men. The Czechs called him the "Butcher of Prague."

As Deputy *Reichsprotektor* of Bohemia and Moravia, Heydrich answered to only *der Führer*, Adolf Hitler, and *Reichsführer* Heinrich Himmler. Heydrich's genuine power lay in his position as Chief of the RSHA—*Reichssicherheitshauptamt*—Reich Central Security Office. He was the ravenous spider of an omnipotent web: SIPO—Security Police; KRIPO—Criminal Police; *GESTAPO*—Secret State Police and the SD—Security Service of the *Reichsführer*.

Shortened from *Geheime Staatspolizei* to simply *Gestapo* by a postal clerk, this agency investigated internal affairs, dealing harshly with all enemies of the Third Reich. Their smaller cousin, the SD, or *Sicherheitsdienst*, was originally formed by Heydrich to track down internal political opposition much like the *Gestapo*.

The SD was comprised of academics studying not only political matters, but issues of economic, religious and social import. They explored everything from the effect of communism abroad to Judaic influence on economics, the doctrine of papal supremacy as well as numerous implied philosophical threats to Nazi Germany. A sanctified, far more lethal contingent—to which Joachim von Zeitz belonged—adhered to the struggle against Germany's hardline enemies: saboteurs, counterfeiters, intelligence networks and any hardcore criminals causing harm to the State with illegal activities.

Joachim von Zeitz played a key role in many of the Blond Beast's schemes. Though his machinations were often known only to Heydrich, von Zeitz was a rung or two below his champion as they climbed the blood-slick ladder to Nazi triumph.

Setting the handset into the cradle, Heydrich met Joachim's pensive gaze and resumed their conversation, "*Ja*, it's been a long time since we've chatted."

"*Ja*, Reinhard, it has. To be precise, I've not been back since our little clean up foray into Russia last summer." A smile tilted von Zeitz's thin mustache as he recalled the bloodbath in the Soviet Union.

Heydrich motioned toward an informal grouping of chairs. In a somewhat high-pitched voice, he observed, "We've no time for idle chit-chat anymore. Things are neither as pleasant nor as easy as our initial invasion of Russia had been." With a short, Billy goat laugh, Heydrich added, "I've flown so few sorties lately, I feel as if I fly by the seat of my jodhpurs—with a hole in them at that."

While von Zeitz chuckled at his superior's humor, Heydrich poured two generous portions of cognac. Taking the proffered snifter, von Zeitz discreetly asked, "How have you and your lovely Lina been? Does she enjoy Prague?"

"We're well, thank you." Sitting, Heydrich's narrow-set, light-blue eyes met von Zeitz's shrewd gaze. "Lina enjoys the charms of Prague immensely, but it will be the death of me, yet." He smiled grimly. "Damn Czechs never had it so good."

The two men sipped their cognac in companionable silence.

Smiling, von Zeitz contemplated the esteem he held for this man and Heinrich Himmler. The styles of Himmler and Heydrich differed but they made an impressive team: Himmler dreamed of a glorious Aryan race; while Heydrich was a pragmatist bent on eradicating all opposition to the supremacy of Nazi Germany. Himmler was the play's director, creating the actors and their roles, while Heydrich produced results by clearing the stage and made sure the performance ran with brutal efficiency.

Melding facets of both Himmler and Heydrich into his own character, von Zeitz maintained his own harsh creed. When the careers of von Zeitz and Heydrich initially brought them together, they shared ambitions and a cunning, not obvious to any casual observation. The two men's objectives, however, were painfully driven home as their enemies were stomped beneath their black jackboots—if any were even left alive.

Though von Zeitz took the more strenuous role of covert enforcer, Heydrich held the complex task of bureaucrat. War's fiery crucible forged a strong bond of respect between the two men.

Raising his glass to preface his words, von Zeitz asked, "Why did you need to speak with me, Reinhard?"

Heydrich swirled his cognac. "We have a mutual problem," then took a sip. "A mop-up operation after Wolf Gündestein's retirement."

Casually crossing his legs, von Zeitz smiled. Retirement was their euphemism for the elder man's assassination.

"Do you happen to recall Eugen Ulmstein?" Heydrich asked. "My scheduling clerk," he further reminded.

"Mousy fellow, bottle-glass specs always sliding down his nose, worked out the liquidation timetables for our

Einsatzgruppen of Jews and political prisoners in the Ukraine and Belorussia?"

"Yes, well apparently the fellow's more rabbit than mouse. He took a holiday last week and vanished. My agents tracked him to Lisbon, from whence he hopped away to his ultimate destination of London."

Analyzing this news, von Zeitz knew Ulmstein could identify him as a double agent. He told Heydrich, "To be precise, *Mein Herr*, that rabbit will soon be of no use to MI-6 except as an unlucky rabbit's foot."

"Precisely my objective for you, Joachim. I have a conference coming up in Wannsee related to this Jewish matter. I will rest easier knowing you're handling this little problem."

"Not to worry, sir, I'll take personal care to skin this hare."

Raising his snifter, Heydrich said, "I've no doubts you'll succeed, Joachim. Precisely why you command our covert field operations."

Returning the toast, von Zeitz offered, "To *WIRKUNG FLUT*." Though von Zeitz considered Operation Flood Heydrich's brainchild, it was a challenge and would become a plume of honor for him when they succeeded. *FLUT* would not only increase Germany's territory but also the Reich's domination of the world.

After a long, satisfying drink of the exquisite cognac, Joachim von Zeitz asked, "By the way, have you located *Hauptsturmführer* Todt?"

"*Ja*, Serle Todt's returning to Berlin from Stalingrad even as we speak. That was he who called. He won't arrive until late tomorrow but I will brief him on our expectations."

"I trust you'll tell him not to unpack his winter gear," von Zeitz said, grinning. "To be precise, Greenland's weather is equivalent to the Eastern Front."

"True, but for now, Todt will take a long-overdue leave to thaw out his toes." Heydrich's Billy goat laugh rang out again. "Undoubtedly, Todt will also need to thaw out that frozen clangor between his legs. If he even recalls its use."

In his own high-pitched chortle, von Zeitz assured, "No need to worry there, *Mein Herr*. Serle never forgets the needs of his *Schwanz*."

After a brief chuckle, Heydrich became serious. "Joachim, on that note, please do not let your *Schwanz* lead to any fatal mistakes over STARLING. That little beauty of a bird can sing a tune to blind any man, much like the sirens of ancient myth. Use her or abuse her, I don't care. But if she poses a threat: pay special attention to retiring her."

A sneer tilted von Zeitz's mustache. "Orders have been issued to our BLUE FOX in Halifax to eliminate the little STARLING. This is something of a test to see how he fares."

Thoughtfully sipping his cognac, von Zeitz secretly hoped BLUE FOX would fail. BLUE FOX was not a favorite in Joachim's cadre.

VICTORIA GENERAL
HALIFAX, NOVA SCOTIA
WEDNESDAY

Willy Krigeshaald took another slow, deep breath. The trembling in his hands subsided. His heart beat more calmly. Formulating a plan had helped—he never liked doing things haphazardly.

Again pushing open the door, Willy observed the lady sleeping on the bed. Making his way closer, he stole around the end of the bed toward the side table and her water pitcher. She remained still.

Willy couldn't hear her breathing over his own heartbeat.

Now that I'm here, up close . . . I can't do this. She may have been a nefarious spy but she's so pale and ill. How can I possibly smother the life from someone so vulnerable? It'd be like killing a baby bird.

In Greenland, Willy never obtained a hunter's instinct for killing like his younger brother, never cultivated a taste for blood. I would never have survived in the Arctic, much less thrive in it like Hans does. *So why am I here now, in this room, hovering over this woman, with murderous intent in mind? Though God knows it's not in my heart.*

Grabbing her pitcher, Willy raced out the door. Hands again shaking, he poured water from the large pitcher into hers. Water slopped onto the floor. His shaking grew worse as he envisioned placing a pillow over her exquisite face, the struggle when she could not breathe, her hands grasping—

"Son . . . you okay?"

The deep voice startled him from his panic. Willy turned to face a dark haired officer, as tall but huskier than himself. He had eyes of an intense blue-gray. They held nothing but concern.

"Ye—yes, sir," Willy stammered, "I—I'm all right, really."

"You trying to convince me or yourself?" the officer asked with a smile. He then suggested, "Why don't you sit down."

"I—I can't, sir. I have to refill the patients' water jugs."

The man nodded, then gestured toward the woman's room. "You want me to take Mrs. Greer's water in to her?"

Willy felt his nerve crumble like an ice bridge. Thrusting the pitcher at the man, he blurted, "Thanks," and pushed the cart away. Glancing back, Willy decided: *Someone else can do JAEGER's dirty work. I'm truly not a coldhearted murderer. I never will be.*

⊕

Shutting the door, Karney paused inside Ellie's room to set his things on a wooden chair and remove his coat and cap. Lit by a shaft of sunlight angling through the partially open curtains, he could see Ellie slept soundly. He heard music softly playing from the radio. Stepping closer, the desire to kiss her and wake her from the nightmare which had brought them to this place in time was overpowering.

Though she's a Sleeping Beauty, I'm certainly not her Prince Charming capable of waking her from this painful reality.

The slow drip of the IV was a metronome to Ellie's life. Her breathing seemed relaxed. Seeing her so peaceful, yet ashen, Karney did not want to wake her. *I'll just leave the box and go.*

Cat-footing back across the room, he fetched the water and Christmas box. The pitcher went on the bed stand beside a radio. The box he set out of her reach on a small shelf below the windowsill. Leaning the envelope against it, it slid off. He replaced it. It refused to stay. Finally, he stuck it beneath the shiny green ribbon. Turning to take one last look at her, he found Ellie watching him.

In a voice sultry from sleep, she said, "I thought St. Nick wore red robes with white-fur trim and black boots?"

Caught red-handed, Karney grinned sheepishly. When she returned his smile, her eyes lit up. She evidently felt better than appearances indicated. Pulling a chair up to the bed, he clasped her hand in his and said, "Besides red not being my best color, I'd probably be mistaken for a practice target by Coastal Command."

Ellie giggled, setting off a bout of coughs. Karney poured a glass of water and slid his arm under her shoulders to prop her up. "Pretty sad," he said pensively, "when the only comment coming to mind is: 'Seems like we've been here before,' doesn't it?"

"Aye," she agreed between sips, "but this isn't *Zealous* and we need to fix me bein' such a pansy."

"You're no pansy," he disagreed. "You're a rose."

She finished drinking, then grinned. "Thanks, Irish, you're too sweet." He started to lay her back down. "No, please, help me with the pillows?"

Assisting her, he rather anxiously asked, "Should you be sitting up like this? Your doctor might not approve."

"I don't care. I'm just bloody well tired of starin' at the ceilin'. They need to paint a picture up there or somethin'."

He glanced up, then shook his head realizing there was nothing to look at. Changing the subject, he asked, "Do I detect these white-washed walls blanched the color of a Highland lilt out of your voice?"

Ellie rolled her eyes. "I accepted a post at the garrison. I'll be on the radio and *my* uncle wants me to lose *my* Scottish burr," she said in exaggeration. "He's afraid the Canucks won't understand me."

With a nod, Karney said, "Please don't lose it around me though. I find it quite endearing."

Smiling rather coyly, she said, "Should I be askin' how you be farin'? Or wonder what the other fella looks like?"

"What—" he started to ask, then touched his bruised cheekbone with a split-knuckled hand. "Oh, this . . ."

"Aye, that." Ellie grinned. "And that." She lightly touched his split lip, then his scuffed knuckles. "And these."

"While trying to convince a pilot to fly me to Halifax, he sorta got us into a wee donnybrook last night with a buncha Frenchies. I helped, ah . . . bail him out."

"And he repaid the favor by gettin' you to Halifax?"

"Yeah, something like that," he said with a lopsided grin. "But I didn't come all this way to talk about me. How're you doing?"

Unsure how to answer, she stared at Karney a second before responding. "Let's just say, I've been better."

"You'll be better again, sweetheart. It'll just take time."

"Aye, you keep tellin' me that." She closed her eyes for a second, then said in a defiant tone, "Truth is, you told me it'd be God's time. Well, Irish-dear, I be thinkin' God's bloody well late."

"Nah," Karney softly countered, "God may not always be there when you want Him, but He's always on time.

That's another thing Gramma always told me. And Gram was seldom, if ever, wrong. 'Sides," Karney squeezed Ellie's hand, "God doesn't always answer prayers how we think He should, 'cause we don't always know what's best."

Ellie started to ask how losing so many loved ones could be best but knew it wasn't a question anyone could answer. Instead, she took a ragged breath, asking, "So, what did Father Christmas, in the guise of a Yank Coastie, bring me?"

"Santa's not at liberty to say." Karney grinned wickedly, feeling more than a little mischievous. "You can't open it till tomorrow."

"Oh, Karney, that's na fair. Since I'm nae gonna promise to be good, will you stick around to make sure I don't open it early?"

"If I stay," he began, then fell into the emerald depths of her eyes, "I'm afraid I'd soon be the one misbehavin'." Hearing how brazen he sounded, he back-peddled, "Ah, I mean, I wish I could stay, but I'm not supposed to be here at all. If I'm not in St. John's by late this afternoon, your big Canadian cousin'll hang me from the nearest yardarm along with one cantankerous Aussie pilot."

"Mac? How do you know Mac?"

"It's a long story that'll sink ships if I loosen my lips."

"Ships sink all the time and if I know Mac your knowin' him is more than a mere thank you for rescuin' me. Did he freeze you into this Ice Pact deal?"

"You know Mac pretty well. But I can't answer more than I already have, angel. But I still have to leave in a bit, and there's better things to discuss than the war."

Nodding weakly, Ellie turned her face away from him.

Karney gently caressed Ellie's silken cheek. "What's wrong, *meu anjo*?"

"Nothin'," she sniffled, forcing a smile. "You best go. I'd nae be wantin' you to be gettin' into trouble. Mac can be a bloody tyrant if provoked," she said, hurriedly brushing an errant tear away.

"You expect me to leave when you're crying?" He shook his head. "Not a chance till you tell me what's wrong."

"You've already done so much for me, Irish. I just . . ."

Squeezing her hand, Karney softly prompted, "Just what?"

"I think the reason I've been sleepin' so much is I bloody hate bein' alone . . ." Her tears spilled over.

Karney sat on the bed, pulling her into his arms. "Shhh, *meu anjo*, it's all right . . . I'm right here and part of me's been with you all along. Doubt anyone told you, but before your uncle flew you outta Argentia, you gotta blood transfusion from me. I'm one of those oh-negative types who can donate to anyone. And it was you who needed my blood."

He held Ellie, stroking her hair, cherishing this moment, especially knowing he might not see her for a long time. *If I'm taking advantage of this situation, so be it. The opportunity to embrace her is one I definitely do not wanna pass up.*

Sniffing, Ellie pulled back slightly to gaze up at his face and smiled. "That explains why sea chanteys have been runnin' through me head." With another sniffle, Ellie asked, "Dear sweet Irishman, do you still be totin' a handkerchief?"

"Always keep one handy for beautiful Scottish lasses," he said, tugging it from his back pocket.

Ellie daubed at her eyes. "I'm sorry, Karney. You come all this way, and all I do is weep like Scarlet O'Hara over Ashley what's-his-name in *Gone With The Wind*."

"If that makes me Rhett Butler, Scarlet," he said, falling into his very believable Clark Gable imitation, "then, frankly, my dear, I do give a damn." Pulling back, Karney cocked an eyebrow, "However, you still can't open your present till Christmas morning no matter how much you cry and carry on."

Ellie giggled, his facial expression chasing away her

gloom like a fleeting rain storm. The clouds, however, never quite cleared.

Opting to risk a longer stay, he got comfortable. Their conversation sailed over many subjects till he noticed the sun no longer slanted in through the curtains. He unwillingly stood and looked outside. "I better git or Collins will maroon me here. On the other hand, I'd still be here with you. But on the other, other hand," he tilted his head in thought, "I'll pay hell trying to explain all this to my CO and Mac."

Nodding, Ellie took his hand. "What about New Year's Eve?"

He hesitated. "*Anjo*, I won't be back. But when I do return, let's celebrate by painting whatever town we happen to be in red or pink or green and talk or dance the night away. Okay?"

Again nodding, she declared, "I better be out of here soon or I guarantee I'll be as grouchy as a bloody ol' she bear."

"Don't rush things, angel. 'Sides, once you open your gift, tomorrow, Mama Bear won't be quite so alone anymore."

"Then let me open it now, while you're here."

"Nothing doing, doll." He kissed her cheek. "I'm just sorry I won't be with you on Christmas Day."

Ellie caressed his clean-shaven jaw line. Before she lost her nerve, she curled her hand round his neck, pulled him closer and kissed him fully on the lips, far longer than she intended.

Bracing his arm across her on the bed, Karney fully savored the warmth of her lips, the sweet tenderness of her mouth.

Resting back, Ellie softly wished, "Happy Christmas, my Irish dearest. Thank you for all you've done." She gazed into his eyes that sparkled like a sun-drenched ocean.

Caught off base and reeling from her kiss, Karney was at a loss for words. After a moment, he grinned. "You know, sweetie, that's the best Christmas gift I ever got. Did you peek at my wish list to Santa?"

"Nae, but 'tis all I've to offer since I've nae been out to shop for a proper gift to give a gentleman such as yerself."

"Who needs store bought doo-ma-jigs when I have you?"

"Now, I didna say you could have me. Just the kiss." Though feeling shy, she said, "Leastwise, nae till we're together again."

"Then I guess your kiss will have to tide me over."

Sensing his reluctance to leave, Ellie firmly said, "Please, go, Irish, or I'll start cryin' again and you will be late."

Nodding, he continued to hold her hand, stepped back as he gently assured her in Gaelic, *"Giorra cabhair Dé ná an doras,* my darling, and Merry Christmas. I'll be back soon enough, angel."

Trying to decipher his words, she blew him a kiss. A smile again lit his face. It was still there as he slipped through the door. With its closing, the Gaelic translation slowly came back to her. It was a saying her mother often said when she was a little girl: God's help is nearer than the door.

She understood. Karney meant for her to keep prayer a close part of her life in his absence. God was in her heart as was Irish.

Prayer returned hope. Prayers have brought Irish into my life. But might it be a flight of fancy? Or infatuation? Can love lift my spirits? She slapped the bedcovers and chided herself, "Stop thinkin' of love. You barely know the man. Love notwithstanding, Karney's a bloody good kisser."

Turning up the radio Liz had brought her, Ellie heard the song, *I Know Why* by Glenn Miller. The honeyed voice of Paula Kelly and The Four Modernaires sang. Though she liked the song, she turned the radio back down. She sighed not wanting to hear of robins singing in December or stars on her ceiling. *But that would give me somethin' to look at.*

Sagging back against her pillow, she muttered, "Even the radio's conspirin' against me." Then the candy-cane striped box caught her attention. "I never did promise Irish I'd nae open it." Swinging her legs off the bed, the restraining IV tube halted her. "Bloody hell!"

Ellie contented herself with playing her grandmother's game of guessing what it held—like figuring out who posted a letter by reading the postmark. The possibilities created the pleasure. And with this gift from Karney, the possibilities seemed absolutely endless.

ICE SHEILA
EN ROUTE TO ST. JOHN'S, NEWFOUNDLAND
WEDNESDAY

Roughly shaking Karney's shoulder, the young navigator practically yelled in his ear to be heard over the incessant drone of the Sunderland's engines, "C'manda Rork?"

Opening a bleary eye, Karney stared at the Aussie flight sergeant, wondering why the guy had disturbed his catnap—sleep in the military being sacrosanct, never to be violated needlessly.

With the frank smile of a high school kid, Jamie Malcolm answered his unstated question, "We're almost to St. John's, sir. Wendy wanted me to wake ya. It's late, and he can't waste time gettin' you ashore."

Stretching into a yawn, Karney rubbed his sand-scratched eyes, then rolled up to a sitting position on his bunk in the lower aft compartment. "Is Wendy just gonna throw me overboard?"

The young man's face brightened. "He might give you a dingy with an oar if you ask real nice, mate."

"Swell," Karney moaned, peering out the porthole at the haze of a westering sun. He glanced at Jamie. "Why're we running late?"

"Head winds, sir. Front movin' down from the Arctic."

"Can you guys make Torbay before nightfall?"

"Doubtful but no worries. Wendy swears he can set down blindfolded. Least I know he can in the dark."

The aircrews' informality was cheering. It was also probably a lot easier to call Flying Officer Collins "Wendy" as he got promoted and demoted like a barometer's rise and fall.

Even if Wendy's ethics might be doubtful, his flying skills were not. According to Mac, there wasn't a plane built Wendy could not fly. On the way to Halifax, Wendy had given Karney a rundown on *Ice Sheila*. Though she wasn't a particularly elegant looking plane nor the fastest nor the most powerful, her double-deck structure had facilities equal to a hotel and enough firepower to hold her own against most any German fighter. And that included her ability to stay aloft for thirteen hours.

Heading out of the aft section, Karney shook his head. He wondered how Thomas "Dibbs" Dibley—the tail-gunner—managed to not feel like the loneliest guy on planet earth. Dibley's only means of communication was via his throat-mike. During a firefight, he might not even have that. *It sure ain't a position I'd like to fill.*

Climbing to the upper level, Karney passed the waist-gunner positions. To port was Wally Conway and on the starboard guns was Ron Fredrickson. Further forward were the flight engineer, Rick Glendenning; the wireless operator, Davey Grahe; navigator, Jamie Malcolm; and the ASV operator, George Painter, most affectionately known as Puddin for his pudgy build.

In the cockpit sat Wendy and copilot Mike Ahearn, while forward and below them in the nose-turret was the bomb-aiming position. During U-boat runs this held Al Pierce, dubbed "Arrow" after the Pierce Arrow automobile and his uncanny aim.

For their formidable grouping of machine-guns, Sunderland flying boats had earned the proud nickname from the German *Luftwaffe, Fliegende Stachelschwein,* meaning Flying Porcupine. And judging by the swastikas painted below the pilot's window, *Ice Sheila*'s ten-man crew utilized that firepower to her fullest extent.

During their initial meeting over dinner and darts at the French Arms Tavern, Karney got to know the crew fairly well. He considered them both friends and comrades. Though sometimes hard to figure out the Aussies, he knew they were in this war to the bitter end. Their easygoing manners camouflaged an eagerness for combat—whether with the enemy or anyone else who crossed them.

"Come on up here, Irish," Wendy called, motioning him the rest of the way up to the cockpit.

Karney perched behind Mike Ahearn's seat and the rack of flares for the Very pistol, a stubby gun that fired colored flares to signal ships or planes. Seeing Wendy's swollen cheek and the shiner ringing his eye, Karney figured a purple flare might well match his battered face.

Motioning toward the sunlit span of high clouds and the steel-gray sweep of sea beyond *Sheila*'s dog-like snout, Wendy yelled to him, "Ever been to St. John's?"

"Coupla times aboard *Zealous.* Never flew in though."

Hailed by the Harbor Authority, Wendy confirmed his landing instructions and banked the huge flying boat west, then informed Karney, "We'll be down quicker'an a croc' can piss, mate."

Amber rays turned St. John's snow to a mantle of gold dust and ruby shadows. Brightly painted houses marched up the steep streets like blocks from a child's toy box. Most were flat-fronted, trimmed with white and distinguished by the owner's choice of primary color. Smoke tried to curl up from their chimneys but was quickly snatched away by a cold breeze.

The Battery, crowned by Signal Hill to the north, stood sentinel over the Narrows, before opening into the mile-long harbor with small fishing trawlers and much larger ships of war. From St. John's Harbour, the quaint capitol city spread up and out into slightly wider streets with more houses, churches, schools and varied businesses.

As North America's easternmost port nestled in serenity, it was easy to forget a fierce struggle being waged against U-boats on a storm-tossed North Atlantic. Karney briefly closed his eyes in prayer that Newfoundland and Nova Scotia would remain free of the carnage of war with which Nazi Germany threatened the world.

Wendy swung the Sunderland around on final approach. White caps roughened the ice-slushed, slate water. "Hold on, mates."

Karney barely caught his canvas-web seat before *Ice Sheila*'s broad, single-step belly bashed onto the slush, then abruptly hurtled skyward. When Ahearn "reversed" the four Bristol Pegasus engines, they roared in defiance. Gravity slapped the flying boat back to the surface. Her speed dropped rapidly as she began to settle.

Once again a boat, *Ice Sheila* became an ungainly behemoth on the water. Even so, Karney felt more at home on the sea than buffeted by invisible air currents.

Returning to the cockpit, he heard Wendy's vehement cussing, "Piss on me koala! How the hell'd he know when we were comin'?"

Karney shared Wendy's dismay upon seeing Mac on the jetty. He stood with his dog Chelsea. Some officers wore eccentric uniforms; some smoked a pipe or cigar; others carried a riding crop; Mac had Chelsea beside him.

Idling the engines back, Wendy gave Karney a lopsided grin and offered, "Best of luck to ya with Cap'n Mac's firin' squad, mate. And give me regards to ol' St. Pete when ya get to heaven."

Karney back-slapped Wendy's arm. "I'd save you some wings, but where you're headed, mate, you'll probably need a pitchfork."

With a nasty chuckle, Wendy groaned, "Eh, get offa me ruddy plane, ya bloody Mick." Karney obliged.

A Canadian seaman rowed out to pick up Karney. He

barely had a chance to sit on the thwart when he heard *Ice Sheila* power-up for take-off.

Nearing the quay, Karney saw Mac's eyes were hard jade. Chelsea, however, was glad to see him. Her front paws did an elated two step as her tail feathers swept the wharf clear of snow. Snapped fingers ended her elation at seeing her new friend.

Bumping the rowboat against the jetty, the baby-faced RCN sailor tied it up as Karney stepped onto solid ground. *Is Mac more pissed about the tavern's fight report that Marciá held up or our illicit flight down to Halifax? Probably both.*

Echoing the Aussies' hail, Karney greeted, "G'day, Mac."

Mac's countenance remained as hard as concrete. "Dare call me 'mate', Irish, and I'll throw your ass in the drink, eh?"

Without another word, Mac turned on his heel and marched up the jetty. Mac gave Chelsea no prompt, but she fell in at his side, allowing herself a quick backward glance at Karney. He swore she looked sympathetic.

In two long strides, Karney matched cadence with Mac. Hearing the straining Pegasus engines pull *Ice Sheila* from the harbor and hurl her skyward, neither man looked.

Hiking along the harbor edge, a chill breeze in their faces, Karney glanced over at Mac. Before starting up the city streets, he lightly gripped Mac's arm to stop him. "Look, Mac," Karney said, "I don't need this kinda crap from you. You're not my CO—"

"On that bloody note you're wrong." The sunset lent Mac's eyes a wicked glow. "I now am your CO and you damned well would've known it had you not gone traipsing off to Halifax on a whim, eh? Make no mistake, Mr. Rork, your cover-up for Wendy has also been duly noted."

Gulping down his pride, Karney defended, "I cleared this junket with Commander Wharton two days ago. He said nothing about a change of command. I was, however, outta line for asking Marciá to sit on that report. I apologize, Captain MacCalister. It was wrong of me to make such presumptions."

"You're damned bloody right about that, Irish," Mac snapped. He resumed his march up the narrow street more suited to sturdy mountain goats than people. With a whimper, Chelsea trotted after him.

To again match strides with Mac, Karney took a quick jog-step. He didn't want to lose the captain in this unfamiliar seaside town.

More amicably, Mac said, "You've not committed some mortal sin, though, Irish. I'm still Mac. You're just one in a string of chums, who come to that Aussie's defense out of blind loyalty." A pace more, he asked, "Despite Wendy's charm, how's Ellie?"

Karney shrugged. "She's holding her own. Medication plays hell with her emotions, though. Happy one minute, crying the next. Guess it's only natural after losing her baby."

Nodding, Mac turned up another street, its steep way paved by cobblestones of a finer, more peaceful era. His pace eased.

Karney wondered: *Is this the extent of my firing squad?* Further along, aromas of food grew overwhelming. He tried to ignore his rumbling gut. "How'd you know when *Ice Sheila* would get in?"

A smile lit Mac's face. "Simple math. Recall the pretty blonde lass you held the door for when you were coming out of VG?"

Remembering the cutie in a red coat with long, wheat-colored hair and bright blue eyes, he said, "How could I forget her?"

"That was Liz, my wife. She noticed the polite, handsome guy, but didn't know you were *that* Coastie till Ellie told her you'd just left. You were definitely their topic of conversation. Liz called a bit ago, not tattling, just letting me know she approved."

"Approved?" Karney asked suspiciously. "Of what?"

"Ellie's new flame." Mac chuckled. "Hell, man, Liz already has you two married with three kids, eh?"

"Christ sakes, Mac, Ellie's a striking charmer— extremely so—but if she's even remotely attracted to me, it's probably 'cause I pulled her out of the drink. It doesn't mean she loves me, even if—" Karney shut up.

Mac stopped, his look insinuating that he knew Karney's next words. But Karney would and could only speculate if Mac thought Ellie loved him back.

Motioning behind him, Mac said, "We're here."

Karney glanced around the tall Canadian to a long run of stairs, hugging a warehouse. "Your office is up there?"

"No, but the Crow's Nest Tavern is," Mac said.

"I thought we were headed for your office?"

Mac simply countered, "Aren't you hungry?"

"Yeah. Starved. But I don't have any dough left to—"

"No worries, mate," Mac said, mocking the Aussies as he began climbing the stairs. "Tab's on me tonight."

Karney simply asked, "Why?"

When Mac paused to glance back at Karney, Chelsea bounded up the stairs like she was home. "Let's just say, un-pleasantries set better on a full stomach."

Mac continued on up, leaving Karney to stare after him. Halfway, Mac again paused. "Though I've never counted 'em myself, they tell me there are fifty-nine steps to the top. They'll not get any fewer with you gawking at the lot of 'em, eh?"

With no more explanation as to what un-pleasantries he referred, Mac continued up the span of stairs. Chelsea waited for them on the landing.

Muttering to himself, Karney started up the long flight of rickety stairs, "Sweet Mother of Jesus, what the hell am I getting into this time?"

⊕

Roman Catholic Basilica Cathedral of St. John the Baptist towers over downtown St. John's, Newfoundland.

Lower Battery fishing community located on the opposite shore of St. John's Harbour from the downtown area.

U799 rising from Neptune's depths . . .

D.D.O'Lander

CHAPTER ELEVEN

U799
DENMARK STRAIT
WED: 24 DEC 41

Sleek and sinister, the prototype U-boat rose from the hostile depths of Neptune's realm. Despite her massive size of more than 350 feet with a submerged displacement of 3,205 tons, the German submarine skimmed like a ghost along the ice shelf as speed was reduced. Seawater promptly formed icicles on cables rising from the net-cutter—wholly impractical for its purpose—at the bow back to the conning tower and aft to the stern. In mere seconds *U799*'s mottled Arctic camouflage paint rimed with frozen brine beneath the shimmering Aurora Borealis.

The emblem of an Arctic fox, within the curve of an upturned horseshoe, gazed with shrewd eyes upon *U799*'s awesome array of weaponry. Even the U-boat's stepped deck design was unique. Fore and aft, three different sizes of multiple *Flak* guns were strategically placed for maximum firepower. On the foredeck, enclosed in a clamshell to reduce undersea drag, was their 12.7cm *Schiffskanone*. Within *U799*'s hull she carried her most lethal weapon: torpedoes or "eels," a total of thirty-six with twenty-four to be used by *U799* and twelve available for other U-boats. Each torpedo measured more than twenty inches in diameter and twenty-three feet long, fired from four forward and two stern tubes—double other U-boats.

Though *U799* carried huge tanks for fuel, oil and ballast, she was streamlined for speed and presented a very low profile. With a power-plant double other U-boats, *U799*'s top surface speed was 23.3 knots and submerged almost ten. Despite variations in her range, specifications put her at 22,500 nautical miles on the surface at twelve knots and 105 miles submerged at about four knots. If ideal circumstances ever allowed, *U799* could sail back and forth between Lorient, France, and the Panama Canal about five times without refueling. That trial run would doubtless never happen.

Before *U799*'s forward momentum stopped, four *Kriegsmariners* scrambled from the tower hatch, their sea boots a bare whisper on the waffle plates—grating for the central ventilation duct—on which they stood. Raising binoculars to their eyes, they scanned ice-bound Greenland and searched Denmark Strait for enemy ships. The only signs of life from these bundled, silent men were frozen puffs of exhaled air and their slow, methodical motion.

Chief Warrant Officer Hermann Schefflein, Officer of the Watch, joined them. Bracing himself between the spray deflector and the retracted periscopes housing, he hopped up on the half-meter-high rail with ease despite his bulky winter gear. Though the rail dug into the cork-lined soles of his sea boots, Schefflein preferred this to the lookout steps. With his shorter stature, standing on the rail was the perfect height to see over the spray deflector and allow him to brace himself.

In addition to the periscope housing, within the core of the bridge, were the main compass housing and a Target Bearing Transmitter or TBT. The TBT aimed the torpedoes during surface runs and had a removable support and special binoculars fitted on the pedestal to relay targeting data to the attack computer. The computer was basically a calculator which worked more efficiently than a crewman.

Right now, the TBT had been stripped to a two-pin, open-sight aiming device.

The inner wall of the spray deflector was lined with thin-wooden strips to keep men from freezing to the metal surface. The voice tube, hand-held searchlights, bullhorn, binoculars and a slot for *FuMO30* Radar—a retractable "mattress" antenna were also found here. The *FuMO* was the latest in a series of radar, designed to locate enemy ships. But no matter how good the set, U-boats sat too low in the water. In heavy weather, U-boat lookouts could often sight an enemy convoy before radar received a glimmer of their presence. Other aspects of *U799*'s design were exceptional, including the fact her designer had been ordained to become her captain.

Lieutenant Jakob Gündestein Prüsche, as spare as a sailing ship's mast and slightly stooped from backache, painful legacy from a brutal depth charge attack, climbed onto the icy bridge at a leisurely pace. Chief Warrant Officer Schefflein made more room.

Prüsche nodded to him and solemnly greeted, "*Oberfeldwebel.*"

Schefflein knew his skipper was in pain. When *Kaleu* Prüsche's back felt good, he seldom stood on such formality. Concerned, Schefflein replied in kind, "*Guten Morgen, Kapitänleutnant.*"

Despite the stagnant confines below decks, Prüsche didn't like this Arctic cold, it bit into his spine like shark's teeth sinking into human flesh. Turning up the wolf's fur collar of his gray-leather coat, he asked in a low voice, "Contact yet?"

"*Nein, Kaleu,*" Schefflein said, returning to the short form of *Kapitänleutnant.*

Frigid gusts ruffled Jakob Prüsche's dark hair. With his elbows resting on the spray deflector, he raised his binoculars to scan the eerily illuminated Denmark Strait around to the luminescent snows of Greenland. His every movement calm, methodical, precise.

At thirty-three, Prüsche was one of the oldest U-boat captains in the U-boat fleet. He was also the best. From the Arctic to the South Atlantic the skill and luck of the "Ice Fox" had grown legendary. It was a proud distinction Jakob Prüsche shunned. Sooner or later, if the horseshoe tipped, his luck might run out.

He felt Germany's horseshoe had tipped the day Hitler declared war on the United States, barely four days after Pearl Harbor. America's entry into the war spelled disaster for the Axis Powers: Nazi Germany, Fascist Italy and Imperial Japan.

Isolated by broad oceans, the mighty industrial nation had had a stick viciously thrust into its copious hive. Like angry hornets, American forces would swarm out of their prosperous ports, fortified and determined. In Japan's audacious attack, Great Britain and Russia had gained a staunch ally no longer bound by isolationists.

Jakob Prüsche should know. His wife had been born in America and lived there until her father's diplomatic transfer returned the family to Germany. Cynara's astute memories of American culture gave Prüsche a unique insight into his enemy's ideals.

The hues of the rippling Northern Lights shifted, transforming Prüsche's worry to a sigh. He knew the fates of war were fickle; Germany's future along with them. It was a destiny his Uncle Wolf foretold long before Adolf Hitler's rise to power.

Pensively, Prüsche again surveyed the dense pack ice between *U799* and the distant, unseen granite shore. A shiver, having little or nothing to do with these sub-zero temperatures, ran up his spine. He felt uneasy pursuing this particular venture with so many variables, both known and unpredictable.

The tail end of the *Fahneneid* allegiance Prüsche had sworn to Adolf Hitler in August 1934 still echoed in his mind: "to Adolf Hitler, *Führer* of the German Reich and People, and the Supreme Commander of the Armed

Forces." Jakob Prüsche trusted neither Hitler nor his megalomaniac henchmen. Truth be known, he never had. Jakob Prüsche's faith lay in *U799* and his men, as well as the man who had become known as "Admiral U-boats" to them: Karl Dönitz. A short man who carried several laudable nicknames.

Onkel Karl, as his *U-Bootwaffe Kriegsmariners* often thought of him, had developed plans far beyond Hitler's near-sighted view of naval warfare. The admiral had created the Wolf Packs—U-boats hunting enemy convoys *en mass*, the key to their success in the North Atlantic. Had Hitler given Admiral Dönitz the 300 U-boats he requested at war's onset—a war not to start for another five years—Z Plan could have severed Allied convoy routes. Prüsche also held Admiral Dönitz—*Die Grosse Löwe* or The Big Lion—in high regard because Dönitz understood the stakes.

As a senior officer, commanding his own prototype U-boat, Jakob Prüsche often operated outside the restraints put upon other officers. Since her commission, *U799* had overcome each and every obstacle. Wise in choosing his targets, Prüsche attacked with cunning and boldness, tempered by a degree of caution. *U799* seldom, if ever, missed her mark.

Too bad the course for my personal life was not so precise.

In the military, he'd been extremely blessed. In 1937, once his design had been approved, Blohm & Voss Shipyards were given the go-ahead to construct his prototype. Prüsche transferred to Hamburg to assist with design and development of his own prototype and making improvements on several other U-boat classes. During this time he cultivated a companionship with then *Commodore* Karl Dönitz, who backed his design. Dönitz also approved more workers and materials. Despite this, Jakob Prüsche had been obliged to let recognition for his unique design slip into anonymity against the day *U799* went to war.

It was small concession for fulfillment of his dream.

Technically *U799* was designated a Type VIII—a U-boat of only 600 tons. *U799* actually displaced more than five times that tonnage. Only a few slow, unwieldy U-boats known as *Milchkühe—milk cows*— could rival *U799*'s size. But secrecy had masked her true capabilities.

Yet Prüsche had realized he would fail unless he proved his worth as a commander. Against his wife's wishes—a sizeable misstep—he accepted a commission as an *Unterseebootoffizier*. After his naval training, Jakob joined Dönitz's tactical staff. When *U799* neared completion, Prüsche's innate skill had earned him a promotion to *Kapitänleutnant*. Within weeks, he took command of *U799* as she slipped from the quay into the River Elbe on 12 Sept 1938.

His promotion and command of *U799* were unprecedented. Onkel Karl's blessing did not sit well with other U-Bootoffizieren. However, Prüsche was too preoccupied with *U799* to notice or even care.

Regrettably, *U799* would be the only boat of her class. Hitler's idea of sea-power envisioned mighty battleships—like *Bismarck*, also nearing completion at the time—not skulking, undersea marauders like *U799*. His myopic vision decided Type VIIC and Type IX boats—inexpensive, easy to build and proven—should be mass produced.

After the largely German speaking region of the Sudetenland in Czechoslovakia, then Austria and the remainder of Czechoslovakia fell under Nazi rule, Prüsche knew war loomed on the horizon. British Prime Minister Neville Chamberlain's claim of "peace in our time," made after the Munich Conference, couldn't have been further from the truth. Hitler would never be content with such peaceful conquests. Prüsche's Uncle Wolf and Cousin Brandt implored Jakob to resign. He obdurately refused.

Instead, Prüsche fed his passion to test *U799* to her maximum. Events rushed by like seawater past her hull. On 1 September 1939, Hitler's *Blitzkrieg*—lightning war—swept over Poland. Jakob was too blinded by his own shining star to fathom the future Hitler had planned.

Now, the *Gestapo* made it clear, Jakob was left no choice in the matter. Not only were his actions marked, but his wife Cynara, their three children and his cousin's little girl were held under close scrutiny. For their sakes, Jakob remained an exemplary officer. He did his duty.

Fatalistically, he mused: *Perhaps it no longer matters, we may all die for that mad paperhanger in Berlin.* Aloud Prüsche muttered, "*Mein Gott,* what a foul course I've plotted for myself."

"Pardon, *Kaleu?*"

"Nothing. *Es tut mir leid, Oberfeld.* Just mumbling."

A minute bolt of light stabbed the darkness: once, twice, three times. The last the longest.

Needlessly, Schefflein pointed. "The signal, *Herr Kaleu.*"

"*Ja.*" A smile creased Jakob's dour countenance as he considered: *Perhaps my earlier assessment of clandestine operations and the character of our contact was mistaken.*

To Schefflein, he said, "Respond: one long, two short."

With his reply, blinks ensued. Schefflein read:

DUMPLING WANTS ROSES 26 DEC / CASH AND CARRY / STORE CLOSED FOR SEASON / TOAST 4 6 AFTER NEW YEAR.

Prüsche unscrambled the mindless code. DUMPLING was *Kaleu* Wäscht's boat, *U1160.* WANTS ROSES 26 DEC was their prearranged rendezvous point and date. CASH AND CARRY meant he needed fuel, supplies and torpedoes, but no repairs.

STORE CLOSED FOR SEASON was a definite relief. STORE was their codename for a cache of supplies at Ikeq Fjord. In winter it was accessible only by exacting navigation under pack ice and through unpredictable leads—clear channels within the ice. *Trekking beneath the ice is something I do not wish to risk again. Now, we won't have to; ice seals the fjord.*

TOASTS 4 6 AFTER NEW YEAR was also good. *We can go back to Lorient, France, for a well-deserved rest. The men will be ecstatic. Too bad we cannot make it home for Christmas.*

The message doesn't mention U820. Did they forget?

"*Oberfeld*, ask about STRUDEL."

The question flashed toward shore. A reply came rapidly on its heels:

LAST DISH STRUDEL 13 DEC OVER.

"*Verdammt!*" he swore, thumping the spray deflector with his fist. "Treden should have long since reported in."

He took a calming breath. Rüdiger Treden, a boyhood friend, was notorious for his dare-devil stunts. Ego and orders, issued through this Danish contact, had quite probably led to the death of the captain and his crew. Realizing Schefflein waited on him for a response, Prüsche ordered, "Reply: Understood and thanks."

Schefflein did so and verbalized: "'GOOD LUCK' they said, sir," then quietly asked, "Will there be more, *Kaleu*?"

"*Nein.*" His voice cold, Prüsche called orders below, "Get underway. Set course one-thirty-five. Speed, twelve knots." Motioning to the young officer coming topside, he said, "*Oberfeld*, report to the First."

Jakob Prüsche nodded to Garrick Bechtler, his twenty-two-year-old First Watch Officer— *Erster Wachoffizier* or I-WO. Garrick was a trusted colleague and friend as well. "If you need me, I will be in my cabin." Prüsche started down the ladder.

A lookout yelled, "Ship off port beam, *Kaleu*. Low on the horizon."

Climbing back up, Prüsche raised his binoculars. The Aurora Borealis revealed a menacing silhouette, closing rapidly. "She's a Treasury Class cutter, headed straight for us." He lowered his glasses and called out, "Clear the decks. Prepare to dive."

Lookouts raced below. As the last man in, Prüsche shut the hatch. Wincing in pain, he found Garrick there to help him turn the wheel to secure the hatch. "Take us down to thirty meters, First. Remain on course one-thirty-five."

Black seas again swallowed the prototype U-boat. The only sign of the "Ice Fox" melting back into Neptune's depths was a swirling feather of slush, soon stilled.

USCGC *PARATUS*
WEDNESDAY

Stocky Lieutenant Commander Pete Halloran, executive officer of the 327-foot Coast Guard cutter *Paratus*, lowered his binoculars from the barely visible pack ice. The East Greenland Coast itself was almost fifty miles further away; the rugged ice ominously closer. Turning, he waited for his phone talker, watching his body language.

It struck Pete: *Jim Reynolds oughta be playing varsity basketball, not relaying reports from a warship's Combat Information Center.* But on this watch, Jim was Pete's link to CIC. The nerve center of *Paratus*, located behind the bridge, CIC housed the SOund NAvigation Ranging equipment, or sonar, as well as experimental RAdio Detecting And Ranging device, or radar, and other navigational and communications apparatus. Jim's shoulders sagged. Pete knew the answer.

From beneath his oversized helmet, worn to protect him and his headphones, Jim said, "CIC reports radar contact lost, sir."

"Typical bungling," came Commander Dean Tennef's intrusion.

Startled by *Paratus*' pencil-pushing, practiced-drunk of an inept captain, Pete groaned inwardly. With such a pathetic joke for a captain, Pete Halloran often forgot when Tennef was even aboard *Paratus*.

Neither emotion nor hint of interest tinged Tennef's

voice; just sarcasm. "Our new-fangled contraption must be hunting ghosts again."

The phone talker, eyes wide, glanced at Pete, as did other crewmen. *The radar didn't hunt ghosts.* Pete waited for Tennef to request more data from CIC. As usual, he did nothing. Too well disciplined to confront the captain in front of the crew, Pete's anger rose like an upsurge of seawater after a depth-charge explosion.

Pete wondered: *What the hell is Tennef waiting for? Why doesn't he take this one on? They're a sitting duck. We have the advantage. That U-boat is pinned between slabs of unyielding pack ice and the firepower of Paratus.* Gnawing on his unlit cigar, Pete mutely predicted: *Tennef's gonna let it slide like all the others.*

"Stand down, you alarmists," Tennef said, fulfilling Pete's prophesy. "Course zero-one-five. Ahead standard."

With the force of a tidal wave, discouragement surged over Pete.

The helmsman's reply, laden with disappointment, was slow in coming, "Aye, aye, Captain. Zero-one-five; ahead standard."

In the red night-running lights, Tennef gazed with eyes as lifeless as a dead shark. The man's phony New England dialect grated, "No use chasing wild geese this morning. If it was a U-boat, which I seriously doubt, they're gone by now."

The implied behest for consensus knotted Pete's gut. Though Tennef watched and waited, Pete refused to take the bait. Indicating his objection, Pete silently raised his binoculars again.

With a slight 'humph,' Tennef tucked his helmet under his arm. "Send a report with normal radio traffic. No use in getting everyone in a huff over nothing. I'm retiring. XO, you have conn." With that, Tennef stepped off the bridge, no doubt headed to his cabin and a bottle.

"I already had conn," Pete muttered under his breath. Aware that all eyes on the bridge watched him from beneath their helmets, Pete perceived the men's concern. He shared their fear as well. It was the fifth contact since patrol began a month ago. The men wanted a U-boat by Christmas. Today was Christmas Eve. If *Paratus* was to live up to her Coast Guard motto of *Semper Paratus*— Always Ready—things had to change.

Yet sinking a U-boat, wasn't their only problem. Tennef was also negligent in his duty. He blatantly ignored orders to report all U-boat contacts near Greenland. The urge to act was strong, but Pete had to be patient. The gallows was still being erected. They needed more rope to let Tennef hang himself.

Realizing no one had moved, Pete ordered, "You guys heard the captain. Secure from GQ."

The directive didn't quell Pete's ire. *Paratus* should've been his command. Tennef clearly brown-nosed the right jackass at HQ. *He has no business commanding any ship, much less Paratus. If those jokers at the Puzzle Palace would look up from their own paper shuffling, maybe they'd see what's going on out here.*

Having landed a well-paying job as manager of a Lake Erie shipping firm shortly after World War I, Tennef transferred to the Coast Guard Reserve. He hadn't been to sea since 1919. His only hope for a promotion was an active sea command—and *Paratus* had become his meal-ticket when another world war appeared imminent.

Whoever helped grease his captaincy failed to consider the demoralizing effect a weak-willed officer had on a crew primed for action. Tennef sailed *Paratus* toward disaster and defeat.

Does Tennef expect a U-boat to waltz up, pop their hatch and give up? Will he let the wolf-packs have a turkey shoot while he watches, afraid to ruin our Arctic-camouflage paint? What a crock of shit. "Mr. Johnston, code this to GreenPat: Radar contact 0123; 66°N 33°W; no pursuit per captain order; contact lost 0155."

"Aye, aye, sir." The spindly ensign jotted down the

message on his clipboard, repeated it back, then started back to his radio.

"And Sam, put my name on it."

"Yes, sir." Johnston retreated to the radio room.

Sitting in the bridge chair, Pete gnawed his unlit cigar. *I don't like disobeying a superior officer, but Tennef's outta line, and I gotta cover my own ass somehow.*

His sulking was broken when he noticed someone enter the bridge from CIC.

Lieutenant JG Sean Rork was their newly acquired technology expert. He was also Pete Halloran's younger brother-in-law and often his sounding board at moments like this. Though cocky, Sean often made worthwhile observations.

Staring into the false gray dawn, Sean quietly said, "Man, I really hoped he'd go for that pig-boat, sir. It looked bigger than any I've ever picked up before—Pacific or Atlantic. And that's allowing for bounce-back off the ice."

Eyeing Sean, Pete chalked up another strike against Tennef. "Log all contacts. If it's a new pig-boat, CinCLant needs to know. They also need to realize Tennef's shirking his duty out here."

With a glint in his blue eyes, the tall Irish-born Yank nodded and turned away.

"Oh, and, Sean . . ." Pete said, turning Sean back.

The young man noted the wry grin on Pete's face.

"I don't need it in quadruplicate. One copy is fine."

With a two finger salute, Sean smiled. "Gotcha, Commander."

ST. JOHN'S, NEWFOUNDLAND,
COMMISSION GOVERNMENT
OF GREAT BRITAIN
WEDNESDAY

In the chill quiet of Mac MacCalister's office, Karney observed the collage of maps and photos, revealing

Wendy's keen eye. Though a womanizing trouble-maker, the Aussie had a flair. Shots of Greenland exposed more than treeless tundra, rocks and ice in black and white mosaics, shaded by grays. Viewing the photos, Karney's memory filled in colors, smells, sounds, even moods of the awesome ice-laden island. Wendy was focused on the war, but Greenland came to life in Karney's mind.

Pictures of various seasons exposed U-boats on the surface. Some showed eerie dark shapes just below the surface of swirled waters, the only indication of a U-boat's emergency dive. Yet the latent danger was set against a magnificent backdrop.

Summer conveyed memories of resplendent, deep violet fjords with steep, jagged precipices rising from their depths. Beneath the wings of black-backed gulls and gray and white tattrats—doubtless startled to flight by the drone of Wendy's Spitfire—the water sparkled jewel-like. In other shots, guillemots, murres and dovekies rose over iced fishing spots or soared along the craggy cliffs near their nests. Birds numbered in the thousands, perhaps millions. Karney could almost hear their cacophonous cries.

Color film would have revealed a flourish of bright flora: mosses with tiny purple, red or white flowers; dandelions and crowfoot nestled among dainty blue harebells; dark green grasses growing in profusion along angled slopes; river banks edged with red willow-herbs; marshes sprouting downy tufts of cotton-grass sedge. Karney learned the fauna and flora of this huge island from Gunnar Bryannt. The elder Coast Guard officer's keen insights had come full circle.

In the photographs, Greenland's beauty was never lost, just magically transformed. With every click of Wendy's shutter, the rich spirit of life was portrayed; even during the darker, frigid winter season.

Quilted layers of ice were rent by jagged rocks from which incessant winds had blown the snow. In most fjords, ice buckled into ridges, pushed inland by massive ice floes encircling the coast. Some fjords revealed swift currents, keeping channels ice free throughout the winter. U-shaped valleys, carved by receded glaciers, lent an illusion of a snowy wonderland. Beyond the coastal mountains, the icy heart of Greenland sprawled. Here, mighty glaciers churned relentlessly toward the ocean, fractured by mile-deep crevasses which often spelled death to the unwary.

Short cycles of Greenland's freeze and thaw had been captured as well. When summer retreated, thin sheets of virgin ice glistened on the water. Vegetation rusted and shattered with nights of ever-increasing length and growing cold. As winter thawed into spring, gigantic glaciers calved mammoth ice blocks into the fjords, creating tidal-surges of brash ice and frigid water which crested high along the rocky shores.

Closing his eyes, Karney could imagine ice crunching underfoot, feel the wind bite his flesh, trying to tease warmth from the nebulous sun. The fragile fragrance of a forbidden world filled his nostrils. The impression was exhilarating.

The clunk of Mac setting Karney's open Moosehead beer on the table brought him sharply back to war's reality.

"It astounds me," Mac said, after sipping his beer, "how someone as bloody crass as Collins manifests such rare talent, eh?"

Pensively, Karney took his beer and sat. Partially aware of Mac's plan, he knew he'd have to put the puzzle pieces in place. Just not this instant. "The way Wendy makes Greenland look," he said, "he oughta work for some fancy travel bureau like Thomas Cook and Sons."

"He already works for a travel bureau." Mac grinned. "Mine."

Karney snapped his fingers. "That's right, and I'm your first chump, I mean client."

"Here, take a gander at this," Mac said, winging a photo at Karney. It silently spun across the broad table, landing precisely in front of him. "Collins took that a while back. Something about that U-boat bothers me. What do you think, Irish?"

Staring at the enlarged glossy photo for several minutes, Karney confidently answered, "She's bigger and more heavily armed than a Type VII. She looks larger than even a type XI, as well."

"Besides doing your homework, you've got sharp eyes."

"Where'd he take this one?" Karney asked, turning the photo around to look at it from a different angle.

"Off the pack ice, south of Ammassalik. It's fuzzy but the best shot he got. She's the pig-boat who played connect the dots on *Snapper*. Other photos are a blurry haze of tracers but Collins swore she's the most heavily armed U-boat he ever ran into."

Karney gazed through the magnifying glass. "She has six, no eight anti-aircraft guns, but with some of 'em paired, it's more like fourteen. And there's housing for a cannon. He's lucky they didn't blow his sorry ass completely outta the sky. She reminds me of those World War One U-Cruisers Gunnar told me about. And I'll bet this baby carries extra torpedoes, too."

"Either that or extra fuel," Mac speculated.

"Maybe both. Too bad Wendy didn't have a tape measure."

"Well, Irish, while you're gallivanting around on the ice up there, why don't you ask Jerry for her specifications?"

Karney grinned. "Should I ask 'em to surrender, too?"

"Isn't that stretching your diplomatic license a bit far?"

"Mac," Karney countered, falling into his native brogue, "I bloody well kissed the Blarney Stone with the best of 'em, remember? So don' ya be sellin' me short 'fore I even start this mission."

"Ah, Irish," Mac said, lolling his head back, "I see your strategy: If you can't dazzle Jerry with brilliance, you'll baffle him with pure, unadulterated bullshit, eh?"

Raising his ale, Karney said, "*An uair a bhíonn do lámh i mbéal an mhadra, tarraing go réidh í.*"

"My Gaelic's a bit rusty," Mac said. "Enlighten me."

Karney grinned in a knowing manner. "When your hand is in the dog's mouth, withdraw it gently."

RCN TRAINING GARRISON
SHEET HARBOR, NOVA SCOTIA
SUN: 04 JAN 42

Ellie thanked the young seaman carrying her case. On their walk down here, he talked constantly. *Is Al Carter glad to do this as a reprieve from KP duty, or is he just starved for female attention?*

Bowing politely, Al grinned. "Sure ya don't want me to help ya with anythin' else, ma'am?"

Smiling, Ellie backed him off the porch. "Nae, Seaman Carter, but thank you all the same." Hope faded from his eyes as he turned and headed to the front gate of the white-picket fence. Though his help was greatly appreciated, she craved solitude.

Ellie strolled around the outside of her new home, admiring the fresh paint job: trimmed all in white, bright canary siding made the cottage stand out among the pines, while the shutters and door were a welcome azure blue. A basic rectangle, the cottage perched near the abandoned lighthouse. Set at an angle, the front faced southwest. To the east Ellie glimpsed the blue-gray waters of the North Atlantic. A pleasant assortment of aromatic pines surrounded the property, creating a natural windbreak. A broad porch protected both the front and back. Though several gardens lay barren under the snow, they held potential. She'd plant vegetables in some, flowers in a few.

From the backdoor, a trail wound toward the lighthouse. If storm waves hadn't changed the contours, the path used to lead to a broad, sandy beach. Now it was a thin beach of sand, rock and the occasional piece of driftwood. A second trail meandered northwest to a road which ringed the property. The part of the road she would use most led north to the manor house. South, another trail led to the tiny village of Mushaboom. This was a place of pleasant memories and adventure.

Ellie had loved this cottage long before now. It was often where she stayed with her mother when they visited Uncle Richard and her cousins.

Going through the entry, she stepped into the living room where plush sage-green carpet—remnants from the manor—welcomed her tired feet. To the left were the bedroom and a bathroom. Straight back was a tidy kitchen, complete with an ice box, a two-burner gas stove, hutch and oval table seating four. The larder nestled near a handy mudroom where the backdoor was located.

Tile countertops felt cool to her touch. She smiled at the convenient pass-thru. She and her mother had played various pretend games there and used the surface to cool freshly baked cookies, pies and breads.

A cozy fire was already burning in the fireplace. Twirling around the tightly-spaced, rich pine furniture, Ellie felt home at last. A princess in her castle.

Her smile fading, Ellie stopped. What was missing in this cozy pintsize castle were her own little girls—Anna and Nikki. Closing her eyes, Ellie let the sadness recede, then returned her thoughts to here-and-now.

A Victrola phonograph and records, her most costly purchase in Halifax, waited to entertain her. A varied collection of books selected by Uncle Richard lined the shelves. The Motorola radio, courtesy of Mac and Liz, completed the decor. *Bless all their hearts! Nothing's been spared to make me feel 't home. 'Tis perfect.*

Turning on the radio, Ellie took her case to the bedroom and tossed it on the double-bed. After peering into the closet, she checked the dresser from bottom to top. It was a burglar's trick to save time by not having to close the drawers again if you didn't care about being obvious.

She had learned it for quick searches and often did it out of habit. Again closing the drawers, she heard the radio crackle to life.

Ellie returned to the living room and rolled the dial through static. The gesture was eerily reminiscent of her last hours aboard *Glasgow Bonnie*. She closed her thoughts to the still vivid images and the tragedy that followed. A distant station soon hummed into clarity. With Duke Ellington's band brightening her mood, she went back to her charming bedroom to unpack.

Opening the case, Ellie set her new Teddy bear on the bed, then shook out and put away her few new clothes. Most of the articles were sensible with the intent of warding off the permeating chill of Nova Scotia's winter. All but one.

She scowled as she withdrew a red silk negligee.

"What a waste of your hard-won money, Irish," she chided.

Bought after jovial prodding from Liz, Ellie's smile softened, then she considered: *I doubt Irish will e'er see me in this anyway. New Year's Eve has come and gone with nary a word from my errant knight in Coast-Guard-blue.*

She stuffed her crimson hopes in a bottom drawer, trying to convince herself it was the best place for fantasies.

Soon enough she'd be wearing uniforms. *Probably the best and only attire Irish should see me in. Duty has to come first.*

Double-checking the case's side-pockets, she found an envelope. It held the note Karney had penned at Christmas. Carefully unfolding it, she once more admired his precise penmanship. "'Tis more reminiscent of Celtic runes written by some Irish brigand than a stalwart young American sea captain."

Ellie slumped back onto the bed, a sense of loneliness sweeping over her as she read:

My dearest Ellie,   *24-Dec-41*

Her heart fluttered anew at this affectionate greeting, and she recalled Liz's teasing comment: "Oh, my! He sounds like a keeper already." Since Liz had been the mischievous elf to deliver Karney's package from the windowsill into Ellie's hands, it only seemed fair and more fun to share opening Karney's gift with her. Even though Liz hadn't asked, it seemed rude to leave her sitting there.

> *Sorry I can't be with you on*
> *Christmas Day. I don't wish to*
> *neglect you, but I'm slated to run one*
> *of those what-nots to wherever, for*
> *which this particular Coastie seems*
> *destined to accomplish lately.*

Obviously, Irish hadn't expected to talk to her. And though he never explained his "what-nots to wherever," Ellie was glad she'd awakened in time to see him and chat. She read more:

> *When I return, I'm sure you'll be*
> *your old self, a self I dearly wish to*
> *know. Till then, here are some things*
> *I hope will help:*
> *1) The 125 bucks are my take from*
> *   Lady Z's on-going poker game.*

Ellie recalled thumbing the tens, fives and ones, then laughing when she caught the correlation, telling Liz, "'Tis *Lady Z's* length: one-hundred-twenty-five feet, though she's called a Buck and a Quarter." Ellie read on:

> *I know you have family in Canada*
> *for other needs. In fact, I already met*
> *Cousin Mac and spoke with Uncle*

Richard. But I want you to buy
something pretty with this.
Something special, just for you.

When she first read this suggestion, she agreed with
Liz that it would be nice to buy something lovely and
feminine to wear just for Irish. In part, that's why she
bought the red negligee. But, she realized, other necessities
came first. Regardless, Ellie intended to return his money.
She owed him too much already. The note went on:

2) Walked by a store and this caught
my eye. Sorry, I couldn't resist.
Please open small red package.

When she had torn the red tissue, a delicate necklace
fell into her lap. Braided gold glimmered in the sunlight.
Savoring Karney's choice, she had Liz help her put it on. It
still circled her neck. Ellie told Liz, "This probably cost a
bloody fortune. I almost feel guilty wearing it."

To which Liz replied, "He must've wanted you to have
it or he would not've purchased it, eh? And it's not like it
suggests any sort of commitment." Liz's cornflower-blue
eyes sparkled with mischief as she had added, "Yet."

Flustered anew, Ellie continued to read:

The proprietor also showed me these.
Please open white package.

Upon ripping this tissue, matching earrings had
tumbled out to adorn her ears. *I dinna know why Irish is*
so generous but the least I can do is graciously accept.
Brandt never gave me such finery and he could well
afford it. Irish, I'm fairly certain, canna.

Ellie had rationalized to Liz, "Well, if he's fool enough
to waste his hard-earned cash on me, who am I to
complain?"

Liz promptly pointed out, "It's not like you twisted his arm to buy these things, El. His money is his to do with as he pleases."

Ignoring his extravagance, Ellie returned to the note:

3) Please open small, green package.

Tearing the tissue, she'd found a longer silver chain with one of his sea-tarnished dog tags engraved with his full name: KARNEY LIAM RORK, his serial number, USCG, blood type "O-" and an "E" representing Episcopalian. Somehow she still thought of Irish as Catholic as he had been raised. Little did it matter. She'd worn his dog tag day and night, a place near her heart.

Why he gave it to her made no sense until she read:

Against CG regs, you hold one of my dog tags. Madame Arseneau's Boutique, Valerie's Fine Apparel for Women and McBrand's Half-Penny Drugs, will extend credit when you show my dog-tag. Though not as fancy as the other necklace and earrings, I should probably get the dog tag back.
Please keep the silver chain forever.

"Forever, eh?" Liz had repeated.

Agreeing, Ellie had said, "Even for Irish 'tis quite impassioned." It had rattled Ellie, specially sensing the sincerity behind his sentiment. *Does this mean his heart is mine forever, too? The way we kissed, it might. And truly, 'tis nae such a bad thing.*

"Stop this day-dreamin'!" she scolded. "Focus on his practical side. The side that knew I'd need everyday necessities . . . though his thoughtfulness is certainly sweet.

Then there'd been more, explaining the big present:

*4) Last, but not least, is the big box.
Inside is my personal envoy to the
beauty of Clan MacCalister. Since
your Scottish bear Baird was lost at
sea, I thought a new recruit should
be mustered in. May he brighten your
spirits and ease your pain, as I wish I
could. Hope you don't mind that I
took the liberty of naming him.*

Ellie remembered eagerly sliding the green ribbon from the red and white candy-striped box and lifting the lid. Smiling up at her had been a stuffed bear holding a wee, block-letter sign:

HI, ELLIE, I'M LI'L JAKE.
I'M ALL YOURS TO HOLD
AND HUG AND MAKE YOU
FEEL FOREVER LOVED!

"There's that forever again," Liz had said. "Li'l Jake's precious."

Ellie had to agree, but she still didn't known whether to laugh or cry. Picking up the bear, she asked, "How'd Irish know to recruit you, Li'l Jake? I only mentioned losin' little Baird once, and I didna think Karney had noticed. But here you are and I'm glad of it."

Hugging the stuffed bear, Ellie momentarily closed her eyes in gratitude. "Obviously, Irish had paid closer attention to what I said than I thought."

Li'l Jake was about eighteen inches high with tiny stuffed bagpipes, kilt and tam. *How did Irish even find you. With a kilt and wee bagpipes to boot.* Before she continued reading, tears stung her eyes.

Brushing them away, she grew angry. She felt stronger each day but cried too easily. *Is Irish right? Are tears the cleansin' rain to wash away me sorrow as his Irish grandmother said?*

Regardless of my emotions, Irish knew I'd need somethin' to hold, to fill the emptiness in me arms and ease me sadness.

She looked back at his note to distract her thoughts. Irish had penned through several more formal closings before finally settling on:

> *Faithfully Yours,*
> *LtCmdr Karney L. Rork*
> *Or, if you prefer,*
> *Krazy Rork, The Wild Irishman*

"Leftenant Commander Rork. It has a nice ring to it, love."

Ellie again sighed, wishing him congratulations. When she saw him, she hadn't noticed the oak-leaf cluster pinned to his uniform blouse. *I still feel bad about that.*

Once more, the loneliness of his leaving engulfed her. With it came a panicked feeling she might never see Karney again. Her emotions warred between desire to be with him and fear of loving and losing him. They made for unsettling bedfellows.

Ellie fought back her tears. Deep down, she wanted Irish to worry about her, to love her and care what happened to her. Searching for excuses not to love him, she came up dismally empty-handed. Karney's positive attributes far outweighed the negatives: kindhearted, generous, tall and handsome, as well as strong and brave. *Besides, Irish knows exactly how to touch me heart with a wee stuffed bear.*

Still, she worried about falling in love with him.

Negatives came ponderously and were easily countered: *Irish is military—like Brandt. There's the war—Karney could be killed like Brandt.* "Aye, and Irish might die crossing a bloody street in Boston as easily as

Brandt and Anna were killed in a tragic plane crash."

Pushing away these dreads, Ellie decided her other, uninvited-self was merely playing Devil's advocate. She carefully refolded the note, slipped it in the envelope and tucked it in the bottom drawer on top of her red negligée.

She plumped up her pillows, grabbed up Li'l Jake, plopped down and opened the dog-eared copy of *Beat to Quarters* by C.S. Forester she'd borrowed from Karney. The story was about Horatio Hornblower, another stalwart sea captain, but he was in the British navy during the Napoleonic Era; not the U.S. Coast Guard in these modern times.

The words soon blurred as her thoughts meandered back to Karney. "Why do I keep thinkin' of Irish today? Surely he does nae need me as badly as I wish. He has his own life to live."

But Ellie couldn't help but wonder: *How's Irish doin' right now? Where'd Mac send him in the midst of winter? How long will he be gone? Will Karney be in danger wherever he is? Will he miss me?*

SECTION THREE
CLAIRE-MARIE

CHAPTER TWELVE

Karney Liam Rork watched red tracers cross the Sunderland's bow. Hearing their loud kerthwack into the fuselage, he had no trouble translating their message of death from the German planes.

"Two more 88s. Ten o'clock high. Comin' outta the clouds," screamed the waist gunner. "That makes four of the buggers."

"Hang on, Irish," Wendy Collins needlessly called to where Karney sat in the uncomfortable canvas-web seat behind the co-pilot.

Wendy and Mike Ahearn flung the flying boat over in a steep dive. Every bolt, rivet and mounting-screw shuddered. Had he not felt the strain of their violent descent himself, seen the roll executed, Karney would've thought the feat impossible.

With this drastic maneuver, the *JU-88*s overshot their

prey. Karney recalled the *Junkers*-88 was classified as a medium-bomber. But their efficient twin-engines gave them power equal to most Allied fighters while their maneuverability worked against *Ice Sheila*'s slower bulk.

To starboard, the Germans came around for another strike. *Ice Sheila*'s guns chattered an angry warning. Glancing below, Karney saw only unforgiving slate-blue waves clawing up to reach them with the same animosity as the fighters. *"Between the devil and the deep blue sea"* suddenly took on a new meaning.

Wendy and Mike still did not pull up.

Karney closed his eyes. *Sweet Jesus, how do I get into these pickles? Bein' volunteered'll be the death of me yet.*

Though positive the impact would be his last sight, he opened his eyes. All four Pegasus engines snarled in protest as power was poured on to pull *Sheila* out of the dive. Wendy and Mike hauled the dual yokes back. Taut faces and white-knuckled fists emphasized the strain of leveling the giant plane.

A split-second too late, *Ice Sheila* began to recover. Death eagerly waited. Huge waves churned into white-capped mountains with deep frothing valleys. One of their floats slammed into a wave top. Wings tipping precariously, *Sheila* surged upward.

"Bleedin' Christ," Wendy moaned through clenched teeth. "That float hits another fuckin' wave, we'll cartwheel 'cross the bloody sea like a damn boomerang. 'Cept we ain't gonna be comin' back."

Gaining a few precious feet of altitude, *Ice Sheila* steadied with about ten feet between her broad hull and the ocean's malicious peaks. Though the distance was minimal, it was enough. Barely.

"Puddin," Wendy yelled to George Painter, "gimme a damage report?"

More tracers danced toward *Sheila*. "Bleedin' H. Christ," Wendy swore, straining to see the fighters. "Damn Krauts loaded up with petrol 'steada ammo. Jerry shoulda buggered for home by now. We're at the bloody edge of their range."

"Two more comin' back in," came a high-pitched warning over the intercom. "Eight o'clock high."

"Jerry doesn't think he's outta fuel," Karney remarked.

"Nor does he seem to be lacking for munitions."

Holding *Sheila* to the water to shield her vulnerable belly, Wendy said, "No bloody shit, Irish. The fuckers must've used drop tanks."

The tracers blazed red as *Sheila*'s waist gunners hammered Jerry with relentless fury. At the same time, bullets ripped the Sunderland like spiteful hailstones. German tracers zinged past the big flying-boat's arrow-straight flight path toward the Orkneys at the northern tip of Scotland. Dwarf geysers peppered the raucous sea where spent bullets hit only to be instantly swallowed by a new surge.

Pressing their air speed to the limit, Wendy swore, "Bloody hell, this'll never cut the rug," then again yelled, "Puddin?"

"Behind ya." Out of breath, George Painter leaned closer to be heard. "There's a bloody huge hole in our hull where one of the plates ripped off. Glen's tryin' to keep a second one from joinin' it."

Without being asked, David Grahe, *Ice Sheila*'s radioman, sent a MAY DAY to Scapa Flow, still miles distant. Wendy climbed from his seat to check damages himself.

"Irish," he said, slapping Karney's leg as he passed, "keep me bloody seat warm and help Mikey fly our wounded lady."

Objections raced through Karney's muddled mind. He ignored them, taking Wendy's seat a split-second before bullets ripped through the cockpit. Gauges shattered. Glass and metal fragmented in every direction. Bitter winds howled viciously in through the new ventilation system. Opting not to contemplate how terribly close the bullets came to slicing his legs and family jewels, Karney strapped the mike around his neck and adjusted the headset.

Nervously scanning the overcast skies for the enemy, Karney asked, "Ahearn, how much further to Scapa Flow?"

"Too damn bloody far for the likes of me, mate."

"Splash one Fritzy. 'Nother's smokin' . . . he's done for," yelled a gunner.

Hoarse, disembodied cheering immediately followed.

Karney's gaze darted toward the smoking plane. Exploding in a violent ball of aviation fuel, the *JU-88* performed a slow-motion cartwheel before slamming onto the ocean. Her crew departed to an unknown oblivion, dead long before impact.

The intercom burst to life. "Wally, where's the other two?"

"Comin' in off the deck, three o'clock. Got 'em dead—"

Machine-gun clatter cut off his words as the Brownings opened up from their beam positions. Another torrent of tracers thunked into *Sheila*. Bullets tore into the broad wing. The cockpit window beside Mike splintered in a shower of Plexiglas. Rushing wind became a frigid blast. *Ice Sheila*'s inside starboard engine erupted in flames, spreading fuel and fire over the wing.

Wiping blood from a gash across his cheek, Mike yelled to Karney, "Irish, feather Number Three."

As Wendy had taught Karney in the numerous days of near-constant flying, Karney ceased the flow of fuel and power to their damaged prop. "Three feathered," he stated in a cold monotone.

Making brief eye contact, Mike grinned despite the blood soaking his collar. With a wink, he yelled over the howling wind, "No worries, mate. Remember, we're Irish. And if you're lucky enough to be Irish, mate, you're bloody lucky enough."

Karney smiled weakly, the knots in his gut wholly unconvinced of anyone's Irish luck as *Sheila*'s machine-guns continued arguing with Jerry.

The *JU-88*s started a new assault. *Ice Sheila*'s tracers marked a path of destruction. Karney's gaze shot past Mike's profile to see a third *Junker* burst into flames.

"We got 'em this time," the intercom voice asserted. "Last Fritzy's buggerin' for home. No worries, mates."

To front starboard, Karney found plenty of worries. The fiery *Junker*'s port wing and engine sheared off, creating a mad whirligig of potential death. It hurtled straight for *Ice Sheila*'s cockpit. In the only recourse left to him, Karney simultaneously ducked and muttered the start of a prayer.

Before he could finish, "Dear, God—" the wing struck a glancing blow, clipping off the ASV antenna. In one clattering mass the conglomeration carried past *Sheila*. Plexiglas and metal fragments showered their already damaged cockpit. Karney clutched the madly vibrating yoke and checked the instrument panel only to see that most of the remaining gauges were shattered. "Whadda we do now?"

Receiving no answer, he took his eyes from the worthless instruments to glance at Mike Ahearn. Slumped in his seat, blood darkened more than his collar. The Aussie's Irish luck flowed down his neck and over his leather flight jacket.

So close to the deck, Karney dare not let go of the yoke to assist Mike. The shuddering plane demanded his full attention. He made no pretense of knowing how to fly this airborne behemoth on any wing with a dozen prayers. Especially in *Ice Sheila*'s battered state.

He grasped the throat mike. "Collins, get your ass up here. Ahearn's hit and the instrument panel's shot to hell."

Silence came over the com-link. "Collins?" he again yelled for Wendy only to hear his answer come from directly behind.

"I'm here, Irish, don't cast a kitten." Dragging Mike from his seat, Wendy pressed his hand against Mike's bleeding neck and yelled, "Jamie, come here. Mikey's bleedin' like a bloody stuck pig." The navigator appeared almost instantly.

Sliding into Mike's seat, Wendy wiped blood on his pants and took the yoke. "Irish, feather Four. Her goose is cooked."

With two engines gone on one side, *Ice Sheila* lurched like a bull staggering beneath the final strike of a picador's lance. They worked the rudder pedals to compensate for her ungainly yaw. Wendy seemed to take it in stride until Karney noted sweat beading on his face and the pallor of his skin.

Even though his face was pale, Wendy's sense of humor remained colorful. "I swear, Irish, can't leave you alone for a bloomin' second without you runnin' us up the bloody billabong."

In the same breath, he called his radioman, "Davey, gimme an open channel." Wendy keyed the mike to send an urgent plea, giving their heading and dilemma. As an afterthought, he added, "For any mates waltzin' us home or fetchin' us outta the drink, if we hafta ditch, supper's on me. Channel clear. Out."

In mere seconds, the radio crackled with the cockney voice of a newly acquired escort. "Wendy, you maniacal roo. You ever gonna learn to fly that beast? And don' you be forgettin' ya still owe me a bloody supper for the last time I covered yer arse."

The banter continued as two Spitfires streaked toward them at wave top level from Scotland. Karney's tension eased.

The smaller fighters danced and swooped around the Sunderland like eager cliff swallows circling an albatross. The pilots, drinking chums of Wendy and his crew, kept up the running malarkey, never straying far from the limping plane.

Karney didn't care what they said so long as the Spitfires stayed near. *A dip in the North Sea ain't on my wish list today.*

An agonizing hour later, at Scapa Flow, *Ice Sheila* made a regal, albeit rough, touchdown. Dozens of sailors and officers alike gawked. Oozing petrol, with a gaping hole in her side and countless bullet holes aerating the fuselage, she was an awesome marvel of determination in the fading twilight. Too bad no war correspondents were on hand to record the phenomenon.

Wendy cut power. "'Cept for Mac's orders to pick up this Limey pom, I'd tell this bloody Brit to go fuck 'is bloody self for gettin' Mikey and *Ice Sheila* shot up. Least you help out, Irish. This Brit prick demands first class service just to cart some hush-hush bloody shite to Canada in person."

Pushing up his Ray-Bans, Karney leaned back and eyed Wendy speculatively. He had known they were to pick up some British major from MI-6; not that anything about it was considered hush-hush. Karney shook his head. *If Mac's chess game is this cryptic, I'm screwed. But I'd wager even a goddamned searchlight wouldn't reveal that man's maneuvers to guard this mission.*

LIMEHOUSE, ENGLAND
MON: 05 JAN 42

Untersturmführer Eugen Ulmstein, formerly an officer of the *Allgemeine SS* and also the ex-clerk to Reinhard Heydrich, stared out a soot-smeared, partially boarded window. Sitting back in the sparsely furnished parlor of the rundown shanty, he hoped he was not visible from the rubble-heaped roadway. Of course, he had no idea what roadway it was, he just knew he was supposed to be safe here. And since no one ever seemed to come down this street, he needn't have worried about being seen. The majority of buildings in the area were bombed to ruins or deemed unsafe for habitation. When Eugen braved a look down the block yesterday, the few buildings still standing seemed to glare back at him. Why, he couldn't imagine, because this place should've been condemned as well.

Unfamiliar with London, Eugen knew only that this area was called Limehouse located somewhere along the Thames River. He remembered seeing the water on the drive over. Now he could feel and smell its dampness, as well as hear ships' deep-bellied horns. This wasn't where Eugen expected to be sheltered. He had hoped for some nice cottage in the countryside. Not this ramshackle flat where *Luftwaffe* bombs might kill him in the next raid. He would speak to Commodore Greer about his living arrangements when he saw him later today.

Muttering phrases in German, then haltingly in English, Eugen's fingers fidgeted with the clasp of a scuffed leather satchel. It had been with him, day and night, since he fled Prague. Though he felt relatively smug with his escape, he knew until he met with Commodore Greer of British Military Intelligence, he wasn't safe. Wolf Gündestein had warned him not to trust anyone but Greer and Brumble, whom he'd already met.

Chief Petty Officer Gerald Brumble was a burly, barrel-chested sailor. His face was hidden behind a walrus mustache and dark glasses, hiding a disfigured eye—token of the Great War. To Eugen, the chief looked, waddled and even sounded something like a walrus he'd seen at the Berlin Zoo. The only item missing were tusks. Brumble had brought Eugen promptly to this safe house on Friday, but today he was late.

Nothing unusual there, Eugen supposed. *After all, this is England. Nothing runs on time.*

"Eugen?" the plump, middle-aged widow who ran the safe house called from the kitchen. In high school German, Mrs. Petrie asked, "*Trinken Sie eine Tasse Tee mit Milch?*"

"*Ja, gerne*—I mean, yes, please, that would be fine, *aber keine* milk." Though he struggled with this new language, there was no going back. Having betrayed his Nazi taskmaster, he must learn to function in the world of his former enemies.

Distracted by her interruption, his view returned to the road. Startled to notice a man snaking through the debris, Eugen's emotions cascaded from momentary panic to irritation, finally settling on relief when he recognized Chief Brumble. Shuffling through the gate, the war-lame sailor made his way up the cracked sidewalk.

Mrs. Petrie set her mismatched tea service on the table the same instant the door buzzer sounded its precise long and short code. "Oh, my goodness," she said, smoothing her graying auburn tresses, "Gerald is here already."

It was obvious to Eugen, the isolated Mrs. Petrie was sweet on Gerald Brumble but the chief's reticent mumbling made it tricky to pinpoint exactly where he stood on liking Mrs. Petrie, or any other account for that matter.

Eugen heard Mrs. Petrie giggle as greetings were exchanged. Lightly holding his hand, she led Chief Brumble into the parlor, apologizing again for her home's disarray. Having heard it in German and English, Eugen felt the Luftwaffe would have done her a favor by leveling the dump in their last raid.

Prepared to greet Chief Brumble with the English phrases he had meticulously rehearsed, Eugen stood. However, as the thickset man behind the mustache removed his dark glasses, Eugen realized it was not the chief. His heart lodged in his throat as his stomach clenched and his mind went numb.

Unable to speak, Eugen motioned with his hand. But before Mrs. Petrie turned, a double 'pfft-pfft' ended her lonely life. Mrs. Petrie crumpled to the faded Oriental rug. A crimson splotch spread on her starched, flower-embroidered apron. Trembling like a petrified hare, Eugen stared into the golden-green eyes of his executioner. The familiar scar near the man's eye was like a white dagger. Knowing the man and his reputation, Eugen knew there was no redemption.

The lieutenant colonel's voice bled condescension and disgust. "A pity you must die such an untimely death,

Eugen. To be precise, you have always been such an excellent keeper of schedules."

The weapon spoke again. Eugen collapsed next to the housekeeper, his English lessons terminated. The colonel scooped up the leather satchel of Third Reich secrets. Sorting the purloined contents, von Zeitz retained a number of documents and flung the rest into the fireplace. Flaring brightly, incriminating morsels flamed to ashes.

After checking his Rolex, von Zeitz hurried to catch the next train. He debated burning the building down but knew the bodies served as warning enough that the Reich was in charge. "It also serves as a snub to 'Cripp-odore' Greer. That old sea-fart's life will soon ebb as well."

Pausing at the front door, von Zeitz, once more the mumbling, seemingly bumbling chief, called over his shoulder, "That would be splendid, Mrs. Petrie. I will see you then." With no telltale glances to betray his self-assurance, he turned and shuffled down the street.

EUSTON STATION
LONDON, ENGLAND
MONDAY

With a quick glance, the dapper gentleman decided no one in the busy station was watching him. One chap seemed to stare, but his uniform, white cane, dark glasses and curious manner of turning his head, marked him as a blind sailor. No threat there.

Smoothing his mustache with a manicured forefinger and thumb, the fop set down his tan valise to compare his ticket to the timetable. With a scowl, he stepped toward a ticket agent, then kept going . . . his valise left behind.

Exactly four minutes later, the blind sailor rose, tapping his cane, head gently swiveling side to side, listening. People glanced away, shamed by his loss or fearful his affliction might befall them. Their emotions, however, blinded reality.

Closer scrutiny marked the still-youthful face masking many years of hard-earned acumen. Underneath his neatly trimmed, ginger-blond hair a cunning mind calibrated the exact number of seconds needed for this snatch. Though a jagged scar lent credence to his blindness, his lucid blue eyes perceived everything with feral intensity.

In one, seemingly ill-fated step, the man collided with a vivacious gabber and her equally talkative friend, both so intent on their chat they hadn't seen him. The blind sailor sprawled, knocking over the tan case. Mumbling an apology, he fumbled for his lost belongings. As planned, the two mortified women helped him. They handed him the valise, lying beside his cane. Hearing the boarding call for Bristol, he thanked the two women profusely and tapped his way toward the platform.

On the train, a slight smile creased the sailor's face. Intel on a crucial U-boat officer was back in safe hands.

As the train whistle faded away, a frantic Nazi agent hunted for a tan valise supposedly left behind by a top British double agent. He could not find it anywhere. Fears of retribution blackened his thoughts.

LIMEHOUSE, ENGLAND
MONDAY

Commodore Angus Greer of MI-6 slumped deeper into his wheelchair, staring at the sheet-covered corpses as if willpower could bring them to life. His thoughts circled the same roundabout: *'Tis sad to think I offered this job to Mrs. Petrie to keep her from wasting away after her husband's death. But Eugen Ulmstein . . . I don't even want to consider those ramifications. If I had been in town when he arrived, could this all have been avoided? I do hope this blaze can be put out before it spreads any—*

Hearing a car drive up, Greer rubbed his weary eyes and glanced out the dirt-smudged window. Geoffry Sloat had returned.

"Commodore," the lanky lieutenant began as he stepped past the detective, vainly dusting for fingerprints.

"What is it, Sloat?" Greer asked his stalwart adjutant.

Sloat cleared his throat. "The body pulled from the Thames was identified as Chief Brumble from his dental records, sir. No doubt but he was murdered. A garrote fashioned from telephone cord was still embedded in his throat, neck broken, larynx crushed. Poor bloke never stood a bloody chance from the looks of it."

Greer nodded absently, having already presumed the worst for the chief. Turning to the Scotland Yard technician sifting the smoldering ashes, Greer asked, "Have you found any bloody thin' worth a whit, Henley?"

Ponderously, the soot-smudged lad shook his head, then once again focused on the charred debris before him.

"Too bad about Mrs. Petrie, sir," Sloat said. "Guess we can chalk Ulmstein up as a Nazi win." Indicating the body, he asked, "Since he can't tell us anything, where do we go from here?"

Greer dismissed Sloat's overt callousness toward the bodies to the lad's tenure with Scotland Yard. "I'm not sure. Ulmstein may not've been able to reveal the name of the Nazi wolf hiding in English sheep's wool, but I'm certain," he angrily thumped his aching leg, "Ulmstein knew the damned bastard we seek."

"You suppose," Sloat ventured, "whoever shot the two of them was actually the double agent we've been huntin' so damn bloody long?"

"Bugger all if it might've been him in bloody person," Commodore Greer muttered.

RCN TRAINING GARRISON
SHEET HARBOUR, NOVA SCOTIA
MONDAY

"Eleanor, welcome to the garrison," Admiral Richard MacCalister set his pipe in his cork-knocker ashtray, then rounding his desk. He pulled his niece into a brief hug. "I am so glad you're here. Considering all you've been through, you look grand."

Ellie kissed him on the cheek. "Thank you, Uncle—I mean, Admiral." Stiffening slightly into a professional manner, she said, "I'm glad to be here, too, sir."

Flustered by his own emotions, the admiral retreated behind the bulwark of his black walnut desk, motioning his niece to take the comfortable, leather wing-backed chair. He began straightening his papers.

Once seated, Ellie felt enveloped in the past. The scent of leather and furniture wax mingled pleasantly with the aroma of her uncle's pipe smoke. A subtle mustiness wafted from scores of leather-bound tomes lining the shelves from floor to ceiling. She fondly recalled Uncle Richard reading from such classics to his sons, Ellie and her older brothers on wintry nights in 1912, the last year they had all been together.

But that had been thirty years ago: four years before Kyle was killed in the trenches of France; seven before Aunt Janine died of influenza; ten before Ellie's mother committed suicide.

How she had wished in the years since that those daring-do tales of courage and fortitude with *Robin Hood*, *The Three Musketeers* and *Ivanhoe*, among other tales, could have been the reality of her cousins' and brothers' lives. Those endings were known. Yet the threads from those stories were woven into the sturdy fabric of the young listeners to become a resilience they shared as adults. For herself, Ellie learned of honor and bravery. Despite Joan of Arc having been burned at the stake, Ellie learned what a powerful combination faith and belief in one's self could be. She knew it was here that her bold other-self had been born and nurtured.

And here she must find herself again.

That other-self who casually strolled through fancy parties officiated by high-ranking Nazis in order to eavesdrop on any careless conversations; her beguiling other-self who engaged in idle chitchat in order to tease tidbits of potentially vital intelligence from unsuspecting guests. The resolute-self who made a vow to Brandt Gündestein on their wedding night to fight Hitler till death tore them apart.

Death had taken Brandt. Anna as well. Ellie felt that dire Nazi measures had ultimately killed Nikki—

"I'm sorry I wasn't here yesterday," her uncle said, ending her trance. "Are you settled at the cottage?" he asked, puffing on his meerschaum pipe. "I hope Rob Roy's boys cleaned up their mess. He assured me they'd finish in plenty of time, eh?"

"Yes, sir, they did. It's lovely. They did a bonnie job."

Uncle Richard fidgeted with his pipe as she considered his word choice. Mac had explained "his boys" were an elite assembly of Special Forces, handpicked for ICE PACT. Each a veteran with unique skills, posted here for advanced training and battle scenarios to meld them into cohesive teams. When the mission received final approval, they'd be ready to go. Most doubled as instructors or assistants.

Officially, the garrison trained sailors in such basics as climatology, ASDIC (the British term for sonar), radio-telegraphy, Morse code, semaphore and cryptography. These regulars, however, provided Mac and his boys with a handy cover for their own more covert and far-reaching intent.

"From what I heard," she said with a wry grin, "paintin' my cottage was a bloody lark compared to Mac's forced marches with full packs and numerous obstacles thrown in for good measure."

"Yes, quite so," the admiral agreed, knocking the tobacco from his pipe against the cork centerpiece of the ashtray. "Bloody wartime tobacco. Haven't had a descent smoke since '39." With a *harrumphed* sigh, he sailed back on course. "I daresay, house painting is also not what that hobnail bunch of pirates considers their cup of tea."

Her uncle's chivalrous view of war clashed with the clandestine operations she and Mac had been involved with for so long. And Ellie's marriage to Brandt, a German working against his own countrymen, even if they were Nazis, was something he would never understand. Wars were supposed to be fought on the high seas with guns of mighty battleships belching death or on land by soldiers slogging it out on muddy battlefields with rifles and bayonets; thundering cannons and charging cavalry, swords raised in a frightening display of honor, their horses' hooves pounding.

"I daresay," he said, squaring-up the tidied stack on his mirror-polished desk, "if Rob Roy's boys had known it was for such a winsome lady, they'd have stampeded the bloody paint lockers."

"Thank you," Ellie said, feeling her cheeks flush, "but you don't need to flatter me. I already agreed to work on whatever hush-hush tasks you may have. But, Mac's hidden the intent of ICE PACT more thoroughly than Mae West tries to hide her legs."

"Ahem, yes, well, I'd like it concealed more but, with so many foreigners involved, it's hard to hide a well-turned ankle, eh? I only hope Rob Roy knows what he's doing."

Ellie didn't doubt Mac had already appraised every angle of this mission and then some. Ignoring her uncle's skepticism, she asked, "Is Commander Rork involved because he rescued me?"

"Leftenant Commander, is it now?" He sounded annoyed. "So, Rob Roy pushed through his bloody promotion, eh?" Noticing his niece's raised eyebrow, his comeback was typical. "Ahem, yes, well, this Rork chap's function has little enough to do with you." Grumbling to himself, he added, "And the less that bloody Irishman has to do with you, the better."

Though the admiral's words were soft, Ellie heard them and gave Uncle Richard an accusing glare, wondering: *What's Irish done to irritate him?*

Flustered, he said more loudly, "Rork's doing an odd bit of reconnaissance for Rob Roy. Left on Boxing Day. Don't know the particulars. That's Mac's concern. And Rork's undoubtedly."

So, she thought, *that's why Irish suggested celebratin' New Year's late. He really doesn't know how long he'll be away.*

"Rob Roy chose this Irish chap over several other candidates, any of whom I felt were more qualified. Naturally, we disagreed."

Stuffing more tobacco into the bowl of his pipe, the admiral clenched it between his teeth and lit a match to it. As he puffed it to life again, he hefted a thick file from the corner of his desk. Ellie glimpsed Karney's name on the tab.

The admiral scanned a few pages. "Well, I suppose this Irishman will—"

"Admiral, Commander Rork may have been born in Ireland, but he is, as they say, as American as apple pie and baseball."

"Yes, well, I suppose so." He scrutinized the file further, pursing his lips at some odd fact. "Says he graduated with honors and is working on his master's degree." Her uncle read more with an occasional *humph* over a point. "Ahem, well, Rork seems to be well-educated, though he seems to favor those odd 'gyrotating' aero-machines that allegedly go up and down without any wings." His hand made an erratic fluttering motion in the air. "They'll prove a worse bungle than dirigibles, except for use as barrage balloons. God save the King and all of us from inventors and their bloody new-fangled gadgets."

Not quite sure what her uncle was babbling about, Ellie knew she'd have to find a chance to examine Karney's file, it sounded fascinating. Quietly, she asked, "Why are you so reluctant to concede Karney is a good choice, Admiral? He did save my life and has proved to be a very capable officer. Well-liked by his men, too."

With a scowl, the admiral closed the file and set it aside. "Yes, well, this is not a bloody popularity contest, my dear. Though Rork may have rescued you, I shan't pardon his insolent behavior, eh?"

Though curious, Ellie dropped the subject. A minor infraction to anyone else might be a major insult to her uncle. She'd learn the rest of the story later. For now, she merely said, "Karney did take excellent care of me, Admiral. 'Tis a debt I would be hard pressed to repay."

Her uncle pulled his pipe from between his teeth, again knocking the embers into the ashtray. "So, it's Karney now, eh?" Stuffing fresh tobacco from a different pouch into the bowl, he lit a match to it, his gaze watching her over the flame. The aroma of this new tobacco filled the room.

Ellie could almost hear the laughter of bygone years, long since shadowed by time and tragedy. Talking around his pipe stem, his harsh words yanked her sharply back.

"Be that as it may, Eleanor, my first choice was not Rork."

A knock sounded on the door, quashing her retort. When a yeoman entered the room with a message for the admiral, Ellie let her thoughts drift back to Commander Rork. She repeated his full name in her mind: *Karney Liam Rork. His name is like a soothing breeze compared to my uncle's stormy gusts of irritation.* Yet thinking of Karney right now disturbed her—as if her fantasies would be exposed and ruin her performance of quasi-indifference toward Irish.

Once the yeoman left, she noted her uncle's visage and thought it best not to bring up Irish again.

Ellie sought safer ground. "What are my duties to be, Admiral? I trust you'll not assign me to a desk to pound typewriter keys? I need to fill a more vital role for ICE PACT? My training with MI-6 is extensive as you probably know. I'm quite certain only a handful of people at the garrison have my credentials or experience."

Following a wisp of blue smoke rising toward the oak-beam ceiling, her uncle's eyes turned a hard jade. An umbra of gloom descended over the study like the shadow of an eclipse. A chill permeated the room. *Perhaps bringin' up me past was nae safer ground,* she grimly realized.

Admiral MacCalister settled his gaze on her. "Yes, well, Eleanor, I'm well aware of your various credentials and background. Your cover story, however, is angled toward your last posting back in England. You will be on loan to us from the Women's Royal Naval Service to organize a similar branch in the Royal Canadian Navy. The RCN is thinking about incorporating WRENs but, so far, no ink has bled on paper. Therefore, you'll be given duties suited to a leftenant commander, starting in the radio room to get you back up to speed with codes and intel."

"Admiral," her frustration resurrected her brogue, "'tis barely a month since me every bloody thought was in code. 'Tis nae somethin' I'd easily forget."

"Well, no, I suppose not, but you must start somewhere and that's where it shall be. Rob Roy will disturb your tedium with oddball trips, running errands hither and yon. This will allow you time to acquaint yourself with our wee operation here."

Suitably snubbed, Ellie forced a cheerful, "I guess I've evolved from STARLING to WREN. Perhaps next time I can be a chickadee."

The admiral scowled. "Don't be so glib, Eleanor. You sound like Rob Roy. And one of him is enough at this garrison."

As she watched him sort papers, Ellie realized Uncle Richard could never know the wounds she hid. *Though my life's been shredded and parts totally ripped away, my proficiency is unimpaired. I must be tolerant and rely on my trainin' and expertise to exact retribution from the Nazis. Arguin' with me uncle is futile.*

The thought suddenly occurred to her: *With my regular duties, I can learn what Karney's mission entails without arousin' my uncle's suspicion.* Ellie squared her shoulders and cleared her throat before pointedly asking, "Admiral MacCalister, may I take midwatch?"

SIR SANDFORD FLEMING PARK
HALIFAX, NOVA SCOTIA
WED: 7 JAN 42

Barely a shade within a shadow, Willem Krigeshaald waited for the taillights of the Ford to vanish. The woman who gave him a lift to Purcell's Cove Road asked little of the blond Dane's final destination. She simply assumed he lived nearby.

Cold frosted Willy's every breath. A bitter wind blustered through hemlock and oak near Frog Pond, tugging at his clothes. He scrunched his flat cap down a bit further on his head, not that it helped. Seemingly angered by his calm, the wind rushed on, searching for easier prey. The chill night remained Willy's faithful companion, the darkness his ally.

Satisfied no one was about, Willy strolled into "the Dingle," drawing its name from the tall stone tower. In the western sky, ice-crystal wintry clouds shrouded the waning moon, its light as useless as wearing clothes in Cyndi's flat. At least in her bed, where he would rather be, was warmth.

In glum silence, Willy followed a footpath toward the cove.

He reached the hill upon which Dingle Tower rested, overlooking the North West Arm waterway just across from Halifax proper. The imposing structure, built shortly after the turn of the century, loomed over him menacingly. Ignoring this implied threat, Willy already knew its height was ideal for his purpose.

Climbing the snowy steps located on the cove side, his footprints mingled with hundreds of others left by daytime visitors to the park. He paused next to one of the great bronze lions, listening to the night sounds. Willy backed up into the shadows, deftly picked the heavy padlock, then opened the massive door to steal inside.

Halfway up the long stone stairs, Willy paused to catch his breath. The icy air felt like it burned his lungs. Reaching the last flight of stairs, where they became iron, spiral steps, he again paused, forcing himself to breathe more slowly. He listened to an emptiness more telling than his life. Only the hateful wind protested his presence.

Under the iron landing, aligned with the top floor, he slid an iron rod back and jerked out a black case. He lugged it up the last few steps. Crossing to one of the arched windows with two smaller rectangular openings on each side, knelt and opened the case on the floor.

The cumbersome radiotelegraph inside measured about eighteen by thirteen by seven inches. He efficiently unwound a long wire and ran it up the wall, hooking it on a masonry nail he'd driven in months ago. Time was short. He had to be punctual.

Squatting beside the radio, Willy turned it on. He withdrew a leather book, not unlike a wallet, wedged at the side of the case and opened it. With a glance, Willy's "photographic" memory—technically referred to as eidetic—engraved the day's code on his mind like taking a photograph. Trading tactics, he pocketed the code book.

Willy warmed his bare hands under his arms as he listened for any noise from below. Since the war had begun, Royal Canadian Mounted Police had taken to patrolling the park at odd intervals, but with tonight's cold, he was sure no visitors would be about nor any coppers.

Satisfied all was quiet outside, Willy put on the hard, uncomfortable headphones and waited. At exactly seven minutes past midnight, he tapped the key in a rapid, syncopated rhythm of long and short key strokes:

1ST US TROOP CONVOY NA-1 / SAIL 10 JAN /
HALIFAX LONDONDERRY / 2 TRANSPORTS 2 ESCORTS /
BLUE FOX OVER

After seventeen minutes, Willem had received no response and so sent it again. Though he didn't mention STARLING, Willy hoped news of the Americans sailing to Northern Ireland, eventually to deploy for England, would satisfy JAEGER.

His message had to be received to do any good.

Ten more minutes passed. Worried, he resent it. *Is the transmitter working? It's impossible to tell with this shoddy equipment. But JAEGER seldom takes this long.*

With no way of knowing what was wrong, he sent the message one last time at seven minutes to one. Almost at once an answer came back:

COPY / IS STARLING DEAD / JAEGER

His anxiety peaked with the nasty reply. *What can I say? I can't find her in a province the size of Nova Scotia? With such pathetic resources, I can't draw suspicion by making any blatant inquiries. And once I find her, what then? Will JAEGER demand I kill her for the glory of the Third Reich or some such tripe?*

Irate, he thought: *JAEGER and the Reich be damned. They've not seen her face, her beauty, her vulnerability—* Willy cut his reminiscing short when he recalled JAEGER waited. Hesitantly, he rested his finger on the key, then transmitted:

STARLING LOST / NOT IN HX / CHKG PROVINCE / BLUE FOX OUT

Barely a breath after his transmission ended, a reply came back, cold as the wind, snappish as JAEGER's temper:

CHECK HARDER BOY / FINISH JOB / OUT

Clearly, failure to kill STARLING fueled JAEGER's anger. Remorse seeped into his heart. Willy wished JAEGER's hatred against STARLING would freeze in the Arctic cold. Bearing the burden of JAEGER's hate isolated Willy more than the ocean's breadth.

He remained motionless. Regret replaced resentment and fear. Warring with his emotions, he knotted his fingers in his blond hair, trying to keep from giving up. The cold claimed a victory after all as Willy sat crumpled in defeat.

Why did I ever believe in JAEGER or the Reich? I should've seen through their bloody lies. Felt their hate for everything and everybody. Understood the Nazis' true mission for me. Now I'm trapped, wholly miserable and bloody fuckin' alone.

After a while, he broke down the set and returned it to its hiding place under the landing, thinking: *Saturday, I'll hitch a ride to Sydney, verify the departure of that big SC convoy in the Gulf of St. Lawrence, then get my other radio at the ferry terminal. Once I transmit the new data, maybe JAEGER will get off my back for a while.*

He sighed. *It won't make any difference. Results are all that matter to JAEGER. And JAEGER's in Greenland. Greenland! I hate the thought of that frozen land.*

Yet how can that frozen place seem more hospitable than beautiful, quaint Nova Scotia? Here I can never lower my guard. At least in Greenland I was, more or less, at home. Christ, I must be desperate.

Willy sadly realized: *This change of heart is an indication of the depth of despair to which I've sunk. Greenland home?*

Smuggled into Canada, Willy had created a new life, worked into a prime post as harbor master's assistant, went to night school, made a pretense of being happy. Yet he navigated a complex life: shrewd spy, loyal worker, straight A student. With no compass nor sun nor stars, sooner or later, he'd run aground. Willy had learned as a boy, from his officious father navigating Denmark's waters, life was also tricky.

Alone in this foreign country, the only link to his

former self were his radios. In spite of his undertakings, he received no reward, no encouragement. Intimidation and terror forced him to come here and now kept him here. In the last eighteen months, fear and coercion had transformed into heartache and humiliation.

His life tangled with his mission as if shackles bound his every stride. *If captured or killed, my family won't know. They think I died when the Nazis took Denmark in April 1940. Of my supposed friends, the only one who might miss me is Cyndi, at least till she finds some new stiff to warm her bed. No one would really care. No one.*

Willy glanced out the window, then descended the stairs. Cautiously, he opened the door a crack to peer out, listening intently. Stepping outside, he locked the padlock behind him. He turned up his collar and plodded toward Purcell's Cove Road, shoved along by a mocking wind.

Bitterly, he thought, *What's it matter if I walk all night? I've only a cold, empty flat and a lumpy bed awaiting me. My burden is heavier than my naivety believed I would have to bear when I started this bloody covert operation. Sweet bugger all as the Canucks say.*

RCN Training Garrison
Sheet Harbour, Nova Scotia
Thurs: 8 Jan 42

Shortly after midnight, Ellie intercepted a cryptograph from Blue Fox. While decoding it, she heard it sent two more times. She waited for a reply with the same anxiety she was certain Blue Fox felt: never knowing when you might be discovered because you waited too bloody long.

No answer was sent until almost one o'clock. The responding code name—Jaeger—however, evoked painful memories, as well as fear and anger.

She tore the flimsy off the pad and rolled her chair back, wheels protesting like scalded mice. The squeals garnered Chief Clevell's stern gaze. Ben was an odd duck to

say the least, clearly more at home with cryptograms than
people, thus his preference of midwatch. *Heaven knows
how Ben fills his free time,* she thought. *Probably solves
crossword puzzles for excitement.*

Waving the flimsy, her anger simmered. "Be right
back, Ben."

Chief Clevell nodded once and went back to listening.

Ellie marched out of the communications bunker and
up the stairs, following the pleasant aroma of fresh coffee,
stout as a ship's mast. The KPs were hard at work fixing
breakfast for the throngs of garrison seamen. Only the
chief steward nodded a greeting as she passed him.

On the main stairs, she greeted several officers
returning from some late night maneuvers. Grubby
fatigues, exhaust-drawn and blackened faces made them
difficult to recognize. But they knew her. Since she was the
admiral's niece and their captain's cousin, word of Ellie's
identity spread like an oil fire.

Smiling at their weary faces when they saluted, Ellie
returned the salutes and assured them, "No worries, fellas,
'tis Admiral MacCalister I be huntin', nae ye."

They grinned. Quick-witted Lieutenant Kevin Rodgers
called, "Kindly give 'im hell then, Commander. We don't
dare, eh?"

With a wave of the flimsy, she pounded up the
staircase to her uncle's quarters in the south wing. A ship's
chronometer at the end of the hall chimed in unison with
the huge grandfather clock downstairs. *One AM. So what?
This canna wait.*

Her uncle's quarters were marked by his sentinel,
Ensign Jeremy Folks. He sat on a wooden chair, reading.
Only Rodin's "The Thinker" could be more focused.

"Ensign Folks," said Ellie, "I must speak with Admiral
MacCalister. Is he about and available at this late hour?"

Ever reluctant to disturb the admiral, his cool gray
eyes took her in. "I'll have to check, ma'am. Please, wait for
me here."

"Tell him it's important . . . please."

Disdainfully, Folks said, "Yes, ma'am. Isn't it always?"

He came back shortly. "The admiral's in his study to the—"

"Yes, I've been here before." Not wanting him to think her wholly impudent, she added with a smile, "Thank you, Mr. Folks."

Closing the door, she entered her uncle's private domain, a proud gentleman's sanctity from a troubled world. Usually.

Forest-green drapes, plush sage-colored carpet and chairs upholstered with rich brocaded satin of the same greens, soothed weary eyes. Wood paneling was broken by original oils of swift clippers and great man-o-wars. Polished black walnut furniture endowed the room with a subtle, dignified warmth. A crackling fire and glow from a green-glass floor lamp enhanced the mood.

Ellie had only been in here once before, and that on a dare from Mac. The sense of awe she felt then still remained.

Uncle Richard, in a smoking jacket and slippers, placed a marker in his book, set it on the table and rose to meet her. "My dear girl, what is so critical this late?"

She stowed her awe and handed him the message. "This. I just intercepted it."

Scanning the flimsy, he looked at her, his eyes turning a harder, jaded green. "So? What's the problem?"

Ellie exploded. "Why wasn't I told JAEGER's alive?"

"No need to get all in a huff, Eleanor. By all reason, I doubt it's the same agent, just the same code name. JAEGER ceased to exist in 1940."

"That's a bunch of hooey and you bloody well know it. This isn't an obscure agent using JAEGER's code name. This tells me JAEGER is very much alive and obviously able to receive messages from BLUE FOX, who is transmitting from here in Canada. And judging by the strength of the reply, JAEGER is definitely closer than Denmark or Germany. I bet 'tis probably Greenland or as close as Newfoundland."

Uncle Richard's features did not soften. He sat down before the fire, holding his leathery hands toward its warmth. After a moment, his gaze met hers. "I sincerely hoped you'd not learn of JAEGER's . . . reemergence quite this soon." Leaning back, he sighed, then said, "I guess it's my fault for starting you in the radio room. You've always been wiser than most. More bloody headstrong, too."

Seeing she had yet to budge, the admiral lifted a gnarled hand to the wing-back chair opposite him, motioning her to sit.

She did so, asking more civilly, "Why are you tryin' to protect me?"

"Rob Roy and I agreed you shouldn't know about JAEGER until you had a chance to settle in . . . especially after your recent . . . mishap." A loud pop of sap drew his gaze to the fireplace.

"Settled or not," she said, "I think you should fill me in on the rest." A disturbing thought shot through her mind like a bullet. "Does Karney's mission in Greenland have anythin' to do with this?"

"I daresay, Rork's mission is merely the tip of a huge iceberg, Eleanor. Though inadvertent, his involvement began with your rescue. One of the German prisoners from *U820*, the boat *Zealous* encountered, also happened to be the radio operator aboard *Glasgow Bonnie*."

Swept by a chill colder than any North Atlantic swell, Ellie incredulously asked, "George Mathers? The out-of-work actor?"

"Yes, well . . ." Admiral MacCalister consulted one of the files stacked on the coffee table. "It seems his real name is Georg Aldistreich and his starring role as an actor was that of a bloody ne'er-do-well Nazi agent."

With his absence after *Glasgow Bonnie* was torpedoed and the missing port-side lifeboat, she knew he must have abandoned ship before the attack. Her gut knotted recalling their camaraderie.

"What Mac and I fear, Eleanor, is you have made some serious enemies in high places within the Nazi regime. To have a U-boat target one bloody ship in hopes of killing one person is quite extreme. But the bigger picture is more complicated than just JAEGER's resurgence." The admiral again sighed and glanced at his watch. "I will have Jeremy bring us some coffee as this will take some time," he said, standing to leave before Ellie could protest.

She phoned Clevell, asking him to cover the frequencies on her radio as well. Sitting back down, she pondered the problem.

Knowledge of JAEGER's resurrection transformed her. Senses sharpened, the commitment to ICE PACT deepened. JAEGER's undying hatred tore like a bird of prey ripping at her heart. Though it had been more than a year ago, nothing had seemingly changed. The threats of this virtually invincible agent would continue to haunt her if she didn't ignore the intimidations and galvanize her resolution.

Another intrigue rose: *Is JAEGER two agents usin' the same bloody codename? How could I tell? Yet I know whoever lurks behind that codename 'tis key to my predicament. My life's come full circle. I know I'll meet JAEGER again. And this time I must defeat them once and for all. If not, I'll be the one left for dead.*

CHAPTER THIRTEEN

Waking from a cold, uncomfortable sleep, Karney felt his eyes assaulted by the erratically bobbing glare of a flashlight. In its wake, however, came the pleasant aroma of fresh, hot coffee.

Groggily, he sat up on the rickety cot, the only furniture in the vacated back office of the seaplane hangar. It was one of the few places where the clamor of rivet guns, hammers and the hiss of welding torches didn't quite penetrate.

From behind the bouncing flashlight came the hesitant voice of Corporal Davey Grahe. "C'manda Rork, Wendy's doin' pre-flight on our *Sheila*. We'll hit the sky by oh-eight-hundred. He wanted me to get you rollin' now."

Karney looked at his luminous watch dial: 0715. Glancing up, he forgot there was nothing to see, the lone window was painted black in lieu of a blackout curtain. At this northern latitude, dawn would not tinge the sky anyway. Karney accepted the proffered coffee, mumbling between sips, "I take it the British have landed?"

Grahe flipped on the light switch and answered in his slow Queensland drawl. "Wendy's pissed, so it must be the Brit. If you ain't noticed, Wendy don' like the bloody poms, officers that is." He grinned askew. "Present company 'cepted, o' course, sir."

Karney gave him a dubious look. "Course, Davey. With my run of bad luck at poker lately, I'm this crew's open coffer."

"Better 'an an open coffin. Sides, your Irish luck'll improve. Just don' try drinkin' Wendy under the table again, mate. That Fosters'll get ya every time." With a wink, the young corporal left.

Catching the smirk on Grahe's face, Karney wondered if he would ever win back his losses. Irish luck or not.

Needing a hot shower, Karney drank down his joe and squared away the area. He shambled toward the locker room, kit-bag, semi-clean uniform and boots in hand.

After tugging off his socks, Karney's feet recoiled as soon as they touched the glacial-ice tile. When he stripped off his clothes, frigid air struck him equally hard. He turned on the hot shower water full blast. Lathering the stubble on his face, he luxuriated in the steam while he shaved. Karney took his time—no telling when, where or what hot water he might be in next time.

But where they'd been for the past week was in a virtual limbo. *Ice Sheila* was repaired in record time, whatever they needed, they got: royal service courtesy of a slew of directives for any eventuality, signed by Admiral MacCalister, RCN, no less.

Co-pilot Mike Ahearn, head and neck bandaged, as well as Wally Conway, grazed in the arm, had been released to rejoin the crew. Major Strafford, the British pom Wendy already loathed, had been delayed on military business.

Karney knew better.

Night before last, over ales and a long dart game, a Scapa Flow wing commander confided in Karney—along with a glut of other juicy tidbits—Strafford was on holiday. The major might be entitled, but his snub to *Ice Sheila* and her crew was more than a little irksome. They had no duty except to wait, punctuated by an occasional flight, crap games or poker and guzzling a seemingly bottomless supply of Foster's.

Strafford's let-them-wait attitude pissed Karney off, but he didn't dare mention it to Collins. The Aussie already leveled verbal salvos on just about anyone who dared look at him wrong. And they hadn't even seen the whites of Strafford's eyes yet.

Stepping from the shower, Karney was toweling his hair when someone entered the locker room. He thought nothing of it till a nasally London voice asserted, "You must be Commander Rork."

He turned to find a solidly-built man in the well-tailored uniform of a British Royal Marine major, with an intent, but guarded expression. Glancing down at his nudity, Karney snapped his fingers. "Damn! I thought I found the perfect disguise."

Puzzled, the major guffawed, "The perfect . . . found the perfect disguise . . ." He gave a snort, squeezing his nostrils between thumb and forefinger self-consciously.

His affected laughter rasped on Karney's nerves.

"Oh, jolly, Commander, simply jolly." He grabbed Karney's hand in a bear-like vise, pumping vigorously. "But I forget my manners. I am Major James Fenton Strafford, the Third," he said. "Sorry if I caught you at an awkward moment, old chap." Poignantly glancing at Karney's nakedness, he added, "My, but it is rather nippy in here, isn't it?"

Unruffled by his crass, though accurate observation, Karney casually tucked the towel around his waist. "Not as cold as a dip in the Greenland Sea, anytime," he said, sizing up the man.

Standing at nearly six-feet with dark-blond waves of well-oiled hair, Strafford sported a pencil-thin mustache. *That's gotta be hell to shave around every day,* thought Karney. Hazel eyes shifted constantly, never pausing on any one thing for more than a second or two. Shadows rimmed his restless, almost golden eyes, reminding Karney of a pair of wild tigers pacing in their cages. Only a jagged white scar near his eye marred the dapper facade.

"Yes," Strafford said, clearing his throat, "to be precise, that would be a chilly dip. Quite." Trying to look at ease, he leaned against the sink. "I looked you up, old boy, to chat before we get underway. That is the proper term for you Navy chaps, is it not?"

Sensing Strafford being an irritant, Karney didn't look at him as he said, "I'm not Navy, Major. I'm Coast Guard. Ships get underway. The Sunderland's supposed to fly."

"Right you are, old chap." His high-pitched chortle didn't quite hit full throttle this time. "Forgive the mistake. So many blokes in this operation, I can't bloody well keep track of who's who."

Karney raised an eyebrow. *Who the hell does this guy think he's kidding? He has a line on every correct ass to kiss. Or maybe, he plays it dumb like a fox slipping into the chicken-coop. For God sakes, the guy's Military Intelligence.* Karney knew the major's type: *James Fenton Strafford never loses track of anyone. He always knows where he stands in the pecking order.*

Evidently, Strafford didn't miss Karney's skepticism as he amended, "Well, I did get your name correct, didn't I? Irish, aren't you?"

Wiping steam from the mirror, Karney heard the spurn in the term "Irish," and saw the hate reflected in the major's golden eyes. Coldly, he said, "No, sir, actually I'm an American. Irish is my nickname."

Karney had recognized Strafford's Irish campaign ribbon. *I recall Pa pointing out the Black and Tan of the Royal Irish Constabulary during and after Sinn Fenn in 1919. I may've only been a lad when we visited Derry, but I remember their angry stares all too well. Since the major's about forty-three or five, I bet he fought with the Black and Tans. That'd be reason enough for him to hate Irishmen and the Republic. We gave 'em good reason.*

Mentally, Karney sighed: *Be that as it may, I won't be*

baited into Strafford's petty game. This war's between the Allies and the Axis. Not the Orange and Green.

Despite knowing they were allegedly allies, Karney wisely let the Limey's rancor simmering on a back burner. Saying nothing, he bent over the sink to brush his teeth.

"I've never had the pleasure of working with a Coast Guard chap before. To be precise, it should be a splendid treat."

While Karney dressed, Strafford prattled on like a Gatling gun. Listening with half an ear, Karney continued to assess the British major.

He could see Strafford prided himself on being a cake-eater. *He undoubtedly fancies himself quite the lady's man to devour their sweetness. With his sophisticated speech and well-cultivated veneer, Strafford could outflank and beguile an unsuspecting female before she has a clue she's under attack. God, I loathe that tactic.*

Yet Karney had no doubt Strafford used this strategy often and favorably—for himself. *Whatever this Limey might lack, he more than makes up for with his ego.*

Pinning his gold oak leaves to his collar, Karney noted the fine fit of Strafford's uniform. He seemed to be a powerhouse: broad shoulders, solid arms, muscular legs. Though Strafford sported a silver-topped cane to help with his limp, he looked to be in peak physical condition. Karney wondered: *Is he like an aging prize-fighter ready to take on the world, whether the world wants to go another round or not?*

"By-the-by, Rork, I'm sorry you've been saddled with those bloody kangaroo fly boys so long. To be precise, that pilot's an insolent churl, straight out of Botany Bay. I'm glad you'll be along for some intelligent conversation. What I might possibly have in common with those koalas is beyond me."

Karney zipped his kit bag, ignoring Strafford's provocation for or against the Aussie crew. He refused to bite. Never liking people with holier-than-thou attitudes, his Irish birthright naturally sided with the down-under crew and their Irish bonds.

"Collins' only saving grace," Strafford grumbled, "is he's reputedly a bloody good ice-pilot. He wasn't my first choice but this is a Canadian show. If Captain MacCalister wasn't my dear friend Eleanor's cousin, I'd have challenged him in a heartbeat."

Though certain Strafford was too enamored with his own oration to take note of Karney's brief surprise at hearing Ellie's name, Karney nonetheless busied himself with his tie. *How long has this joker known Ellie? More to the point, what sorta knowing might be involved? With Strafford, "dear friend" could mean chatting at a cocktail party more than ten years ago.*

Karney let his initial alarm cool. *Is this just Strafford's attempt to get me to fold my cards? How does he even know I know Ellie? If he's trying to call my bluff, it failed. I play poker too well—even if the Aussies have turned my pockets inside-out.*

Rattling on about taking it on the chin, Strafford finished his soliloquy, "Then again we all must swallow our pride in time of war, mustn't we, Commander?"

Absently nodding, Karney wondered: *How the hell does this buffoon keep from drowning in his own conceit?* Sitting on a bench, Karney pulled on clean socks and jammed his feet back into his boots.

Curiosity, finally won out as he casually asked, "How long've you known Ellie?"

"Eleanor? Oh, my, we go back years. Met her in '31. Or was it '30? To be precise, I recruited her into MI-6 with the blessings of her father, Commodore Greer. First rate officer if not for that bloody wheelchair confining him. Yes, anyway . . . Eleanor was my best agent until she married that Brandt Gündestein chap!"

Strafford spoke Brandt's name with contempt—no doubt fused with bitterness because Brandt won Ellie's heart. *It really shouldn't matter to Strafford since he's already married.* This was another ale-tipped tidbit Karney picked up while in limbo.

"After the wedding bells pealed," Strafford continued, "it seems Eleanor lost all sense of direction. She got even worse after she gave birth to a daughter. I can't recall the little girl's . . . ah, yes, Adrianna or some-such-thing."

Since Strafford obviously assumed Karney knew Ellie's intimate history, it proved difficult not to ask what the hell Strafford was talking about. Karney only recognized the names as those Ellie spoke in her morphine-laced sleep aboard *Zealous. But Gündestein? Brandt must've been German. Ellie married a Kraut while working for MI-6? Talk about a conflict of interest. Yet being a Kraut doesn't necessarily mean being a Nazi—at least I hope not. And although Ellie called out "Anna" in her sleep, it's a likely nickname for Adrianna. Just like Nicole became "Nikki."*

Strafford's buttery voice slid Karney's speculation aside.

"Both of them died in a plane crash in 1940. Upset Eleanor something awful. Her damnable hubby didn't even die honorably. Seems the no-good was running some sort of smuggling venture, chasing wealth and jewels his own family already possessed. Eventually, he'd have been caught. Too bad he took the little girl with him."

Karney thought: *What's behind that remark? In light of what I know, Strafford probably won't die honorably either. And why smuggle into Germany in 1940? As a way to help Jews get out? Funds for the resistance? Why would Strafford object to that? Either would probably benefit MI-6 somehow.* He decided to write off his confusion to Strafford's eccentricity and obvious resentment of Brandt.

"Eleanor resigned from MI-6 after they were lost," Strafford rambled on. "Went over to MI-5. Dammit, but we needed her more in foreign security than in their bloody domestic branch. It was a tragic loss . . . simply tragic."

Dubious, Karney asked, "Their deaths? Or Ellie's resignation?"

The major shot a furtive glance toward Karney. "Well, to be precise, both were a tragedy. The whole bloody thing was sad, terribly sad."

His tone sounded anything but sorrowful to Karney. *I doubt the major gives a crap. Hell, the Tin Man in Oz has more compassion by accident. Even without a heart.*

In the same, insensitive tone, Strafford said, "It's sad Eleanor lost this other baby, though she couldn't perform her duties very well with a brat hanging off her teat, now could she?"

With the major's crass remark and his icy chortle, molten anger steamed inside Karney almost bubbling to the point of eruption. *Which is precisely what the bastard wants,* Karney warned himself as he tucked his tied laces into the top of his boots. He left his rage simmering on a backburner and stood to meet Strafford's gaze. "You know, Major, Ellie's desire to go back to Canada, was to get far away from the war and her obligation to duty. For God's sake, Strafford, Ellie never wanted to be anything other than a mother to Nikki."

It was Strafford's turn to be surprised. Though he assumed Karney knew Ellie's background, he plainly didn't expect him to have such insight into her personal intentions. Nor, apparently, had Strafford expected Karney to defend her so vehemently.

His defense was more ardent than he intended as well.

Strafford recovered, however. "Well, yes, I suppose so, but to be precise, without such domestic burdens tugging at her apron strings, she will be a much better asset to our ICE PACT team. Personally, I never wanted Eleanor to give up the game, but I couldn't offer the dear lady anything to keep her on the playing field. Any woman can be a mother; I needed Eleanor for the bloody cause."

Still trying to sound indifferent, Karney observed, "Sounds like you wanted Ellie to marry the cause, Major, so you could keep her as your mistress to relieve the stress and boredom of war?"

"What? Eleanor my mistress? Never gave her a second look beyond credentials, old boy. Why she's like a sister to me," he said with a wink. "And Shebas are never allowed in my billfold. Too costly and too much risk of upsetting the bloody apple cart."

Karney gathered his things and offered, "Wasn't implying anything, Major."

Strafford merely shrugged, smoothing his hair as he took a quick glance at himself in the mirror.

What Karney planned to say next went against his codes, but he needed a chink in Strafford's vanity. "It strikes me that a man with your panache would wanna bit of calico fluff waiting in every port, Major. But I do agree: Shebas and billfolds don't mix." As intended, the major's ego took the bait; Karney's line reeled out nicely.

"On that we agree, Rork. My wife's my golden goose, has the wit of a pigeon and chatters like a magpie. Even has the gall to tell me how to run my affairs. Only reason I married the hen was to maintain an inheritance and title rightfully mine by birth."

Karney backed away from the subject of Ellie to ask with a raised eyebrow, "I do have to apologize, Major, I'm not quite sure of British protocol. Should I be addressing you as 'Sir Major Lordship Strafford' or is it 'Your Lordship Major Sir Strafford'?"

Seeing his half-cocked grin, Strafford slapped Karney on the back and let loose a chortle. "You bloody Irish. Always kissing the Blarney Stone. Sir Major Lordship, what? Jolly good, Rork. Your Lordship Major Sir. Even better, but simply 'Major' will be fine."

His contrived laughter rose, then died away. Karney held the locker-room door for Strafford, who leaned heavily on his cane. They walked in awkward silence toward *Ice Sheila*, floating between wood-planked jetties within the seaplane hangar.

Eventually, Strafford asked, "By-the-by, how do you know Eleanor, old chap?"

Ah, so you are curious about my connection to her as well. If I wouldn't reveal my feelings to Mac, I sure's hell won't to the likes of you. Karney took several steps before nonchalantly saying, "I rescued Ellie after *Glasgow Bonnie* was torpedoed."

"Oh, so you're the bloke Mac mentioned. To be precise, I'm most assuredly in your debt, Commander. I didn't realize—"

Strafford was cut off by one of *Ice Sheila*'s engines coughing and sputtering to life. A deafening roar echoed throughout the hangar. Waving his cane toward the huge flying boat, he yelled, "Escape is at hand, Commander. Best not miss our ugly, albeit magic carpet."

RCN TRAINING GARRISON
SHEET HARBOUR, NOVA SCOTIA
TUES: 13 JAN 42

A bitter wind thrashed Ellie like some malevolent beast intent upon tearing her from the bluff near the abandoned lighthouse as she made her way through the scraggly pines and a few errant oaks. She brushed snow from the large, scarred rock left eons ago by a glacier and sat. Below, turbulent seas swelled black, except for wave caps whipped to froth with each raging breaker. This spot, not far from her cottage, had become her sanctuary from the garrison's madness—the haven Sandy had taught her years ago to always seek, no matter where she lived.

Now, as at other times, Ellie needed this refuge.

Danger stalked her. Though she again intercepted BLUE FOX's message—an innocuous missive of failure—it was Mac's men who had brought to light the closer peril endangering her life.

In the wee hours last night, they apprehended an intruder. Thinking of this man sent a chill down her spine, having nothing to do with the icy wind. Her thoughts unraveled again.

Her empathy to BLUE FOX was a more benign reflection, allowing her to slide back to this other agent and considered the unknown spy's transmission into the black ether of space. His message last night garnered no reply from JAEGER—apparently a common response.

Though Ellie didn't forget BLUE FOX was the enemy, sending intelligence to a ruthless master spy, she felt she knew BLUE FOX. Though not personally, as with any agent, there was a bond of similar circumstances and hazards.

Often, under threat of discovery by the Germans, Ellie had sent messages and received no reply, leaving her to wonder: *Did MI-6 receive my broadcast? Do I send it again? Is my transmitter working? Do I wait and jeopardize my position? Or simply pray it reached England and trust my orders haven't changed?*

Despite JAEGER not answering BLUE FOX, Ellie was sure the master spy decoded each word and calculated its worth, deciding whether to reply or ignore it. Ellie also knew that JAEGER not only learned she was alive, but now knew where to find her.

BLUE FOX had kept tabs on her since before Christmas.

Two days ago, trying to establish a transmission pattern to help Mac and the RCMP locate BLUE FOX, she inadvertently learned of a message sent to JAEGER just before Christmas which simply read: *STARLING ALIVE.*

When confronted with this information, Uncle Richard acted rather blasé and not at all surprised she had found out. He merely shrugged, explaining it was Nazi Germany's knowledge of her survival which prompted Mac to offer her the post at the garrison.

Even after several discussions with Uncle Richard, Ellie felt completely in the dark regarding ICE PACT's depth. Her uncle did, however, reveal MI-6 believed they had a double agent, deep within the infrastructure of British Military Intelligence. Yet for all his Sherlockian theatrics, he said nothing Ellie hadn't deduced from her own father's questions upon her escape from the Nazis.

Though Uncle Richard revealed JAEGER's location had been narrowed down to Greenland, the vast area that encompassed wasn't narrow at all. And Karney's excursion to Denmark's northernmost Territory remained as vague as shifting shadows in the fog.

Since her run-in with JAEGER, Ellie believed MI-6 still didn't have an inkling as to the identity of the elusive master spy. If Karney encountered this ruthless agent, he wouldn't know the extreme danger he faced. And knowing your enemy was tantamount to survival. Even Ellie hadn't known her peril until it was almost too late.

After that first missive, matters had grown worse. The next transmission had revealed JAEGER still wanted Ellie: *What of STARLING?*

Realizing BLUE FOX hunted her hadn't truly been the problem. After all, Mac guaranteed Ellie's safety with hundreds of men at the garrison, many of them Mac's handpicked Commandos. She felt quite secure in their presence.

At least I did till a few hours ago. The fact that the Nazis had found her so quickly was unnerving. *If Mac canna protect me at the garrison, can anyone protect me anywhere? Yet I am still alive.*

Ellie sighed with the wind and thought of her past—as dark and tumultuous as storm tossed waves. "Brandt and Anna were always me moorin' lines in Germany," she whispered to herself. "They grounded me, held me safe and secure. Then their lives were severed from mine with a keen-edged blade."

Many were the memories she struggled to forget. At times like this, they fell upon her in thunderous torrents. *Like what happened this mornin'.*

An unidentified man was captured near her cottage. Before Mac's men did a strip-search, much less interrogate him, he drew a frisk knife—a thin-bladed weapon designed to be missed in a cursory search—and killed himself. Not as posh as cyanide but a slit throat was just as effective.

Instinct told Ellie: *He came to kill me.*

As expected of a would-be-assassin, he had no papers, only weapons: frisk knife, a garrote and a pistol with silencer. *One of them to kill me.* However, one mark, more telling than the rest, was his blood-type tattoo, beneath his left arm. *The man was SS.*

He probably assumed I'd be sleeping at the late hour of his approach. But I work midwatch and sleep mornings. Thank God he didna known me schedule or—

"Ellie?"

Startled by the interruption, she took a deep breath, staring toward the eastern sky, barely tinged by dawn's arrival. Not until her name was called a second time did she force herself to answer, "I'm sittin' 'neath the split oak, Mac."

Cat-paw footsteps brought him up beside her before she knew he was even present. Mac sat down beside her on the broad rock slab.

After a few minutes, he asked, "You going to let pneumonia finish what the hit man couldn't, eh?"

"No, but you obviously agree with what I've been thinkin'."

"Just 'cause we caught that joker sneaking up here doesn't mean he was after you, love." Mac's back-peddling was in vain.

The faint morning light hid much of her irritation, but when she glared at her cousin, Mac knew better than to lie.

"All right," he relented after a second, "so he probably was after you. I learned Strafford warned you about the Huns, and Irish filled us in on *Bonnie's* radio operator who'd kept in touch with Jerry. I've also read the messages you pulled that BLUE FOX sent to JAEGER . . ." He paused, "You don't suppose—?"

"No," she stated, knowing Mac's thought before he spoke. "The man you caught was nae BLUE FOX."

"You don't know that for sure," Mac lamely argued. "Maybe we killed two birds with one stone."

"Mac, believe me, he was nae BLUE FOX. I saw the body when Rodgers asked me to see if I knew him. His haircut, his attire, just his whole look was too . . . too military. BLUE FOX's key stroke indicates a dynamic person with finesse. If that chap were BLUE FOX, I'd be lying on a slab, or you'd be interrogatin' him right now. BLUE FOX is nae suicidal."

"I know you're good, Li'l Elf, but how the hell—?"

"I canna explain it. I just know. Please, believe me."

Though Mac fell silent, Ellie hoped he wouldn't push for any more explanation. He would be totally unimpressed to learn her judgment was based more on feminine intuition than expertise.

Rising behind dark clouds, the sun burst forth with streaks of copper and red. Its pattern reminded her of the day Nikki had been buried at sea. Her heart momentarily sank. She still mourned her baby. And missing Irish like she did, Ellie realized: *He's filled that older, wider gap in my life left since Brandt's death. But I know Karney is right: healing takes time.*

Mac drew her attention back to the sunrise when he quoted the mariner's phrase, "Red sky in the morning, sailor take warning . . ."

Without thought, she asked, "Will Irish be worrin' about bad weather where he is?"

"I doubt it. He's still stuck in Scotland."

"Scotland? What the bloody—?" she stopped. "Never mind. I imagine that falls under need-to-know business."

"Actually, in this case you'll need to know, just not quite yet, eh? How 'bout I treat you to breakfast in town?"

"No thanks, Mac. What I need in town is nae breakfast."

"I can save you the trouble, El. Besides you'll never find what you're looking for in quaint little Sheet Harbour."

While her gaze was still locked on the horizon, Mac pressed something against her arm. Taking it, she immediately recognized the comforting heft of a Walther PPK. She dropped the box magazine, fully loaded with

7.65mm rounds. With practiced ease, she methodically inspected the weapon.

The Walther PP was a German pistol, introduced in 1929 for police officers. The later Model PPK was a more compact edition made for plain clothes policemen. It had been her weapon of choice while working in Nazi Germany for MI-6. Weighing a little more than a pound, its magazine held seven rounds. Besides its simplicity, a PPK was easily concealed under clothing or in a handbag.

That weapon lay at the bottom of the North Atlantic.

"Do I dare ask how you came by this in Canada?"

"No," Mac said with a soft chuckle. "Just don't get arrested while carrying it, or we'll both have hell to pay trying to explain this to the Old Man, eh?"

"Ammunition?"

"See Chief McGuire on the gunnery range." His tone became big-brotherly. "And please don't go shooting every Tom, Dick and Heinrich givin' you the once-over around here, or I'll not have any men left to fight Jerry. Just so you know, I've posted sentries closer to your cottage, so don't get trigger-happy with them, either."

"Oh, Mac," she groaned, feeling a sense of control over her life. "Don't you be thinkin' I'm a gun-crazed Bonnie Parker. I just want to make sure it's properly sighted."

Mac sighed wearily. "Just be careful is all I ask, eh?"

"Have faith in me, will you, Noble Elf?"

"I do have faith in you," Mac said, standing, "absolute and unfailing faith. More than you know." He reached to help her up.

Grasping his hand, she sensed more to his remark than Mac revealed. She let go of her distress as she slid the Walther PPK in her pocket. Its weight felt reassuring. However, she also knew: *I'll nae be safe till I view JAEGER's dead body and know for certain that's exactly whose body I'm standing over. Not some Nazi imposter.*

⊕

AMERICAN-BRITISH NAVAL BASE
HVALFJORDUR, ICELAND
TUESDAY

On the Sunderland's dreary hop from Scotland to Iceland, Major Strafford had imparted to Karney what intel MI-6 had about U-boat bases along the East Greenland Coast. It was pathetically little. But Strafford was convinced a base existed somewhere along the vast coast. As the debate ensued, Karney's hackles rose, especially considering the role *Lady Z* would be forced to play.

Worse, Strafford wasn't telling him everything. Too much "need-to-know" crap left him wondering why they needed *Zealous* at all. In part, he understood the major's reluctance to reveal more than need be. On the other hand, Karney was the one responsible for initiating talks with the Danes. Ignorance might be his ruin, not to mention the danger *Zealous* would inevitably encounter next summer.

And no one had yet told Karney when and where he was to meet the elusive Dr. Krigeshaald, whose erratic schedule kept him far from Ammassalik for weeks on end. Not to mention, communications with the good doctor, since well before Christmas, had been virtually nil.

Never having worked covert operations, Karney wondered if he was just not used to this hush-hush malarkey. Or brombyshit as Wendy quaintly put it. But with each step deeper into the mire, Karney felt less secure. Despite misgivings about Wendy Collins, Karney realized the Aussie would share the truth if only to spite Strafford.

Karney felt like he was the catcher in a baseball game with Abbott and Costello and their radio routine. With no idea Who, What or When were on any of the bases, Karney figured Strafford wanted to keep it that way. And the major had made it clear he didn't even like the comedy team. *What does that say about him?* Karney wondered.

⊕

THURS: 15 JAN 42

Since their arrival in Iceland, Karney spent the short days studying charts and reading explorers' notes on the East Greenland Coast, plotting possibilities, as well as reviewing journals of his own travels to Greenland. Evenings, measured by a clock since the short daytime hours were constant twilight, dragged by in the Foster-sloshed poker games, playing his guitar by himself or entertaining others stuck here.

Strong winds, howling like banshees, divined nothing good to come. Gales kept them ice bound. After having lost a virtual fortune to *Ice Sheila*'s crew over the past couple weeks, Karney prayed these spiteful winds stranding them would die. His bad luck had blown away last night and he didn't want to risk it returning. For once, Karney was ahead in the money game with the Aussies.

But even flat-busted was better than Strafford's flat-ass pomposity. Jonathan Swift's term for the Whinnen's opinion of humans in Gulliver's Travels fit well: James Fenton Strafford, the Third, was a definite yahoo.

Ill luck had also dealt Karney quarters to share with Strafford. The man rudely awakened him again as he huffed and puffed his way through a regimen of push-ups, sit-ups and jumping jacks. Though physical exercise was crucial for military personnel, Strafford's intent seemed to be pure exhibitionism. Karney was sure he could best the major. However, he chose not to demean himself with petty rivalry.

Besides a nasty hangover checking his every move. Karney watched, an eye half-open, as the major began his pull-ups on the flimsy door frame. Disgusted, Karney pulled his equally flimsy pillow, reeking of hair oil, over his eyes. It did nothing to stop the drum solo inside his head. *I almost wish I hadn't played poker all night. But damn! I won everything back and thirty-five bucks more!*

Despite lack of sleep, Karney knew his true error was

ignoring Davey Grahe's warning about matching Wendy lager-for-lager. Even his Irish hardhead and drinking stamina couldn't ease the wallop of a Foster's punch. Karney dozed off again.

"Good morning, Commander Rork," the loud greeting exploded inside his head. "Rise and shine, old boy," Strafford called.

Guardedly, Karney sat up. Running a hand through his sleep-ruffled hair, he did not see much good in this dismally cold, dark morning. He viewed Strafford's primping with disdain.

Having already showered, shaved and dressed, Strafford put the finishing touches on his glossy-blond locks with a sweep of his pocket comb. The major glanced at Karney in his tiny shaving mirror, then turned to take Karney in with a chortle. "To be precise, Rork, you look absolutely pitiful. Perhaps today will return the twinkle to your bloodshot eyes and brighten your ailing aspirations."

"What ailing aspirations?" Karney grumbled.

Ignoring him, Strafford packed his toiletry bag and marched past him. "Better get a move on, old boy. Wouldn't want you to miss the bloody war, now would we?"

On his way out of the room, Strafford slammed the door with what Karney could only interpret as gleeful animosity. His head reverberated as if his mainmast had been shattered by a broadside. "Son of a Buck and a Quarter," Karney moaned, holding his throbbing head. *That damn Limey's skating on thin ice with my Irish patience. I think Wendy pegged him for exactly what he is: A bloody pompous ass.*

Favoring his pounding head, Karney slowly rose and walked to the locker room, certain the war would wait till he took a piss.

By the time he ambled over to *Ice Sheila*, three engines ran smoothly, the fourth, just coughing to life, sounded like he felt. He headed for the galley aboard the massive flying boat and poured a mug of fresh joe. Dumping in some sugar, he stirred his mug as he crossed through the wardroom. With a bare nod of his sensitive head, Karney greeted Tom Dibbs—*Ice Sheila*'s baby-faced tail gunner—and George "Puddin" Painter—the pudgy, often gloomy ASV operator. From the central corridor, Karney took the ladder up to the flight deck where Wendy worked.

In *Ice Sheila*'s cockpit, Karney sat in the co-pilot's seat as Wendy finished the pre-flight. "Where're we headed?"

Wendy checked gages and fuel mixtures, then shouted over the engines, "We're buzzin' up East Greenie's Coast on a recon, weather holdin' clear of course. Little Lord Prickleroy," as he now referred to Strafford, "wants to acquaint his-holy-self with the lay of the coast . . . or some such frozen brombyshit."

Drinking the sweet, black coffee, Karney let it purge the cobwebs from his mind. Talking loud enough to be heard over the engines and not make his head throb any worse, Karney asked, "How the hell's he gonna get familiar with Greenland by flying over it?"

Listening to Number Four, Wendy enriched the mixture, then grinned wickedly. "Maybe we'll shove him out at two-thousand feet. That'd get his bloomin' ass familiar with the icescape, at least the few square feet he'd splat on, wouldn't it, mate?"

"'Fraid Mac wouldn't approve, 'specially after we tell him his arrogant Ice Pact coordinator coordinated an impact with solid ice."

Frowning, the Aussie shrugged. "Yeah, I forgot Mac's ruddy orders regardin' his prickship. Just picture it, though, mate!" Wendy grinned. "The Little Lord'd definitely be one precise frozen stiff."

Karney tried to stop a chuckle to save his aching head but failed. Gripping his forehead between thumb and fingers, he waited for the pounding to subside before he asked, "What happens after Strafford looks Greenland over?"

"We come back here tonight, Mikey flies the pom-ass to Nova Scotia in *Ice Sheila* on the morrow, and I fly you to Am . . . Amma . . . goddammit, Aunt Maggie's Slick and dump you over there." An image of Ammassalik, the Danish settlement south of the Arctic Circle came to Karney's mind. The small village sprawled on an island amidst a convoluted maze of islands, mountains and numerous narrow fjords. Denmark Strait lay to the east with thin Sermilik Fjord to the west— in summer they were fluid. Now, in the midst of winter, land and water frozen solid for miles appeared as one and the same. Staring hard at the Aussie pilot, Karney softly voiced his shock, "You're kiddin', right?"

Wendy shook his head. "Sorry, mate. Got orders to fly you in so yous can meet up with Doc. Here, read 'em for yourself," he said, tugging a crumpled, many-folded flimsy from his sleeve pocket.

Unfolding the paper, it took Karney's unfocusing eyes several seconds to read the words. "Fly me over there in what for God's sake? Even if we wait for Mike to come back with *Sheila*, you sure's hell can't land her near Ammassalik. The water's frozen for miles."

Making a notation in the log, Wendy grinned at his friend's dazed expression. "Ever flown in a Traveler with skis, mate?"

A long stare was the only answer the Aussie received.

Mike Ahearn suspended Karney's dismay as he joined them. Bandages evidenced Mikey's run-in with Krupp munitions, while a pallor revealed his earlier loss of blood and his weak state of health.

His greeting, however, remained cheerful. "G'day, mates."

Mikey's voice melted the frozen tracks of questions tramping through Karney's mind. He mumbled a reply, drained his mug and vacated the co-pilot's seat as he retreated to his cubby across from navigation without another word.

Glancing at Wendy, Mike asked, "You told Irish the news?"

"Cancha bloody well tell?" His gaze was perturbed. "Mac shoulda told him before we got this far. Fuckin' Greenland in January. Irish ain't thrilled in the least." "Cracky, Wend, can you blame him? Bloody suicide if you ask me. But then no one ever asks me a bloomin' thing in this bloody war."

Sagging into his seat across from the navigator, Karney felt buried by an avalanche of concrete misery.

The young flight sergeant watched him for a moment, finally clearing his throat to ask, "Ya all right, C'manda Rork?"

Glancing up, Karney forced a grin. "Yeah, I'm okay, Jamie. Too much Foster's last night's all," he lied. In part.

With a sympathetic grin, Jamie returned to scrutinizing his charts; the whole crew more than likely knew the mission at hand.

Karney wondered: *How the hell did I get into this ice jam?*

The answer came quickly: *The war.*

The war Strafford's so damned worried I'll miss.

This damned bloody fuckin' war.

CHAPTER FOURTEEN

Karney again attempted to not think about flying across Denmark Strait in this enclosed biplane. Commonly known in Britain as the Traveler, *Claire-Marie* was designed by Beech Aircraft in the early 30s as a business executive's plane. The war transformed the little plane's role; now Wendy used her as a light transport plane.

Called a Staggerwing in the States—because the upper wing was set slightly behind the lower wing—Wendy assured Karney she was reliable. Wendy even boasted about Jackie Cochran, America's heroine of the air: "Jackie flew a specially equipped Model D17W Staggerwing. That li'l gal broke all sortsa speed and altitude records. And she either placed or won the Bendix Trophy Race a numbera times." Wendy beamed as he said, "Why Jackie even set a transcontinental speed record. And it was a record for anyone, not just Sheilas." From the way he affectionately called her the Speed Queen, Karney figured Jackie Cochran placed a close second to Marciá in the Aussie's heart.

Although this Arctic-camouflaged biplane was the same basic model Jackie Cochran had flown, Karney had serious doubts about *Claire-Marie*'s capabilities in the dead of winter. All pilot talents considered equal.

The little Staggerwing could haul four passengers and supplies, or as in this flight, a Yank and more supplies, up to a max take-off weight of 4,700 pounds. A far cry from the 58,000 pounds *Ice Sheila* lugged into the air. Equipped with retractable landing gear, *Claire-Marie* had been further modified to handle skis for landing on ice.

Having inspected the plane and skis with Wendy during preflight, the thought kept running through Karney's head: *Those thin, awfully-flimsy-looking slats are gonna hold up for a landing?*

But Wendy assured him, "I make runs in *Claire-Marie* all the bloomin' time, mate. This baby's gotta bloody powerful Pratt-Whitney supercharged engine. Ain't no worries, mate, no worries at all."

Maybe, Karney thought skeptically. *I'd still feel safer surrounded by Ice Sheila's bulk, even if they both reek of aviation fuel.*

Powering up, Wendy eased up on the brake and *Claire-Marie* began a bumpy race down the snow-packed runway. The landing lights punctured bright cones into the night, but offered Karney little to see through the angled windscreen. As the ice sped by under them, he felt certain: *We're gonna hit the water before Claire-Marie hits the air.*

He was about to ask Wendy how long the runway was when the little transport's tail came up and she lurched skyward. With a terrier's tenacity, *Claire-Marie* clawed steadily into the air, then gracefully banked west as if to say: "See, love, no worries."

Dawn chased them across Denmark Strait, casting a glow over the water, which defined the line of sea-ice below. Far to the west, Karney could see Greenland spread out beyond the horizon. The sun rose in a brittle sky. Crimson and copper hues shifted hauntingly over indigo-blue seas, dancing with glints of silvery-diamond fog.

Nearing Greenland, wind-stripped mountains and promontories loomed above stark iced-rock ridges. Mesmerized by this ever-shifting display, Karney let his thoughts, as they often did, drift to Ellie.

Tragically, what he remembered most was how she looked during Nikki's funeral. Though pale and weak, it had been Ellie's green eyes which had held him transfixed: emerald fires sparked by a setting sun; their strength as she scanned the waves beneath which her daughter's tiny body had been consigned; stark emptiness and loss expressed when she met his worried gaze.

There had been much he wanted to tell her that day, much he wished to share in empathy. Yet wary of seeming too bold, Karney had held his thoughts. Then the tranquil moment was snatched away.

Karney sighed. Desiring Ellie created a deeper sadness. His heart hadn't ached like this since Jen-Mai's departure for China—a journey from which his exquisite China doll never returned.

Last night, Karney tried to write a letter to Ellie. It only magnified his longing. *No, it's more than longing. What I feel is love. His spirits hit rock bottom. If only I—*

Claire-Marie violently jerked sideways, losing altitude. Buffeted by unseen wind-gods, Karney watched Wendy battle to regain control from their forceful hands. Wendy's more-than-usual customary swearing indicated the situation was critical.

The thought of crashing onto the frozen wastes below turned Karney's melancholy into alarm. Wind, whistling at increased velocity, tore away his half-baked prayer for deliverance. As the craggy coast rose closer, monstrous mountains brought their salvation. The icy precipice formed a windbreak, allowing Wendy to wrestle the transport back onto a level, controlled flight path.

The Aussie was quiet—unusually so. *Does he, too, wonder at our fate if we'd crashed?* Then again, Karney questioned: *Would that sorta thing even cross his jackaroo mind? Isn't this the kind of danger Wendy always navigates?*

Karney took a deep breath of the frigid air, forcing

himself to remain as unruffled. They flew on.

After untold minutes, Wendy stabbed his finger down, yelling over the whine of *Claire-Marie*'s engine, "There's Amma ... Amm ... ah shit, the bloody place we're goin' to. Aunt Maggie's Slick, the Eskie settlement Doc calls home."

Wendy's mutilation of the English language brought a smile to Karney's face. In truth, he was simply thankful the Australian's dead-reckoning navigation was better than his dreadful articulation.

As Wendy banked *Claire-Marie*, Karney gazed down on the cluster of snow-draped houses. From the air, Ammassalik seemed make-believe in a virgin veil of white. Mountains pressed the houses to the sea. Among the numerous fjords, Karney barely perceived the flat surface of Sermilik Fjord cutting north, separating Ammassalik from the vastness of Greenland. All surface water frozen solid.

Leaning closer, Karney yelled, "Where're you putting down?"

When the Aussie pointed toward Sermilik, west of the isolated settlement, Karney stared incredulous. "You're kidding, right? That's nothing but ice and snow over very cold water."

"What'd ya expect, Irish, Logan Airport? It's the frickin' fjord or nothin'. Can't land on a glacier or we'll fall into a creev-ass. So, we slide in between Aunt Maggie's sweet lips. Sorta."

His analogy painted a crude but apropos picture.

Wendy made a pass up the long fjord between ridges of snow-streaked granite rising like eager fangs from the ice—not sweet lips to be kissed. Two fur-clad figures waved from their sledges, large versions of dog sleds designed to haul heavier loads. Twenty-some Inuit dogs curled in apparent oblivion. Further up Sermilik Fjord, Karney caught sight of a makeshift windsock streaming stiffly south-southeast.

Banking sharply over a jagged precipice, Wendy flew

Claire-Marie south, then turned into the wind. "All set to go, or go to set, mate?"

Karney glanced to either side of *Claire-Marie*, sliding up his Ray-Bans as if the lenses hid an unseen, prayed-for landing strip. Only blinding glare assaulted his eyes. Snugging the glasses back on his nose, he caught a glimpse of Ammassalik to the east. The petite settlement seemed even more surreal from this angle.

Winds pressed under the staggered wings, then just as quickly vanished leaving gravity to flex its unwavering muscles. Wendy compensated in slow motion. Karney keenly felt the lack of *Ice Sheila's* protective metal while Wendy whistled as if flying a kite.

Eyeing their imaginary landing strip, Karney leaned closer. "How the hell d'you know it's smooth enough to land on?"

"We put down and, if we don't crack up, it's smooth."

The Aussie adjusted his speed and elaborated, "Doc and his Eskie friend check the ice with their dog teams and smooth out the worst rough spots. They mark my path with blood by draggin' a dead seal down the middle. Sometimes paint but that's even harder to come by. The first pole indicates where to touchdown, the windsock marks how far up the fjord they checked."

Karney wasn't consoled by this Nordic technology.

Sensing Karney's misgivings, Wendy called over to his friend, "No bloody worries, mate, I haven't cracked up yet."

"Maybe the plane hasn't, Wendy," he scoffed, "but I think you already went round the bend."

Unruffled, Wendy eased the throttle back. *Claire-Marie* was assailed by snarling ground winds. The skis hit, bounced upward, then settled down. Wendy feathered the prop. Coasting into a turn, the propeller stopped inches from a rock as huge as a humpback whale.

Opening his door, Wendy patted the fuselage. "Good girl, my sweet *Claire.*" He stepped on the lower wing and glanced over at Karney. "Irish, you are now ready to solo.

Next time, you fly us wherever we're headed, and I'll bloody well sleep."

Karney climbed from the cabin, grumbling, "The day I solo will be the day I go to heaven and put on my damned angel wings with clouds for a landing field."

"There ya go again with them bloody angel wings," Wendy barked as he headed toward a snow-buried shed. "What if ya end up in Ginny Gall with me, mate?"

Jumping down to the ice, Karney worked his stiff and tense muscles. "Then we'll roast hot diggity-dogs and neither of us'll fly."

A gust of frigid air hit Karney as he rounded the plane and headed for the waiting men, dressed almost identically: fur-inside caribou anoraks with *nanus* (polar-bear-hide pants) and knee-high sealskin *kamiks*. However, Dr. Krigeshaald towered over his companion, a *Tunumiu* or native Inuit in their tongue, by almost eighteen inches.

The doctor greeted Karney, "Hallo, you must be my American contact." He waved at Wendy. "That character already I know."

His English was broken, but intelligible. Despite the snow-glare, Karney pushed up his Ray-Bans. "Dr. Krigeshaald?" Firmly shaking hands, he introduced himself, "I'm Lieutenant Commander Karney Rork, United States Coast Guard."

There was little to see of the Dane's face. His full red beard, shimmering with ice particles, spread beneath dark goggles and a hank of darker red hair protruded from his fur-lined hood. When Doc lifted his goggles up, his eyes were stark blue, holding the warmth of an iceberg, though his smile seemed friendly enough. Karney recalled he was a stern man with little room for misunderstandings.

Squinting his eyes and cocking his head, Dr. Krigeshaald asked, "Do I know you, Commander?"

"We met a couple years back, sir. Captain Gunnar Bryannt introduced us when our cutter, *Zealous* put in here on a supply or a mail run."

"Ah, yes, Captain Bryannt. He was supposed to meet me. Why did he not make this trip? Is he all right?"

Uncertain of Gunnar's true condition, Karney vaguely said, "He's on medical leave, Dr. Krigeshaald. Appendicitis."

"Sorry to hear that," the Dane said, then added, "but we do not need to stand on formalities. You call me Doc. Did you not have a nickname?"

"Irish, sir." He grinned self-consciously. "And I'd better call you Doc rather than butcher your name every time I say it."

"You say it fine." He indicated the Inuit. "This is Ooqueh, my friend. He is also a spokesman for the Ammassalimiut, the people who live where ammassat or capelin fish are. They are their main food source. But as the fish dwindle, so do the Ammassalimiut. I fear their very existence is threatened here in Tasiilaq, as the People call what Danes call Ammassalik."

Karney greeted Ooqueh in East Greenlandic. Ooqueh's cracked-toothed grin grew broader. They shook hands. Though the temperature was below zero, Ooqueh's brown, weather-roughened hands were bare. Karney knew, from his Arctic odyssey ten years ago, this was common for these hardy natives.

Introductions made, they got to work.

With Karney's help, Wendy manually swung *Claire-Marie* about, to face into the wind for take-off and onto smoother ice. While he and the Aussie rolled fifty-gallon drums of petrol from the shed out to the plane, Doc and Ooqueh unloaded the various supplies from *Claire-Marie* onto the sledges. Wendy had to hand pump the fuel into the plane's thirsty tanks.

After the Aussie and Yank returned the fuel drums to the shed, Wendy said, almost as an order, "Irish, come help me with the bloody pre-flight, will ya?"

Hearing the tone of his voice, Karney obeyed, squatting on the lower wing beside the cockpit. Karney watched Wendy run the checks, seemingly oblivious to his presence. Then he got to the point.

"I learned somethin' earlier but forgot to tell ya. Someone up here, maybe one or two somebodies smack in the middle of Aunt Maggie's Slick've been relaying convoy intel to Fritzy. There's gotta be Kraut collaborators up here, Irish. Figured you oughta know." He glanced at Karney's seabag. "I trust you're armed." It wasn't a question.

Conscious of the Navy Colt's weight, carried in a shoulder holster, Karney nodded. Wendy's caveat simply justified Karney's impulse to stuff a second Colt and extra ammo into his seabag.

Gazing past the whirling propeller, Karney wondered again what he'd gotten into. "Thanks for the heads-up. Hell, with all this goodwill," he quipped, "you're gonna earn your angel wings in no time."

"Eh, get the hell off me plane with yer angel crap."

Karney started to hop down when a thought came to his mind. "How will you know when to pick me up?"

"Doc'll radio Iceland. I'll get ya first chance, de—"

"—pending on the weather," Karney finished. "I've heard that pick-up line before. What if Doc's our spy?"

"Then pray you're the one alive to work the friggin' radio, mate." Wendy looked serious. "Watch yer bloomin' ass, Irish."

"I will, don't worry." He backed down off the wing.

Watching *Claire-Marie* take off, Karney felt the rift widen between his life and survival like a lead between ice floes expanding. The Traveler grew smaller and smaller, until the speck disappeared entirely. The persistent drone faded into silence. He felt only cold wind keeping him company. Suddenly, the frigid, fuel-reeked and cramped cabin of the staggerwing became as longed for as his beloved easy chair before a well-banked hearth on a wintry night at home in Saugus, Massachusetts.

⊕

RCN TRAINING GARRISON
SHEET HARBOUR, NOVA SCOTIA
FRIDAY

Major Strafford waited impatiently for the alluring blonde secretary to cease her dillydallying and let her Canadian captain know Major James Fenton Strafford the Third had arrived after his deplorable layover in Iceland. Rapping his silver-handled cane on the floor gave no satisfaction. The thick carpet absorbed his irritation.

Should I wrap my cane around someone's neck?

His wait for Mac MacCalister brought back irksome memories of London. Ten months ago, he'd been forced to sit while Commodore Greer and the captain conferred about ICE PACT. He'd cooled his heels with old news from the London Daily and prudish Beth, Greer's secretary who was nowhere near the caliber sex-pistol as Marciá.

Appreciating Marciá's headlights and well-rounded bumper, Strafford thought: *To be precise, Marciá is a vast improvement over old Greer's chunk of lead. Though I daresay, Marciá bears a marked resemblance to Ice Sheila's nose-art. I wonder—* He cautioned himself. *Nose-art aside, I cannot yet taste her sweets with so much resting on this meeting with MacCalister. I will reserve a more private time for Marciá Therkilsen.*

Pocketing his lust for the blonde, Strafford let his mind march back three years to his first encounter with Mac MacCalister at a pre-war conference, also in London. *We didn't see eye-to-eye then. But today, I need to make a better impression on that rangy Canuck. The core of my credibility is an exemplary service record, my expertise and the clout I carry with Military Intelligence. My words can neither cast doubt upon myself nor reveal my preoccupation with Eleanor.*

Strafford had to persuade Captain MacCalister that Eleanor's true nature was devious and that she had played them all for fools. Once Mac believed Eleanor was a liar, the pedestal on which he'd placed his winsome cousin would begin to crumble.

Again stomping his cane against the carpet, Strafford's ire flared anew. *It galls me to think of brownnosing that Canuck bastard, two bloody grades above my rank. But he cannot doubt the shocking truth of my disclosure about Eleanor. If he does,* Strafford thought with dread, *my entire bloody cause might be—*

To his surprise, the subject of his focus suddenly stood before him. Arms laden with files, Eleanor had entered the room. Strafford's heart seemed to stutter, not only distracting his thoughts but causing a great deal of irritation at himself.

Though startled to find Strafford sitting in Mac's waiting room, Ellie recovered quickly, inquiring in her sassiest tone, "Why, James old boy, drop by to mooch a spot of tea? Or would that be liquor? Sorry, cocktails aren't served till after six."

Flustered by her sudden appearance, Strafford wasn't nearly as swift with a glib comeback. "Eleanor . . . ah, of course not, I have a meeting with your cousin, Captain MacCalister, you know?"

"Why, yes, James, I am wholly aware Mac's my cousin. Couldn't you have just dropped him a line? Or rung him on the tellie?"

"To be precise, I've been assigned here. I wasn't aware you were at the garrison yet. I daresay, this is a rather pleasant surprise finding you here today. How long—"

"James, cut the bloody crap," she sneered. "You knew before Christmas I'd be here. Mac told me how you practically begged him to be part of this mission, certain he needed your competence to solidify this muddle into an ICE PACT so he'd be free for field work and how elated you were to know I'd be on the team. Or some such drivel."

"Well, Eleanor-dear, it wasn't drivel. At the time you were still in hospital, and he wasn't certain of your commitment."

Captain MacCalister came out of his office. Marciá took Eleanor's reports. The captain barely glanced at Strafford. Obviously more concerned with garrison paperwork than the fact Strafford had just flown more than seventeen-hundred miles in a deafening, cold and uncomfortable monstrosity of a flying boat, the big Canadian turned to the ladies.

"Great, Ellie, you finished the training requirements, eh? Marciá, I know it's late, but—"

"Yes, Cap'n Mac, I'll have 'em all typed before Commander Sanders arrives in the morning."

"Thata girl. Why don't you take tomorrow off, eh?"

Marciá mumbled, "Tomorrow's Saturday, Cap'n Mac. Aren't I supposed to have it off anyway?"

Strafford *harrumphed* in annoyance at their plebeian bargaining, then slumped back into the sofa,. *Though this wench must have security clearance and quite magnificent bubs, she's still just common help.*

MacCalister still didn't acknowledge his presence. Instead, he turned again to Marciá and dictated instructions on how he wanted the reports broken down.

Indignant, Strafford turned to Eleanor. "I say, Eleanor-dear, is that Royal Navy Leftenant Nigel Sanders of British Commando infamy arriving tomorrow?"

"Aye, but he's leftenant commander now. Mac's lucky to have his expertise. It seems nothing but the best on our shoestring budget for this operation."

Strafford gave a pretentious nod. "Of course, my dear, to be precise, that's why they recruited us. A better team there's never been than you and me." Leaning toward Ellie, he said *sotto voce*, "In or out of bed."

Ellie took a step forward, ready to slap the damn Brit as she said, "You bloody son of a—"

"Major Strafford," Mac said, turning toward them.

Mac's interruption saved Ellie from doing something she might regret, though it would undoubtedly have felt damn good at the time she did it.

"Welcome to Canada, Major, let's go in my office. You, too, Ellie."

Clearing his throat, Strafford planted his cane and didn't move. From Eleanor's stance, all too familiar from numerous past quarrels best forgotten, Strafford knew she was more than pissed.

When Mac realized no one had budged, he asked, "Is something wrong, Major?"

"Captain, what I have to say is for your ears alone." His tone grew patronizing. "Much as I'd love to chat with Eleanor, I cannot allow that to occur. My orders are, after all, orders."

Ellie tensed. Since arriving in Nova Scotia her clearance was TOP SECRET. She had never been left out of anything. But tired from a long day, she snapped, "Fine, have your bloody chat with my cousin. Mac can fill me in later. I'm going home. Goodnight, Mac, Marciá."

With the door's slam, Mac MacCalister remarked, "What's eating El? She never throws in the towel that quickly, eh?"

Implacable to the last, Strafford retorted, "To be precise, Captain, I can assure you, it's for the best. Nor, might I add, will you tell any of this to Eleanor later. Is that understood?"

Mac glared at the Brit with a look filled with venom, and when he spoke, his tone was menacing.

"I understand my orders perfectly well, *Major*," he stressed the Brit's lesser rank, "and they do not come from you. You don't make decisions regarding disclosure, and to be precise, you are not in command of this operation."

Inwardly, Strafford seethed, but he said nothing more. With a curt nod, the major stomped into Mac's office, his cane softly thudding in precise accord. A second later, the major was backed out the door by Chelsea's deep-throated growl.

As if speaking to a person, Mac said, "It's alright, Chels." Strafford glared at him. "Major, you may sit on the sofa. I will be in shortly. Chelsea won't mind, will ya, girl?"

Tail hesitantly wagging, Chelsea, her eyes on Strafford, backed up and lay down by the desk. Strafford went in more gingerly to sit down.

Mac looked at Marciá, but before he opened his mouth, she replied, "Yes, I know, Cap'n Mac, don't disturb you, but, Cap'n, don't forget you've a meetin' in Hali' tonight."

Annoyed at having forgotten, Mac rolled his eyes, then looked at Marciá. "Are the reports for the attending officers ready?"

She hefted a thick stack of manila folders off her desk. "Ready, alphabetized, new data sheets inserted, as well as British Admiralty's projected losses for the next four months, as well as the long range prospects for when the Yanks get rollin'."

He took the reports in one big hand. "Why do I ever doubt you'll get the job done?" he asked rhetorically.

As he glanced at the wall clock, Marciá saw the irritation Major Strafford's early arrival created. Since Mac's transfer of offices from St. John's to Sheet Harbour, a day didn't go by with this sort of unexpected interruption. Marciá almost wished they were back in the far off, boring confines of Newfoundland. *Poor Mac*, she sympathized.

"This better not take long," Mac said, storming into his office. "I don't have much time, Major, so whatever you have to say, make it snappy."

Mac's agitation was punctuated when he slammed the reports down on his desk at the same instant the door banged shut. It was an exclamation point which jump-started Marciá back to work.

A second later, Marciá heard Mac's voice over the intercom. She started to ask him to repeat what he had said, then realized he wasn't talking to her. The files that he dropped on his desk had, inadvertently, pressed the intercom button, allowing her to hear what was supposed to be confidential.

About to let Mac know, Marciá overheard Strafford's nasally London sneer when he said, "Eleanor's working for the Nazis."

Mac's voice boomed, "BULLSHIT!" Marciá again jumped in her seat. "Ellie's as loyal as an Arctic summer day is long."

Marciá found it impossible to interrupt now.

"Captain," Strafford replied, "she may be loyal but it is no longer to our side. Last year, after her mission in Denmark, it was learned Eleanor had compromised that operation. Four key agents were killed, while she vanished for weeks into Nazi Germany."

Marciá strained to hear past the silence of her intercom.

Sounding wary, Mac finally said, "Go on, Major Strafford."

"Eleanor claimed, while returning to Great Britain, a Danish agent code named JAEGER turned her over to the *Gestapo*. MI-6 learned of her arrest, but their hands were tied. At great risk to my own life and wholly unauthorized by my superiors, I posed as an *SS* officer and secured her release. Not until our return did it ever occur to me our little venture went much too smoothly. The Nazis let us escape because your dear cousin is working for them. And I've proof."

Faintly, Marciá heard Strafford's cane thud on the carpet as if in emphasis of his statement. Papers rustled when he ostensibly handed over the supposed evidence on Ellie.

As expected, Mac was quiet as he read.

Marciá leaned closer.

"Goddammit, Major," it sounded like a whip cracking when Mac snapped his hand against the paper. "That's all the evidence you have? That's a fire I could piss out blindfolded. I'll need more bloody proof than this before I accuse Ellie of treason."

"Captain MacCalister," Strafford whined, "don't blow

your top. I am merely the messenger. More proof is forthcoming. To be precise, your Aussie charioteers arrived at Scapa Flow as I waited for the necessary corroboration. It was delayed, and since I have been unable to hand deliver it, other means of conveyance had to be employed."

"Well, Major Strafford, if you don't mind . . ."

Mac's voice held enough sarcasm to indicate to Marciá he wasn't buying any part of the major's story.

"I have my own sources to contact about this situation."

"Suit yourself, old boy. However, I strongly advocate you curtail Eleanor's part in this operation."

"But you were the one insisting she be included."

"Yes, well," Strafford said, "to be precise, I did not want her slipping the noose, as it were, before I could speak to you, old boy. As coordinator of OPERATION ICE PACT—"

"Coordinator, yes, Major. Bloody rumormonger, absolutely not. Goddammit man, you expect me to believe, hook, line and sinker, that Ellie works for the Nazis when you haven't given me one shred of solid proof. If and when, and I'm extremely doubtful of when, I receive any corroboration about my cousin being a Nazi double agent, I'll take appropriate action. Until then, I'm far too short handed and her expertise is much too valuable to waste rolling bandages or darning socks or some other menial, no-security-needed task."

"Captain MacCalister," Strafford said huffily as his cane thumped the carpet, "I will not have my integrity questioned nor the intelligence which I've presented to you so blatantly ignored. Especially since you are, by no means, fully aware of our situation."

Venom spat through the intercom with Mac's next words. "Then why the fucking hell don't you enlighten me, Strafford-old-boy."

From his swearing, Marciá knew, Mac was utterly pissed. The pause widened as Strafford presumably prepared another salvo. When he spoke, she heard the restraint of his own anger.

"In the early thirties, while Eleanor worked for MI-6 in Germany, her cover story was working as Wolf Gündestein's personal secretary, a position I went to great pains to arrange for her. During those years of employment with him, her ties became strong, a bit too strong. What you feel you could 'piss out blind-folded' was a flame ignited by *Herr* Gündestein himself. He had his own ties to *das Dritte Reich*, of which MI-6 wasn't aware."

Mac snarled, "What ties to the Third Reich?"

"Wolf Gündestein was an aristocrat, who happened to be a shrewd businessman with an honorary rank of *Obersturmbannführer* in the *Allgemeine SS*. A leftenant colonel, if you don't happen to be familiar with—"

"I'm quite familiar with *SS* rank structure, Major."

Derailed by Mac's snapped retort, Strafford cleared his throat and continued, "To be precise, Gündestein's ties were deep within the *Sicherheitsdienst*, the *SD*, the Nazis' most nefarious spies of—"

"Major, I realize you're not aware of my background, but I do not need to be lectured like an imbecile."

"Yes, of course, Captain. Forgive me."

Strafford's cane thumped again, giving Marciá the distinct impression the meeting wasn't going as Strafford had planned.

"Eleanor's situation is complex," Strafford said ultimately. "When she crossed into Germany, it was to see the old man. In the past, Gündestein gave her stolen gems and, more recently, substantial funds of which—"

"That's the corroboration you're waiting for?" Mac broke in, clearly irritated by the major's drawn out tale.

"Yes," he snapped, barely bereft of impertinence. "At least in part. She has since received more funds, though not directly from Gündestein."

Cautiously, Mac asked, "Why not directly from him if he's working with MI-6?"

"The old boy's quite dead, Captain. Wolf Gündestein was assassinated."

"How can you be so sure he's dead?" Mac asked skeptically.

Strafford flatly stated, "Because I killed him."

The hush grew ponderous as Marciá awaited a response.

Quietly, Mac asked, "Also of your own volition?"

"No, it was a sanctioned kill from MI-6. The old boy's wealth as well as influence within the *Kriegsmarine*, in particular the U-boat arm, had grown. Gündestein pushed for increased production of U-boats, which would ultimately benefit his own shipping business. And I do not need to remind you, Captain, of the devastation wolf-packs have wrought on our convoys. Any escalation in production could lengthen the war by years, perhaps even give Nazi Germany an edge."

Hearing Strafford shift position on the sofa, followed by a soft but distinct growl from Chelsea, Marciá whispered under her breath, "Good girl, Chels."

"As for the money, it's been, how do Yank gangsters put it, laundered through a Swiss bank account, which has left MI-6 with a bloody cold trail. I'm sure you know, Swiss bank accounts are held in tight confidentiality. However, there's a body of evidence to indicate the majority of the money came from confiscated funds of wealthy Jews now in concentration camps or dead. Gold, silver, diamonds, gems: Swiss bankers handle it all. And they do not care where it comes from, profit is their bottom-line. All they see, all they want to know, what?"

Strafford briefly paused, then apologized, "Excuse me, Captain, I digress." He again cleared his throat. "To be precise, all we know for certain is Eleanor's funds originated from a Swiss bank."

The silence again engulfed Marciá's senses.

So softly, she barely heard, Mac asked, "Is there more?"

An equally soft *harrumph* preceded Strafford's next words, "Gündestein's nephew is *Korvettenkapitän* Jakob Prüsche, a U-boat captain with a nautical engineering degree. He designed and built an advanced *Unterseeboot*, the prototype Gündestein encouraged Dönitz to mass produce. Both Prüsche and Uncle Wolfie," Strafford mocked, "are tight with Naval High Command and *Herr* Hitler himself. And we have absolutely no useful data on this prototype. MI-6 feels, in part, our efforts have been thwarted because Eleanor has kept in touch with—"

Mac laughed outright. "Strafford, you make it sound like she rings up Adolf and his cronies on a daily basis to chat."

"Captain," Strafford's voice oozed disdain, "you should not need to be told of Eleanor's skill as an operative. If she needs to contact Germany, she can, any number of ways, most obviously with the powerful radiotelegraphs right here at the garrison. Your radio towers are quite obvious, despite the forest. I saw them when your driver let me out at the portico. To be precise, Captain MacCalister, I'm sure they have more than ample strength to reach Europe."

The silence deepened. Unconsciously, Marciá leaned forward, fearing Captain Mac weighed Strafford's words and found them laden with truth. Footfalls thudded out in the hall. Marciá jerked back and buried her own intercom under files. A minute elapsed. No one came into the office. She took the files off. Whatever Mac said—

"Marciá!" Mac's voice thundered behind her.

Her heart lodged in her throat. Turning slightly, she found him standing in the doorway. "Yes, Cap'n Mac?"

"Assign Major Strafford private quarters in the north wing." Mac noted the duffle bag and suitcase at the far end of the sofa. "Have Petty Officer McGuire escort him and carry up his gear."

"Yes, sir," Marciá said, a sigh of relief escaping. Fearful she had been caught red-eared, her hands shook slightly as she rang up the armory, the most likely place to start looking for Chief Dunstan McGuire. Marciá felt an incessant urge to peek over her shoulder. Though she had not heard it all, she heard enough.

Marciá glimpsed Major Strafford strolling out of Mac's office. He took up residence on the leather sofa like he lived there. The major brought a brittle enigma to the garrison and she resented him for it. *Strafford might be a sharp looking fella, but he sure has it in for Ellie.* That in itself bothered Marciá. *What if there's more?*

Heading for the outer door, Chelsea at his side, Mac said to Strafford, "I'll see you at mess in the morning, Major. Oh-six-hundred. Good afternoon."

She saw he was empty-handed. "Cap'n Mac," Marciá called to him. Like an agile mountain cat, Mac spun on his heel. "You forgot the reports . . . I'll get—"

"No, you work." Mac pointed to her desk, then at the floor beside him. "Chelsea, sit." Both obeyed.

Inwardly, Marciá cringed. She acted industrious, all the while dreading to hear Mac's voice boom through the still open intercom. He emerged, reports in hand, and paused before her, his back to Strafford.

Marciá glanced up. His green eyes were iced as he stared down at her. "Yes, Cap'n Mac?" she timidly asked.

Though he rifled through the reports, his gaze never left hers; silent warning he was aware she had heard what Strafford had told him. The fact Mac said nothing in the major's presence, also made it clear she wasn't to mention anything to anyone.

Trying to swallow, she found her mouth drier than a burlap sack of Alberta wheat after the last harvest. She eventually forced out, "Is anything wrong, Cap'n Mac?"

His gaze softened. "Just checking, Marciá. By the way, when Sergeant Boudreau arrives, ring me up, eh?"

"Sure thing, Cap'n Mac," she said with a nod. Only then did Marciá notice Strafford staring with interest, his arms spread over the sofa back, his cane twitching restlessly in one hand. After Mac and Chelsea left,

Strafford's gaze zeroed in on her. A surly half-smile tweaked his thin mustache out of kilter.

Clearing her typewriter, Marciá turned to find Strafford perched on her desk. She hadn't heard him move. *These spy-types give me the creeps*, she thought. *Mac moves on cat's paws, too, but at least he has the decency to betray his position before spooking me.*

Coldly, she asked, "Can I help you, Major?"

"Does that slave driver ever give you a break, Marciá?" Strafford leaned close and sniffed her perfume. "I could take you out to dinner? Some wine, a little conversation, you could fill me in on local attractions." His gaze lingered hungrily on her bosom. "You could help me settle-in while we get better . . . acquainted . . ."

"Yes, no, I mean no, sir," she floundered, falling under the spell of the major's golden eyes. Then she recalled what he'd told Mac and realized: *This guy changes gears too fast for me. He just accused my friend of being a Nazi spy and now he's trying to screw me onto his pecker. Did he kill that old man, then sit beside a cozy fire, sipping hot toddies while relishing his triumph?*

"Major," she said, calming her jitters, "I must finish all these reports, so no, I can't leave. Besides," she stretched the truth to the Yukon and back, "I'm spoken for."

He caressed her left hand. "Marciá," his light tone scoffed, "I see no proof of anyone having spoken for you."

Gracefully retrieving her hand, despite feeling like ants crawled over her flesh, she simply said, "Physical evidence does not prove matters of the heart, Major."

He twirled a strand of her hair. "I've always adored blondes, and your flaxen hair curls are so inviting . . ."

Marciá didn't miss his gaze down her blouse, not on her locks. Yet she felt almost hesitant pushing his hand away. "Major, my curls and all my everything else are off limits to any man stationed at this garrison." She reached for the phone. "If you'd prefer, I'll have Cap'n Mac explain his definition of no fraternizing—"

Strafford intercepted her hand. "I'm sure there's—"

"Absolutely no need to introduce yourzelf, Major," came a French-accented voice from the door. "However, you are not aware of me. I am Sergeant Vance Boudreau, Royal Canadian Mounted Police. RCMP for short. Though personally, I've never found myzelf short on ability nor insight in the line of duty, eh?"

Striding into the room, there was no ignoring the challenge in Boudreau's eyes as he met Strafford's annoyed gaze. Though he couldn't have heard it all, the blond Mountie perceived Marciá's bind. *Sergeant Boudreau,* she thought, *you have most decidedly just become my knight in shining armor.*

Strafford recovered quickly. Leaning heavily on his cane, he offered his hand to the tall Mountie.

In an obvious snub, Boudreau ignored Strafford, turning to Marciá. "We're still on tomorrow, *Chérie?*"

Not sure if he acted out a scenario for Strafford or if he was really asking her out, Marciá mutely nodded. Testing the water, she hesitantly ventured, "Yeah, what time?"

"I'll pick you up at the usual, about six, eh?"

"Swell." A smile tickled her lips, recognizing the honesty in his eyes. Not hard jade like Mac's, but light gray-green like summer sagebrush in Alberta. Marciá picked up the phone. "I'll let Cap'n Mac know you're here, sweetie," she added as she stuck her whole foot into the water, hopefully not her mouth.

Receiving a teasing wink from her newfound heartthrob, Marciá also noted the iced snarl in Strafford's tiger eyes.

As Mac answered the phone, Dunstan McGuire showed up. Some unspoken warning must have shot from Boudreau to the gruff-looking sailor after the two men greeted one another as chums and equals.

The solidly built Irishman roughly grabbed Strafford's luggage. "Chief Petty Officer McGuire here, sir. Hope you don' mind a wee bit of a hike. Jus' lemme know if I walk too bloody fast." McGuire turned on his heel, leaving Strafford no choice but to follow.

Strafford gave a quick, "Cheerio, Marciá," as he hastily hobbled out of the office.

With a heavy sigh, she closed her eyes. Opening them, Marciá realized Boudreau watched her intently.

"Are you all right, *Chérie*?"

"Yes, thanks, but you really didn't have to ask me—"

With a hurt expression, he touched a finger to her lips. "I never do what I don't have to, *Chérie*. If I didn't have to go to this meeting with Cap'n Mac, I'd take you out tonight. At least the major banished my procrastination and shyness, eh?"

"A shy French-Canadian Mountie?" she teased. "That's like callin' Cap'n Mac wishy-washy. It just doesn't jive."

"I guess you learned that on your own. Besides," he timidly said, "I already ran into Cap'n Mac. He requested I deliver you from the drooling jowls of that lecherous Limey. I already have the definite impression that our good captain is none too impressed with Major Strafford's caliber."

Mac's voice arose from the doorway, "That's a damn bloody understatement." He flopped on the sofa as his gaze met Marciá's eyes. Chelsea raced to Boudreau. "Were the Mountie's skills as a bouncer needed?"

"Almost, Cap'n, but Chief McGuire did the bouncin'."

Though Mac was quiet, Marciá knew he mulled something over.

Finally, he leaned forward, elbows on his knees. "Knowing you overheard some or most of our conversation, Marciá . . ."

Her face flushed with the heat of guilt.

"Do me a favor."

"Name it, Cap'n Mac."

"Run a check on our sublime Limey, a tad more personal than usual. Use your feminine wiles on the guys to beguile unofficial tidbits from those who've worked with him. Then see what flotsam rises to the surface from the gals. Start with Commodore Greer's secretary, Beth. It would help if you handled that part of my investigation, so I can check on some other matters, eh?"

Though not quite sure what he hunted, Marciá nodded as she answered with renewed verve, "Sure thing, Cap'n Mac."

"*Sacré bleu*, I pray this gorgeous lady never has to do any sort of background check on me."

"But, Vance," she mocked, "I thought you were chaste?"

Glancing at his watch, he avoided her eyes. "Cap'n Mac?"

Mac stood. "Aye, let's go, or we'll be late. Marciá, you're a clam: blonde, smart and beautiful, but a clam nonetheless."

Boudreau winked and whispered, "Tomorrow at six, *Chérie*."

Marciá smiled briefly, but her suspicions already dug through the slimy can of fat worms Mac had opened. *And I suspect Strafford is probably the only worm at the bottom. Though I haven't known Ellie long, she seems virtuous and trustworthy. But, I know, the stuff Mac's checkin' deals with Strafford's claims against her.*

What if they prove right? What if Ellie really is, God forbid, some sorta Nazi spy? Has she fooled all of us? Even her own cousin?

On the icy edge of the East Greenland Coast.

Photos taken by Ron Eidlemann during one of Lady Z's mail and supply runs to Ammassalik in late May of 1941.
Karney later pasted them into his journal.

Looking north from Ammassalik (Tasiilaq), Greenland.

CHAPTER FIFTEEN

Karney slid from his perch atop Dr. Krigeshaald's sledge when the dog team halted. In short order, a young Inuit man showed up to take charge of Doc's sledge and the team. Doc did not introduce him, although the fellow gave a brief nod, almost as if he knew Karney. Seeing the resemblance to Ooqueh it was an easy jump to figure they might be related. Hearing him call the older man father, the relationship fell into place. Karney didn't remember his name, but they had met several summers ago, when *Zealous* had brought medical supplies and mail into Ammassalik.

When they got the dogs moving, Karney waved in farewell and turned to take in his surroundings as he thought: *Good to know I've got another potential ally on this hunk of ice.*

On the northwest fringe of Ammassalik's houses, of which there weren't many, Doc's house perched closer to the twenty-one-hundred-foot tall mountain Doc had labeled Aammangaaq than to the main settlement itself. Winter raiment gave Ammassalik the impression of a ghost town compared to the pristine, vibrant apparel of summers Karney recalled from previous visits.

Yet the settlement held inhabitants. Smoke trails of

life rose from numerous stovepipes. It still amazed Karney how people had survived here for centuries. Perhaps Greenland was "the land of man" as the Inuit called it. On the other hand, Karney knew from history, Scandinavians and other Europeans had settled here and lived quite contentedly. Karney had to admit, despite its starkness, Greenland was incredibly beautiful.

The shadows he and Doc cast elongated with the early sunset as they trudged up a snow-blanketed slope near Tasiilaq Inlet. Looking back, Karney realized the dollhouses he saw from the air had been blasted by the incessant *piteraq* winds off the icecap. The homes held only faded remnants of original reds, yellows or blues. The bit of exposed siding on Doc's house showed cinnamon-red laced with white gingerbread trim, scarred by the wind as well. No icicles hung from the eaves—this time of year was too cold for anything to thaw.

Doc paused. "Irish, you meet my Valya now."

To match Doc's stature, Karney's mind pictured his wife as some big, horsey Viking Valkyrie with thick, braided-blonde tresses to her waist, over a steel breastplate, ready to wield a shield and spear or perhaps a finely engraved battle axe.

Karney ducked through the doorway to enter the vestibule, warm and welcoming. Holding back a thick curtain to keep the cold at bay, Doc motioned Karney into the living room. Karney's numb senses quickly thawed to his gross fallacy—Valya was anything but horsey. Long, blonde, braided tresses fit a portion of his vision, while her bosom definitely lived up to Doc's stature.

But Karney's erroneous image halted there.

Shaking her diminutive hand, Karney found himself inspected from head to toe by the cool, gray eyes of a Norse Siren stranded in a treeless world of frozen water. As if to further emphasize her daintiness, Karney barely felt her hand within his. When she spoke, each word was precise King's English, her voice feathery soft and seductive.

"I am pleased to make your acquaintance, Commander Rork."

"And I you, Mrs. Krigeshaald," Karney mumbled, chagrined.

The moment he released her hand, Doc grabbed Valya up off the floor in a wild polar-bear hug. Though Doc had only been gone a few hours, like a hungry dog missing his master, it could have been weeks from the intensity of his impassioned display. Feeling an intruder as they kissed, Karney gazed around their home.

Brightly colored vases of dried flowers lightened the dreary winter atmosphere. Candle glow flickered off highly polished oak paneling, an extravagance in this northern clime. Heavy, maroon drapes hung at the few small windows. A collection of tapestries with provincial scenery of forests and hunters provided color and extra insulation against the harsh Arctic weather outside.

In the living room, a red horsehair sofa, four needlepoint chairs and a battered ottoman gathered around a mirror-luster coffee table; each item carefully placed near the stone hearth, where a well-banked fire crackled. Neatly laid out on crocheted mats was a silver service containing a lavish coffee urn, china cups and a platter heaped with sweet-rolls and Danish butter cookies.

Valya looked flustered as Doc set her on the floor. She quickly smoothed out her skirt and apron, then patted her hair to make sure it was in place. After Doc and Karney washed their hands in the kitchen, Valya beckoned them back into the living room to sit down. Eyes flickering with an inner luminosity, she filled three cups from the urn.

"I am sorry it is only ersatz coffee, Commander Rork," she said. "With the war, our supplies are limited. I hope the treats will make up for the lack of real coffee?"

Before Karney spoke, his stomach growled in anticipation of tasting the delights. Laughing with, as much as at him, Doc and Valya simultaneously pushed the plate of pastries toward him.

Doc smiled. "Do your Coast Guard cooks starve you, Irish?"

Taking a glazed cinnamon roll, Karney chuckled. "Not my cook, just lousy food on this trip. Up until now." He took a bite. "By the way, ersatz coffee is just fine," he said, sipping the bitter brew. "As long as it's hot, anything'll do." He licked the icing off each finger. "And this roll is absolutely delicious."

Valya beamed, obviously pleased. "Help yourself, Commander, but don't spoil your appetite before supper," she warned.

"If supper's this tasty," Karney said, selecting several butter cookies, "I'll make sure I leave room." Though he noted the grin on Doc's face, he also caught the knowing glance Valya gave her husband, as if I-told-you-so was the unspoken phrase.

With the ice broken by Karney's grumbling gut, they settled in to deal with the questions he needed to have answered. Though dozens filled his head, he stuck to a simple roster: population of Inuit and Danes; sizes of nearby villages; possibly new or unfamiliar visitors; where were the best hunting grounds?

The last question clearly threw Doc off track. He stared blankly, then, almost defiantly, answered, "This you must ask the Inuit or my son, Hans. I do not hunt."

Doc glanced uncomfortably at his wife. She returned a scathing look of warning which obviously had no effect on the big Dane. "I order Hans to not have such close fellowship with the Inuit. He never listens. And, Commander, your people shall not consort with them either. The war makes the situation worse. Inuit bloodlines will be steadily diluted by foreigners escaping Nazi occupied Europe. This must not continue unrestrained. Inuit blood must remain pure."

His voice having risen with his diatribe, now fairly boomed with implied threat. "Furthermore, Commander, I will not abide you Americans, Canadians nor Englanders, bringing your numerous depraved habits to the Inuit, infecting them with venereal diseases and maladies for which native peoples have no immunity or medicine."

Raising a hand, Karney tried to defuse the Dane's growing indignation. "Whoa, Doc, we don't plan to invade Greenland with criminals or diseased malcontents. Our intent isn't to establish another Botany Bay or some sort of penal colony."

Yet Karney knew Ammassalik would soon be the site of their radio-weather station to be dubbed Bluie East Two (BE-2) and a larger endeavor, LORAN short for LOng RAnge Navigation, was also in the hopper. LORAN utilized radio signals to triangulate a plane's position allowing them to establish an accurate "fix" for navigation. The East Greenland Coast was slated for LORAN bases which would be manned by mostly young, lonely guys, far from home. The exact sort of influx Doc feared.

Right now, however, that was not Karney's problem.

"Doc, the only bases I'm interested in are ones the Germans might be building. I asked about the hunting because if areas are frequented, the Nazis will avoid them."

Though clearly still skeptical, Doc repeated, "You must ask Hans. He is probably holed up in some Inuit igloo, even as we speak, keeping himself much too warm."

Valya quietly interceded. "I am certain Hans will be home soon, Bross. You judge him too harshly. He is a responsible young man and the storms of the previous few days, I'm sure, have delayed his travel time. He will arrive before supper."

"Yes," Doc said, frowning. "He never seemed to be late for Valya's meals if he's nearby." Then Doc had to qualify, "If only that young man were so timely with his school studies."

Karney remained quiet. *My mission isn't to help a young Dane appease his father.* Yet beneath Karney's silence, thoughts clamored for attention which did not foster trust in the Krigeshaalds. *Am I just borrowing trouble? Or maybe my usually-right sixth-sense is trying to warn me that something is outta line here. I'm sure time will tell.*

U799

DENMARK STRAIT

FRIDAY

Kapitänleutnant Jakob Prüsche shrugged deeply into his gray-leather coat. His white-cloth captain's cap proved worthless against the wind shrieking past the conning tower. The scarf his wife Cynara knitted helped only marginally. Emotionally, however, it was a God send.

This storm had closed rapidly. Winds had whipped to gale force in a matter of seconds and the temperature plummeted. Trying to sustain an even keel, *U799* remained partially submerged. The effort was useless. The swells rolled violently; no quarter given by these Furies.

Wind keened in the overhead cables like a malevolent demon, echoing a sharp pain in Prüsche's spine. Even the insignia on the conning tower of their bold little Arctic fox appeared to recoil beneath this vicious wind.

Four lookouts, crowded around the horseshoe-shaped conning tower platform, were all at the mercy of the Arctic cold. Icy water drenched them with battering waves, the spray deflector of virtually no use against the onslaught. Layers of ice built up on the deck-plates making the already slick footing even more treacherous. The gale seemed set on pummeling the boat into submission.

Prüsche swore under his breath. Several men suffering from frostbite had already been relieved of duty. Though always frigid off the East Greenland Coast, the option to leave was not his tonight.

How many more will succumb before this Dane shows?

He was livid at having to battle this tempest, causing the calm of his U-boat to deteriorate. Yet it was neither his men nor the boat's fault. No, Prüsche blamed it all on a haughty Dane who couldn't tell time and thought *U799* had nothing better to do than loiter off the pack ice.

"*Kaleu*," a lookout yelled, "I think I see something."

Staring at the blackness, Prüsche barked, "Maurer, either you see something or you do not. Which is it?"

Halden Maurer was quiet. Prüsche knew this new man, not yet seventeen, was too terrified to speak. Maurer wasn't the only one. Since this mission began, the crew grew wary of the skipper's unpredictable outbursts. It was not like Jakob to fly off the handle, yet none of his men understood what lay beneath their skipper's rage and frustration.

Prüsche knew his crew was not to blame. If anything their efficiency had vastly improved. However, he neither pardoned nor praised. Things were just this way—no reasons given. Though his attitude might be justified, it remained a private matter.

Raising his binoculars, he asked more softly, "Where do you think you might have seen something, Halden?"

His reply was immediate. "One-hundred-thirty-five degrees, *Kaleu*. There it is again, sir."

It took a moment for Prüsche to see the minuscule pinprick of light flash across the pack ice beside which *U799* lingered. He set a hand on Maurer's shoulder. "Good eyes, son."

Turning slightly, Prüsche spoke to Hermann Schefflein, his quartermaster. "Schefflein, verify their identity and answer in kind." When he did not respond, Prüsche asked, "What's wrong?"

"*Kaleu*, the code is correct, but the sender is not JAEGER. I can tell by their hesitancy with the blinker, sir."

"Who are they and what the hell do they expect us to do?" Prüsche snapped.

Schefflein sent the question, then read back the reply. "It says: 'AM SKUA. JAEGER BUSY. RETURN 4 NIGHTS HENCE'."

"Busy? *Heilege Scheisse!*" Taking a frigid breath of the

night air, Prüsche glared upward, slowly letting it escape. "Are we pathetic marionettes for them to control?" he demanded of no one in particular, his tone as icy as the wind. Then, to himself, Prüsche muttered, "No, the damn war has made us all puppets. We will cut the strings and find a convoy on our own."

Looking hesitant, Schefflein asked, "What do I reply, sir?"

"Tell this damned skua, we'll return six plus four chimes."

Not waiting to see if this arrangement, six nights and four hours later than the present time, was acceptable, Prüsche ordered, "Clear the bridge. On diving stations."

After sending the message, Schefflein was the last to go below, sealing the hatch behind him.

Free of banshee winds, Prüsche's voice sounded stiff and hoarse when he ordered Chief Petty Officer Konrad Tauben, "*Stabsfeldwebel*, dive operations are yours."

The chief gave a series of follow-up orders which were quickly relayed down the boat. The leviathan gracefully sank beneath the churning icy waves. Seawater began to slash past *U799*'s sleek hull.

When semblance of harmony was restored, Prüsche turned to his First Watch Officer, the 1-WO, young, reliable and loyal Garrick Bechtler. "*Oberleutnant*, calculate course and speed to take us into the convoy routes southwest of Iceland by daybreak. We hunt tomorrow. Now, I need some sleep. Wake me if you require any assistance."

"*Ja, Kaleu*," Garrick softly intoned. "We'll be fine," he assured.

Prüsche had barely taken a step when the cynical voice of *Leutnant zur See* Karl Habicht rose from behind him. Habicht's presence on board was an ever-tightening turnbuckle of self-perpetuated tension.

"*Kapitänleutnant* Prüsche, those are not our orders."

Formerly a *Hitlerjugend*, now a staunch Nazi Party member, Habicht had no sense of command, just street-tough bully tactics against Jews. His uncle was a rear admiral and had much to do with his posting to *U799*. Before this, diving for Aryan artifacts in the Mediterranean was Habicht's only real sea experience.

Having joined *U799*'s crew days before she sailed from Lorient, France, it seemed crewmembers avoided him for more than just his contemptuous bearing. From week one, Habicht made sure everyone knew he expected them to live up to Nazi Party ideals: absolute obedience and devotion to *der Führer*.

Had he not replaced a well-liked communications chief in a questionable manner, Habicht's acceptance might have met with less opposition. As it was, he gained more enemies than friends. Only diving expertise for conceivable underwater repairs, as yet unnecessary, had kept Habicht's hide intact.

Staring at Prüsche, Habicht puffed up to his impressive 5'-6" height and jutted out his chin, darkened by downy fuzz it served only to accentuate his youth. "Admiral Dönitz has never approved of this departure from our operation, *Kapitänleutnant*."

Eyes like ice on steel, Jakob Prüsche glared at the brash Nazi. "*Leutnant zur See*, you dare to question my orders?"

"I'm merely pointing out, *Kapitänleutnant*," Habicht droned, "you have not, to my knowledge, cleared this with headquarters."

"So," Prüsche's grin was the serrated edge of a shark tooth, "you have read my sealed orders from HQ?"

Habicht's eyes widened. Stammering, he said, "*Nein, Kapitänleutnant, Nein*, I only, I only mean I . . ." His voice trailed off.

Prüsche waited to see if the Nazi stooge would try to swim clear of this watery grave. Wisely, he said no more. Prüsche, on the other hand, held the menace of a depth charge arming itself as it fell toward its victims. "In my cabin, *Leutnant*. Now."

The crew glanced furtively at the two, fearful of letting either man see their interest: Prüsche out of respect; Habicht to enjoy him squirm. Brushing past the ensign, Prüsche was a shark testing his prey before moving in for the kill.

Schefflein noted the shock on Habicht's face. Like speakers at any great Nazi Party rally, Habicht needed a captive audience before whom he could expound on party ethics or his grand fealty to Hitler. But fidelity was a difficult lesson Habicht would never truly grasp. Men of any U-boat owed loyalty to no one but their captain. For it was his wisdom and his skill standing between their lives and the cold, dark depths of a stark and violent death.

Glancing at Garrick Bechtler, Hermann Schefflein barely noticed the nudge of his head toward Prüsche's cabin. It was enough gesture to know Garrick wanted Schefflein to listen to whatever transpired.

Shortly after leaving the base at Lorient, France, Garrick told Schefflein of his concern for *Kapitänleutnant* Prüsche, and how they needed to guard the *Kaleu* against Habicht. Schefflein did not know why, but it did not matter. Prüsche and Garrick had already stuck their necks out to save Schefflein from an awkward predicament. The young quartermaster's devotion to both of them was guaranteed.

Schefflein gave Garrick a nod of acknowledgement as he moved in the general direction of Prüsche's cabin.

The cabin door clicked shut. Knowing he violated a sanctity, Schefflein edged closer. He felt wholly uncomfortable. Leaning toward the door, he heard the captain's voice slash like a knife.

"You're my communications officer and *U799*'s diver. Nothing more. Your job is limited to those fields of expertise. You are not to question my authority, interpret my orders and especially not try to take charge on my boat. As for our agenda, it is not a dance card agreed to by potential targets. I do not need Admiral Dönitz to tell me when I can take a piss. And I do not give a damn if your uncle is a top admiral or Adolf Hitler himself. Never presume to challenge my orders again, *Leutnant zur See*, or you will suffer the consequences. *Verstehen Sie?*"

Except for the whir of their twin E-motors and frigid ocean whooshing past the pressure hull, only silence answered. Tensely waiting, Schefflein wondered if Habicht would back down. Then he heard Habicht's snarly voice.

"Need I remind you, *Kapitänleutnant*, your loyalty to the Third Reich is under suspicion? If you ever fail to execute your orders properly, it may very well have grievous consequences on your naval career. Not to mention the welfare of your family in Hamburg."

Barely loud enough for Schefflein to hear, Prüsche answered this unmistakable threat. "I do not need to be reminded that my wife and family are being watched. But my sworn duty is to destroy enemy shipping whenever and wherever I find them. In a few days, a convoy will sail through Denmark Strait, unscathed if we sit on our collective asses and do nothing. Will you report this to Admiral U-boats, since you don't think it a good idea for me to attack enemy shipping?"

Again, only silence met Schefflein's ears.

Then, in a more congenial tone, the skipper added, "On the other hand, if you fear a depth charge attack, *Leutnant*, we can arrange to leave you on the pack ice. After we accomplish our little war-junket, we can come back to pick you up. That is, if we survive and locate exactly where your ice floe has drifted."

Habicht's voice was caustic. "Are you threatening me?"

"Whatever gave you such an absurd idea, *Leutnant*? I am merely pointing out your options. The choice is wholly yours. But right now, get out of my cabin, so I can sleep."

Schefflein started to withdraw when he heard his captain's voice again. Though congenial, Schefflein imagined the leer of some stealthy shark eager to consume Habicht's flesh.

"And, *Leutnant*, if you ever question my orders in front of the men again, you will find yourself hauling garbage across Spitzbergen and fighting Russians over the ice at forty-below. And *that*, Habicht, is not an idle threat. It is a promise."

Schefflein beat a hasty retreat into the control room where Garrick engaged him in conversation as if he'd been there the whole time. Habicht slipped back into the radio room like an eel retreating into its lair after a failed attack.

The conspirators exchanged glances before Schefflein softly expressed, "Did you know *Kaleu*'s family is under some sort of scrutiny in Hamburg? Why, for God's sake?"

Garrick gazed anxiously around, then spoke just loud enough to be heard, "You met *Kaleu*'s wife, Cynara, *ja*? A most gracious raven-haired beauty. Her mother was American. Prior to the Great War, Cynara's father was a German Ambassador to the United States. Cynara was born in Washington, D.C. and has dual citizenship. Her mother died when she was young. She grew up in Germany, but the *Gestapo* feel, since we're at war with them, Prüsche may lose his focus because of her."

"He would never do that," Schefflein fiercely defended.

Garrick met his eyes. "Perhaps not, but the noose around his neck explains his temperament of late, especially with our Nazi snitch. As for myself, I'd like to put a noose around the neck of Habicht the weasel."

Eyes on the radio room, Schefflein remarked, "You know, it is a long way from here to Lorient. Any number of perils might await one not familiar with our boat."

With a cold grin, Garrick agreed, "You are so right, Hermann, many perils."

AMMASSALIK, GREENLAND
FRIDAY

Karney's chat with Doc and Valya turned to other subjects as the afternoon wore into evening. Valya's curiosity about fashion was insatiable. Karney was of virtually no help whatsoever. Though he never failed to turn an eye to a good-looking gal, he had no idea what was trendy. From the sparkle of animation in Valya's eyes, he evidently gave her the tidbits for which she longed.

Yet not knowing the Danes well, other questions Karney answered with deliberate obscurity. Doc played the same wait-and-see game with vague responses. It didn't matter. In a habit perfected under Gunnar Bryant, his guardian, mentor and captain, Karney gleaned as much from what Doc and Valya didn't say as by what they did.

Valya was setting their dessert plates onto the serving tray when Hans entered the house with an icy gust of wind. Though Doc jumped up to meet him, Karney noticed Valya gaze poignantly at the young man. Hans curtly nodded his head.

A silent greeting? Or answer to an unspoken question?

Unsure which, Karney was distracted when he noticed she now watched him and not her son. Karney met her gaze. Averting her eyes, she retired to the kitchen. Though disturbed, Karney ignored it to focus on Hans. He couldn't shake the feeling he had seen the lad somewhere before, though where was an elusive shadow.

Outwardly, Hans looked Inuit: a fur-side-in caribou anorak, which he shrugged out of; prized *nanus* or polar bear fur pants, indication he killed the bear himself; and *kamiks* on his feet. Almost as tall as his father, Hans lacked the older man's broad girth. Beneath his Arctic trappings, however, Hans was no gangly youth. He had the brawn of a college line-backer and probably the speed to match.

Removing his cap and goggles, straight, flaxen hair tumbled across his brow. His cheeks, weathered by wind and cold, bore the raccoon-marks of his snow-goggles. Even though his eyes were blue, a slightly darker shade than his father's, they held the icy cunning of an Arctic fox. Hans eyed Karney with suspicion.

Dragging Hans into the room, Doc said, "Irish, this is Hans." Practically pushing him in front of the American, Doc ordered, "Hans, shake hands with Commander Rork."

Embarrassed by this forced politeness, Karney was hesitant. Hans seemed just as reluctant. Though Karney was an outsider, it was clear that Hans had grown into a man his mulish father refused to recognize. Finally, their hands met in a power-assertion grip. Karney ignored the forceful grasp as he asked, "So, how was the hunting, Hans?"

The young Dane's gaze rose to meet Karney's with the warmth of a welcome hearth. Hans started to answer, but his father interrupted.

"This boy spends too much time hunting. He should study for entrance exams. At this rate, he will not be admitted anywhere."

Eyes again turning a glacial blue, Hans glared at his father.

"You cannot eat books, Father. I put food on our table and extend what meager supplies we receive, but you choose never to notice."

Disregarding Hans, Doc turned to his guest. "Hans is almost eighteen and quite smart. He is to start university with Willem, my oldest boy . . . next fall . . ."

Doc's voice trailed off, his eyes grew distant. His younger son's eyes, however, spat hatred. For whom, Karney was not sure.

After a moment, Doc said, "Hans speaks good English. Maybe he should attend university in America. What think you, Irish?"

Awkwardly, Karney shrugged, saying nothing, but Hans' face reddened and his gaze lowered. As if rethreading bare spots in the worn carpet, he seemed torn between humiliation and annoyance. His ever-shifting eyes reminded Karney of Valya's furtive looks. *Is everyone in this family afraid to make eye contact?*

Eyes narrowing, Hans again raged, "Maybe you've

forgotten, Father, there is a war going on in the real world. Willem is dead and the Nazis rule Denmark. Books and fancy schools cannot change that or bring him back. Only fighting can set things right."

Hans stormed from the room. Though Hans had spoken to Bross Krigeshaald, his gaze met Karney's for a brief instant. In their depth, Karney perceived frustration and bitterness. Trapped in Greenland, hate devoured this boy, without giving him a chance to truly live. *Or is he perhaps more ready to fight and die?* Karney wondered.

Obviously angered by his son's exit, Doc excused himself.

As if on cue, Valya emerged from the kitchen. Only when she heard the door to Hans' room slam a second time did she speak.

"Hans and Willem were very close . . ."

She daubed crocodile tears that failed to moisten her eyes.

"You see, Commander," a delicate hand touched his arm, "they are not my sons. Their mother was my friend. She died when the boys were little, creating a close bond. Though Hans is younger, he was always stronger, more aggressive. Willem is—was more like Helga. Both he and his mother were extremely bright, sadly neither were robust. Hans is convinced, had he been with his brother, Willem would still be alive. Now, all Hans ever thinks about is killing Germans."

Hesitantly, Karney asked, "How did Willem die?"

"When Germany invaded Denmark, he and some other students tried to resist, they were arrested and later executed."

Karney studied the dainty woman. The sorrow Valya's words were intended to convey was absent from her cold Nordic features.

"I was a language professor at university," she continued. "Willem was my star pupil, truly my pride and joy. Bross and I met at an award ceremony for all the honor students. I reintroduced myself and we became friends. Bross was a lonely man. Then when Willem died . . . well, we grew closer. We married only recently, but, I am sad to say, Hans has never quite accepted me."

Valya took a shaky breath, her feigned emotions barely held in check as she withdrew a laced hanky from her apron pocket. *Is she trying to convince me? Or has she rehearsed her little spiel so often the gestures come automatically?*

Yet Valya's tale did reveal some of the lad's angst. If vengeance was part of the equation, Hans would be hard pressed to extort revenge from this remote, icy corner of the world.

"Forgive me, Commander," Valya said, putting her kerchief in her apron. "I'll show you to your room, then start supper. I do hope the stove has had time to warm the guest room. We normally do not have visitors in the midst of winter."

Following her through the doll-like house, Karney expected Lilliputians to pop out. Similar to shipboard sizes, the rooms were typical of Greenland where lumber was an indulgence. Forced to duck through each door or suffer the consequences, he knew how Gulliver must have felt. *Is Doc's head so hard 'cause he forgets to duck?*

Once Valya excused herself, Karney dumped his sea bag on the floor and surveyed his living quarters.

Though its furnishings were sparse, the craftsmanship was exquisite. A stout four-poster took up most of the space. Pressing down on the mattress, a long-standing habit, Karney was delighted to find it was eider down. The door swing barely cleared a bureau with a washbasin and pitcher on top; though chipped, both were of Dresden china. The pot-bellied stove glowed with cordiality and warmth, though it scarcely chased the chill away. Whistling from the stovetop, a dented tea kettle sang its own greeting. Space for one chair remained at the foot of the bed but no desk for writing.

Mixing hot water with cold in the washbasin, Karney removed his thick sweater, then stripped off more of his layered garments. He scrubbed his hands and face, taking what guys in the military called a whore's bath to rid himself of the grime and residual stench of aviation fuel. However, a sense all was not as it seemed in this household was not so easily washed away.

Though Karney liked Doc, the Dane didn't seem to have the Allies' best interests at heart. Nor his son's for that matter. Doc's concern for Greenland and her people was evident. Regardless of any code of ethics, he didn't seem to care if the Nazis used this strategic island for their own ominous design so long as they steered clear of the Inuit inhabitants. *Some trade off,* Karney thought.

He perceived what irritated Doc with Hans was the father's inability to control his son. And, from all indications, Doc was a man who definitely liked to be in control, no matter what the circumstances.

Then there was Valya. Though Doc apparently worshiped his wife, her welcome toward him seemed rather stilted. She might regret Willem's death, but her behavior didn't convince Karney she truly mourned his loss. Had Greenland frozen her tears? On the other hand, even if it meant enduring bitter cold and isolation here, had Doc been her meal-ticket out from under the Nazi thumb of tyranny in Denmark?

And what of Hans? If he hates the Nazis, maybe he can lead me to the resident spy. After all, Bross said Hans knows the area like a native. Does Hans perhaps look to me for rescue from this barren existence? Or was that parting glance from Hans a plea for me to treat him like a man? Something his old man fails to recognize.

The questions were confusing, eliciting empty answers that reaped more complex issues. Though he didn't consider himself a Sherlock Holmes, it would have been helpful to have a humble Dr. Watson with whom he could bandy his concerns.

Pulling on a clean sweater, Karney finger combed his hair as he reexamined the use of a Watson character.

No, Watson's not who I need. Elli's be a better choice. She's been doing this spy malarkey stuff a helluva lot longer than some fictitious Dr. Watson. And it's more than just a matter of intelligence. Not only is Ellie a damn sight prettier, she also gives a fine back rub. And right now, those elegant fingers of hers would soothe a helluva lot more than the aches in my body. Sighing, he turned to leave the room. *And Ellie's the only woman who might be able to patch this hole in my heart.*

CHAPTER SIXTEEN

Though wearied by his return trip from Prague, Czechoslovakia, *Reichsführer-SS* Heinrich Himmler felt he must visit his office before going home tonight. On Tuesday, the Wannsee Conference chaired by Reinhardt Heydrich, would begin. While things were fresh in his mind, Himmler wanted to make sure his representatives had everything they needed to facilitate this Jewish question once and for all.

Opening the tall double-doors, his aide-de-camp rushed to turn on the array of lights, revealing rich wood paneling and thick red carpet. Himmler strolled around his desk, then sat down. He adjusted the photograph of himself, taken with *Herr* Hitler and Jakob Grimminger, the first official bearer of the *Blütfahne*, or blood banner, the Nazi ritual flag from the 1923 *Munich putsch*.

Himmler couldn't pinpoint why this picture was so special, but it was. Perhaps because it epitomized Himmler's closeness to *der Führer* on that particular day in Nürnburg. During this annual ceremony, Hitler sanctified all new regimental colors by holding the bullet-riddled and blood-stained *Blütfahne* and touching each unit's flags with his other hand. It was a great personal honor to be there.

The few other items atop his mirror-polished desk seemed mere necessities: the photo of his family, a pen and inkwell, books held between bronze eagle bookends and a small lamp. With his arms stretched straight across the ink blotter, Himmler made eye contact with his tall *SS* bodyguard. "Franz, check for any new communiqués."

With a snapped but silent "*Heil*," the young officer left.

Breathing in the essence of power, Himmler closed his eyes. The scent was very exhilarating. He opened his eyes to gaze upon the huge portrait of Adolf Hitler—the colossal canvas scarcely did admirable justice to such a great man of vision. Himmler was wholeheartedly honored to serve under *der Führer*.

A sharp rap drew his attention to the door. Entering, his blond adjutant, a prime example of Aryan masculinity, marched up to the desk. Franz turned the file around to face Himmler and set it down, then took a precise step back, awaiting further orders.

"*Danke, Obersturmführer,*" Himmler said, silently praising his stars for the day he found this young officer.

On an impromptu visit to a field hospital near the Eastern Front, Himmler felt providence had led him to Franz Niedermann. Severely wounded by shrapnel in fierce fighting near Archangelsk in the Ukraine, as part of Operation Barbarossa, Franz had been highly decorated for bravery. The *SS Leutnant*, barely twenty-one at the time, so impressed the *Reichsführer* that Himmler offered Franz a staff posting in Berlin. When Franz concluded his medical leave in September, Himmler found he needed an aide to handle some delicate intelligence matters. With Franz's insight, language skills and battle experience, he proved an ideal candidate.

Even *der Führer* agreed. After all, Franz was an elite officer of *Leibstandarte-SS* Adolf Hitler. Though this was the first *SS* Division created and had become quite heroic, they were commanded by Sepp Dietrich, a foul-mouthed troublemaker whom Himmler despised. Once separated from Dietrich, Franz proved to be discreet, savvy to Himmler's needs and extremely competent. Himmler's trust in Franz Niedermann wasn't misplaced.

Returning to the business at hand, Himmler read through the messages, pausing with a frown on the third one. "This is from von Zeitz," he shared. "Perhaps I should have sent you to Canada to handle this problem. The assassin failed to eliminate STARLING, though he managed to commit suicide after he was captured."

Blue eyes hard, the robust Aryan came to attention. "It will be my honor to assassinate her, *Herr Reichsführer*."

Himmler replaced the flimsy in the file. Closing it, he set his folded hands on top. "I know you are capable, Franz, but von Zeitz believes he has the situation well under control. And since I truly do not wish to interfere with *Obergrüppenführer* Reinhard Heydrich's grandiose plans for *OPERATION FLUT*, perhaps we should let von Zeitz resolve this problem or see if he can tie his own noose. We also do not wish this problem to come to *der Führer*'s attention or he will be reminded of Greenland, a most inhospitable place. And *der Führer* isn't overly fond of snow and ice."

Himmler smiled benignly. "And this despite his residence near *Berchtesgaden*. In winter, the Bavarian Alps cannot be too disparate from Greenland." With a shake of his head, Himmler continued, "*Nein*, Franz, we will not send you there yet. Let's allow von Zeitz some more time. Eventually, we may rid the Reich of two potentially dangerous problems. He might fail, then you may take care of STARLING at some future date."

The younger officer gave his superior a curt nod and grinned in a shy manner offering no sign of his abilities as a cold-blooded assassin.

⊕

RCN TRAINING GARRISON
SHEET HARBOUR, NOVA SCOTIA
SUN: 18 JAN 42

Ellie stabbed a half-burnt log further into the flames of her hearth as she waited tensely for Mac to arrive. The peace and warmth of her cottage on this wintry day should have been wonderful. But no, agitation kept any hope for peace at bay. Trouble was, Ellie couldn't decide with whom to be more angry: Major James Fenton Strafford or Dear Cousin Mac. Apparently this weekend: Captain Rob Roy MacCalister.

Years ago, when Strafford had recruited her into MI-6, he had locked her into circumstances which led to her recent hardships. Mac now held the key to release her.

Yesterday at Mac's office, she had asked him what Strafford had said that was so secretive. Mac glared at her, grabbed his coat and growled, "I don't have time for this now. I'll talk to you tomorrow afternoon at two."

Mac had stormed out, leaving her to stare after him. Hoping for an explanation, she had glanced at Marciá, who shouldn't have been working yesterday anyway. Marciá suddenly became very busy, and without making eye contact, said, "Mac's been under a lotta pressure lately, El. I'm sure he didn't mean to sound so . . . brusque."

"The hell he didn't," she snapped. "'Tis his way of lettin' me know I'm in bloody trouble before he tells me to me face."

"But, Ellie—"

"Forget it," she said. Then, recalling how Karney's "forget it" had cut, she more softly amended, "I'm sorry for barkin' at you, Marciá. 'Tis just James Fenton Strafford's been here less than twenty-four-bloody hours and he's already got things in a bloody turmoil. 'Tis what he bloody well does best."

Marciá met Ellie's gaze again, a strange expression in her hazel eyes, telling Ellie she knew more than she was letting on. Much more. But Ellie respected Marciá's loyalty to Mac and didn't push the issue.

So now, she waited for Mac, uncharacteristically late, and time froze to a crawl. Turning from the hearth, Ellie folded her arms and ambled to the side window. Fluffy snow fell outside, thick and white. No wind disturbed its descent. The cold matched the chill in her heart, though it could not cool her ire.

Unbidden, gentle thoughts of Irish settled in her mind and warmed her soul. It brought memories of the Canadian Rockies and the warm chinook winds causing an unusual rise in cold temperatures, often melting the snow. Irish was her Chinook wind, thawing the ice of her heart. Karney was strong, immobile and enduring like the lofty peaks from which those chinooks blew. He helped stabilize her temper.

Oddly, considering Mac's attitude, Irish had begun to emerge as her protector. The role heretofore entrusted to Cousin Mac. Love for Irish, however, fought her vow to distance herself from him. She didn't want loving him to lead to tragedy.

"Oh, sweet bugger all," she swore, dropping her arms to lean against the windowsill. With a sigh, Ellie added, "And that's only the iceberg's tip of me pesterin' worries."

But, she knew, absence from Karney was only making her heart grow fonder. "I miss that Irish hunk of heartbreak terribly."

Jolting Ellie from her reverie, Mac's sharp rap sounded at her door. She'd been so wrapped in warm thoughts of Irish, she hadn't noticed Mac walk up the snowy path. Adjusting her bulky shawl sweater, she stepped to the front door and opened it.

Still slapping snow from his uniform with his maroon beret, Mac glanced at her from where he stood on the porch. His eyes revealed nothing more than iced-jade. Beside him, as always, stood Chelsea. In a cloud of white, the Border Collie mix shook snow from her fur and proceeded Mac into the cottage to take up a post in front of the hearth, where she began licking ice balls from her paws.

Sounding annoyed, Mac demanded, "May I come in?"

Without a word, Ellie stepped back, thinking how Mac suddenly sounded as aloof as Strafford. She watched Mac unbutton his overcoat as he ducked through the door. He tossed his beret on top of the radio and draped his coat over the back of the easy chair. Strolling to the fireplace, he squatted beside Chelsea to warm his hands before the fire.

Dryly, he commented, "Bit cold today, eh?"

More frigid than the cold air which flowed in upon Mac's boot heels, a chill had penetrated the room. Ellie said nothing as she sat in the chair closest to the fire and scratched behind Chelsea's ear. The dog's fur was too wet to do more.

After a moment, Mac stood and began pacing. Chelsea's eyes followed his every move, even though the room didn't allow many steps for Mac's long legs. Ellie tensed when he finally stopped. His gaze pinned her with a complete lack of compassion or mercy.

Mac was unsure where to start with the allegations Strafford had made against his younger cousin. Ellie knew Mac thought of her as more a sister and friend whom he had trusted his entire life. After Friday's punch, Strafford's secrets had somehow cracked that long-standing bond between Mac and her.

"Where'd you get the £200,000?" Mac's voice held an undeniable tone of accusation. "Money recently transferred from a Swiss bank in Zurich to the Bank of Nova Scotia?"

Ellie was at a loss, not sure how that son-of-a-bitch Strafford got his hands upon such personal information. What he did with it was obvious.

Mac's insinuation hit Ellie like a torpedo strike. Her mind raced to battle stations. She knew her only recourse was to tell Mac about Wolf, Brandt and Anna; people Mac had never known about. But, before she did that, she had to know the position of the enemy she faced.

"Exactly what did Strafford tell you?"

Twisting the tip of his mustache, Mac glared at her and sighed heavily. "He said you're a double agent."

She burst out laughing. "Oh, that's rich." In mock gravity, Ellie looked penitent. "But 'tis true. I've been a double agent for years." Mad over such ridiculous drivel, she snarled, "Bleedin' Christ, Mac, Strafford was my controller." She stood and paced away from him. "Of course I'm a double agent." Raising her arms in vexation, she snapped, "He bloody well made me one."

Softly, from behind her, she heard Mac clarify, "I didn't say for us, Ellie. Strafford said you worked for the Nazis."

Spinning back around, Ellie stared at him. She was stunned. "And you bloody well believed the bastard?"

Rather than answer, he countered, "You need to explain the money." Seeing anger and shock on her face, Mac sat in the chair opposite the one she had vacated. "Let's take this one step at a time, eh?" He motioned toward her chair.

Reluctantly, she sat. "All right, Mac, one bloody step at a time. Regardless of what you hear, don't be passin' any judgment till I'm through. And I mean completely bloody well through."

With an eyebrow raised, accusation shaded his voice as he spoke, "All right, no judgment, but you must answer all my questions. I need your full cooperation."

Raising her own eyebrow, Ellie said, "I've always given you my full cooperation, Mac. Even to the point of lyin' to me Dad to get you clear of your whorin' expedition during your convalescent leave."

As expected, his face reddened. "That's not the cooperation I meant, and you damn well know it. Disguising yourself as Aunt Elaine was quite an actin' coup for a fourteen-year-old, but I'm not interested in cover-ups and lies." Mac's gaze pinned her. "Get on with your defense before I walk out with nary a look back."

Fearful he'd do exactly that if she pushed her luck to
say, "All right, already, Mac. Dinna be slippin' a bloody cog.
I was just teasin'."

"Teasing me right now will not cool the hot water
you're in, dear cousin," he growled. "Start talking and let
me hear the truth."

AMMASSALIK, GREENLAND
SUNDAY

Wholly stuffed, Karney sat with Doc and Hans around
the hearth, while Valya washed dishes. Supper, the third
since his arrival in Ammassalik, was, as were all her meals,
delicious. Most of Saturday and much of today, he helped
Doc and Hans work on the sailboat the family had sailed
from Denmark to escape the Nazis. A fine craft, the ketch
evoked fond memories for Karney of when he had worked
with Gunnar on *Zephyr Cross*, their gaff-rigged sloop.
However, this was nowhere near as pleasant with the
mission hanging over his head.

Though Karney still gained useful information from
these casual conversations, he needed intelligence on likely
sites for U-boat bases. Doc, however, always tacked back to
the subject of the Inuit and their plight. Karney grew
frustrated.

A momentary impasse came when a loud knock
sounded at the door. Like a dutiful servant, Valya answered
it but soon summoned Doc. Hoisting himself from his easy
chair, Bross gave Hans a poignant look as if in warning.

Studying the charts before him on the glossy coffee
table, Karney half-listened to the muted Danish voices
from the vestibule. He gave an inquisitive glance to Hans.

Quietly, Hans translated, "They need him in
Sermiligaaq, a settlement to the north and east." He
gestured in the general direction.

Within an hour, Doc was gone, probably for days.

In his father's absence, Hans became more affable. No

longer a reticent teen, he became a buoyant young man, dropping the formality his father forced upon him. He now referred to the visiting Coast Guard officer by his nickname.

Sorting through the charts, Hans pulled out one and pointed to a fjord south of Ammassalik. "This is it, Irish," he said, stabbing the map. "I found something here."

Skeptical, Karney asked, "You couldn't tell what it was?"

Hans stiffened defensively. "It's too hard to reach alone. We can leave tomorrow. You will see for yourself."

Thoughtfully eyeing the map, Karney estimated the distance to be more than a hundred miles. His mind raced over whether a trek of that distance, in winter, would be worth the peril to look at an unknown something of dubious import.

Prodding him for a decision, Hans said, "The fjord is quite deep and accessible to U-boats. I saw one there last spring."

"Why the hell didn't you tell me earlier?"

"Always before, my father was here. He accused me of lying when I first told him about it. He ordered me not to repeat such foolishness to anyone." Contempt filled the young man's voice. "My father is blind to what's in front of him. The Inuit mean more to him than I do. He's a pacifist and doesn't believe the war will come here."

"I hate to break it to him but the war's already here." A massive yawn overtook Karney, causing him to reach the only decision he cared to make at this late hour. He began gathering the charts into a bundle. "Let's sleep on it."

"But Karney, I must show you—"

"Hans," he held up his hands to halt the defense he knew was about to erupt. "It's not a decision I wanna make in haste. Let me sleep on it. We'll discuss it over breakfast."

They said goodnight, each going to their respective rooms.

Tugging off his sweater and unbuttoning his shirt,

Karney started to unlace his boots but sank back into the eider-down softness of his bed. He rolled into the quilt's cozy embrace.

Awakened some time later to a subtle tapping, he groggily unwrapped himself from the quilt and rose. Karney figured Hans had prepared some new argument to show him his guarded secret. Opening the door, Karney instead found Valya. Her long braids undone lay in soft ripples over her ample bosom, provocatively bulged up by another comforter draped over her arm.

"Forgive me for disturbing you, Commander, but I felt you might need this. A very cold *piteraq* blows tonight."

Barefoot, Valya brushed past him, shaking out the comforter. Too sleepy to offer a protest, Karney let her play out her role of genial hostess as he splashed water on his face. Drying off, he said, "I truly doubt I'll need it, Mrs. Krigeshaald. That stove keeps the room plenty warm." Lowering the towel, he turned to find her smack in front of him, the door swinging shut.

Valya's cool eyes gazed up into his as her hands parted his open shirt, her fingers caressing his chest hair. "I was not able to sleep knowing you were all alone and might be cold."

Though dumbstruck by her presumptuous overture, he was not blind. He pulled her hands away, holding them cuffed together. "I'm fine, Mrs. Krigeshaald, so you can go on back to your room and get a good night's rest."

She pulled free of his grip, whirling to the bed to turn down the covers. Valya's pink satin robe, far too flimsy to provide any warmth, left little to his imagination. If she wore anything underneath, it wasn't obvious—too much rounded ass and bare leg below the tie, too much bosom demanding attention above.

Despite the tantalizing temptations she flaunted, Karney didn't want to be her sex quarry. Though he enjoyed getting a little as much as the next guy, he hated to have a tryst crammed down his throat. Valya was also quite married, and this was the home of her loving, devoted, ill-tempered, not to mention gigantic husband.

Knowing where she wanted this to go, Karney wasn't at all prepared for her next move. In a fluid twirl, Valya untied her robe, letting it fall in a rippled heap. She wore only lace panties. Sliding back on the bed, she spread her legs and leaned forward to emphasize the volume of her breasts. Her rosy nipples peeked out invitingly from the curtain of her glossy tresses.

She licked her pouty lips and, in a sultry voice, said, "You may be warm, Irish . . ."

He stood transfixed, not sure what to say or do.

Running both hands slowly along her shapely thighs, across her pink panties and over her abdomen to cup her breasts, Valya regarded her own lush body with narcissistic adoration. Her eyes came back to Karney's face as she finished her sentence, "But I'd rather we both be hot . . ."

He couldn't believe how crude and brazen Valya had become after seeming so demure and reserved the last few days. The equation, however, he realized was simple: *Me + Valya − Doc = an illicit affair.*

Not sure how to deal with her tactfully, if that were even remotely possible, he stammered, "I—I really think you'd better go."

Valya slid off the bed, but rather than head for the door, she dramatically flung her long hair over one shoulder, gliding toward him like a snow tigress. Her eyes never leaving her prey.

"Don't tell me, Irish," she said, lifting her large breasts in her hands, "you don't want to suck on my warm and lush, pearly orbs?"

When Valya took a step closer, he took a step back only to run into the bureau. Karney warily watched her. What Valya offered was indisputably attractive. And, as a red-blooded horny male, his body responded accordingly.

But it was not from the woman he loved.

With no space to retreat, Karney was trapped. Molding

her body to his, she slid her leg between his, pressing it up into his groin. One hand stroked his hard-muscled chest while the fingers of her other hand slid around the waistband of his pants.

"I don't know what you want to prove, Mrs. Krigeshaald, but I suggest you get out before I throw you out."

"You wouldn't throw me out, Irish. I can feel how hard you—"

He grabbed her hands, cutting her words off. Valya shrieked, startled he'd follow through with his threat. Her flashing grey eyes revealed she expected submission.

Opening the door, he shoved her into the hall, tossing her robe after her. "Like I said, I think you better go."

Valya was furious. Her eyes no longer burned with seductive fire; they erupted with molten hatred. Her face flushed angrily. To his surprise, though, she said nothing. Storming to her room, she left a chill breeze of contempt in her wake.

Closing the door, he discovered no lock. He leaned against it, mentally barring her from further intrusion. Searching his memory, he tried to recall any inadvertent sexual innuendo he might have made. He found none. Karney sat down and finished unlacing his boots as he mulled over the dilemma in which he now found himself.

Is Valya trying to seduce me for secrets: Mata Hari of the Far North? If so, who's she working for? Or is she so starved for sex from Doc that she throws herself at the first available guy to come along? Unfortunately me, in this case, he realized.

It was an unsavory predicament either way. *Lord sakes, I sure as hell don't relish facing that woman in the morning.*

And what will happen when Doc returns? Will she fabricate a lie to retaliate against me for jilting her? Or strike back in some other more devious way? Karney didn't doubt she was a vain and resourceful woman, but he certainly didn't know her well enough to know if she'd resort to revenge or drop it like her robe.

An even more unnerving thought slid into his mind. *What if Doc and Valya planned this together? As domineering as Bross appears to be, turning Valya into a whore to gain information wouldn't be unreasonable if it achieved his or the Nazi's goal.*

With an uncontrolled shiver, Karney reached for his sea bag, pulled his Colt .45 out of its holster, chambered a round and slid it under his pillow. He expected to be left alone, but he also wanted a proper welcoming committee. Just in case.

Finally kicking off his boots, he heard a sharp rap on the door. Karney groaned inwardly and took an angry stride to answer it.

He jerked it open, growling, "Look—" then stopped.

Hans leaned nonchalantly against the jamb, a knowing grin on his face. Raising a bottle of Aquavit and two hefty tumblers, he asked in slightly slurred words, "Need a drink, chum?"

Apparently Hans knew what had transpired. Taking a tumbler and a step back, Karney gestured for him to enter, then glanced down the hall to make sure Valya did not lurk in the shadows.

From behind him, came the reassurance, "Don't worry, Irish, my schtep-mummy has been sufficienwy snubbed for one nigh. She won' make another pass on you, at least naw for a while."

Hans slid onto the lone chair. Karney sat on the bed, holding out his empty tumbler for Hans to fill. "Does your step-mother do this sort of . . . thing . . . often?"

"Evewy fuckin' chance she gets when daddy's a way, way off." Hans chuckled at his pun, then his blue eyes hardened, his grin turned vengeful. "She is a nym . . . nymph . . ."

Karney supplied the answer. "Nymphomaniac."

"*Ja*, tha's the word. She is a nymphomaniac," he

repeated with a crooked grin, apparently happy to remember the proper word.

"So," he asked, eyeing the syrupy, pale-yellow liquid, "to whom are we drinking?"

"To you and me, Karney Irish Rork." He raised his glass. "De only two men, in my restricted sphere of existence, to've told that vixen no. And that, my Americaner pal, includes my brother, who lost more than jus his wirginity to her at university."

It sounded to Karney as if Hans blamed Valya for Willem's death; not himself. He raised his glass, "To you and me then."

The tumblers clinked together, then they bolted the viscous Danish liquor. Unlike his younger companion, with a jumpstart on drinking, the first kick took longer to fizzle out for Karney. He declined a refill while Hans poured himself another.

In a conspiratorial tone, Hans said, "Valya will be a bitch the next few days. She thinks no man can ever refuse her, 'specially with those jugs of hers." Hans cupped his hands out from his chest in mocking pantomime. "We can go hunting tomorrow. Or I could show you my ice cave at Ikeq."

Hesitating a second only to weigh what he already suspected about Valya's temperament, Karney said, "Either sounds fine."

Hans smiled, pouring himself and his friend another drink.

"We'll weave in the morning. My doggies iz always eager to go ou'," Hans slurred, then continued in a more deliberate tone. "My dogs are the stwongest, bwavest and best on awe de East Coast. Take me anywhere an' protect me, too. They he'ped me take ou' a powlar bear not two years ago."

Ignoring Hans' drunken bragging, Karney asked, "Other than your hunting rifle, do you carry a pistol?"

Looking stunned, Hans drained the bottle by tipping it

straight up, waiting for the last drop, then said, "Always, my friend."

If Hans had answered differently, Karney would have been surprised. "Good, then I won't need to loan you my spare."

"Do you carry the Navy Colt .45 Model 1911?"

Somewhat startled Hans knew what weapon a Yankee officer would carry, Karney nodded. The young man's eyes lit up.

"Colt mayes a better weapon than Bergmann-Bayard, the pistol daddy-waddy gave me. The wines awe cweaner and they're more rewiable. May I see it?"

Digging his spare from his sea bag, Karney judiciously dropped the clip, locked the slide back and handed Hans the weapon.

While Hans admired the pistol, smiling appreciatively, Karney hoped he wasn't venturing into the wilds of Greenland with the equivalent of a voracious polar bear. Yet the thought of staying here with Valya, not knowing when Doc might be returning nor whom to trust, he'd rather take his chances on the ice.

At least, Karney reasoned, *ice I know.*

Tossing the .45 back, Hans said, "Ikeq takes severaw days to weach." Apparently through with their weapons chat, Hans stood, then fell back onto the chair, looking dazed. "And I sink I drinkted too much."

"Take some aspirin and drink lotsa water before you go to bed. You'll be fine come morning." Mentally, he added, *I hope.*

Nodding, Hans shuffled out, leaving the empty Aquavit bottle on the bureau.

Karney shut the door once more. The Aquavit still burning his throat, he stripped off his clothes. Blowing out the lamp flame, he slid between the cool sheets and listened to the ice banshee's howl, thanking God for the warming stove in the corner.

Karney closed his eyes, but disturbing outcomes of

Valya's wanton lust appeared. Distress caused by this Nordic siren did not make for peaceful rest.

Imagining Ellie in a similar scenario in this cozy room, Karney found himself grow hard. Though not entirely sure this was where he intended to go, he kept her lovely face and svelte body in his mind and resolved the matter. Rolling over, Karney soon drifted off to sleep.

Hans listened outside the door long enough to make sure the American went to bed. In thick greased-wool socks, Hans made no sound as he tiptoed down the hall; evidence of any drunkenness gone. However, he did not head to his own room.

Before reaching the opposite end of the hall, a door softly swung open. Warm golden light spilled onto the floor. Hans gazed inside and grinned hungrily.

Valya's face was in shadow. Her voluptuous curves, however, were distinctly silhouetted by the lamp's glow. Flaxen tresses, falling to below her naked buttocks, flowed like silken threads behind her. He knew her nipples would be erect.

Taking her outstretched hand, his cock hardened with eager anticipation. Hans followed Valya inside, closing the door behind him.

CHAPTER SEVENTEEN

RCN TRAINING GARRISON
SHEET HARBOUR, NOVA SCOTIA
SUN: 18 JAN 42

Ellie removed the whistling tea kettle from the small burner and lowered the flame. Before she turned, she found Cousin Mac beside her, teacups in hand. Glancing at him, she said with an exaggerated brogue, "My, my, 'tis indeed a brave Scotsman to be puttin' those cups afore his manhood when boilin' water's 'bout to be poured."

With a soft snort, Mac rolled his eyes. However, he did set the cups down on the counter.

With tea made, they sat at the table, a plate of macaroons between them. The tea kettle whistled softly, reminding Ellie of when they were kids, sitting with their brothers, sharing fresh-baked cookies and mugs of hot-cocoa on chilly winter days.

But Mac, she knew, was in no mood to reminisce.

"So," he resumed his questioning, "you started working for Wolf Gündestein in 1932 as his personal secretary, but, as far as you know, he wasn't working for MI-6 at that time?"

Shaking her head, Ellie said, "Mac, you need to understand, Wolf Gündestein works for nobody but himself. Any help he gives the Allies will be out of cooperation. Though Hitler's Munich *putsch* failed in '23,

Wolf began keeping an eye on nasty old Adolf, especially once *Mein Kampf* was published. Wolf joined the Nazi party solely to determine what Hitler's long-term plans might be. Not that everyone in Nazi Germany didn't hear the propaganda speeches. But once Hitler threw out the Versailles Treaty and began his armament build-up, Wolf offered his services to MI-6."

"And Commodore Greer became Wolf Gündestein's controller in the same way Major Strafford was yours?"

"Aye. Dad felt it best to keep Wolf's intelligence work and mine separated in case Wolf was, in fact, loyal to Hitler. This also resolved the sensitive issue of a German aristocrat dealing with a lower-ranking British intelligence officer."

Pondering Strafford's version of Wolf being a devout Nazi, he wondered how Ellie could not've known. "Which is why Strafford never knew Wolf worked with MI-6?"

She nodded, then further clarified, "He only knew I worked for Wolf. Strafford also never knew that Wolf is my father-in-law."

Mac stopped cold, his teacup halfway to his lips. Setting it back on the table, he softly said, "Pardon?"

"Wolf Gündestein became my father-in-law when I married his only son, Brandt Rösspitz Gündestein in 1933."

Staring at Ellie as if she had thrown hot tea on him, Mac wasn't quite sure what to say. *During all my meetings with Uncle Gus, he never mentioned his only daughter married a Hun.* All Mac could manage to mutter was, "Brandt Rösspitz Gündestein? Your husband?"

Ellie slowly nodded, her bombshell still fragmenting. "When I married Brandt, he was a second leftenant in the *Gestapo*, but was later promoted to first leftenant in the NA SS-VT."

Mac stared, incredulous. Finally, he pushed past his mental block to clarify, "NA SS-VT as in *die Nachrichten-Abteilung Schutzstafel-Verfügungstruppe*?"

"Aye, the Signal Battalion of the *Gestapo*'s Special

Purpose Troops, now it's the *Waffen-SS*-NA," she stated as if that tidbit would reduce the shock in Mac's eyes. "Before Brandt died in 1940, he'd been promoted to captain."

Without a word, Mac stood. A soft whine came from Chelsea, who watched him intently. He gulped his tea and grabbed the Dewar's Scotch from the pass-through into the living room. He poured the amber liquor into his cup, drained it all and refilled it before sitting back down, bottle in hand. Once Mac was settled, his dog laid her head back on her crossed paws.

Ellie met Mac's gaze. In the depth of his eyes, she saw a sense of betrayal and the unspoken question: *How could you marry someone and never let me know?* Anxiously, she waited for him to ask whatever question rose to the surface of his stupefaction.

Shaking his head, he quietly remarked, "I guess those funds Strafford thinks you took as a payoff is something of a molehill when buried under this avalanche, eh?"

How typical of Mac to downshift and take another road.

Taking a liberal swig of Scotch before meeting her eyes, he softly asked, "I take it there's more to your tale?"

Finishing her own tea, and feeling a need to brace herself as well, she reached for the bottle. "Brandt wasna the devout Nazi that he presented to the world. But as a tall, strapping, very-blond police detective, the *SS* wanted him inside their vast hierarchy. They offered Brandt a commission. 'Twas quite an honor," she formed quotes with her fingers, "nae refused without repercussions. When this happened, I'd nae seen Brandt for several weeks, though we were engaged at the time. He invited me to *Oktoberfest im München*. When he met me at the train station, he was wearing a black *SS* dress uniform. You can imagine my shock—"

"Doubt it was worse than you informing me you were married to some Nazi *Gestapo* officer. His heart in the bloody job or not."

Understanding Mac's shock at her revelations, Ellie took a long, slow sip, giving him a chance to recover. After a moment, she said, "Like all *SS* officers in Himmler's Black Order, with their secret ceremonies and death's head rings, Brandt had to swear his loyalty to Hitler unto death. Truth be, Brandt would rather have slit the bastard's throat as look at him. Hitler's cronies as well."

Ellie took another drink, recalling the early days. "When Wolf first introduced us, I thought Brandt was an overbearin' braggart, using his position as a police officer to gain gratuitous favors and make all sorts of illegal deals. One bein' an extremely thorough background check on me."

"How thorough?" Mac asked, absently swirling his Dewar's.

Ellie peered at her cousin over the rim of her cup. Setting it down, she said, "He somehow learned I worked for MI-6."

Shock again registered in Mac's eyes. "He knew you were with MI-6 from the start?"

"Aye," she said. "He had connections in Britain of which I wasna aware until Dad became Wolf's controller." She noticed a brief frown cross Mac's face before he spoke.

"How, in all those years," Mac quietly asked, "did Brandt manage to avoid being detected by the Nazis?"

Sensing his skepticism, Ellie knew only one answer. "Brandt was a master at smoke screens and mirrors. He was more suited to espionage than I ever was . . . except maybe for one thing . . ."

Mac raised his eyebrows. "One thing?"

"Brandt had done such an exhaustive check on me to make sure I wasna a Nazi plant, because, as he later confessed, he'd been smitten with me from the start—"

"I can't imagine that ever happening," Mac lightly scoffed. Yet he knew full well the power of Ellie's charisma. *After all,* Mac mused in silence, *wasn't I one of her first captives when we were just kids. Earned a bloody drubbing from her older brother after I gallantly came to her defense?*

Though blushing, she continued her tale. "It didn't matter who loved whom first because I'd fallen in love with Brandt, too."

Topping off their cups, Mac asked, "How'd you manage to pass Himmler's racial purity screening, not to mention getting the go ahead from MI-6 and your Old Man to marry Brandt?"

"To answer the last first, Dad already knew Brandt and held a grudgin' respect for him. How they met was a classified matter neither would bother to explain. In light of my father's experiences in the Great War, Dad wasna keen on me marryin' a Hun. But he knew I'd marry Brandt whether he approved or nae. So to safeguard my cover while in Germany, he ordered me not to tell anyone. Especially you."

Mac nodded absently. *So this was the reasoning behind the madness. It seems the measure of Ellie's loyalty to MI-6. I never believed she'd hold anything back from me.* Twisting his mustache, he asked, "What about the *SS*?"

"Brandt worked it out before he proposed to me. With Dad's help, they peppered my past with unverifiable lies. Nae effort was made to hide my Anglo-half, since, at that time, Germany desired to stay in Great Britain's good graces. It probably also helped when Brandt introduced me to *Reichsführer* Himmler at a dinner party. I appealed to the gentleman farmer in Heinrich by sharing some of those cozy childhood memories of Granma Gunda's farm—"

"*Oma-Gunda und ihre weiblichen Reize auf Himmler?*"

Smiling shyly, Ellie said, "Nae, I didna use my feminine wiles on Himmler. Nae deliberately anyway." Though Ellie felt her cheeks warm, she went on, "In part, doctored records of Oma's family going back to the 1700s, when the church burned, were probably what did the most to sanction our marriage."

"When were you married?"

"Secretly, we were married on 28 October 1933. According to *SS* records, our wedding occurred the day after the Night of the Amazons in an official *SS* ceremony, crossed sabers and all."

"Night of the Amazons? Hitler's grand celebration of women in all their natural, bare-assed glory as God created them, parading on horseback through the streets of Munich? That same exhibition?"

"Aye, the same brazen spectacle."

"Since you're an accomplished rider, were you one of those naked beauties?"

Rose tinged her cheeks again as she replied, "Besides the fact Brandt was training at an *SS* cavalry school and I was able to ride a gorgeous Friesian mare, I didna want them to suspect I was pregnant with Anna by nae participatin'. It was imperative I make a good showing as the virgin I was supposed to be."

Mac blinked as if he struggled to see through a pall of thick billowing smoke, the Night of the Amazons completely forgotten. "You had a daughter by Brandt?"

"Aye," Ellie said, smiling gently, as if seeing Anna across the table. "Oh, Mac, you would've loved her. Adrianna was such a beautiful child, filled with equal parts mischief and sweetness. Her eyes were clear blue-green like Brandt's. She also had his mile-wide stubborn streak, which I'm certain she didna get from me. That part of her had to be all Brandt's doing," she grinned, then went on, "Her hair was blonde like his and always a disheveled mass of curls. When she laughed, you couldna help but laugh with her. Her spirit fairly bubbled like a mountain brook in springtime."

For a few moments, Ellie bubbled with the memory of her daughter. In cheerful empathy, Chelsea's tail thumped against the linoleum floor.

Ellie smiled as she continued, "And did Anna ever have her *Vati*'s charisma! One generous smile and a beseeching look with those twinkling eyes and there went your heart."

Though Mac heard Ellie's description, in his mind, he saw Ellie as a little girl: sparkling green eyes, tousled curls, a quick, easy smile, radiant sunbeams of mirth. Anna had already stolen Mac's heart—stubborn streak, impishness and all—though he had never even met her.

In a heartbeat, Ellie's eyes welled with tears and her face took on an expression of immeasurable sadness.

Gently, reluctantly, Mac asked, "What happened?"

Slogging through her painful memories, Ellie dug out a hanky from her sweater pocket and wiped her tears away. She took a drink as she considered her next words.

"At some point in early 1937, the *Abwehr*, German Military Intelligence . . ." Ellie looked up at Mac. "Sorry, you know all that. Anyway, having no idea I already worked for MI-6, they asked me to spy for them. I voiced my reluctance. Of course," sarcasm dripped from her words, "there was no pressure on me as a loyal German, wed to one of their finest *SS* officers to do my duty. I stalled till I got word from Dad. Needless to say, he gave me the go-ahead to accept the Nazi request, officially making me a sanctioned double agent."

Ellie reluctantly went on as memories filled her mind. Finally, she said, "This meant more trips to England, without Brandt and Anna, barely three when I had to leave the first time. My job with Wolf became my cover. It was very credible. His health wasn't the best, and I was already serving as his proxy. With so many Nazi sympathizers in Britain, businessmen in the Reich were eager to keep those lines of trade open. 'Twas amazin' the number of doors opened for me in that guise."

Alarmed at Ellie's admonition, Mac demanded, "So you did spy for the *Abwehr*?"

"I most certainly didna," she snapped, eyes flashing. "Never in the sense you be thinkin'. Any intelligence I gave the Third Reich had been cleared with MI-6 as either planted misinformation or data verifiable through other sources. MI-6 tended to be more curious with what interested Hitler. Little if anythin' I passed on was of military value." She hesitated, knowing where her story led. Softly she said, "But there were risks . . ."

She fell silent and drained her cup. Mac refilled it with Scotch, topping his off, then patiently waited.

Slowly, Ellie she said, "Before Germany invaded the Low Countries and France in May 1940, I was ordered to England to learn what British Intelligence knew. 'Twas ironic how the *Abwehr* gave me the means to tell MI-6 of the planned invasion. Not that it changed the outcome a whit anyway." Ellie's memories drifted.

Sun-drenched images of Brandt and Anna romping on pristine Atlantic beaches and strolling with Anna through busy Portuguese marketplaces, while Brandt met a contact, flooded Ellie's thoughts. She blinked, but could not force the visions to recede.

"And?" Mac gently prompted.

Afraid to speak too loudly, lest her emotional dam break, she gently said, "Before I was to leave on my mission, the three of us flew to Lisbon. We enjoyed an absolutely splendid holiday. I left the day before they were to fly back to Berlin. Their plane never made it. It crashed in the Pyrenees during a storm. All on board supposedly killed."

"Supposedly? You didn't think they were dead?"

With a limp shrug, Ellie said, "When Dad first told me, I couldn't say why, but I felt certain Brandt had died."

A vacuous look crept into Ellie's eyes, which rapidly clouded with tears. Daubing them with her hanky, Ellie balled it up in her fist, then continued as if she remarked on something as mundane as the table's wood grain.

"Some months after the fall of France, Frederick, a German agent with whom I'd worked, and who knew Anna, was sure he'd seen her in Berlin, well and very much alive. If Anna had indeed survived, because I was no longer in

Germany, she might have been assigned to a foster home. There are hundreds of foster children, many from conquered lands who are suitable for raising as Himmler puts it," she again used her fingers to make quote marks, "good Aryan breeding stock."

Ellie again fell silent. This time Mac was not willing to be patient. "What do you mean 'if Anna survived'?"

"With the way the war had been goin', MI-6 had ordered me to remain in England. Ironically, the *Abwehr* ordered the same. I didna get back to Germany till November but couldna find Frederick. Perhaps he'd been killed. Without his direct help, my leads were months old, contacts had vanished, clues evaporated. It seemed like someone ran a step ahead of me, slammin' every door in me damn face. I tried Wolf, hopin' he might know what'd happened, maybe even where Anna might be. Supposedly, Wolf was in Switzerland on a business trip."

In his heart, Mac wanted to believe, for Ellie's sake, Anna was alive. Yet there was something in his cousin's tone which discouraged hope. He shook his head. "There's that 'supposedly' again. Why'd you believe Wolf wasn't away on a business trip?"

"Because no one would give me straight answers. Wolf seldom traveled. Maybe he didna want to see me because it would reopen the recent wounds of losing his only son and granddaughter. Not to mention that wouldna done his health any good. Financially he's a powerful man and guards his private life closely. Though I dinna think he meant to hurt me, I'd married into the family; nae been born into it. That's part of the reason I never want to return to Germany: my husband and little girl are both gone and my father-in-law didna wish contact. Even Dad doesna seem to know Wolf's situation now."

Ellie glanced past Mac's shoulder as if seeing an image of her past. "Before I met Brandt, Wolf's daughter, Brianna had committed suicide. After losing Brandt and Anna, as well, I imagine Wolf become an even worse recluse, but regardless, I never found out any more about Anna."

Suddenly looking exhausted, as if once again reliving the entire trip and all its futility, Ellie closed her eyes.

Mac knew this period was the unaccounted for "weeks" of which Strafford had spoken. Yet he still didn't want to give the charges credibility. As Mac promised, he wouldn't pass judgment until Ellie finished.

Opening her eyes, she finally went on, "The only person who did welcome me was Cynara Prüsche. Jakob Prüsche, her husband, is one of Brandt's cousins. Although I didna know Cynara well, we always got along. Cynara said she and Jakob, the captain of a U-boat, had visited Wolf the previous summer, but she'd nae seen Wolf since. At the time I visited them in Hamburg, Jakob was out to sea, so I was unable to ask him anything either."

Gazing at his cousin, Mac realized Ellie might know Prüsche, but it evidently was not the tight-knit association Strafford had implied. Conscious of Ellie's dejection, Mac offered, "Even if this agent's leads didn't pan out, Ellie, it doesn't mean your little girl's dead. Any country in time of war has all sorts of communication breakdowns. Even Hitler's vaunted *Deutschland* isn't impervious."

A gaze of emerald ice met his.

"You know, Mac, that's exactly what I kept tellin' myself. Right up until the day I spoke with the physician who had signed Anna's death certificate and touched the chill marble of me baby's gravestone. She survived the crash but her injuries lead to complications. Alone and afraid, without Brandt or me . . . Anna died before I reached Berlin. That guilt will haunt me till the day I die."

With a frown, Mac countered, "Then how the hell could Frederick have seen Anna three or four months earlier, alive and well?"

"Frederick was mistaken," she flatly stated. Her Mac-fortified dam unexpectedly crumbled, tears poured forth.

Ill at ease with feminine tears, all Mac could do was take hold of Ellie's hand. Giving a sympathetic whine,

Chelsea sat up and rested her head in Ellie's lap. Mac knew it was all either of them could do. Karney Rork was who Ellie really needed. Even if Irish wasn't familiar with the nuances of espionage, Mac was damned certain the Yank would provide the strength Ellie needed right now.

With Shakespeare's "what a wicked web we weave when first we practice to deceive" running through his head, Mac wondered: *Does anyone truly grasp the nuances of espionage? It's a dicey game at best; at worst, it's a deadly campaign of moves and counter ploys. And in this bloody war, it's such a tangled mess of double-deals and triple-crosses, does either side really know who's friend or foe?*

Pulling her hand back, Ellie blew her nose, then put the hankie away. Not sure where to go from here, she gave Chelsea an affectionate rub, stalling for time.

"So, Macaroon," Ellie began, using his nickname from when they were kids and the fact he'd always loved the chewy delights, "I didna mean to fall apart. Please, forgive me?"

"There's nothing to forgive, Li'l Elf. I understand." Watching Ellie for a moment as she gazed out the window, Mac pondering the complications of her story before asking, "Do you feel up to answering some more of my questions?"

"Aye, though you've heard the worst already." Sniffing, she withdrew her hanky. With a grimace, she held up the soggy linen. "Let me run to the Lou, rinse my face and get a hanky not as limp as this one." She stood and clarified, "Just in case another cryin' jag hits."

Chelsea trailed Ellie toward the bathroom. Mac stood and looked out the frosted window at the blanketing snow. For a long while, he simply stared, letting the Dewar's Scotch strain the jumble of thoughts in his head. Eventually, they sieved out into more questions: *Where did Strafford get his misinformation? Or if he has it right, what's Ellie trying to hide? Are they both in the dark and someone's trying to play them off each other? If so, have I been appointed judge, jury and bloody executioner for someone else's devious machinations? Like maybe this* JAEGER *bastard whoever he might be?*

"Christ Almighty," Mac swore, "wicked bloody web is right."

CHAPTER EIGHTEEN

Ellie came back from the bathroom. Turning, Mac smiled. Her face was framed by wet hair where she splashed her face with water.

"Feel better?" he asked, picking up a macaroon and chomping into it. Chelsea sat, waiting expectantly for her morsel.

With a nod, Ellie fixed herself another cup of tea, not bothering to remove the last bit of Scotch. She sat at the table, feeling resigned to explain things to Mac.

Mac refilled his cup with Dewar's and again sat in the chair across from his cousin. After tossing Chelsea her tidbit of cookie and taking a slow sip, he started the questions once more. "If you never saw Wolf on your return to Germany, how did you come by the £200,000? Which is apparently Strafford's only damning evidence."

Ellie looked decidedly uncomfortable. Mac wondered: *Is she trying to cover up something which links her to the Nazis?*

With a sigh, she said, "The money was already there. 'Twas a weddin' gift from Wolf. If I'm guilty of any bloody thin', 'twas my means of retrievin' it. I had the account number but, after my mission in Denmark was completed,

I had to have documents to pass through Germany into Switzerland. My papers were forged. I also hoped I might find Wolf if he truly was on a business trip."

Recalling Strafford's declaration, Mac interrupted with a briskly asked, "What was the outcome of that mission?"

Ellie tilted her head, then said, "Despite the eventual outcome, it went quite smoothly. Far too bloody glass smooth."

Her phrasing brought to mind Strafford's words of his daring rescue of Ellie from Berlin, which also went too smoothly.

Ellie spoke of her mission as if relating a Sunday brunch. "I was the one responsible for linkin' four separate resistance cells within the Odense operation and ultimately with our team at MI-6."

Knowing four agents were killed, according to Strafford, Mac asked, "So you made contact with each cell?"

"Nae. Since I'd already established contact with the primary agent, I only met up with him. The other three were blind drops."

Digesting her words along with another chewy macaroon, Mac asked, "What was the eventual outcome?"

Ellie arched an eyebrow. "You know, Mac, it just occurred to me, you and Dad discussed this shortly after I came back. Why're ye now dredgin' it all up again?"

He shrugged. "I want to hear your version. Go on."

Looking skeptical, she finally said, "It went fine. After I left, I learned JAEGER, a nefarious Danish agent workin' for the Nazis, had ripped through those cells like the nasty seabird the bastard's code-named after. He knew just who, where and when to hit. The *SS*, with help from their Danish brethren in the *DNSAP*, ripped what little was left of the Odense operation to shreds. Many were arrested, interrogated and most ultimately executed . . . I'm sure." Her voice trailed off.

In the gray cast of Ellie's eyes, Mac saw the raw

memories exposed. Though she apparently hadn't been there, Ellie clearly felt responsible. Mac had learned from her father that the *Gestapo*'s sweep of Denmark's resistance, especially the Odense cells, had taken hits from which they had yet to recover. "Who else besides yourself knew what the Danish operation entailed?"

She thought back. "Dad, possibly his aide, Leftenant Sloat, and maybe Chief Brumble, but he's since been killed anyway."

"Yes, your Old Man told me," Mac conceded. Not elucidating that Commodore Greer wanted to keep the death of Eugen Ulmstein under wraps since he might be the key to unmasking the double agent deep within MI-6. "Anyone else?"

"I dinna think so. Strafford handled the initial set-up but nothing more. I think he left for Norway right after I headed to Denmark. It was the mission on which he'd been wounded."

"That's when his cane appeared," Mac confirmed.

"Aye, though he was obviously well enough to pull my bacon outta the bloody fire in Berlin when I was captured."

"Obviously," Mac echoed. "When did you run into JAEGER?"

"Never had that bloody pleasure till I got back to Copenhagen in early January, and I was totally unaware of any problems."

"What happened?"

Ellie stared at her cousin. "You're bein' as bloody obtuse as Strafford. I dinna want to be rehashin' this whole damn scenario. Besides ye're makin' me digress from me bloody defense."

Though Mac was debriefed by Uncle Gus, Ellie's father, after her narrow escape, Mac recalled that was when Strafford had first been mentioned in connection with ICE PACT—at that time a droplet with no real substance. The meeting with Commodore Greer had been as strained as this one with Ellie, because of the old man's insistence on Strafford taking part. Mac hadn't wanted the British major involved. Mac lost his case.

He now held his ground with Ellie, however. "I want the story, to put it crudely, straight from the horse's mouth."

Ellie glared at him. "I'll comply but your bloody choice of words leaves a lot to be desired, big cousin. You be makin' me sound like some old nag." Leaning back, her gaze never left his eyes. She sipped her tea before continuing.

"I thought I'd slipped back into Denmark undetected, but after six days of failed attempts to reach my contacts, I was arrested and dragged off to Berlin. The prick of a Nazi in charge of my interrogation was quite vocal in his praise of what a wonderful job JAEGER had done in destroyin' the cells and findin' me."

"So you never actually met JAEGER face-to-face?"

She shook her head. "'Tis why JAEGER's identity remains a mystery. I've a feelin' I'd be dead had I met him."

"Was there anything unusual about your imprisonment?"

Her eyes lost focus and wouldn't meet his gaze.

"Only that after they transferred me to Berlin so fast. My captivity was primarily psychological. They must've expected me to break with what they *might* do to me. I was stripped and left in an ice-cold cell. I heard the screams of less fortunate prisoners at all hours. As for the times they interrogated me, I was blindfolded and tied to a chair, but they never really asked me any damn bloody questions of any worth. 'Twas like they were waitin' for somebody who never showed up. Consequently, the officer who was in charge often left and the guards wiled away their time by fondlin' me—"

Seeing the angst on Mac's face, she paused. "Nae, Mac. Thank God, they never raped me, though I'm sure they would've bloody well gotten round to it eventually."

His voice sounded strained as he asked, "Beyond

molesting you, was there any other torture involved?"

"Nae really. Horribly uncomfortable and terrifyin' and, as they intended, 'twas the possibilities goin' through me head that played bloody hell with me. That nae knowin' what to expect."

"Did you receive any . . . therapy when you returned?"

"Nae. Dad wanted me to, but I refused." Ellie took a deep breath and continued, "Anyway, Strafford intervened before they raped me or actually tortured me. I've never been sure if he preempted their game plan or if they had somethin' completely different on their perverted minds. 'Twas almost as if someone oversaw what they did and kept it all from getting' out of hand."

A myriad of unpleasant possibilities crawled through Mac's mind as to who might have been that overseer.

Sitting in silence, Ellie watched him weigh her words against what he knew and what Strafford might have told him. She endured Mac's silence stoically. But barely. She revered her elder cousin and to have him suspect her like this was painful.

Eventually, he motioned with his hand. "Please, resume your story concerning this little detour through *Deutschland*."

Ellie again raised an eyebrow at Mac's choice of words but went on, "As I told you before, MI-6 forged my visa and travel papers, but since Strafford okayed the mission, no one asked any questions."

Skeptical, Mac asked, "So Strafford knew you were going to Germany, then on into Switzerland?"

"Nae necessarily. He only knew I might need to contact some agents in the Reich. As for Switzerland, if routes to Portugal or Sweden weren't available, Switzerland was an alternative. Besides, Dad didna want Strafford knowin' I was gettin' money from my Swiss account to find his granddaughter and, if need be, purchase her freedom. In Dad's words, quote, 'Tis none of his bleedin' bloody business, end quote."

With a shrug, Ellie sighed. "Truth tell, I'd hardly touched the money by the time I learned Anna was dead."

Again nodding, Mac wasn't sure why the money so convinced Strafford that Ellie worked for the Nazis. Another long moment passed before he asked, "What'd you do with the money after that?"

"I redeposited it." Ellie looked down, her cheeks blushing slightly. "Then when I became pregnant with Nikki, I had some of the money transferred to the Bank of Nova Scotia to live on till she was in school and I could resume fulltime work." Ellie's voice broke. "I just never imagined I'd lose her as well . . ."

Though he didn't want her to dwell on her more recent loss, curiosity prompted him to ask, "Who was Nikki's father?"

Ellie debated keeping her answer as vague to Mac as she had to Karney, but it might lead to worse consequences, though how she truly couldn't say. Far more serene than she felt, Ellie quietly confessed, "James Strafford."

His face again fell. "No wonder you and Strafford were going at it like a Scottie and an English bull terrier." Emphatically, Mac said, "And I imagine he made you indebted for his daring rescue in Berlin."

"In part." Looking down, she cautiously said, "Strafford was also the only one who believed I was bein' stalked when I returned to London. I never found any substantial proof nor any real idea who it might be, 'twas just . . . well—"

"After nine years in Nazi Germany, you could sense someone following you."

"Aye." She sighed. "After a particularly harrowing night, when someone took some potshots at me just before the start of a bombin' raid, I found myself at Strafford's flat and . . ." Recalling the phrasing Karney used, she said, "Things just happened. At least James believed I was bein' stalked. Dad was positive I had battle fatigue or whatever the bloody hell spies experience once they get back to the real world and try to adjust."

His tone insinuating nothing, Mac said, "Strafford understood, gave you succor and got you into bed. D'you suppose his infatuation for you set you up for that end?"

Mac's question gave Ellie a strange sense of confusion, like trying to remember a dream after waking up. She shook her head, finally answering, "James may be a bloomin' royal skirt-chaser, but I dinna think he's nae that twisted."

Mac mentally chewed on this before getting back on track. "How much money is left in your Swiss account?"

"A little under 400,000 Marks."

Another curiosity prompted, "In your position for Wolf, did you ever have need to know what his assets might be?"

"Nae, Wolf did his own bookkeepin'." Ellie tapped a finger to her head. "All up here. But I do know they're considerable. Despite setbacks in the Twenties, he gained it back well before Hitler was sworn in as Chancellor. A lot of his money was spent funding his resistance network, though."

"Any jewels or valuables, anything like that?"

"Occasionally. Before the war, Brandt would meet wealthy patrons in Lisbon. They were American or British Jews, as well as former German Jews, who covertly funded the crusade against the Reich through Wolf. Sometimes negotiable bonds, uncut gems and jewels were smuggled in to help relatives escape. That ended when Jews were no longer allowed to leave Germany at all."

"Was helping Jews a large part of Wolf's operation?"

She gently shook her head before saying, "Nae a large part but 'twas definitely an important part. I believe Cynara Prüsche was even involved for a while, but I never knew for certain."

"With her husband a U-boat captain?" Mac asked in disbelief. "That's a bloody dangerous venture." Recalling

Strafford's boast of assassinating Wolf, Mac wondered: *Did the Brits murder an innocent German? Or was Wolf set up to be killed?*

Derailing the thought, Mac asked, "And MI-6 offered Wolf no support?"

"Nae. Except to give him decent radiotelegraphs. Truth be, Wolf doesn't want to rely on MI-6. He says they waste too much time with their bloody red tape and politics. He wants results."

Nodding, Mac registered Ellie's use of the present tense in reference to Wolf. Mac realized Ellie didn't know her father-in-law had been killed. But now didn't feel like the time to enlighten her. Yet he understood Wolf's reasons for self-reliance. Knowing Wolf might have been a Nazi, however, Mac also wondered: *Did Wolf wish to keep MI-6 from knowing the exact nature of his operation? Was he just a greedy SOB, who kept contraband for himself? No, I doubt Brandt would've gone along with that scam nor been able to keep Ellie from knowing.*

As pieces fell into a semblance of order, a new question popped into Mac's head. "Was Brandt smuggling anything on that last trip?"

"I dinna know. His contact had postponed. They rescheduled for late Friday and my flight left early that mornin'. I dinna know if he even met up with the chap . . . although . . ."

"Although what?" Mac prodded.

"I later ran across a report at MI-6 that Brandt's contact was assassinated a few weeks later in Tel Aviv."

"Were you always aware of who Brandt was meeting?"

"Generally, aye. I was his backup in case problems arose. Like his duty to the *SS*."

Weighing Ellie's answers and Strafford's insinuations, Mac felt a growing sense of anxiety about this entire situation. He felt something stirred just beneath the surface, out of sight, with lethal ramifications to far more than Ice Pact alone. And nothing in the course of their conversation had unequivocally cleared Ellie's name of Strafford's allegations. Yet.

Though not sure what Strafford told Mac, Ellie suspected an ulterior motive. *Even if James thought he did the right thing by revealin' his distrust of me, there has to be somethin' in it for him. There always is. But what?*

Barely above a whisper, she asked, "Do you really believe I sold out to the Nazis after all that's happened?"

Rubbing his hand over his bristle of burnished copper hair, Mac sighed forcefully. He glanced up, his gaze not lingering on hers. "I honestly don't know what the hell to think anymore."

"I didna say think, Mac. I said believe."

Ignoring Ellie's emphasis, Mac swallowed the last bit of his Scotch. Nor could he tell Ellie that Lieutenant Commander Nigel "Sandy" Sanders—a topnotch officer and instructor, responsible for training many MI-6 agents—had been transferred here by her own dad, as much to protect her as watch for any breach of security on her part.

Mac's jaded gaze pierced Ellie's soul, making her decidedly nervous. This day was becoming as unpleasant as she expected.

"Ellie, what I think or believe no longer matters. However, for the time being, it might be best to alter some of your duties."

"You bloody well think I sold out to the damned Nazis, dinna you?"

Mac's silence fell like a guillotine dropping.

"How can you suspect me when the Germans are tryin' to kill me? Oh, wait, I get it. You think I'm BLUE FOX's contact? Or I'm in league with JAEGER, who wants me dead?" Ellie threw up her hands. "How could I've been so bloody stupid. I've set up these bloody attempts on me own life to throw off suspicion, hopin' they'd all fail. 'Tis all so bloody clear now. Thanks for lettin' me know what the hell I've been doin' with meself lately."

Ellie felt gripped by the same panic as when she found herself alone aboard *Glasgow Bonnie*. Finally, she forced out, "'Tis a deep slash to have you suspect me, Mac. My God, we've known each other since we were little kids."

Mac looked away. *How can I tell her—a woman I love like a sister, who's been a vital part of my life for years— that her own dad has suspicions but is afraid to admit the possibility?* With a heavy sadness, Mac countered, "People change, Ellie."

"I'm nae a bloody Nazi, Rob Roy MacCalister!" She stood, turning away from him. Her sudden motion reeled her Scotch-pickled senses, forcing her to grab the counter edge. The tea kettle's soft whistling suddenly seemed an annoyance. She snapped off the burner as she fought to regain her equilibrium.

Chelsea nudged Ellie's leg. Kneeling to pet the sweet dog's head, she received a generous face licking. *At least Chelsea knows me heart.* Standing, cautiously, she faced the window and focused on the falling snow. *I wish Irish were here. Nae Mac—even if he is me cousin. Me Irishman would know me heart, too.*

Quietly, from behind her, came Mac's ambiguous reply, "I didn't say I believed Strafford, Ellie."

Still careful, Ellie turned back. Her brogue rose with her accusation, "Ya sure as hell're nae disbelievin' him either, ya sanctimonious son of a bitch." Shocked by her own words, She hastily added, "Meanin' no disrespect to dear Aunt Helen, of course." Feeling flustered, Ellie stepped toward the living room.

Mac checked her escape. She tried to move around him, but he stopped her and gently rested his large hands on her trembling shoulders. Gazing down at her, his eyes were kind and forgiving. As he spoke, his voice settled like a feather.

"Things will take time, Ellie, some longer than others."

She supposed it was an answer. Of sorts. Evidently Mac's investigating the charges and needs more time.

Still, she felt trapped. Trying to calm herself, she shrugged off his hands and poured a stiff belt of Scotch. Ellie downed almost all of it, hoping to quell a dram of her anger. It did little more than spin the room faster.

Mac wondered: *Was her affair with Strafford, then rejection of him—whether or not he knew she was pregnant with his child—motive enough for Strafford to fabricate these accusations?* With Ellie's heavy sigh, Mac decided to keep that thought to himself.

Setting her cup down, Ellie faced Mac. "So what am I to be doin' in the meantime? Take up knittin' for the boys?"

"Meanwhile, you'll analyze data from miscellaneous recon flights and supervise the training of these new baby-face recruits. After Commander Sanders gets settled in, he'll need your help with the training agenda. After the perils of espionage, such a task may seem mundane, but since you worked with Sandy before, you can both shift gears more smoothly to adapt to ICE PACT's demands."

Briefly glancing away in consideration of something, Mac said, "When our Irish Coastie returns, you'll go to Argentia, Newfoundland, to debrief him." Mac refused to expand on his fear for Ellie's safety if she stayed here, nor his dread if she was a Nazi. Though Mac knew in his heart, and was certain her dad knew Ellie wasn't a Nazi, Mac needed irrefutable proof for all the other skeptics who might create problems for her and ultimately ICE PACT.

To Ellie, he finally said, "For now, it's the most latitude I can allow."

Nodding, a sense of defeat overwhelmed her. She had never in her life been weighed under a burden of suspicion like this. Even in Nazi Germany where it was typical. It amazed her how much power Strafford still wielded. Power that could ruin her life. Remorse suddenly provoked a wholly uncharacteristic response: "Irish should've let me die with *Glasgow Bonnie* when she sank."

Mac swiftly embraced her. "No, Ellie, he shouldn't have. And I do not want to hear that kind of bullshit from you again. This will all work out. It will just take time," he emphasized.

His words, echoing Karney's time-sentiments, provided some comfort, but the fervor of Mac's embrace spoke more than words could convey.

Holding her close brought to Mac's mind better times of love and laughter and how close death had recently come to Ellie on too many occasions. Quietly, he asked, "Do you have any idea who might've targeted you for assassination?"

Ellie sagged away from Mac as the war came back to the forefront. "Obviously JAEGER. That bloody prick's had it in for me even before Denmark I think."

Pulling further away, she took another sip of Scotch. "It could be someone as high up as Himmler. He may feel responsible for allowing my marriage to Brandt, and now I've betrayed *der Reich*. If JAEGER keeps in contact with little Heinrich, and I'm sure they keep in touch somehow, my name's surely been sullied across Europe. It might even be Heydrich, the Blond Beast, though I've never crossed paths with him. And if Joseph Goebbels feels I somehow harmed the image of Hitler and *das Dritte Reich*, he'd have a say in my demise with more than just his propaganda machine."

She set her cup down. "Then there's the Danish resistance. They might've been led to believe I betrayed them and want revenge for the agents they lost. In spite of the fact I was captured, who knows what seeds of evil JAEGER may've sewn."

Sighing, Ellie met his gaze. "In short, Mac, I truly have nae any bloody clue beyond JAEGER." She gulped the final slug of Dewar's.

Mac stood speechless, feeling helpless and pained as he sensed Ellie's frustration and anxiety. *How'd we come so far from those innocent days of frivolity and mischief? I think I finally understand the meaning of that novel I started to read by Thomas Wolfe:* You Can't Go Home

Again. *Even if circumstances were different, you truly can't return to the life you've had before.*

Turning from her empty cup on the pass through, Ellie changed subjects. "Have you any idea when Irish will be in Newfoundland?"

"Not really, since he just reached Greenland on Friday. More than likely it'll take several weeks. It depends on what he finds, weather conditions, any number of factors. But you, Li'l Elf, are my immediate concern. Not Irish. He can handle himself. Though I'm sure he'd do wonders for your morale, eh?"

Nodding thoughtfully, it occurred to her Mac was taking some grave risks to clear her name. She hesitantly said, "I dinna want you to be puttin' your head on any choppin' block for me, Mac. 'Tis my neck under the blade, nae yours. Only one of us need fall."

"Neither of us will fall." Though Mac grinned down at her, Ellie's expression was still downcast. "Li'l Elf, please try not to worry. Right now, Strafford's got a damned weak case against you, and I'm sure I can stack the deck in our favor with a strong, legitimate case. If not for Strafford's connections and seemingly implacable record, I'd have him assigned to a goat cart in Greece. But he'd undoubtedly terrorize the poor ewes till they'd quit giving milk."

Ellie smiled slightly, knowing full well the insult Mac made against the major. In other circumstances she might have laughed. But not tonight.

Mac sighed at his flopped joke. "Trust me, Li'l Elf, the only heads to roll will be the ones that are supposed to. Especially if I've any bloody say about it." He stepped into the living room, then turned back. "And I damn well do!" Gazing expectantly at her master, Chelsea wagged her tail.

With arms folded, Ellie strolled after the pair and quietly asked, "What am I to do if Strafford starts quizzin' me about any of this?"

"You answer directly to me or the admiral. Not Strafford." Mac shrugged into his coat. "With the legwork

I've slated for you, he'll trip over his dandy little cane if he tries to keep up." Putting on his beret, Mac asked, "Supper at the Tartan Banks?"

"Are you callin' a truce?" she asked suspiciously.

"I wasn't aware we were fighting. Frankly, I'm starved and would prefer some beautiful female companionship. I've already seen too much of my camouflage-painted, unshaven, smelly lads in the last few days. Although a goodly portion of them may be at the tavern anyway, at least they should be cleaned up. To paraphrase the Lord: 'And on the seventh day, we shall rest.' At least for part of the day. Let's head to town, get some great chow and maybe find a few good laughs, eh?"

Hunger won out over mulish pride. Retrieving her red coat from the closet, she asked, "And you're buyin'?"

Mac grinned. "Come on, Chelsea, let's treat my gorgeous cousin to a steak and seafood dinner she won't soon forget." Helping Ellie on with her coat, he hugged her from behind and gently kissed the top of her head before opening the door.

Ellie placed a red tam on her head as if to trap Mac's kiss and be there as a reminder of her cousin's love.

However, trudging through the snow to the mansion, twilight shrouded Ellie with an even deeper gloom than Strafford's allegations.

Must fate always intervene for the worst? I dinna wish to involve Irish in me life of espionage and perils. On the other hand, as he says, I've a feelin' that Karney could deal with me own troubles and his without battin' an eye. Perhaps me wild Irishman's love can see us both through these difficult times? I just wish he were here now.

CHAPTER NINETEEN

Lieutenant Commander Pete Halloran waited for the captain to read another redundant report. Pete stood rigidly. The cabin reeked of booze, but Captain Tennef showed no signs of intoxication. A practiced drunk seldom did. Pete knew—his father had been very practiced, a virtual mirror-image of Tennef, except Pete's father, when home from sea duty, became a brutal lush.

Signing the report, Tennef scanned the next one and finally got back to why Pete stood waiting.

"Well, Mr. Halloran, you don't need me at this Canuck meeting ashore. You handle whatever problems vex them. After all, you are my executive officer. I expect you to execute your duties," he gave a wry grin at his cleverness, "because I certainly have better things to do than play a game of patty-cake with our sniveling Limey cousins."

Pete bit back a retort as Tennef shuffled a stack of paper to exaggerate the magnitude of his job. It didn't impress Pete. Tennef's vanity did not negate the fact that Pete Halloran kept *Paratus* and her crew welded into a cohesive unit. Without Pete, this cutter would slip into an abyss of quadruplicated forms and hundreds of flawlessly typed reports. Battle-readiness was not Tennef's priority. It galled Pete to have this desk-sailor command a cutter with the potential of *Paratus*. If Wellington J. Tennef had not found the right asses to kiss, he would no doubt still be rationing toilet paper at the Ninth Coast Guard District's office in Ohio with an occasional cruise on Lake Erie.

Close to blowing a gasket, Pete said, "Sir, the request was to discuss our part in OPERATION ICE PACT. GreenPat wants us to work closely with the Canadians. I feel it's imperative we comply."

"Well, Mr. Halloran, I don't agree. GreenPat's aficionados are not here, are they? They think all there is to running a boat is briefings and afternoon teas. If HQ gave me a proficient crew and more competent officers, such as yourself . . ." Tennef's smile was as condescending as the tone of his voice.

Inwardly, Pete grumbled: *And we're a ship, specifically, a cutter, not a goddamned boat.*

"I'd have time to attend to such trivial meetings. If you want companionship, take that J-G what's-his-name, your young upstart expert in modern technology."

"Lieutenant Rork is his name, sir," Pete furnished, knowing Tennef would never bother to learn his officer's names—especially Sean's.

"Yes, the smart aleck who's related to you somehow, with all his mumbo-jumbo answers to the future of warfare. He can answer their technical questions or at least take a stab at telling them about that damned contraption he always has in pieces."

Pete's temper ratcheted up a notch. Besides being his younger brother-in-law and friend, Sean was a top-notch officer. He knew sonar and radar could win the war if utilized to their full potential. But technological warfare was beyond Tennef's pencil-pushing dogma. Even if Pete didn't grasp how the complex equipment worked, he knew its worth and most assuredly respected Sean's opinions.

More than ready to escape, Pete straightened to attention. "Very well, sir. I'll report back tonight."

"No, no, don't bother to disturb me this evening. Write a report and put it on my desk. Triplicate will be perfectly acceptable."

"Yes, sir," he said, knowing Tennef would drink the night away.

In the wardroom, Pete found Sean pouring a stout mug of coffee. "Rork, you're comin' with me to meet this RCN captain. Dress blues on the quarterdeck at noon."

Baffled, Sean looked up. He'd pulled a double watch to inspect and calibrate their radar while moored in Sheet Harbour; nor had he slept much in the last two days. And he felt it. His brain slogged through the maze of diodes, wires and connections leading to the cathode-ray tube's eye-numbing green squiggles. But he knew Pete was pissed about something. No, not something. Someone: Tennef.

To the receding thud of Pete's boots, Sean gave a two-finger salute. "Dress blues, twelve-hundred. Aye, aye, sir, with bells on my toes."

IKEQ FJORD
SOUTH OF AMMASSALIK, GREENLAND
FRIDAY

The midday sun, invisible to Karney Rork in the isolation of this ice cave, sat low on the southern horizon. Filtered through a thick expanse of blue-green ice, it captured the cavern in perpetual twilight. A faint world, neither day nor night, with an almost overpowering aura of cold and stillness.

After the long trek across glaciers, snowfields and ice, Karney and Hans had taken refuge in an abandoned Inuit stone and turf hut, mostly buried in snow, near Ikeq Fjord. Late this morning, actually before a feeble dawn, they set out for Hans' ice cavern.

They'd reached the cave by crawling through a long, slick tunnel, bored out by last summer's fast run-off. After autumn's freeze, the water flow had ceased, leaving a passage from the glacier above to this cavity beside the fjord. In order to reach the icy floor where he now stood, Karney had slithered down a rope secured to a climbing piton hammered into stone-hard ice.

Hans waited twenty feet above him, a bodiless voice attached to a flashlight, its agitated bouncing aping the lad's impatience.

Throwing back the corner of a stiff tarp, Karney beamed his flashlight over the equipment and gear set on pallets. Though frost obscured the cache, it definitely was not from any glacial deposit.

In the light's orb, Karney scanned tool boxes, emergency pumps, voltmeters, gauges, dials, a welding torch, two acetylene tanks and several fifty-gallon drums. He rubbed his gloved finger over a dial face and read the writing beneath: German.

Shifting toward the rear of the cave, gravel crunched under Karney's crampons. He uncovered steel plates of various sizes and enough electrical cable and copper filament to rewire a ship the size of *Zealous*. Most any damaged U-boat could easily be repaired and made seaworthy with the gear and implements at hand.

Anxiously, Hans called from above. His voice echoed with a chill resonance in the glacial cavern. "Is this it, Irish? Isn't this exactly what I told you? This is it, isn't it?"

Focusing on the indigo shadows swallowing the beam of his flashlight, Karney did not immediately answer. The actual size of this cavern was impossible to determine with such a puny light. He needed to explore further.

"Irish," Hans sharply yelled, "is this what you look for?"

"Sorry, Hans, didn't mean to ignore you. Yeah, this stuff's probably for a U-boat all right, but I don't think they'd get more 'an a dingy in here to pick—" Karney broke off as his beam vanished on the far side of the cavern. "I'm gonna work my way around to the other side," he called up to his companion.

Though Hans kept up a litany of questions, Karney gave no heed to the young man's third degree, except for one remark.

"You've got to remember, this opens onto the fjord and the ice recedes almost every summer."

Hans kept his light dancing like a spotlight waiting for some celebrity to appear on stage. His enthusiastic narration accompanied the erratic motion. "If you ask me, Irish, this is more than big enough to accommodate any U-boat. Even the one I spied here last summer would surely fit. I'm sure it is deep enough, too. Don't you agree? It's like a sub pen. It's just made from ice, not concrete."

With the other side of the cave appearing no closer, Karney noncommittally said, "Yeah, suppose so . . ." His breath, illuminated in the frozen air by the flashlight, hung like fog. His crampons were the only thing keeping him from sprawling on the glassy ice. Reaching the far side, Karney shined his light on a markedly larger, black tarp, invisible from the opening through which Hans observed the hideaway. Size alone made it seem more menacing.

"Where are you, Irish? Did you find something?"

Dragging the heavy waterproof canvas back, rounded noses of double racks of torpedoes were exposed.

"*Heilege Scheisse,*" Karney swore in German, as if shit had any means of being holy. Running his hand over the cold steel, he felt icy fingers stroke down his spine in turn. With a shiver, he hoped he'd never experience the devastation of these harbingers of death. He muttered, "It's a damned cinch no dingy unloaded these babies."

"What, Karney? What did you say? I can't hear you."

Aware the young Dane hated being left out of the action, he rolled his eyes and yelled, "Torpedoes, Hans. Twenty-four of 'em."

"Are you going to disarm them?"

"I'm not even gonna try," Karney hollered. "I'm sure the warheads aren't armed, but I don't wanna blow us to Kingdom come."

"Is there anything you can do?"

"Yeah, if I can find—"

A single gunshot cracked like thunder, drowning Hans' cry as the two sounds merged and echoed in the ice cave. Despite his layers of clothing, Karney cleared his Colt from its holster and racked a round into the chamber in one swift, fluid motion.

Working back to the cache, he saw he was too late. Hans lay in a heap on the gravel. The rope Karney had climbed down lay coiled in uneven loops over Hans' inert form. Keeping his flashlight off, Karney dragged Hans behind the stash of equipment and felt for a pulse below his jaw. The pulse was strong, but Karney's hand came away sticky with blood. Hans would have to wait. Their party crasher might want to create more trouble.

Peering up and around, Karney saw only the indigo void. Then, ever so faintly, he heard footsteps receding. Apparently, whoever attacked Hans wasn't willing to kill them outright. But they'd certainly insured neither man would report to anyone anytime soon. If ever.

Hans stirred. Flipping on his flashlight, Karney checked him over for any broken bones.

Groggily mumbling, Hans said, "I tried to defend myself, Irish, but they knocked me out. I'm sorry."

"Forget it. Did you maybe see who it was?"

Hans gingerly shook his head, then touched the gash oozing dark crimson into his blond hair and staining his parka frozen russet.

"Well," Karney scowled up at their escape route, "if they didn't wanna kill us, they sure's hell did the next best thing under the circumstances."

Darkness crept over them. An icy chill with it. Though warm enough with his insulated Arctic gear, Karney felt chilled. *Like someone just walked over my grave and took their sweet-ass time about it.*

⊕

RCN TRAINING GARRISON
SHEET HARBOUR, NOVA SCOTIA
FRIDAY

Mac met the placid gaze in Pete Halloran's blue eyes as he shook the officer's beefy hand. Though only about five-foot-ten, Pete's build, ruddy complexion and his rusty-blond hair reminded Mac of a sturdy red-brick firehouse. With massive shoulders and a barrel chest, Pete looked like a bull-dozer would have trouble dislodging him. Mac wondered if his temperament was as steadfast as his appearance seemed.

"Captain MacCalister, a pleasure to meet you." Pete turned to his companion. "This is Lieutenant Sean Rork, sir, one of the best Combat Information Officers in the Coast Guard."

Shaking the hand of the lanky young man, Mac knew, without asking, Sean was Karney's younger brother. The resemblance was striking. "This is quite a coincidence, Leftenant Rork."

Cocking his head slightly—a habit of Karney's as well—Sean gazed at the taller Canadian. Sean registered only bafflement as he said, "I don't understand, sir."

"Your brother's working with ICE PACT, too, eh? And at the moment, he's a bit north of where you lads were hunting U-boats. But Irish is trying to recruit polar bears for me. Not sink a U-boat."

Sean nodded, though clearly not tracking Mac's remark. "I thought *Lady Z* left Greenland for Boston weeks ago?"

Amused by Sean missing the tongue-in-cheek humor, the two senior officers locked gazes. Pete barely withheld a chuckle. Sean could be too scientifically literal.

Captain MacCalister bulled his way through, answering, "So she did, Leftenant. Irish, however, is doing recon for me on his own in Greenland. I'd have sent a battle buddy with him but with ICE PACT's shoe-string budget that wasn't possible. Who knows where next he'll end up, eh?"

"Oh, I see," said Sean with another slow nod, still unclear what his older brother was doing. When Mac didn't elaborate, Sean made no further inquiry.

Mac was relieved Sean didn't ask too many questions. It was best if he be kept in the dark. No sense in settling muddy waters.

Indicating the chairs around the fireplace, Mac said, "If you don't mind, we'll catch last lunch." Noticing Sean's eyes widen, he added, "Don't worry, lad, there'll be plenty of chow left, especially since they know I'm comin'. Some ale beforehand?"

Nodding in unison, the Americans sat down while Mac got the ale.

Pete offered, "I'm sorry Commander Tennef couldn't attend, sir. I hope it won't hinder our involvement in your operation."

Handing each of them an opened bottle of Moosehead Ale, Mac remarked, "That's quite all right, Commander Halloran. I'd just as soon deal with just you and Leftenant Rork anyway, eh?"

Mac sat down. "Marriage ties aside, Pete, Irish speaks very highly of you. After reading your file, I feel we've already met. I'm duly impressed by your credentials. To say the least, I was surprised you were passed over for command of *Paratus*. It seems your present captain is a little, how should I put it, off his game."

Cynically Pete thought "under the wagon" would fit Tennef's state better, but to Mac he said, "No figuring the Puzzle Palace, sir."

"Puzzle Palace? Coast Guard headquarters, right? I recall Irish using that term a time or two."

Taking another sip of his brew, Mac set the icy bottle on a coaster along with his congenial manners. "Truth of the matter, gentlemen, I don't give a bloody damn who commands your cutter, so long as they engage enemy raiders, whenever and wherever they meet them."

Mac got the expected reaction as the Yanks glanced at one another, confirming his suspicion: *Tennef couldn't command a bloody rowboat on Griffin's Pond.*

Diplomacy, however, turned him to another concern. "At the moment, I'd like to hear about the U-boat that *Paratus* caught on her radar. Yank Naval Intelligence thinks it may be a prototype sub, and I've received support for this theory from MI-6."

Knowing he could trust these men, Mac stated, "Personally, I suspect this U-boat is causing a great deal of the trouble we've experienced in Denmark Strait, eh? My recon pilot caught a blurry image of her on film. Jerry, however, submerged before he got a more definitive shutter click. I hope you gents can give me a bit more information. Your report indicated she seems larger and faster than other U-boats you've encountered."

"You, sir, did your homework," Pete remarked as he wondered: *How the heck does this Canuck know so much?* "I didn't know the RCN had access to Coast Guard communiqués."

"Routinely, we don't but Leftenant Commander Eleanor Greer, one of my intelligence resource officers, has a way of locating all sorts of information for me. Your logs were comparable to cutting ice with a blowtorch when it came to her not inconsiderable feminine wiles. She can be a very engaging inquisitor."

Seeing Sean's eyes light up, Mac wasn't surprised when he asked, "Will we have the pleasure of meeting her today, Cap'n?"

"Doubtful, Mr. Rork. I don't believe Commander Greer's returned from Halifax yet, where she's charming RCN admiralty out of at least one corvette to hunt this phantom U-boat with you lads. Knowing my sweet cousin, she may well come back with an entire flotilla."

Taking a swig of his ale, Mac leaned forward, elbows on his knees. "Enough small talk, gentlemen. I want to hear about this U-boat, what *Paratus* is capable of and, more importantly, whether your captain wants to hunt Jerry or not."

Pete sized up Mac MacCalister as an honest man, calculating and very resourceful. Perhaps he'd prove the key to ousting Tennef from his paper-puff command. Catching Sean's eye, Pete knew his thoughts tracked the same course. It was confirmation enough.

With a wry grin, Pete admitted, "We'll share all we have, Captain MacCalister, but before *Paratus* can fully help ICE PACT, we need to resolve a dilemma aboard our beloved cutter. I believe it's a situation Karney Rork might be able to help settle if his next TDY, while *Zealous* is undergoing refit, assigns him to *Paratus*. Then, I'm fairly sure, all our sea gulls can perch on the same mooring line."

FRIDAY

"Ah, Eleanor-dear, you've returned from Halifax."

Cringing upon hearing the aggravating pitch of James Strafford's voice, Ellie knew her hopes of fleeing the manor house without running into Strafford had just died. Her escape route was blocked by the vermouth swizzling jerk.

Maybe I shouldna chatted with Mac and his guests so long. Returning from Halifax this afternoon, she found Mac eating a late lunch with Karney's younger brother Sean and Pete Halloran, his brother-in-law. Ellie had joined them for dessert. Getting the go-ahead from Mac regarding the American's part in OPERATION ICE PACT, Ellie gave her report to all three. Now she realized she should not have enjoyed that second mug of coffee when their business concluded.

Setting her thoroughly jam-packed overnight bag and parcels on the floor, Ellie turned, ready to do battle if the Limey said a single word about her parley with Mac last Sunday. Ellie stood her ground in silence, waiting for the major's first salvo.

Martini in hand, Strafford strolled across the vestibule as if at a cocktail party. "I say, Eleanor, when is your Yank hero due back from his icy venture? I daresay no one's heard from the lad in days. You don't suppose he's gone native, do you? I've heard Eskie girls have no compunction about throwing themselves under any man. And to be precise, that would be quite a cozy position for those long, bloody frigid nights. Gives me shivers to think of that weather."

Ellie recoiled from his insinuations. *What I ever saw in this lout must've been a measure of me misery at the time. He's one pompous ass, who loathes not bein' the eye of his own ruddy hurricane. Here at the garrison, besieged by all these Canadians and servin' under Mac, Strafford's definitely not the center of anythin'.*

"Why worry about Irish, Major? You're the one stranded in a martini gutter. I dinna doubt Karney's virtues. He has a mission to do, not an Arctic harem to bed. On that note, 'tis a good thing you didna go, eh? Irish takes his duty seriously. After all, the Coast Guard motto *Semper Paratus* does mean Always Ready."

She put on a sultry voice as she added, "Karney's always ready for whatever difficulty might arise, Major. And quite distinct from you, Irish takes responsibility for his own actions and has no need to embellish his war stories to look heroic. Irish is genuinely brave and lives a bold, honest life."

Though the scar near Strafford's eye was stark against his mad-red face, he spoke with calm control, "To be precise, Rork is just a stupid Mick—in his element when drunk with moronic Aussies or over-sexed Eskie girls. He has no notion of protocol. You should agree, Eleanor. Or has he clouded your judgment with that Gaelic malarkey he spews?"

Ellie never liked playing Strafford's insipid games and took no exception to this one. While she chatted with Mac, Pete and Sean, the day's travels overtook her. Weary and grimy, she now felt every shudder of the lumbering supply lorry that had given her a lift from Halifax. All she wanted was a steaming bath, a stiff drink and a hot supper. Not necessarily in that order.

Instead she had to endure Strafford's asinine glibness. She gave him a mocking smile. "You know, Major Strafford, besides the fact that Mac and I are both a goodly portion of that Gaelic stock to which you refer, Mac will be delighted to know you've such high regard for his key operational staff. Especially when they're out puttin' their lives on the bloody line while you swill your time away in the lap of luxury, meddlin' in affairs about which you know bloody nothin'. 'Tis a real shame your timing is so . . . retarded."

Taking up her bundles, she asserted, "The pecking order was established long before you came aboard at the garrison, Strafford. Tough luck, old man."

If the major wanted to say more, he missed his chance. Leaving him like a statue, if stone could be indignant and pissed, Ellie brushed past him to catch up to Marciá.

Once outside, Marciá eyed Ellie shrewdly. The ladies burst into giggles. Marciá said, "That went swell. I used you to sneak past Major Conceit and you used me to cover your escape from the lush. What a bloody good team we make, eh?"

Ellie giggled more. "A good team indeed." Walking into the brisk night air, she asked "Have you plans for this weekend?"

"Weekend?" Marciá groaned. "What weekend? Hey," she said as they reached her beat-up but reliable '34 Chrysler Airflow, "lemme give you a ride down the road so we can talk some more, eh?"

Sliding onto the cold, leather seat, Ellie asked her soul friend, "Does slave-driver-Mac ever give you a break?"

"Truth is, I told him I'd work tomorrow if he'd let me have this Sunday off. Vance is takin' me ice-fishin'—"

"Ice fishin'? Oh swell, how bloody romantic?"

Marciá grinned wickedly. "It's not about the fishin', Ellie. It's all about the warmin' me up afterward that I wanna reel in."

Smiling, Ellie asked, "Who's Vance anyway?"

"Sergeant Vance Boudreau, that dreamboat of a Mountie who's been helpin' Mac track down your BLUE FOX character."

"Marciá, please, BLUE FOX is not my character."

"Oh, I know, El," she assured with a touch of her beautifully manicured, slender fingers, "but according to Martini Jim, BLUE FOX has a thing for you."

Ellie smiled at another of Marciá's monikers for Strafford. "The major seems to know everybody's business but his own, doesna he?"

"If you ask me, El, the major isn't happy unless somethin' excitin's happenin'. If nothin's capsizin', he starts rumors to churn up the bloody waves. Even the garrison's semi-tranquility's been upset since that royal pain-in-the-ass Limey dropped into our world to mix with us bloody commoners."

Ellie nodded thoughtfully, recalling incidents at MI-6 when mysterious stories had cropped up about some officer, an agent or a staff worker. These rumors, some utterly vicious, were never resolved. Eventually, the person transferred or, worse, was killed on a mission. *Was James Strafford the culprit behind that hearsay?*

Skating to a safer subject, Ellie said, "Listen, Marciá, when I was down in Halifax, I bought Artie Shaw's new record and some nice fabric I think you'll like. When you get off tomorrow, why don't you come over. We can listen to records while I cut your dress out and get it fitted." Ellie giggled. "Not that you'll need it ice-fishin', but Vance may take you dancin' some time."

"That'd be swell, Ellie. What time?"

"How 'bout we scrounge up our own chow rather than sufferin' through the mess hall's Saturday-night surprise?"

"Swell, last meal you scrounged up was the cat's

meow," Marciá said. "Hey, maybe I can teach you some of those new dance steps while I'm over."

"Brilliant." Reaching her stop, Ellie slid out. "Say about six o'clock or eighteen hundred dependin' on your clock's tick?"

"Six o'clock. Leave that military protocol for the office. See ya tomorrow, Els." Waving, Marciá drove off.

Marciá's comment reminded Ellie of Strafford's snide remark about Irish. *Thank God, I got away from Martini Jim.*

No sooner had Marciá's taillights disappeared round a bend, than Ellie heard a soft-spoken, cockney-accented voice, "Evenin', Commander. I was out hikin' around, wonderin' how you'd want to proceed with these bloody recruits comin' in Monday, and, lo and behold, there you were. Or, I guess now, here you are."

The voice was attached to Royal Navy Lieutenant Commander Nigel Marcus Sanders, unassumingly known as Sandy. His youthful tranquility hid the fact that he was at least forty-five as well as an eminent hand-to-hand combat instructor and bloodied British Commando. He had taught Ellie the key disciplines of self-protection and more crucially: self-reliance. She thought the world of Sandy.

"Here, lemme help ya with those things," Sandy offered, being a gentleman as was always his fashion.

"Oh, thanks, Sandy." She handed over her packages. "Glad you came by. I fear that half-mile from the road to home was goin' to seem more like a bloody ten tonight. And this gives me a chance to congratulate you on your promotion, too."

"Thanks, maybe I can keep it this time," Sandy quietly replied with a grin as he launched into the garrison's training agenda.

Though Ellie answered Sandy's questions, she kept thinking: *Did Strafford start those rumors at MI-6? Is he trying to stir up trouble here, as well? Tryin' to create a rift between me and Mac would appeal to Strafford's trouble-making intrigue. With Mac top-dog of ICE PACT, Strafford's malice might throw a monkey wrench into the works. Even if it gummed up the war effort.*

Once inside the cottage, Sandy, looking serious, set her things down and rested his elbow on the counter. "You answered all my questions, luv, but I sense you're not exactly here. When we dubbed you Lithe Ellie at Achnacarry, I always knew your mind was as lithe as your body. And right now, you're weighted down by some very somber thoughts. What the bloody hell's wrong?"

Ellie removed her coat, tossed it on a chair and started to put away the items she purchased in Halifax and considered what to say to her longtime friend. Pausing to turn on the tea kettle, she absently said, "Care for some hot tea, Sandy?"

Raising an eyebrow, he asked, "Would I be safe in assuming Strafford is who's on your mind, and explainin' things will take some time, so it'd be best to sit comfortable?"

His words evoked Mac's decree: "things will take time." She nodded. "Why dinna ye take yer jacket off, while I finish up in the kitchen and make tea. Would ye mind startin' the fire?"

"No, not at all." Removing a wool scarf, fine leather gloves and his waist-cropped Commando jacket, he neatly set them all on the back of the chair beside Ellie's coat. He set his cap on top of the lot. Rolling newspapers for kindling, Sandy wondered: *What the bloody hell's Strafford done now? Is he still causin' her trouble? My job'd certainly be a helluva lot easier if I could eliminate him from the field of contention. He's been like an exhilarant to mayhem before Brandt even came into her life. Now, I get Ellie alone for a few quiet moments and it's sodden Strafford on her mind. What a damn pisser.*

⊕

BEDFORD BASIN HARBOUR MASTER'S OFFICE
HALIFAX, NOVA SCOTIA
FRIDAY

Willy Krigeshaald filed the day's end reports: number of ships, their tonnage, cargoes, comings, goings and the transfers within the deep harbor. These activities—which went on without cease 24-hours a day—had been handed over by Willy to the auxiliary terminal for the weekend. His last concern before leaving was this paper war.

Worn-out and alone in the office, he wanted to go home but refused to leave any of his work unfinished. Unlike his boss, returning Monday morning to a cluttered desk was not acceptable.

The phone jangled. Willy debated not answering but that, too, was not in Willy's nature. He picked up the receiver. "Harbour Master's office, Willy Christensen speaking. How might I assist you?" Nothing came from the other end of the line. Was it a bad connection? "Hello? Is anyone there? Hello?"

Irritated, Willy was about to hang up, when he heard a series of light clacks as if the caller tapped a pen on the mouthpiece.

He grabbed a pencil and jotted down the Morse coded message on a pad. Only the last word made any sense. As before, Willy needed today's code book to decipher this message from KRÖTE—TOAD.

Though no one was around to hear, he spoke as if receiving instructions. "Yes, sir, I'll tell him, thank you." Hanging up, Willy tore off the top several sheets, so no imprint remained, and slipped them in his trousers pocket. After making a show of putting a note on Boggs desk, he shrugged into his coat, put on his wool fedora, tugged on his gloves and left.

Strolling out of the building, Willy gave a casual wave to the Mountie making evening rounds. But eagerness drove Willy's mind like an engine racing without its wheels engaged. The memo was from his Nazi controller in Canada. KRÖTE was someone he'd probably never meet but whose rank presumably topped JAEGER. *Whatever I copied down must be important. This is only the second time KRÖTE ever contacted me. Maybe it's some obscure errand that might improve my standing with JAEGER.*

Realizing he was just short of breaking into a run, Willy chided himself. *Slow down. It can't be so bloody vital that you draw undue attention from the RCMP.*

CHAPTER TWENTY

Listening intently to the icy emptiness, Karney holstered his Colt. Faintly, from somewhere above, came a turmoil of barking dogs. Eventually it faded to silence. He tried not to equate it with the stillness of a grave.

Karney tried Hans' flashlight. The lens was broken. Turning on his own, he tried to peer into the corners of their ice tomb. "Guess we better find a way out of here before we become frozen delicacies for a polar bear come Spring." He reached a hand down for Hans. "You stand?"

"Yes," he answered through clenched teeth. "I'm fine. I'm fine."

Slowly, Hans stood, his eyes troubled. Karney couldn't help but think: *Hans looks anything but fine. But definitely more shocked than frightened or hurting. As if this happening to him is worse than being trapped here. Maybe it's just I'm used to dealing with the unexpected and Hans isn't.*

To his younger companion, Karney directed, "Let's clear off the pallets. If we can get enough of 'em free of ice, maybe we can rig some sorta ladder. With all these tools, copper wire and steel plates we should be able to come up with something."

As Karney began working, out of habit, he softly whistled. The tune was Glenn Miller's "*Stairway to the Stars*." After a few bars, Hans began humming along, off-key.

In little more than an hour they cleared off and extracted the pallets. Karney wired them together, leaning the assembly against the ice-slick cave wall. Hans took over the job of bracing the bottom pallet with the heavier pieces of equipment, steel plates and crates.

Stopping every few minutes to warm his numb fingers, Karney was assured of his task. But his mind jumped through hoops trying to figure out who trapped them here.

Doc? Not if he truly went north. But a possibility. Valya? Doubtful even if she's majorly pissed at me. But did one of them order someone to follow us? Maybe.

Was this the work of Wendy's real Nazi spy? Another possibility. It's not like the Krigeshaald's are the only Europeans in the area. But why didn't our mysterious guest just kill outright? Why wait till we reached this ice cave?

Ooqueh or his son Duneq? Again doubtful. Neither of them are nefarious types. Besides, Duneq's allegedly with Doc, and Ooqueh left to go hunting with his brother-in-law, way up north.

When no solutions emerged from the half-frozen bog of his mind, Karney let his worry sink into a dark oblivion.

"Well, that's that," Karney stated with a shudder. "My damn fingers can't feel the wire to wire another anything together. Gloves on my paws or not."

Hans braced a spool of copper wire against the bottom of the leaning pallets and stood to stretch his aching back. "I, too, am finished, Irish. Everything else is frozen too fast to loosen."

Karney noticed that daylight had pretty much vanished. Beginning the cautious climb down, he explained to Hans, "The top pallet's about four-feet short of the ledge. One of us'll hafta stand on the other one's shoulders."

Near the bottom, Karney hopped down. His *kamiks* crunched in the stiff gravel, painfully reminding him how frozen his feet were as well. It took another few seconds to speak. "Before we make our grand exit, let's do a number on those torpedoes."

Sledge hammers in hand, Karney trudged back to the torpedo racks. Hans came at a leisurely pace. With a vengeance, Karney smashed the wooden blocks protecting the propellers to disable the blades. He prayed with each swing that he wouldn't inadvertently blow a torpedo up. Though Hans helped, he seemed a little too ginger with his approach. Karney wrote it off to the lad's aching head.

When the torpedoes were rendered useless, even the faintest glimmer of light through the aquamarine ice was gone.

Karney's flashlight flickered in exhaustion but still emitted a wan glow. Feeling as drained as the batteries, the Yank and the Dane plodded back around to their makeshift stairway to the stars. It looked pathetic. Then his flashlight died altogether.

Hans retrieved his broken flashlight, removed the batteries and handed them to Karney. Inserting them, Karney coaxed forth a dim halo. This second set was also weak. "We'll use it sparingly."

Resigned to the dark, they removed their crampons, again. They'd had them on and off so often it was like wearing slippers. Karney felt his way up their jerry-rigged ladder. Hans didn't follow. Flicking on the light, Karney gazed down through the gloom. In his Irish brogue, he said, "Might as well start climbin', laddie. Ain't no one gonna carry ye up here."

"But, Karney . . . I'm . . . well, I'm afraid of heights."

"Hells bells, Hans, you can't see a damned thing up here anyway. Just think about freezing to death if we don't get outta here. The height won't mean diddly."

Without further comment, Hans resituated their rope over his broad shoulder and across his chest to begin climbing. When level with Karney, he asked "What now?"

"Since you've got the rope, climb on my shoulders. Once on the ledge, tie it off for me to climb up. Ready? Wait." Karney reached for something. "Here, take this."

The Dane's only answer was to take the flashlight and accept Karney's boost up. Hans then clambered awkwardly onto Karney's shoulders. Balanced precariously on the top pallet, Karney grimaced with the lad's weight. "Thank God you don't have your dad's girth or we might be stuck here forever."

With clenched teeth, Hans said, "Willy should be here. He's a bit taller but doesn't weigh as much. But he's also weaker and not as brave as I am. He would be useless."

Karney didn't miss the hostility when he spoke of his older brother. Yet the enmity seemed born more of spite than grief. *Why'd he use the present tense? Does he refuse to accept his brother's death? Or does remembering Willy bring their father to mind, which creates some of the malicious riptide I sense in their family?*

As Hans struggled to reach the icy ledge, Karney ignored the thought. Their ladder creaked and wobbled. Realizing he was headed for a plunge, regardless, he gave Hans a massive shove up.

Their starry stairway went to hell in an icy hand basket.

With a potential fall of nearly twenty feet, Karney managed to slow his plunge by pushing off to the side and scraping the ice with his gloved hands, knees and boots. He crashed with a resounding oomph, the wind knocked out of him. Fortunately, he missed the jumbled heap of sabotaged equipment by inches.

Ice, however, made no sort of a soft landing mat.

"Irish? IRISH?" Hans cried out. "Are you all right?"

Unsteadily rising, Karney held his shoulder and swung his left arm in a painful arc. He squatted down to make sure both knees worked. Head spinning, body aching, Karney replied, "Yeah, I guess so." In the pale flashlight glow from above, he glanced up, trying to sound hopeful, "I'm still alive anyway."

"I'll secure the rope. Your torch is almost dead."

"So I see," agreed Karney. Digging into his coat pocket, he withdrew his Zippo. He flicked the lighter to life. Grinning at Hans, barely visible on the ledge, Karney quipped, "And the Lord said, 'Let there be light'."

It took several minutes for Hans to tie off the rope. He threw the line down, its length snaking open as it fell.

Crampons refitted, Karney grabbed the end of the rope and dug into the glassy wall. The rope seemed to lengthen a mile. It also felt as if it took a century before he felt Hans grip his arm to help him over the edge. Struggling to catch his breath in the frigid air, Karney lay on the ice, lungs heaving.

After a moment, he asked, "Did they take your gun?"

"I don't know. May I borrow your lighter?"

Digging out the Zippo, Karney handed it over. A tiny sun burst forth in the inky cave. After several minutes of scuffling around on his knees, Hans declared, "Found it."

Karney struggled to his feet. "Let's get the hell outta here then."

RCN Training Garrison
Sheet Harbour, Nova Scotia
Friday

Ellie cocked her head to the side like the starling of her codename as she gazed at Sandy in confusion. "But you're Navy. How'd you meet Strafford in the trenches durin' the last war?"

Sipping his tea, Sandy leaned forward, returning the cup to its saucer. Resting his elbows on his thighs, he clasped his hands. "Like Cap'n Mac, I traded services after the first bloody go 'round. Didn't fancy more time in the bloomin' mud."

Sandy sat back and crossed his ankle over his other leg

as he grasped his knee. "Of course with the way this war's pannin' out, good ol' Adolf's *Blitzkrieg* tactics should keep us outta the damned trenches, though not outta the blood and mud."

With a scowl and eye roll, Ellie simply said, "Aye." Then, after another sip of tea, she asked, "What'd you do before you got back in?"

Sandy gave a lopsided grin. "Learned how pretty ladies can get a chap so lost in their allurin' eyes they beat-all-around-the-bloody bush of what we originally were goin' to discuss!"

Smiling coyly, she wouldn't meet his gaze. "We'll get back to that soon enough, Sandy, but do you realize, in all the years we've known each other, this is truly the first chance you and I have ever really taken to just sit and chat?"

His gaze became serious again. Sandy knew there was no way Ellie could realize the many times he'd wished for moments like this: to be close to her, talk, laugh, touch and . . . and more. Even now, with the opportunity in front of him, he simply said, "Duty never allowed for much more with as bloody seldom as our paths've crossed."

"Aye, 'tis a sad truth."

Uncrossing his legs, he stretched them out to the side to get more comfortable, folding his hands over his lean waist. His eyes never left hers. "Between services I did a lot of this and that: traveled the world, barely stayed out of prison more than once, scratched a living any bloody way I could. Then I met your father. 'Twas Commodore Greer convinced me I needed a meaningful career."

"Sounds like Dad. Is that when you joined the navy and got tied into MI-6?"

"Your Old Man's an excellent judge of characters and what role those characters need to play. Probably why he gets so brassed off at Strafford. The major tends to want the bloody role to be tailor made for him, not the other way round."

"But Strafford's been at MI-6 longer than you, hasn't he?"

Sandy shook his head. "Joined before me but our time averages about the same. The major was in Belfast, then Derry for MI-6, workin' with the Black and Tans. It was around the time of the Sinn Fein Rebellion. Took a bloody beatin'. Damned near killed him from what I understand. After that he dropped out of the bloody picture for years. Lived off his wife's inheritance, got her pregnant with a girl and two or three boys, hobnobbed with the aristocracy on the Continent."

Again Sandy sat up straight. "Least till the depression hit and Commodore Greer got his daughter hooked into MI-6 as well."

With a frown, Ellie argued, "Oh, for heaven's sake, Sandy, you canna believe that Strafford came back just because of me?"

Sandy shrugged. "Perhaps not because of you, but he certainly was interested in working with you. Strafford weaseled his way in as the only available controller when your assignment for Berlin came up. Even then, the lout seemed to access most secretarial panties. Those gals unwittingly gave him intel he never should've had. Probably knew as much about your upcoming Berlin mission as your Old Man."

Staring at Sandy, Ellie sorted through rumors and suspicions she recalled from her early days at MI-6. In a replay from last Sunday with Mac, Ellie slowly stood and went to the pass-through to pour some Dewar's in her almost-empty teacup. Before she turned back, Sandy's cup slid onto the counter.

"Mind?" he softly asked from close beside her.

Blinking, she said, "When'd you start drinkin' again?"

"Only when faced with Strafford-created dilemmas and don't quite know how to bloody well handle it."

Ellie poured the amber liquor into his cup, hesitantly asking, "Am I your Strafford-created dilemma?"

"In part . . ." Sandy took a generous gulp. "Another part is what scares the bloody hell outta me, luv, and I've never figured a way around it for sure."

Turning slightly to face him, she asked, "And what might that be?"

Sandy reached up, sliding his hand around the back of her neck and drew her into a heartfelt kiss. Seemingly of their own accord, Ellie's arms wrapped around his waist as Sandy pulled her in closer. His lips parted. He tasted like Scotch, sweetened with sugary tea, fixed the same way Karney liked his coffee—

As awareness crashed in, Ellie pushed back, breaking the kiss. Letting go, Sandy stepped back, looking flustered and embarrassed.

"I'm sorry, luv, I should never've been so bloody bold. It was totally wrong of me to presume—"

Her fingers gently ceased his words. "No, Sandy, 'twas not wrong of you, and you presumed nothin' that hadn't crossed my mind years ago. Ye remember when ye were my trainin' officer, and I fell apart when I reached the end of me rope that one miserably cold day, and you held me to keep me from leavin' altogether?"

Sandy merely nodded, recalling the day like it was yesterday.

"I thought about you a lot then but nothin' more happened between us, and I was sent into Nazi Germany. And now, well, there's another fella I'm involved with, and 'tis not fair to him for me to be encouragin' you while he's away."

To her surprise, Sandy grinned with a short laugh. "Ah, bloody story of me life. A day late and a kiss shy." Leaning on the counter, he topped off his Scotch. "So, who's the lucky chap who's won your heart this time?" he asked, glancing sideways at her, a smile still in place.

Feeling the heat rise in her cheeks, Ellie said, "A Yank commander by the name of Karney Rork."

"Ah, Irish, the Coast Guard officer who rescued you

and is now traipsin' Greenland's icy wilds. Mac mentioned him in my briefin'." Sandy gazed at Ellie. "At least if I'm forced to admit defeat, it's not to a bloody scoundrel like James Fenton Strafford."

Taking his Scotch, Sandy sat back down and crossed his legs again. "So, even if he's a Yank, is Irish a gentleman?"

Ellie sat down as well. "He seems to be . . . I'm just . . ."

"Just what, luv?" he inquired, leaning forward.

"I just fear lovin' him may get him killed or wounded or—"

"Stop right there," Sandy ordered. "That's bloody shite and you know it. Wars kill people, bullets and shrapnel wound 'em. Not love. Least ways, not more 'an a broken heart. And that's not permanent."

She looked ashamed. "Aye, that's what logic dictates."

"What does your heart say? I won't bloody ask if he's told ya he loves ya, 'cause God knows I've loved ya for years and just got 'round to kissin' ya, and that's not really tellin' ya anythin' 'cept I'd like to make love with ya."

Cheeks flushing, she giggled. "Lord sakes, Sandy, 'tis definitely nae a side of ye I expected to see today. Ye've always been the barkin' drill instructor with nary a wisp of compassion for us poor mud-caked, cold buggers sloggin' through yer bloody obstacles at Achnacarry: rain, shine or snow with live rounds zingin' over our bloomin' heads and charges blowin' up way too close for comfort."

"Amazin' what one sweet kiss from a lovely lady can do for a chap's outlook, ain't it? So, do you think Irish loves you?"

"I'd like to think so. He said so and certainly gave me some sweet and thoughtful Christmas gifts."

Noticing Ellie touch the expensive, unique necklace, which matched her lovely earrings, Sandy smiled. *Aye, Irish loves her, and he knows how to show it without sayin' a blessed word.*

"Well, pretty lady, I'd best be on my way before I do

some bloody fool thing we might both regret later."

"Won't you stay for supper, Sandy?"

"I could, but I won't, though thanks." Standing to leave, he put on his jacket and cap, draped his scarf around his neck and held his gloves.

Feeling guilty, confused and somewhat overwhelmed by what had transpired in the short time they'd been together, Ellie said, "I know you don't much care for Strafford, but what do you think of the man professionally, officer to officer?"

Sandy's clear blue eyes had been as guileless as a spring sky, but they gradually darkened as storm clouds gathered.

Ellie quietly amended, "Strictly between you, me and my resident mouse."

"Luv, I wouldn't trust the major to know you have a poor mouse livin' here. He'd likely catch the wee blighter and feed him to a bloody stray cat for grins." He placed his hands on her arms and leaned in to tenderly kiss her forehead. "My dear, sweet Ellie, everything that I said and did this afternoon must remain between you, me and your poor li'l resident mouse as well."

"Sandy, I—"

It was his turn to stop Ellie with a gently placed finger. "Listen, luv, I honestly did mean what I said, and shoulda said it years ago, but such is Fate. Please know this, if the major ever does anything more than annoy you, and Irish isn't around to safeguard you from him, I hope to God I will be."

Hand on the doorknob, he hesitated, "The next time we kiss, luv, I pray it'll be to kiss the bride of Karney Rork at your wedding."

Ellie smiled warmly, sensing the deep sincerity behind his words. "You're a very sweet man, Sandy. Just knowin' you'll be around with Strafford here eases me worries tremendously."

"The major does hava way of showin' up with trouble

at his heels, doesn't he? Or maybe he's drivin' it ahead of him with that dandy cane of his." Lightly touching Ellie's cheek, he said, "Take care, luv. Rest up. Since I'll be a barkin' DI come Monday, you'll hafta be my purrin' counterpart to coax on those fifty poor new recruits shippin' in. Day after that let's change roles so they'll never know what to expect."

"Brilliant," she groaned. "Well, at least that explains the bloody games you and Sergeant Havel used to play with us." With a sigh, Ellie added, "Sandy, in all honesty, thank you for everythin' we shared. You truly are a sweetheart."

Glancing around, he said, "Lord sakes, luv, please don't be tellin' anybody that or me bloody despicable reputation'll be sunk as deep as *HMS Hood* lyin' on the bottom of bloody Denmark Strait."

With a wink, Sandy left. Gently closing the door, Ellie rested her forehead against the cold wood and sighed before turning the lock. "Dear God, what a peculiar day of remarkable clashes."

HALIFAX, NOVA SCOTIA
FRIDAY

Shoving the code book and message away, Willy Krigeshaald slumped back in his rickety chair. Blank pages, torn from the pad at the harbor master's office floated to the floor. He made no effort to pick them up. He just sat.

A train whistle shrilled in the night. The sound pierced his being as readily as a bullet ripping flesh. Willy rested his elbows on the desk and buried his face in his hands. Desolation wrapped him like a burial shroud, his thoughts just as black.

Ever since JAEGER's indifference became apparent, coupled to his failure to kill STARLING and now this new mandate, Willy began to think a bullet might be the easiest way out of this cesspool into which he'd fallen. Efforts to impress JAEGER only mired him more deeply.

He slowly read the paper's terse orders once more:

STARLING OBSTACLE / ELIMINATE / KRÖTE

Lighting a match to the piece of note paper, he muttered, "My dear TOAD, if I even had a bloody weapon to use on STARLING . . ." Watching as flame consumed the paper, he dropped it in an ashtray, then finished his sentence, "I'd sooner use it on myself than do your vile bloody bidding."

Picking up the papers from the floor, he added them to his mini pyre and watched them burn like a sacrifice.

Willy switched off his desk lamp, pushed his chair back and stripped from his shirt and slacks. Crawling in between the cold sheets of his lumpy bed, he muttered, "Lord, who am I kidding? I had no courage to stand up to the Nazis when I was in Denmark, how the hell could I find the guts to kill myself now?"

Hugging his pillow reminded him of the previous night. "Besides, my old chum," he snuggled under the wool blanket, "think of all the hot nookie you'd miss with groping Cyndi. That alone has gotta be worth living for, even if no one else is pleased with what I do."

IKEQ FJORD
SOUTH OF AMMASSALIK, GREENLAND
SAT: 24 JAN 42

Karney flexed his cold and cracked fingers before a modified train-oil lamp, staring into the dancing blue flames as if wholly mesmerized by their undulations.

Working last night, most of the day and well into this evening, he and Hans repaired the slashed dog harnesses: another parting gift from their mystery assailant.

Unable to work with gloves on and with the poor tools available, the work was crude but adequate. Their fingers were sacrificed to frigid temperatures like raw meat to an insatiable, clawing beast, demanding fresh blood.

Piteraqs wailed over the snow-buried, sod and rock walls of this Inuit hut. Built by nomadic hunters, Hans had explained, Ooqueh restored it years ago and now kept it repaired. Hans and the elder Inuit used it on extended hunting trips. A vague thought crossed Karney's mind when Hans had mentioned this: *Why did Hans never seem to spend time with Ooqueh's son, Duneq, who was closer to the same age?* Karney didn't ask; knowing Duneq was married with a family was probably reason enough.

For now, it was good to be here. Despite sub-zero temperatures outside, the interior remained warm. The walls and floor held a chill mustiness, along with the ever present smell of the chopped up seal-blubber they burned for oil. Moss wicks were arranged around the edge of the lamp provided their meager light. The mingled scents were pleasant enough when the alternative might be freezing to death.

Luckily, after trudging through the glowing rays of the Aurora Borealis yesterday, harnesses in tow, they found most of the dog team near the hut. The rest eventually returned, their keen noses guided by the cache of meat inside. On the other hand, if loyalty brought the half-wild dogs back, Hans had truly mastered this untamed land. It seemed he'd also mastered sleep as well.

Doubts kept Karney awake. He also didn't mention his concerns to his traveling companion. Misgivings led to questions, which grew like hoar frost on a window pane. Exhaustion clouded his objectivity and ignorance intensified his sense of betrayal.

The Dane stirred restlessly, drawing Karney's gaze to where Hans curled under a polar-bear skin. *Perhaps he isn't as free of anxiety as the ease with which he fell asleep led me to believe a few hours ago.*

After leaving the glacial tunnel from the cave, Hans seemed startled to find his dogs missing, harnesses cut. He was visibly shaken and bewildered. Karney knew from past Arctic experiences, the dogs were kept in a near-wild state, fed only every few days in winter, faithful only to their master, sometimes the family. Hans' immediate family was Doc and Valya, possibly Ooqueh.

Who could get close enough to cut the dogs' harnesses without getting ripped to shreds? Does someone Hans know strand us here? Is Doc really up north on a medical call? Or is he much closer? Did Valya request someone hinder our return? If not one of the Inuit, whom I have trouble suspecting, is there another possibility? Is the elder boy of the Krigeshaalds, Willem, alive, living in Greenland and the Nazi spy who's been relaying convoy information to U-boats?

Feeling stymied, Karney realized that even though Hans was trapped here with him, he shouldn't exclude him from all suspicion. The how and why of that possibility seemed ludicrous but such was Karney's bewilderment.

He lacked evidence for all but speculation.

With the dogs' return and the harnesses repaired they would start back to Ammassalik tomorrow before daybreak. Tonight, however, a sense of defeat rose above Karney more ponderous than the wavering shadows on the hut walls.

Having come here as Mac's envoy to find evidence of a U-boat base and to establish a rapport with Dr. Krigeshaald, Karney felt what he'd accomplished was pretty paltry. *Could those German supplies have been left years ago by some U-boat that now lies on the bottom of the Atlantic? And I didn't meet anyone besides the Krigeshaalds on this junket. How could I determine who was trustworthy and who's not anyway? Do I suspect everyone or rule them all out?*

Karney sighed and shifted his crossed legs.

Having avoided one petite but buxom nymphomaniac seemed a poor consolation to Karney's peace of mind at the moment. *I've neither learned what Valya's influence over Doc might be nor if he's truly as good a Samaritan to the Inuit as he alleges. Doc might be my Nazi spy. His travels*

*to visit the sick certainly offers him freedom of movement.
That in itself's a damn good cover,* Karney realized.

*And though Hans might be a momentary ally, his
reaction to this pickle didn't ease my sense of isolation.*

*And to bottom out this fuckin' day, I ache like hell
from head to toe after my fall in that cave. My hands feel
more rigid than the damned harnesses, and I know the
blood-dried cuts in 'em are gonna hurt like hell when any
real warmth lets 'em thaw. And to boot, my damned
mind's so foggy, I can't remember if I volunteered for this
mission or if Mac out-finagled me somehow.*

Hell, wat's it matter? I'm here and I feel like shit.

Karney was cold, tired and miserable. It was easier to
feel sorry for himself—something he tried not to do—than
sort through the enigma of his mission. Finally, eyes
drooping, his despondency blurred. He curled up under his
own polar bear skin and slept.

Karney's slumber, however, was fretful, rife with lurid
images he never seemed to escape and unnerving
nightmares carved out of an indescribable ice-encrusted
hell which seemed to have no way out.

2nd SUBMARINE FLOTILLA
LORIENT, FRANCE
TUES: 27 JAN 42

Kapitänleutnant Jakob Prüsche paced the concrete
quay next to where *U799* was moored. Overhead lights cast
a sickly glow on the submarines moored inside the massive
pens. Each bay held U-boats in mixed states of refit: one
stripped of her outer skin, fuel tanks exposed like
saddlebags; another with damaged deck plates to be
replaced after repairs were completed on her mangled hull;
three more, damaged by depth charges, would receive
hasty, superficial repairs to make them seaworthy again.

U799 fell into the latter category.

Jeweled showers of sparks from hissing arc-welders

careened over submarine hulls and into the oily water like sputtering fireflies. Long cables, ropes, hoses and electrical cords, running in disarray, coiled and slithered with artificial life as workmen tugged and jerked them to numerous work sites among the boats.

Jakob's stride again brought him to the rear of the cavernous structure. After a parade-ground about-face, he admired *U799* as compared to the other U-boats: she was not only longer, but wider and had a greater submerged-displacement. His boat was a beauty, the absolute best. Her service record proved it. It saddened Jakob to think she would never have a sister to share her class.

His attention was drawn past the mouth of the pen when a band struck up a lively march. Another U-boat, victory pennants unfurled after a triumphant mission, sailed into the inner harbor, past a scuttled French tanker.

The quay was lined with a boisterous throng, cheering and waving excitedly to the returning crew. Though he couldn't see the faces of the U-boatmen, he knew the mixture of fatigue and relief, excitement and composure they felt. Her grimy crew, many topside and breathing fresh air for the first time in weeks, stood in rigid lines, not quite knowing how to respond—disbelief of having returned hadn't set in.

Only U-boatmen who'd survived the fury of depth-charge attacks and endured deprivation aboard their boat, would understand why anyone cheered for them. Assurance of a victory party—or standing orders—had brought most of the onlookers here to welcome them.

Jakob saw nurses from the infirmary and the usual ensemble of lightning girls, German servicewomen, waving and holding flowers for the men. Not to be outdone, numerous Nazi party officials met the returning boat as well. Though unable to see the flotilla commander, Jakob knew he was here, as he always was, to greet the crew of an indispensable U-boat.

"Stupid posturing," Jakob mumbled, knowing his

gripes wouldn't be heard over the workmen's racket. Extracting a French Galois cigarette, he packed the tobacco by tapping it on his silver cigarette case. "This merry reception, pretty maidens, flowers, lavish banquets, tons of cheap medals, champagne and beer . . . For what?"

Cigarette dangling, he growled, "So the flotilla commander can lull us into a false sense of security. When cornered, we'll get the only true thanks we sons of bitches ever get: new orders for an even worse mission." He flicked his lighter to life.

"*Kaleu?*"

Glaring over the lighter's flame and the rising smoke wisp, he hardly recognized his First Watch Officer with a clean shaven face and trimmed hair. Garrick looked like a teenager.

"*Guten Morgen, Kaleu,*" Garrick Bechtler greeted with a hesitant smile as he fell in step. A guarded look shadowed Garrick's hazel eyes.

Icily, Jakob grumbled, "Wait until you've heard the joyous news before passing judgment on this morning."

"Have our orders changed again?"

Stopping, Jakob took another drag of his smoke. He scrunched up his face as he glared at it. "The French will kill us yet with these rank cigarettes." Casting it down, he ground it underfoot. "We sail Tuesday with the tide. All leaves are cancelled."

"But, *Kaleu,* with the three-ring circus we endured for the brass, half the men haven't even left yet. And—"

Garrick's protest evaporated with one look at his commander's face.

"Forgive me, *Kaleu.* It was not your decision." Considering the time allowed, he asked, "You can't go to Hamburg either, can you? I'm sorry, I shouldn't have—"

"It's all right, Garrick," Jakob said. "My feelings are much the same." Withdrawing a second cigarette, he tapped it on the case.

"*Kaleu,*" Garrick said, nudging his chin at the smoke.

Jakob glanced down. "*Ja*, you're right, First. Another one won't help my mood any more than the last." He pocketed the case, then suggested, "You'd best spread the cheer to the men."

"Ha!" Garrick snorted. "Good cheer like a funeral." He turned to go, then paused. "What do we do with Habicht, *Kaleu*? He left late yesterday to visit his *Vati* or *Onkel* or guardian or whoever the hell Admiral Habicht is to him."

Jamming his hands in his pockets to keep from extracting yet another smoke, Jakob sighed. "Since *Konteradmiral* Habicht is in Kiel, we may have to sail without our intrepid *Wunderkind*."

Garrick cocked his head, baffled by this cynicism. "*Kaleu*?"

"Send the usual leave-cancelled notice to his *Onkel's* HQ. Either Karl gets back or he won't. Who knows, now that he has so much sea-duty under his belt, maybe he craves a warmer assignment back in the Mediterranean, diving for Teutonic relics with *Herr* Himmler's madcap archeologists again and will depart our wily *Eis Fuchs*."

Gazing at the fox emblem, usually iced over, Garrick said, "*Kaleu*, I do recall a posting to Greece. It seems that *Herr* Goebbels needs a propaganda assistant there." Garrick shook his head. "Ach, but alas, poor Karl could only talk about himself, not Adolf."

"And," Jakob added, with a wry smile, "I'm sure there's a long waiting list. Far too long for Karl's patience."

Garrick turned again to leave but stopped. "*Kaleu*, do you know where we are to go that we must leave in such a hurry?"

Gazing out into the harbor, Jakob heard the final strains of a march and shook his head. "Garrick, you know I can't tell you, even if I knew, which I don't. Our orders won't be opened until we clear Biscay Bay."

Jakob chewed the inside of his lip as his mind ventured into the Atlantic. With a worry he was hard-pressed not to reveal, Jakob gazed down at his young protégé. Resting his hand on Garrick's shoulder, he pointed toward Lorient. "Go, First, round up the boys. It will take till next week to peel them off all the colorful ladies in the French brothels and get them sobered up for duty. Needless to say, they won't be happy."

AMMASSALIK, GREENLAND
WED: 28 JAN 42

Karney and Hans reached Ammassalik at dusk. The sun appeared as a smoky-silver orb, barely shining through the grimy pane of another storm, a constant procession this time of year. Luckily, the travelers would be inside when this one hit: safe and warm.

At least, Karney thought morosely, *I'll be warm, if not safe.*

Helping Hans unload his sledge and store their gear in the shed connected to the boathouse, Karney felt as if he slogged through cement just short of solidifying. A quick glance at Hans indicated his young companion also felt the effects of their long trek. His movement was just as labored, his eyes dull with exhaustion, as Karney was certain, his were as well.

Even knowing his suspicions were intensified by fatigue, he almost felt guilty for believing Hans was a party to their near demise. Unfortunately for Hans, nothing on the return trip occurred to sway Karney's misgivings. The roots sank deep into reality.

Bross Krigeshaald entered the shed. "You both look exhausted. Storms made hard traveling, no? When you were sighted south of Ammassalik, Valya began supper. You two wash and change, it will soon be ready."

To Karney, the suggestion had the ring of an order.

Neither Hans nor Karney moved immediately, prompting the big Dane to ask, "Is something wrong? Was there trouble at Ikeq?"

His back to Doc, Karney's glare nailed Hans. *If Hans*

hadn't told anyone, how'd Doc know we were at Ikeq? A new salvo of questions fired inside the Irish-Yank's mind.

Looking away, Hans gave a half-hearted shrug.

It took a while for Karney to calm his irritation. "No, no trouble, Doc. We just had to cover a lot of ground to beat out this storm." Forcing a grin, Karney said, "Our only big problem was damaged equipment." Fiercely gripping his companion's shoulder, he asked, "Right, Hans?"

Not meeting his gaze, the younger man grunted, "Yes."

"Good," Doc said. "Now get washed up, wanderers. We talk after supper."

Inside the house, Karney went straight to his room. Washing his cut, swollen hands, he knew the best thing was to get the hell out of Ammassalik. *If not, I figure Arctic scavengers'll be gnawin' on my frozen carcass by next Spring. I don't know anyone else around here, much less anyone I might be able to trust. And putting my life on the line won't help a damned thing.*

Even if I peg the spy, there's little I can do without any evidence. And proof won't help if whoever I show it to turns on me like a rabid wolf. Ammassalik—this house—is fast becoming a labyrinth from which I won't be able to extricate myself.

As soon as this storm passes through, I'll get Doc to radio Wendy and pray that crazy Aussie gets here with Claire-Marie before I become a permanent stiff in the permafrost of Greenland.

EPILOGUE
SHEET HARBOUR,
NOVA SCOTIA

Ellie silently breathed a sigh of relief when Mac informed her that Irish was out of Greenland and on his way back to *Zealous*. Why *Lady Z* was still in Argentia, Newfoundland, was a mystery, but Ellie also knew military red tape tended to stretch a long way before it severed. In her case—dealing with Mac, Uncle Richard and her father at MI-6, each one tending to pamper and watch out for her wellbeing—it was more like a scarlet ribbon.

Orders, as well as her official reinstatement in the Royal Navy WRENs and a promotion to lieutenant commander, had already come through. Though her uniforms were still at the tailors, it was a minor inconvenience. She had the paperwork necessary to open most any hatchway aboard Canadian, American and British ships. Too bad she couldn't access some of the *Kriegsmarine* vessels to figure out the next move of *Admiral* Dönitz.

A lingering concern, however, was the hatchway to Karney's heart. It was a threshold she was unsure about crossing. Ellie also didn't wish to dwell on her personal feelings for Irish until she stepped foot aboard *Zealous* to debrief him—her next assignment. One cautious step at a time was all she wanted to take where Karney and OPERATION ICE PACT were concerned.

Other problems hovered beneath the surface of which she had no control. Recalling the anxiety when a U-boat had stalked *Glasgow Bonnie*, Ellie knew she could neither drop her guard nor ignore one other major, unresolved threat: JAEGER's sites were still trained on STARLING.

Read on for a short preview of
D.D.O'Lander's
EMERALD TARGET
BOOK II— IRISH

Though configuration is similare to Paratus, this is a wartime photo of USCGC Taney.

USCGC PARATUS
WED: 04 MAR 42

"Commander Rork," Dawson said as he straddled the opening to stop Karney from crawling into the bilge. "You can't go down there, sir. You're an officer."

Trying to lighten the stark fear in Dawson's eyes, Karney asked, "I am?" Seeing it had no effect, he said, "That's why I am going, Dawson. If I need bodily force to get Tennef outta there, it's my responsibility, not yours. Especially, if it comes to deadly force."

Paratus lurched, almost knocking the two men off balance. Karney gave Dawson a worried glance. "Just make sure Commander Halloran knows where I am."

With Dawson's nod, Karney lowered himself into the imprisoning stench at the underbelly of the cutter's core.

⊕

Moments after the freighter silhouetted against the burning tanker exploded Lieutenant Commander Pete Halloran spotted the Navy destroyer. *Paratus* had lined up for a run on the U-boat's last periscope sighting when the destroyer sliced through the sea at flank speed toward the same point. The vessels would collide if neither changed course.

Pete groused, "And they call us the Hooligan Navy."

"Mr. Halloran," Johnston called from the TBS, "the destroyer's captain ordered us to break off. They've got the U-boat lined-up."

"So the jerk thinks," he growled. "Helm, right hard rudder."

In the same instant, a lookout bellowed, "TORPEDO OFF THE STARBOARD BOW!"

Pete immediately countermanded, "BELAY RIGHT RUDDER! Torpedo reference?"

"One point on starboard bow," the man clarified in a voice slightly higher than normal.

"HARD TO PORT! BOTH ENGINES AHEAD FLANK," Pete ordered, though he feared *Paratus* wouldn't respond in time. Charging onto the starboard bridge wing, Pete saw the phosphorescent trail of death heading straight for them and cursed, "Son of a bitch."

Pete and the lookouts watched the fish race toward them. Holding his breath, he prayed they had enough rudder-on. The torpedo closed. Leaning over, he tracked the menace until it passed safely astern.

A lookout yelled, "It missed us, sir. It missed us!"

⊕

Karney turned on the emergency flashlight, holding it far to his right side in case Tennef took a pot shot at him. Nothing happened. He stayed as low as possible, duck walking forward to see further into the bilge. The captain couldn't go far in the dark, confining space. When Karney's light caught him, he saw the man was a total wreck.

Tennef was crammed into the space where the hull and bulkhead met several feet away from Karney. The good part, he wasn't running anymore; the bad part, he flailed his Colt .45 around in circles with increasing panic.

"Stay 'way from me!" he mumbled, countered immediately with, "Don' come closer!"

At first Karney thought he meant for him not to come any closer, then he realized Tennef's eyes darted side to side, seeing whatever his hallucination was conjuring. "Commander Tennef," Karney called, "we need to get you out of here."

Karney's answer came as several gunshots ricocheted in totally random directions before spending their velocity. The sound was like being inside a fifty-gallon drum as someone pounded on its sides with a Louisville slugger. Dropping the flashlight, Karney tucked himself up against the hull and tried to cover his ears.

Unfortunately, the hammering reverberated into a seemingly endless ringing. Slowly dissipating, Karney realized the distraction of the shots and their racket prevented him from feeling any pain. Sliding back on his haunches, he pressed his hand against his right thigh. It came away sticky with warm, fresh blood. He carefully explored the deep gouge that wrapped itself halfway around his leg.

"Shit," he muttered, gingerly tracing the groove and feeling how close it came to stealing away the family jewels. Though he couldn't tell for sure, he thought the bullet was still in his leg. The pain began to burn ferociously.

"Mr. Rork," he heard Dawson call him, "are you okay, sir?"

Clearing his parched throat, he answered, "Yeah, I think so."

"You need help?" Dawson called. No response came.

⊕

Beginning to breathe again, Pete raised his glasses to where the enemy periscope had been. The destroyer laid a carpet of depth charges. The ocean broiled astern and to either side of her. Blooms of phosphorescent destruction glowed within the sea.

He knew the destroyer's perpendicular approach missed. Though shaken, the Germans would escape. "Sam," Pete called, "get that yahoo on the TBS—"

"Second Torpedo, Three Points On Starboard Bow!" yelled the same lookout. "Closing—"

Staggered by a violent blast jolting *Paratus* from the keel up, Pete realized it'd been a no win situation from the beginning. It still didn't stop him from fervently cussing himself out for ignoring the one-plus rule: If there's one torpedo, there's bound to be a second. And *Paratus* had found it.

"Son of a frickin' bitch," Pete swore more fervently.

⊕

Before answering Dawson's inquiry, Karney leaned around the ship's rib to check on Tennef. In the mis-angled flashlight beam, he made out the irrational captain firing his empty pistol at whatever came toward him. He heard Tennef mutter something about "filthy vermin," and figured Tennef imagined rats attacking him. "No wonder he's still shooting," Karney said with a curled lip. "I hate rats, too."

"Sir?" Dawson questioned.

"Yeah, Dawson, you can come down here. The captain's outta ammo, and I may need your help."

About the time Karney heard Dawson's boots thud, a horrendous explosion rocked *Paratus*. It knocked Karney's head against the ship's rib, then slammed him across the bilge. As a display of stars spiraled into his vision, Karney registered that a torpedo must have struck *Paratus* aft of their location. It was Karney's last conscious thought.

To view some of the places where
the stories of *EMERALD TARGET*
take place or if you wish to make any
comments, please visit me at:
ddolander.com.

Thank you for purchasing my book!
I hope you've enjoyed reading this
as much as I have enjoyed
researching & writing them :)

10/18

84605171R00248

Made in the USA
Middletown, DE
20 August 2018